OPERATION D

RAY PASQUIN

Second Edition (2022) ISBN:
978-1-957351-00-1

Operation D
Author: Ray Pasquin
Co-Editors: R.D. Foster and VicToria Freudiger
Proofreaders: Linda T. Phillips and The Proofreading Divas
Second Edition Proofreader: Jean Sime
Original Book Cover Design: Pamela Trush
Second Edition Cover Layout: Michael Nicloy
Interior Design & Layout: Griffin Mill

PUBLISHED BY NICO 11 PUBLISHING & DESIGN
MUKWONAGO, WISCONSIN
MICHAEL NICLOY, PUBLISHER
www.nico11publishing.com

Be well read.

Quantity orders may be made by contacting the publisher via email:
mike@nico11publishing.com
or by phone: 217.779.9677

Contact Ray Pasquin's management:
g7agent@aol.com

Printed in the United States of America

Dedicated to Rolande who is indeed my better half,
and to my sons Chris and Tim.
Family means everything to me
and they are truly a gift from God.

Author's Note

Twenty five years of hosting a nationally syndicated radio program has occasionally given me the opportunity to meet and interview unique, and, at times, very bizarre guests. Research for two of these radio shows helped garner facts and information later used to mold some of the characters and topics found in this novel.

One of the programs, which centered on cults and demonic beliefs, totally immersed me into the shadowy world of Devil Worship. Doing so via an eerie Satanist who was the show's main guest.

I learned about many of the more terrifying elements of devil worship; the random revenge killings, and their strange satanic traditions. Rituals such as the sacred Purus, an oath of avenging death. And the hallowed Yucid, a hideous skeletal mask, often worn during cult ceremonies and slayings. I was likewise informed about violent, gas-lit 'Satanic Punishment Sessions', popular in the deep south during the '1950s and early '1960s, but still occasionally practiced today. These present day crimes, so my satanic radio guest alleged, are perpetrated by violent Black Mass cults, and are generally written off by the authorities as 'unsolved serial murders'.

I was further informed that Charles Manson and his callous followers had employed similar satanic procedures during their terrible killings and mutilations. And that Manson himself was a practicing Satanist. Whether true or not, I could not confirm. But the torture and disfigurement patterns used on Manson's victims were very similar to those depicted in ancient demonic scrolls.

The admittedly graphic descriptions of some of the satanic customs, and the vile practices occasionally found in my book, are based on fact. They are quite unsettling and shocking. Nonetheless, I have included some of them as a way to show how wrongful and vicious the devil clans were, and, at times, still are.

These demonic sects, thriving and active today, should not be taken lightly. Indeed Satanism, or some type of cult worship, is now the fastest growing spiritual movement in America. The depraved traditions, which I've depicted in my story, only touch on the true brutality of genuine events.

*

A second integral part of my novel was likewise uncovered while preparing for a radio program. That particular show dwelt on 'top secret government agencies'. My guests back then were a retired CIA agent and two former Secret Service workers. During the taping, all three men mentioned a clandestine United States agency and its extremely 'unique' undercover division. I have loosely described this covert department in two of my earlier chapters.

Though further inquiries about this classified security branch were politely brushed off by the higher-ups in Washington, I am now convinced that the agency, or something like it, actually exists. And that it's currently being utilized by our government in the manner I've shown.

The clandestine bureau, which I've renamed G5, continues to be a very effective force, particularly in the area of homeland security and anti-terrorist activity. Its special division, to which my protagonist belongs, is based on an authentic government agency; a top secret department utilizing a select group of incredible looking men, used in similar assignments to the one I've described.

Operating strictly undercover, often in the midst of great personal danger, with only their good looks and guile to aid them, they have proven to be invaluable intelligence agents. It is with great appreciation for their courage and dedication that I present a story based on these secret heroes.

– RWP, New York, NY

*

OPERATION D

Prologue

On a dark, stormy night in 1863, near the Austrian hamlet of Lienz, a weary traveler made his way toward home, traversing a lonely dirt road. Hoping to get some shelter from the violent rain and lightening, he spotted a deserted gravedigger's shed in the small cemetery located on the hill in front of him. The weary trekker was unsure if he should stop there, as ghastly rumors abounded about this particular burial ground. Locals had spoken of strange happenings taking place here. Tortured screams crying out during the night, and loud wails seemingly coming from the dead. On this bleak evening, conditions seemed perfect for those evil tidings to materialize. Although hesitant, the traveler reluctantly decided to seek cover in the graveyard shed until the storm subsided.

Just as he arrived at the abandoned shack, an enormous flash of lightening lit up the entire area. Startled, the man looked up toward the sky, and for a brief moment thought he saw a vestige of the devil. The traveler blinked his eyes and the satanic apparition was gone.

Another bolt of lightning flared, and in its bright illumination the traveler spotted an old parchment scroll buried beneath some rotted logs to his left. The covering logs fully protected the parchment from the heavy rain, and the man's curiosity soon got the better of him.

Reaching down to grab the scroll, abject horror overwhelmed him! Several European night vipers, massive snakes possessing potent venom, had been concealed under the decaying wood. They angrily struck out at the intruding arm, repeatedly biting the traveler's forearm in vicious rage. Several of the bites punctured the man's wrist, penetrating the artery. The terrified traveler screamed and began racing down the hill in utter panic. He didn't get far. The huge quantity of venom now flowing through his body quickly killed him as he tried to run for help.

The incident was soon forgotten and the scroll was never recovered. Had it been found, however, its chilling message of warning would have spread trepidation throughout the region; both then and in the years to come. For the scroll read as follows:

> One day in the distant future, a disciple of Lucifer, Son of the Morning Star, shall rise in the west and lead his satanic legions against all who have opposed the Dark One. He will strike down Satan's foes with a great wrath of fire and destruction, and the world shall never be the same again!
>
> Islavo Fahad Melek
> High Priest of the Yozem sect of Satanic Worship -1803

Blood was everywhere, a dark purple mess crystallizing amidst mutilated body parts. The victim, a forty-year-old white male, had literally been sliced to pieces, his body slashed, torn and cut into an assortment of shapes. It was a crime reminiscent of the murders perpetrated by England's infamous Jack the Ripper, the notorious villain still remembered for his terrible slayings of over 100 years ago. But this present murder, as now shown on an FBI crime scene video, was all too real and current.

The gruesome bloodbath, the handiwork of a truly disturbed mind, seemed to be driven by an almost sexual lust for slaughter. The murderer had obviously taken perverse pleasure in butchering the victim, as evidenced by the carnage left behind. A close-up of what was once a living human face was perhaps the worst of it. As the camera focused on the remains of the vestige it revealed two empty holes where the eyes had once been. Each eye had been cut out of its socket in a neat, yet macabre, surgical fashion. The head's empty eye sockets now seemed to stare blankly at the ceiling.

This particular file footage of a three-month-old murder never failed to bring on a nauseous feeling to FBI Special Agent Loretta Swanson every time she watched it. Yet viewing the film was part of her job, however repulsive, and it had to be done. It was vital to her current assignment, the shocking south Florida serial murders that were responsible for her being transferred from the FBI's SIOC Operations Center in Washington, D.C. down to the North Miami Beach Field Office.

Nearly every day Agent Swanson studied these crime scene films along with the more than one hundred accompanying photographs with hopes of finding clues. While viewing the graphic video tapes, DVDs and photos, she was usually able to stay outwardly poised and alert, as any experienced and highly trained field agent should. But this part of the job was never easy and tonight it had all caught up to her. The young, attractive operative felt exhausted, both mentally and physically, and her fatigue was quite understandable. It had been brought on by six frustrating months of long, tedious days and even longer sleepless nights. And thus far, Loretta had followed nothing but fruitless leads in the deplorable murders that were terrorizing south Florida.

The media was tagging this serial killer with the fitting nickname 'New Ripper'. Loretta Swanson, along with her fellow law enforcement officers, despised the tag mainly because the figure this nickname was based on, London's Jack the Ripper, had never been captured. They took it as another slap in the face by the journalists, who to them seemed to salivate for every chance possible to denounce any member of law enforcement. Yet there was nothing they could do about it, other than catch this madman and stop the ridicule. Nonetheless the New Ripper name had stuck and even the FBI was now using the moniker.

Although the murders had all been committed in the same general south Florida area, the case of the New Ripper, sensationalized in newspapers and on television, had quickly become a national story. It was fast becoming one of the most infamous killing sprees in US history. Seven murders had taken place now on both male and female victims, all tortured and horribly mutilated.

Perhaps the most bizarre twist to this case had been the traces of snake venom found in three of the seven victims. The pathologists' analysis of the corpses indicated that those three bodies contained evidence of a neurotoxin poison, more specifically venom from a rare and deadly cobra. Only vague details about the exact type of venom had been issued to the press in order to keep the species of the suspected serpent known strictly to those assigned to the case.

The authorities were puzzled, unsure why, or even how, the killer had utilized such an exotic reptile as a tool and why he had done so in only *some* of the killings. Everyone, from the local police, to the scientists at the FBI's Laboratory and Investigative Technologies Division in Quantico, Virginia, was genuinely baffled by this inexplicable venom piece of the puzzle. Why did this fiend choose to kill only *three* of the victims with a poisonous creature? Why not kill *all* of them this way? No one was certain.

Having seen as much as she wanted from this particular footage, Loretta Swanson frowned and turned off the DVD player. Leaning back on the black leather couch, she rubbed her tired eyes in frustration. The whole modus operandi of this New Ripper maniac was a genuine enigma, particularly the inclusion of snake venom into some of the crimes. There seemed to be no rhyme or reason to this snake aspect. *Again, why had only three victims shown traces of snake bite? What had set them apart from the other four victims?* Still, it was a traceable clue, the origin of which had to be tracked down in a case where actual clues were scarce.

Loretta was particularly frustrated that her usually reliable *inner instincts* had not produced a single lead, those female intuitions of hers that had always been helpful in the past. Then again, even the best and most experienced minds of her colleagues were baffled, and everyone in the North Miami FBI office seemed to have a different hypothesis.

At one point a rather controversial premise was presented, one which suggested there might be *two* separate lunatics striking in similar patterns; one using snake venom and one not. However this *two-person theory* had quickly been dismissed as soon as the killer's boastful notes, recovered at the crime scenes, were thoroughly analyzed. Written in strangely formed letters, using the deceased's blood in place of ink, the slaughterer's chilling notes were left to taunt the authorities. The handwriting and letter formations were eventually proven to be identical, thereby showing that it had to be the same person responsible for all seven murders.

Bragging of this nature was common for many serial killers, such as the BTK killer in Wichita, Kansas. In that case the letters *BTK* stood for bind, torture and kill. The boastful notes that the BTK murderer had sent to police and the media were signed with a sexually suggestive configuration of the three letters, with the B and T used to form a woman's breasts. Like that Kansas killing spree, this Florida killer had left depraved crime scene notes as well.

The final aspect of these New Ripper murders was undoubtedly the sickest part of all, the killer's bizarre 'trump card'. On all seven bodies, as this and the other videos had so graphically shown, each victim's eyes had been systematically removed from their ocular cavities, cut out neatly with a surgical flair. All of the missing eyes had virtually disappeared without a trace, except for one chilling incident. Five days after murder number four, a suspicious package was delivered to the Miami-Dade Police Department. The label on the box was addressed: *To the FBI Agent in charge of the New Ripper case.* And the handwriting on the tag unquestionably matched the crime scene notes.

Loretta Swanson was immediately called in to view the evidence. Slowly and carefully opening the mysterious package, she found, to her horror, that it contained two human eyes! DNA tests determined the eyes to be those of the first victim, an insurance salesman from Fort Lauderdale.

Recalling that dreadful moment, Loretta closed her own eyes and took a long, deep breath. It was hard for her to think that the eyes she had unwrapped that day had once belonged to someone like herself, or heaven forbid, a member of her own family. The agent frowned and clenched her fists in frustration.

Slowly sifting through the still photographs again, she lamented the utterly unpredictable manner in which this serial killer worked. The only constant in the case was that every murder had taken place on the first day of the month for seven consecutive months. She now asked herself, *what significance does the first day of the month hold for the killer?*

Loretta sighed. Tonight was indeed the 31st day of March. By tomorrow evening, she'd most likely be receiving yet another gloomy phone call. "The New Ripper has struck again, Miss Swanson," a faceless voice from the Bureau would exclaim. "Please drive down to the Pompano police station immediately."

Yes, she mused, it was almost a certainty. The first day of the month was now only a few hours away. By this time tomorrow some poor soul will have been brutally murdered. Instinctively Loretta glanced at her watch. Conceivably the next victim had already been selected, or was presently being stalked, and there was nothing she could do to prevent it. Pondering all this, pangs of guilt slowly began eating away at her mind. Someone would be viciously slaughtered this very night while she sat safe and secure in her little cottage on the beach, the tiny one-story outpost the Bureau was renting for her. The frustrated FBI operative longed to act, to be somewhere doing something, anything, to protect the public from this demon. Yet, the question of *where* had no answer and tonight would doubtless be another ghastly repeat of the preceding seven months. Only this time it would be a morbid April Fools' Day surprise.

The morning headlines were again proclaiming, *No One Safe from Ripper! Authorities Baffled!* Reporters had whipped the public into another frenzy, blaming everyone from the local police all the way up to the White House. In nearly every article the FBI was being particularly excoriated.

As Loretta Swanson glumly considered the depressing facts, there was good reason for her frustration and worries on this muggy Florida evening. Today was the last day of March. Some time after midnight tonight the New Ripper was going to strike again.

Like any highly trained law enforcement officer, Special Agent Swanson knew better than to let frustration, media pressure or lack of real progress get in the way of systematically looking for potential clues. As for these gruesome videos, she'd just have to stick with it. She'd been trained to be as cold and calculating in her work as the Ripper appeared to be in his. The words of her favorite FBI instructor, Professor Thomas Doan, suddenly ran through her mind. *There will be times when you will be totally repulsed by the utter cruelty one human being can inflict upon another. Nevertheless, you can't let your emotions and naturally sympathetic instincts interfere with your train of thought. You should coldly treat each individual crime as a solvable puzzle, merely a riddle to be scientifically solved.* Yet even with Doan's practiced philosophy firmly in her thoughts Loretta Swanson just couldn't rid her exhausted mind of the images of the mutilated bodies. Perhaps it was her understandable feelings of sympathy trumping the role of the aloof, impersonal FBI agent. As a professional, she knew it should be the other way around.

While contemplating her next moves, Loretta glanced around the small beach house and smiled contentedly. She had come to love this little dwelling, no matter how Spartan its decor. It was *her place* now, her tranquil 'home base'. Here, alone on this remote beach, she was able to concentrate fully on the case without being interrupted by phone calls, messages or well-meaning friends.

In addition to the small living room in which she sat, the tiny one-floor residence contained a small master bedroom with a connecting bathroom, an even smaller guestroom with bath, and a tiny kitchenette. The house, which she had taken over from her predecessor on the Ripper assignment, was most definitely an example of location over luxury. Its main feature was solitude, a desolate shore-line site twenty miles from Lauderdale, just north of the small town of Deerfield Beach. Only a narrow one-lane gravel road led to the house, providing the lone pathway in and out. There were no neighbors and the only other people Loretta had seen in the area were the infrequent strolling beachcombers. And though the FBI had offered her a roommate, she flatly refused one, arguing that she needed time alone to ponder the case. Her North Miami Beach Bureau Chief, Benjamin Winslow, had probably known this when he recommended the setting. *The house may seem lonely, Loretta, but you'll be able to do some real thinking in it. Nobody will bother you there. No one would want to!*

Silently she mused; *he was right on both counts.*

Of course the place sometimes seemed spooky to her, particularly at night. During her first few weeks here Loretta had felt the only pleasing aspect of the dwelling was its oceanfront view, as seen through the living room's undersized picture window. This seascape, though rustic, was serene and hauntingly beautiful. In fact, it was this view that had single-handedly allowed her to gradually accept being assigned to the secluded house. Now, after four months, she considered the place home, even with its forsaken locale.

As the attractive agent sat in total concentration, the wind suddenly picked up, the unexpected noise making her jump as the windows rattled. Stretching her aching body, Loretta stifled a yawn, leaned back on the couch and tried her best to relax. She threw her sandals under the coffee table and slowly, almost luxuriously, let her overworked brain wander away from the Ripper murders for a minute or two. Thinking about other things, however briefly, was a welcome change. And there were indeed other things.

In addition to the assignment, with all of its horrible details, Loretta had personal matters to confront. She experienced a slight feeling of guilt even thinking about them at a time when a crazed killer was cruelly slicing up victims. Yet it was unavoidable; she was, after all, only human. And her status as a single woman would never be completely disassociated from her position as a law enforcer, or so it seemed.

Troubling her most was the fact that in just six months her thirtieth birthday would take place. Like other women turning thirty, Loretta had begun questioning her goals and priorities in life. Had she simply married a career? Would she ever settle down and find that certain somebody, a man with whom to share a home and a family? Or, would her sometimes fascinating and exciting life as an FBI agent keep her from a normal married life? *Next year would tell,* she thought. *Either I'll quit the Bureau and go husband hunting, or re-up with the FBI for another three years. After that I can reassess again.*

On a vain impulse she stood, walked to her small master bathroom and glanced into the mirror. On gazing upon her sharp, angular features, pretty face, and striking long, blonde hair, Loretta once more questioned her attractiveness. She was fairly certain that most men found her desirable thanks in part to her almost perfect 5'7" figure, kept fit by the FBI's rigorous physical training. Her shapely body and appealing curves never failed to turn heads. However, while men often seemed interested, there was never really time for any type of meaningful relationship to develop. *That's the problem,* she thought. *My darned career.*

Loretta stared into the mirror again. The lovely blue eyes twinkled back, as if reassuring her of her beauty. However, almost as if trying to dissuade herself, her thoughts quickly returned to the conflict between career and a possible love life. *Was there simply too much work and not enough play*? Before she could answer her own question, the phone rang.

"Loretta, dear. How are you, Angel?"

"Fine, Daddy." She smiled brightly, immediately recognizing her father's deep baritone voice. She still loved it when he called her *Angel*, the affectionate nickname he and his late wife had given their only child nearly thirty years earlier. After a brief pause Loretta spoke again. "Well, actually, I'm not so fine, Dad. I'm completely frustrated with the case I'm working on."

United States Senator Thaddeus J. Swanson knew little about his daughter's actual cases. Time and circumstances had taught him it was better that way and she in turn never gave him any real specifics so as not to worry him. Nonetheless, he was concerned with the obvious disappointment in his daughter's voice. "Hang in there, Angel. Just remember what I always tell my staff; *hard work flushes out frustration*."

"I'll keep that in mind, Dad."

A forced smile returned to Loretta's face. Her father always seemed to have an encouraging witticism for everyone. Senator Swanson was famous for his fighting spirit, his can-do attitude in the senate, and most of all, for his sometimes corny, homespun sayings. Sensing his daughter was not convinced he continued, "Look, Angel, just keep plugging away. Stay in there and keep your nose to the grindstone. I'll be down to visit you very soon. Maybe I can cheer you up a bit. In fact, my tentative schedule has me coming to Florida next week for a meeting with the governor. I'm really looking forward to seeing you. It's been a while since we've spent time together. Wasn't it when we took that crazy fishing vacation last November?"

Hearing that from her father caused the senator's daughter to chuckle at the fun-filled memory of their rare trip, one of the very few she had taken with him. It had resulted in a truly great weekend. His voice quickly interrupted the fishing reverie. "Keep working hard and things will break for you. I personally guarantee it!" Senator Swanson smiled into the phone. "Listen, Angel. As soon as I get down there I'll call you. We can go to *Prime* and have the best strip steak in Florida. And don't forget that chocolate soufflé you love so much!"

"It's a date, Dad," Loretta replied, now daydreaming of *Prime's* delicious zabaglione dessert cream. "And please don't worry about me. I'm just prone to complaining. Actually I'm doing swell. In fact I've just started a letter telling you all about things, although it's still in the end table drawer. Unfortunately I've only been able to get at it piecemeal."

"Can't wait to read it, Angel. Your letters are always special."

"Thanks. And thanks for the pep talk, Dad. Just the tonic I needed. I'll get cracking again right away!"

"That's my girl. Always remember one thing; no one, and nothing, can stop a Swanson when our minds are made up!" The senator let out a small sigh. "Well, so long, Angel. I only had a few minutes, but I wanted to check in with you. Love ya."

"Love you too, Daddy. Talk to you soon."

Just as their phones simultaneously clicked, Loretta inexplicably shuddered. A cold chill rippled through her body accompanied by an eerie feeling, a feeling that for just the briefest of moments made her firmly believe that she would never see her father again. She blamed this particular alert on sheer frustration with the Ripper case and on her constant worry about her father's rather serious high blood pressure condition, one which he himself never took seriously.

Frowning at the negativism she quickly got herself back together again. Although the naturally instinctive FBI operative put great faith in these sporadic *inner-feeling* warnings, she swiftly dismissed the premonition "Snap out of it, girl!" she said aloud. "Time to stop feeling sorry for yourself." The feisty agent walked to the kitchen and made herself a cup of hot, green tea. Then, following her own advice to 'snap out of it', Loretta's mindset quickly returned to the Ripper case.

Ambling over to a four-tiered bookcase located across from the living room couch, she reached up and removed a bronze sculpture of a flying dolphin from the third shelf. Hidden behind the dolphin was a concealed undersized wall safe. Loretta quickly opened it, using a five-number combination code. After removing a thick file marked *FBI – TOP SECRET – NRP*, she spread the papers on the coffee table. Gently placing her teacup away from the files, she methodically began sorting them.

Calm and collected, the efficient agent began studying the documents in an unemotional, almost robotic frame of mind, deciding to once again pursue the only personal theory she had on these Ripper murders; that the snake and venom aspect might relate to possible cult killings. While Loretta concentrated on her admittedly questionable hypothesis something extremely ominous was being planned at that exact same moment.

~

Thirty-five miles away from Loretta Swanson's isolated beach house, a tall mysterious man was likewise hard at work. He was sitting behind a large desk in a concealed townhouse office on the outskirts of Miami. The man was dressed in an expensive beige suit with a matching brown-striped silk tie. Despite his stylish elegance, a shadowy guise surrounded him, giving this man a very sinister aura indeed.

Beside him in a cushioned chair sat a frail, elderly man. Unlike the nattily suited gentleman, this oldster's face definitely showed old age. He appeared to be well into his nineties. This older gent, clad in a wrinkled gray suit, didn't smile or talk. In fact, it would have been difficult to determine if he was even alive had he not occasionally opened his eyes in short, disinterested flashes. His face was gaunt and bony and what was left of his thinning hair was whitish silver.

The younger of the two men casually puffed on an expensive Cuban cigar expelling the smoke slowly and deliberately, as if deep in thought. His smoking had always bothered the older man, yet this elderly gent said nothing. He had long since given up trying to rid his younger counterpart of the filthy habit.

Sensing the oldster's annoyance, the younger man stubbed out his cigar in the glass ashtray to his right. He contemplated deeply for a full minute and then, as if an important decision had just been made, reached under the desk and pressed a hidden button. Within thirty seconds two rather grotesque looking men entered the office from a rear door directly behind the desk. As always, no one had seen them arrive or enter. There was a slight smell of alcohol and stale tobacco emanating from them, although they certainly weren't intoxicated. And though they had given up their former abstinence of alcohol and tobacco, the duo knew better than to ever turn up drunk here.

At first glance, the men who had just been summoned might have been taken for ordinary employees, municipality personnel, or quite possibly, sanitary department helpers. There were, however, two significant things that differentiated them from typical American blue-collar workers. One was the fact that both men came from the Middle-East and had distinct Arabic features; specifically, the hard, angular profile of Iran. Secondly, neither man had ever earned an honest dime as manual laborers. For both were well-trained, cold-blooded terrorists, merciless assassins who had illegally entered America straight from the Afghan training grounds of al-Qaeda.

These two terrorists had systematically murdered many times over, always doing so without a hint of remorse or regret. Taught their trade by high-ranking al-Qaeda instructors, the then youthful pair had been smuggled into the US. They had covertly entered just before the 9-11 tragedy, at a time when it was easier for anyone of their ilk to slip through customs. There was one other distinctive characteristic about them, perhaps the most singular of all. They, like their dapper leader and his aged father sitting across from them, were practicing Satanists, sworn disciples of the malicious *Yozem* sect, the most violent and fanatical of all the satanic clans. All four men in the room were true worshippers of the Devil, devoted followers of Lucifer's dark ways, and sacerdotal soldiers of the High Priest of fallen souls.

The dapper cigar-smoking man sitting behind the desk was the sect's ruler in every way, equally cherished and feared. To the two underlings who had just entered, this charismatic leader, a revered Satanist warrior, was unique in every way, much like bin Laden had been. The two subordinates now wondered why they had been summoned into *his* presence. They were nervously puzzled as to the reason they'd been called upon and that was indeed nerve-wracking. True, this type of private audience was at times a moment of honor, perhaps even an entrée to an important assignment. Yet, being summoned could also be a prelude to unspeakable punishment. Which was it to be now?

Their shadowy leader finally looked up from his desk and spoke in a low, calculated tone. "I have sensed that someone may be getting a bit too close to the truth. Therefore, I have chosen the two of you for the satanic privilege of eliminating this nuisance."

Instantly relieved of their tension, his two subordinates felt as if a great weight had just been lifted from their shoulders. They had done nothing wrong. Indeed the henchmen were about to be rewarded with a notable assignment.

As their leader continued with calculated calmness, the trained assassins listened intently to his every word. "The *someone* that I've mentioned is becoming a dangerous annoyance, and quite possibly a serious threat to our plans. This must be dealt with immediately! You have both studied intensely for this particular mission over the last few weeks and I now decree its implementation. It will act as the opening phase of our sacred Operation D."

His two wide-eyed subordinates nodded respectfully, trying not to show an unprofessional eagerness for the killing assignment. It was one they had hoped for and greatly anticipated. They watched breathlessly as their leader walked to a closet in the back of the office and returned with a medium-sized carrying case, a thick black box with a handle on top. A red skull had been painted boldly on it, along with the sign of the *Madhaf*, the traditional *bird on a pole* symbol of the devil himself. The container also had numerous tiny air holes on both of its sides. The satanic assassins knew what was coming next as their leader nodded and gave further instructions.

"This reptilian instrument of death, this chosen child of Lucifer, shall be used for your assignment tonight." He handed the case to the taller of his two underlings and in the transfer something slithered and stirred inside it. The two subordinates were neither startled nor surprised by the movement inside the case. With a piercing gaze that penetrated deeply into the eyes of both men, their superior spoke again. "May the sacred power of the Fallen Prince be with you."

Again, the two henchmen lowered their heads in veneration, eagerly anticipating the next familiar sacrament. They stood transfixed with eyes closed, as if praying. One of them howled melodiously toward the sky, a wolf-like, guttural wail often heard during the celebration of the Black Mass. Their superior smiled at the sound, walked to a small refrigerator by the far wall, from which he extracted a glass vial. The purple liquid inside the vial looked much like grape juice or wine. Yet to these Satanists, it was far more appealing and powerful. For this particular beaker contained blood, chilled human blood.

Their well-dressed leader next held the vial over the tiny flame of a small gas burner sitting on his desk. Seconds later he seemed to be satisfied and began chanting the familiar mantra of the Yozem blood oath. "Oh Lucifer most high, endow thy servants with the power of death over our enemy. May the forces of darkness and the consuming of this blood guide and protect them. May our foes wither away from our efforts and may Satan rule this world as is his rightful destiny!"

The two underlings knew this ancient chant by heart and also the proper response. They replied in unison. "May it be so. May Satan, who we worship freely, be our strength and liberator!" Their mentor then handed them the vial of blood, used for the demonic ritual called *Druen*, the ancient custom of consuming the warmed blood of Satan's victims or enemies. It would give Lucifer's followers the dark power to carry out any earthly task. The men closed their eyes once more in brief meditation. In turn, each took the beaker, looked up toward the ceiling, and slowly drank long mouthfuls of the warm liquid. Instantly, they sensed a strange and unique energy.

Finished with the ceremony, both assassins bowed, picked up the black carrying case, and waited quietly for their leader to formally announce the target. Unemotionally, the dapper chieftain proclaimed, "The female FBI agent that we have discussed, the blonde woman, Loretta Swanson. Proceed with her execution *exactly* as we have prepared and planned for it. It is to be done later tonight." He then turned toward the old man. "Well, Father, the wheels of retribution against America have now been set in motion. It cannot be stopped! To think, after all these years, revenge against your former enemies and the present foes of the Dark One, will finally be carried out. Our operation, based partly on your masterful plan of so long ago, will be one more blow to the non-believing fools of the West!"

For the first time that afternoon the old man showed signs of life as a thin smile slowly formed on his wrinkled lips. It was more a callous and appropriate expression of evil. The oldster and his son believed, like true Satanists everywhere, that Lucifer would soon rule the world, a destiny prophesied many centuries ago. As Lucifer's followers, it was their shared, sacred duty to help make this happen. They would now do so by unleashing madness and terror on an unsuspecting world; madness and terror with the code name, *Operation D.*

Chapter 3

Alone in the Dark

When her stylish pink cell phone unexpectedly rang, an uncomfortable feeling of dread suddenly overcame Loretta Swanson. *Could it be another Ripper murder?* Instinctively looking up at the wall clock in the living room she saw that it was only 9:05 p.m. Although the first day of the month was still three hours away, her hand trembled as she answered her phone. "Agent Swanson here."

Fellow FBI operative, Kevin Morales of the North Miami Beach office, excitedly greeted her. "Hey, Swanie." Loretta cringed at the office nickname she deplored as Morales continued. "Guess what – I may have some good news. Sunrise cops are about to close in on a guy who fits the profile exactly!"

"Really? That's fantastic, Kev! Fill me in."

Agent Morales, nearly out of breath, spoke hurriedly. "Here's the deal. Sunrise PD has a lead on some weird character, one who definitely owns a reptile. They've had him under surveillance all day after receiving an anonymous tip this morning about a strange man who's employed there as a part-time security guard. The police are ready to pick him up at an old warehouse where he works. Apparently this guy works the overnight shift there. Neighbors and a co-worker described him as a weirdo with a menacing pet reptile. And get this! The man recently threatened to *rip* apart a waitress working at a café near the warehouse. Some chick he was seeing who evidently ditched him."

Loretta gasped as she reflected on what she had just heard. *Could it be true? Would these horrible murders finally stop?*

Her feelings of hope were broken up by the still excited voice on the other end. "SPD's plainclothes guys are staking out the building right now. They've been asked not to go in yet, to instead wait for us. They've agreed. It's a bit after nine now and the suspect isn't due at the warehouse until his shift begins at ten. That's when the cops are planning to confront him. Can you get there in less than an hour?"

"I'm on the way!" Loretta confirmed, grabbing her black leather shoulder holster, which contained a GLOCK 22, the .40 caliber automatic pistol she had carried since graduation from the Academy. She also grabbed a pocketbook containing her ID badge.

"Do you want FBI backup?" asked Morales.

"No backup needed, Kev. Those Sunrise cops should know what they're doing. I'll call you from the warehouse if I think we'll need anything else."

Forty-five infuriating minutes later, after battling the surprising I-95 nighttime traffic, Loretta pulled onto a dark, narrow street and quickly found the unmarked police vehicle waiting. Inside were four detectives. A husky detective sitting in the driver's seat rolled down his window and sarcastically greeted her. "Hello, FBI. Glad you could finally make it. I'm Sergeant Mahoney and these are my cohorts." The men in the car nodded. Loretta nodded back as Mahoney explained further, "We haven't done anything yet, as per FBI orders. Our boy entered the building twenty minutes ago carrying a wicker basket. Could be the snake." The sergeant pointed ahead. "That building across the street is the one he watches over. It's used for storage of auto parts. The suspect has just relieved the second-shift guy and presumably is now alone inside. By the way, the owner of the warehouse, a Mr. Dan Hargrove, gave us permission to enter in any manner we'd like. Even to break down the front door if needed. He also gave us this key." Mahoney held it up. "He said it should fit the back door, although nobody really uses that back entrance anymore. Apparently the suspect only watches the area in the front where the expensive stuff is stored. We were just going to knock on the front door and confront him. I'll post one man at the rear, just in case he tries to bolt. That's our plan, unless you have any other ideas."

"I've been giving it some thought on the way over," Loretta replied. "If he *is* the Ripper, that seldom used back area might be a good place to store things such as knives, a poisonous snake, those missing eyes, or maybe even his next victim." An impressed Detective Mahoney tilted his head in agreement as she continued. "If this guy is our man, and we give him any warning, like knocking and waiting by the door, he could try all sorts of things including possibly starting a fire to burn any incriminating evidence. So, if you fellows don't mind, I'd like to get in there first and briefly look around that rear section for a few moments. I'll use the key and go in through the back door. If I don't see anything to be concerned about, I'll come back out and get you. Okay?" The men in the car glanced at each other and then unenthusiastically nodded. She grinned at them sardonically. "If I'm not out in fifteen minutes, come in any manner necessary, guns a blazing."

The sergeant and his colleagues looked at her questionably. Loretta returned their dubious expressions with a frown. "I take it from the way you guys are glaring at me, that you don't believe I can take care of myself. Let me assure you, gentlemen, I can."

Mahoney smiled admiringly at the cocky federal agent. "I bet you can, lady. Still, I don't like the thought of you going in there alone. But whatever knocks your socks off. My boss was quite clear; we're under your orders, ma'am."

She smiled. "Don't worry, I'll be careful. I have no intention of becoming one of those victims in the videos."

Loretta took the key, walked across the street, and made her way stealthily around the big building until she spotted the isolated back door. There was no outdoor lighting and the rear area was quite dark. If the suspect was indeed in the front of the warehouse, she'd most likely be able to sneak in and out undetected through this rear door. On an impulse, Loretta felt for her shoulder holster and was reassured by its feel. As always in situations like this, the GLOCK was right by her side. She immediately thought of one of her pistol range instructors and his favorite line from a Beatles' song, *Happiness is a Warm Gun.*

Aided by a tiny pocket flashlight, she approached the back door and quietly slipped the key into the lock. It went in easily and the bolt quickly opened, immediately rousing her suspicion. According to the owner this door and lock were seldom used. It shouldn't have opened so effortlessly. As the old rusted hinges creaked, the suddenly nervous FBI agent slowly pushed open the solid wood door. With a scrunched nose, hoping that in some way this gesture would help lessen the sound, Loretta carefully pulled the door toward her. When the gap was just wide enough to squeeze through she quietly slipped inside the building.

The rear part of the warehouse was nearly pitch black, except for a small area beneath a dim, amber overhead light. This thin light illuminated several shelves containing what appeared to be miscellaneous auto parts. Loretta quickly turned off the unneeded mini-Maglite. Having come in from the dark, her eyes acclimated slowly, though the lone dim bulb adequately guided her path.

After a purposeful scan of the immediate area, all she noticed were wooden shelves and some old fenders and bumpers stacked up against the outer wall. *Nothing unusual there*, she thought. She moved farther inside, quietly looking around, intently listening and watching for anything out of the ordinary. Her initial cursory reconnaissance turned up nothing of suspicion, and she found herself quickly tiring of the obnoxious metallic odor of the items all around.

Creeping along silently, while looking for things such as a doorway to a storeroom, a hidden stairway, or even, heaven forbid, the foul smell of a decaying body, she heard the faint sound of music. It was odd-sounding, acid rock music and the strange melody gave the atmosphere an eerie feel. Once more, Loretta instinctively felt for her gun. *Happiness is a warm gun,* she again thought, her senses now fully alert. Although nervous and tense, the agent was still in total control.

She crept closer to the front of the warehouse, hoping to get a look at the suspect himself. Maybe if she could observe him, her reliable 'inner feelings' might send a message confirming if he was indeed the killer who had consumed her life for the past few months. As she cautiously advanced, the pungent, unmistakable odor of burning marijuana filled the air. With a quick drop to one knee, Loretta peeked around a large shelf filled with assorted auto parts and saw a small, unattended desk. The man was nowhere in sight. *Where is he?* she anxiously asked herself.

Lying on the small desk was a stack of *girlie* magazines, along with a pint bottle of Jack Daniels and a partially eaten sandwich. Also perched on top of the desk was a large reptile, at least two feet in length. It wasn't a snake however. It was a lizard, an iguana maybe, or perhaps even a venomous Gila monster. Not being an expert, and loathing all reptiles, Loretta couldn't say for sure the exact species.

The edgy FBI operative took a quick look to the right, and then to the left, much of her view blocked by several massive storage bins. Surveying the area as best she could, Loretta was now extremely troubled that the suspect was still not in sight. *Had he somehow gotten behind her?* She sighed and worriedly wiped the sweat from her brow. *Where the heck is he?*

The entire scene was beginning to give her the creeps, and of course there was the possibility of a sadistic serial killer in the building, high on marijuana! Loretta glanced around one last time. Her fifteen minutes were almost up so she decided to backtrack, quietly exit the building, and then have the waiting detectives enter through the front door as planned. Discretion was now definitely the better part of valor.

Trying to retrace her steps toward the rear door, Loretta found herself walking through a small, narrow aisle that was quite dark. Two bulky shelves on her left were blocking out most of the dim light and she could barely see in front of her. Suddenly, she stopped dead in her tracks! *Was someone breathing close by, or was it merely her imagination? Was that the smell of a dirty man's body?* Standing motionless, the sweat of fear began dripping beneath her arms. Loretta's right hand slowly reached for her holstered weapon. *Happiness is a warm –*

It happened before she had even finished her thought! A huge tattooed arm, covered with coarse, disgusting hair, grabbed her from behind, holding firmly to the nape of her neck. The agent's keen sense of smell detected smoke, grime and stale sweat. Instinctively she wheeled around, breaking the strong grip by countering the aggressor's hold with a classic right-hand Karate parry! The move must have surprised the big man. He stood perfectly still, panting loudly. They were now face-to-face with one another!

Loretta could see that he was a large, grotesque looking individual, sloppily dressed in a blue security guard uniform. From the little she could observe, he had a round, pockmarked, unshaven face with the glazed, hollowed-eyed look of a druggie. The man was breathing heavily and seemed ready to charge. In anticipation of another attack, and with a lightning fast move, Loretta kicked out forcefully with her right foot, which had two-inch heels attached. She scored a perfect hit, directly between the big man's legs. He dropped to the floor, moaning in pain, just as the front door burst open. The four detectives crashed their way in, guns drawn at the ready. "Hold it, fella! Police!" It was the husky voice of Detective Mahoney.

"Relax, Sergeant," Loretta said calmly. "Everything's all right. But our pal here has some explaining to do about the weed on his desk. Unfortunately there's no snake, but there is a large lizard sitting right behind you." She smiled as the four burly men spun around, saw the lizard, and quickly jumped away. Now closer to the desk, Loretta could plainly see that the reptile was a harmless iguana.

They roughly jerked the suspect to his feet, who was rightly complaining that he was simply doing his watchman's job when he had confronted an unauthorized intruder. Mahoney read the man his Miranda rights, which were waived. Although agreeing to answer all questions, the suspect nervously explained himself by claiming his name was Leo Rafalski. He steadfastly declared that he didn't know anything about any serial killings. Rafalski further stated that he had proof of being out of the country up until a month or so earlier.

A quick search of the warehouse turned up nothing of a suspicious nature. Leo Rafalski was arrested for possession of marijuana, and Sgt. Mahoney assured Loretta that they would thoroughly check out the man's alibis. If any further suspicion arose, she and the FBI would be notified immediately. Loretta thanked them politely, but was now all but certain that this Rafalski guy was not the serial killer. His cowardly demeanor, the fact that he'd just come to Florida from Canada just four weeks prior, and finding that he had no snake, only a harmless iguana, didn't add up to his being the New Ripper. Additionally, she was sure that the part about his *ripping up* the waitress would most likely turn out to be merely hearsay or boastful ranting. Perhaps most importantly to Loretta, her trusted inner senses now told the FBI Operative that this man was definitely *not* the Ripper. Unfortunately it was just another false alarm.

Disappointed at the outcome, she got into her car for the uneventful drive home. Arriving at her lonely beach house a few minutes past midnight, Loretta Swanson suddenly realized that the first day of the month had officially begun. She frowned. Her always reliable instincts were now telling her that she'd most likely be dreading what the next twenty-three and one-half hours would bring.

U pon re-entering the beach house, Loretta put away her gun and grabbed a refreshing drink of club soda with lemon from the kitchen. Sitting down on the living room couch, she kicked off the uncomfortable heels she was wearing, folded her smooth legs underneath her and tried to relax. With the adrenaline was still pumping from the warehouse incident, sleep would probably not come for a while, so there was no point in heading to bed yet. She decided, instead, to refocus on the Ripper case and see if something, *anything*, would come to her.

Loretta sat down on the living room couch and tried to force her brain into high gear. Hoping for some type of inspiration, her gaze was drawn to the bookshelf where she focused on one book in particular, the Bible. Loretta's eyes widened, as a sudden thought came. *What if the snake used in these murders was in some way part of a devil worshipping ritual?* She immediately recalled a course she had taken at the Academy, one which had focused on cult slayings. In many of these ritualistic killings, the serpent, the *ancient instrument of the Dark Lord*, was held in very high esteem. Perhaps this was how and why a snake was being selectively utilized. Conceivably the murders *without* the snake were committed simply to throw them off the trail.

For the first time in weeks Loretta Swanson was happy with herself. Her father had been right to chide her into working harder and now his little Angel was really cooking. *After all*, she reflected, *it was often the thinnest of leads that brought down the biggest criminals. Wasn't that what they preached at the Academy? Look for the tiny to bring down the mighty.* During her first year at Quantico she had studied the infamous New York City *Son of Sam* case. There it had been an innocuous parking ticket, again only the smallest grain of information, that had eventually led the authorities to a yellow Volkswagen and ultimately to the capture of David Berkowitz, the notorious Son of Sam.

Loretta grinned excitedly, knowing her admittedly *tiny* theory of a possible satanic tie-in to the New Ripper might similarly lead to something positive. At the very least it would quickly bring about a whirlwind of activity at the Bureau and force them to look in a different direction.

Though thinking of sleep, and despite the late hour, Loretta nonetheless felt an overwhelming urge to phone Washington and tell fellow FBI Agent, Jack Hanover, all about her ideas. She knew Jack was on the midnight to 7:00 a.m. *graveyard shift*, and wouldn't be disturbed by her calling now. Hanover, one of her closest friends in the Bureau, was the agent she had reluctantly replaced here in Florida on this Ripper assignment. In fact, he was the very agent who had first occupied the lonely FBI beach house she now resided in, back when he was *lead dog* on the case. His Miami tenure had abruptly ended because of a perceived lack of progress and for 'being insensitive to a prominent TV reporter'. Despite Jack's reputation and occasional outbursts, Loretta liked and respected him. Even after being pulled off the case and reassigned to Washington, Hanover had remained helpful to her own investigation. Jack was also a genuine character and was often playfully flirtatious with her. And though this flirting made her a bit nervous at times, it always brought a smile to her face. Energized via her new devil worship theory, and also wanting to hear Jack's sexy voice, she grabbed the telephone and dialed the number of the SIOC (the George Bush Strategic Information and Operations Center) in DC.

"Hello, beautiful," Jack began, knowing full well he could always bring a smile to Loretta's pretty face and a reddish glow to her cheeks when he used that moniker.

Pretending to ignore the compliment, but always flattered when he called her that, Loretta replied, "Hi, Hanover."

"And to what do I owe this late-night surprise, beautiful? Insomnia? Loneliness? Or is it what I've suspected all along? You just can't live without me!"

Loretta's cheeks indeed began to redden as she chuckled. "Oh, come off it, Romeo."

Jack grinned as Loretta explained. "Listen, I may be onto something down here and you're the first person I wanted to call."

Sensing a different tone in her voice, Hanover quickly became serious. These Ripper murders continued to trouble him, and despite being removed from Florida, he was still unofficially on the case. He too had seen those awful crime scene videos, as well as three of the actual mutilated bodies. Listening carefully to her he hoped with all his heart that she had indeed found something.

"Tell me, Jack, what do we have on any SRA cases, or devil worshipping groups in south Florida? I'm trying to put a few things together and I need to ascertain if they might relate to this case."

"Satanic Ritual Abuse? Offhand, I can't think of anything, Loretta, although I can certainly run a computer check. But Tom Gibson and I checked into cult possibilities after the very first murder. Not specifically SRA though. No one felt it was a fit. Besides, and you should know this, there hasn't been a confirmed SRA death in this country in over twenty years. Why do you ask?"

"I think there could be a connection with the snake thing."

"The snake thing?" Hanover exclaimed, somewhat disappointedly. "I thought the profile experts ruled out anything significant about the snake, apart from this guy possibly having a weird pet fixation. From what I've heard, there's nothing much to it, except our Ripper friend probably has some type of deadly reptilian playmate. Who knows? Maybe this whacko thinks he's married to it. It's probably just a sick afterthought by the killer."

"I'm no longer convinced of that, Jack. I think the snake and the venom aspect should be looked into thoroughly, only this time from a satanic perspective." Her comment elicited a dismayed sigh from Jack's end of the phone.

"I wouldn't jump to a devil worship conclusion just because there's a poisonous snake around. It happens with lone killers every once in a while. Remember that case in Dallas involving the rattler? The one where the guy tried to murder his three ex-girlfriends with his pet diamondback along with his fists? They got him when one of the victims lived through the snakebite. The woman, still alive, managed to crawl to a neighbor where she called the police. The killer later swore to the cops that the rattlesnake controlled his emotions and had *ordered* him to slay the women."

Loretta shuddered. Gosh, how she hated snakes! She was still shaking as Jack went on. "And surely you remember that sick puppy in Arizona? Tried to kill his ex-wife and two kids with a venomous Gila monster. When that didn't work out he killed the lizard instead and then blew his brains out with a shotgun."

Loretta Swanson would not be put off. "This case may not be like those. Perhaps the snake aspect isn't just some nutty postscript to the murders. Maybe if you and all the others would be somewhat open minded about it you might see that."

Jack Hanover frowned into the phone. "Look, young lady, except for the on-again, off-again use of a snake, the one-man pattern is always the same.

"I can't argue with those facts, Jack, but—"

Feeling the tension of Loretta's need to solve what he couldn't, Hanover cut her off. "Did you hear what you just said? Facts, Loretta. We deal with facts here."

"Okay, I understand that. But hear me out too, Jack. The snake as a symbol, or instrument of death, plays a big part in devil worship, as the serpent generally depicts Lucifer himself. Look at the books by Joseph or Holmen. I studied them at the Academy. And my instincts tell me there may be something to it."

"Oh, I see," Hanover replied acerbically. "To heck with the facts. Let's just go with those famous Loretta Swanson premonitions. Correct?"

"Maybe," she responded meekly.

Jack sighed in frustration, but decided to show some respect for her feelings. "Look, Loretta, if we were simply looking for a group of weirdoes with pet snakes, we'd be checking out half the population of Arkansas."

She smiled into the phone as Jack continued. "Like I've been telling you, nearly every profile expert in the Bureau now feels it's simply one man doing the killing."

Glancing at his watch and thinking about his mounting paperwork, Hanover again sighed and reluctantly decided to placate her. "Listen, why don't we compromise? You promise to dwell on what I've said and I'll voice your theory to the staff tomorrow. Fax me your ideas. I'll go over them with a couple of savvy guys up here who know a lot about cults. If they feel there's anything to it we'll make our recommendations. Who knows? They may see it your way."

Loretta beamed. "You're a doll, Jack. It's just that I'm almost certain that there's more than one person involved in these killings."

"Fair enough, beautiful. Just remember to stick to specifics in your report. I'll present it with the utmost priority. But please keep in mind, I'm putting my reputation on the line in going to bat for you. You're still in the Bureau's dog house. You stirred up quite a hornet's nest up here with your ruckus about that Florida reptile guru, Dr. Klaus Braun."

"Uh oh," Loretta gasped playfully. "I almost forgot that."

Hanover replied with equal sarcasm. "I bet you did! You were told by your superiors to *discreetly* seek Dr. Braun's advice and thoughts as a world-renown herpetologist. Instead, you went down to the Miami Reptile Center and practically arrested the guy!"

"Well, he was a real jerk." Shaking her head at the thought of the creepy snake doctor, Loretta continued venting. "If you ask me, Klaus Braun acted as though he had something to hide. Innocent people don't behave in that manner. Plus he's a pompous snob."

"Braun might be a snob, alright, but he's one of the richest and most politically connected snobs in the world! Snakes are his whole life, along with the venom they supply for his experimental drug formulas. Unique pharmaceuticals that have supposedly helped many ailing people. And Dr. Braun risks his life daily extracting that venom."

Loretta frowned as she responded. "Yeah, and he charges the tourists big bucks to watch him do it at that zoo of his! Klaus Braun knows exactly what he's doing when it comes to fleecing the public."

"The Miami Reptile Center is definitely *not* a zoo, Miss Swanson. It provides scientists around the world with various snake venoms from which they make antivenin and other important drugs. Dr. Braun has developed pharmaceuticals that have apparently helped many people."

"Oh sure," Loretta shot back, "he's *Doctor Wonderful*."

"That's right, missy. And remember, he's got powerful friends."

"I'll remember, coach."

"There's one more thing, Loretta, and I'm serious about this."

"What's that?"

"You've gotta keep a lower profile down there. Don't even think of speaking to anyone again about this case the way you did with that nosey newspaper reporter. The serial killer himself might be the one to read the papers first. Keep in mind that Miami cop who likewise told the papers that he was assigned to the New Ripper case. He recently received the last victim's eyes in the mail and could have easily ended up as one of the killer's targets."

"No need to remind me. I take my job and the risks very seriously." Loretta grinned to herself, purposely withholding the details about this evening's entrance into the warehouse.

Hanover continued his words of warning. "Serial killers have been known to contact, and even seek out, someone who's assigned to their case. And an attractive, young female agent like yourself, particularly one whose name and address was printed in the *Palm Beach Gazette*, could just be in his sights." Jack's tone during this last sentence was deliberately critical, firmly scolding his pretty colleague for revealing her beach house address to an irresponsible journalist.

"Guilty as charged," Loretta admitted. "And that's a mistake I'll never make again. I stupidly trusted a reporter when I should have known better. But I'm not worried about the New Ripper. Hopefully he *will* contact me. The more letters he sends, the greater the chance of his making a mistake. Maybe he'll get sloppy and leave a fingerprint or something."

Loretta grimaced at the memory of the occurrence with the newspaper reporter. She had naively given a female journalist her address and phone number. Then, to her utter dismay, the reporter surprised her with an unannounced visit to the isolated beach house. Caught off guard, the stunned agent granted a ten-minute interview, telling the writer relatively minor details, and saying that she only had a very small role in the case itself. Despite the woman's solemn promises, this brazen journalist then deviously printed Loretta's name in the article. Mention had also been made that they had met at *the pretty FBI agent's seaside cottage,* with a precise description, address, and location. The subsequent story, appearing in several newspapers, unleashed the fury of the entire FBI hierarchy upon poor Loretta's head. It had been a bureaucratic nightmare! Jack's voice quickly brought her back to the present.

"So, please be more careful. There's a real nutcase on the loose, no matter how cavalier you are about it. And right now you've got no backup or bodyguards at your beach house because you foolishly turned *that* down as well. Bad move on your part. Just remember, I lived in that lonely fleabag you're now holed up in. And I know how isolated it is."

"Fleabag or not, at least I'm getting some decent weather," Loretta teased. "I've heard you're up there freezing your you-know-what off in Washington. But what's with the scary Hitchcock jibe? Jealous I'm down here in the Sunshine State?"

"A little," admitted Hanover. "Yet with all of your talk about voodoo cults and devil worship, I'm glad I'm not there alone on that lonely beach; in the dark with who knows what kind of swamp creatures lurking in the shadows."

Loretta giggled at Jack's teasing. "Oh, cut it out. You're not gonna get me all worked up with that Stephen King garbage. I might be in a remote beach house alone tonight. But tomorrow morning I'll be swimming in the ocean right outside my door with 85-degree weather, while you're up there building a snowman!"

"All right, don't rub it in. All I'll be swimming in is dull paperwork with a forecast of sleet. Gotta run. Take care, beautiful."

"Good night, handsome."

Then, just as she heard the click of Jack's phone, it happened again! Loretta unexpectedly got another one of her *feelings*. It came in an almost cold wave, an eerie but definite premonition that she would never see Jack Hanover again. On an impulse she hoped he would be all right up there in the cold, driving on the still icy DC roads, which she knew could sometimes be very treacherous. She chided herself to snap out of it. *Stop these feelings of doom and gloom and just be happy that you may finally have a lead in the New Ripper case.*

Abruptly, a brilliant flash of lightning momentarily lit up the room. It was immediately followed by a loud window-rattling crack of thunder, making the normally calm FBI agent almost jump out of her skin. She giggled at the thought that if Jack Hanover had seen her reaction he would have surely burst out laughing. Perhaps his ghost story chiding had affected her after all. Loretta smiled and looked out the window. Flinching at another flash of lightning, she guessed that it was one of those sudden, fast moving Florida storms blowing in from the sea. Ironically, her guess of an oncoming disturbance couldn't have been more on target!

Chapter 5

The Mysterious Snake Man

"I'm going to show you the most venomous serpents in the world, snakes powerful enough to kill several strong men with one bite!" These were the startling words Loretta Swanson first heard during her astonishing interview with Dr. Klaus Braun, the eccentric owner and curator of the Miami Reptile Center. His greeting had instantly made her skin crawl back then, and did now as she recalled them. Taking a small sip of her club soda, she realized that she hadn't really thought much more about this enigmatic snake man until tonight. Now, while the lightning and thunder continued outside, as if purposely trying to add a shadowy guise to the room, slithering reptiles, particularly deadly snakes, were definitely on Loretta's mind.

Her conversation with Jack Hanover had brought it back full circle, back to Dr. Braun and his incredible reptile collection. She now wondered silently if there was any link between Braun's serpents and a possible satanic connection in the Ripper case. Could some devil worshipping clan have somehow purchased or stolen a rare snake from the doctor's vast collection? If so, how did snakes play a part in their practices?

Loretta strolled over to her computer, situated on a small desk near the couch, and quickly accessed the Internet. Continuing to dig for information, she was led to a lengthy article by a noted authority on cults, Dr. Peter Ludlow. In his article Dr. Ludlow stated: ... *reptiles, particularly venomous snakes, have occasionally been used as a symbol of worship and as a weapon of revenge in devil worship cult slayings of the past. This practice reached its zenith back in the 1940s and 50s. The recurring problem for cultists, however, particularly in the United States, was the actual acquisition of these deadly, but extremely rare snakes; the kraits and cobras from India for instance, or as they were affectionately called by some of the sects, 'Satan's sacred helpers'. For this reason, specifically the difficulty in obtaining the very lethal varieties, serpent use as an instrument of vengeance had gradually ceased over the years.*

Loretta again shivered as her thoughts returned to Klaus Braun and his renowned Reptile Center and to the distasteful memory of meeting with him. She vividly recalled the doctor's rather odd and uncooperative behavior. *Maybe there was some overlooked lead there*, she thought as the recollection of that day slowly ran through her brain.

Thumbing through her files, she soon located Klaus Braun's thin dossier enclosed in its own separate folder. Closing her eyes, the attractive agent leaned into the soft sofa cushion as her mind drifted back to the doctor's reptile hub. With little effort the memories became stark and vivid and she recalled every detail of that fateful day as if it were the present.

Her boss, Special Agent Reese, of the North Miami Beach Field Office, had been cautiously optimistic that morning when he had sent her to see Dr. Braun. "Miss Swanson, there's one person who might possibly be able to help us establish a clue to the serial killer by explaining more about the specifics of the snake used by the Ripper. That would be the renowned reptile expert Dr. Klaus Braun. If anyone knows about snakes and their venom, it's him. I want you to go to Miami and tactfully question the doctor about the venom aspect of this case. And I repeat the word *tactfully*. This guy has powerful friends in Washington."

"What, exactly, should I ask him?" Loretta recalled asking Reese.

"Be subtle. We want to find out if this celebrated reptile authority knows of any other snake collectors in the area. Or possibly any gossip he's heard concerning illegal, black market snake sales. When and if the situation is conducive, discreetly ask Dr. Braun if any of his own snakes could possibly be missing. He's got tons of them so perhaps one might have been stolen, unscrupulously sold, or somehow lost *without* Dr. Braun's knowledge. Asking Braun about this won't be as easy as it sounds though. He deplores hearing anything negative in connection with reptiles. Just remember. Klaus Braun's whole world is snakes. And, over the years he's developed, won FDA approval for, and has sold various venom-related items for his multi-billion dollar pharmaceutical businesses. According to the reports, he's concocted drugs for just about everything. Headache tablets, anti-aging creams, erectile dysfunction remedies, as well as his more controversial cancer-fighting drugs. And, more recently, some trial runs for a new and very promising coronavirus vaccine. All these products have made Klaus Braun the richest snake authority in the world."

Special Agent Reese had been correct on all counts. The *Mysterious Snake Man*, as he'd been called in a recent television interview, had indeed become world famous. Loretta had therefore been determined to be on her best behavior, though, almost from the start, things had not gone well.

First, as she was entering the front gate of the Miami Reptile Center, she looked up to see a giant statue of a coiled, ready-to-strike serpent. Loretta's very real personal phobia of snakes instantly began to take hold. Her dread rapidly rose to a fevered pitch and she worried about what her reaction would be to Dr. Braun's live reptiles, even if they were caged. She prayed that her snake phobia wouldn't affect her professional behavior.

A bureau file she had perused earlier that morning had shown that the Miami Reptile Center had been in operation in Florida for over fifteen years. The place was not just a Mecca for scientists and herpetologists, but also a popular tourist destination with museum-like displays of over two hundred snakes, lizards, alligators, crocodiles, and even the notoriously vicious Komodo dragon. Though the displays were impressive, Klaus Braun himself was the real star here. During his daily shows the gaped-mouth audiences would watch in stunned silence as he deftly avoided each serpent's quick, deadly strike just in the nick of time, ultimately catching the snake and extracting venom from its fangs into rubber topped jars.

Loretta recognized that Braun's reptile shows wouldn't be easy to view for a person deathly afraid of snakes like herself. Before leaving the office that morning, after making sure no one was watching, she had opened a dictionary and looked up the term *ophidiophobia... an exaggerated and persistent dread or aversion to reptiles.* On reading this information, the FBI agent had slammed the book closed. "I am *not* an ophidiophobiac," she had feebly exclaimed, with a frightened shudder that ran through her entire body, causing her arms to break out in chill bumps.

Even now, as she sat on the comfortable couch in her secluded beach home, Loretta's heart raced and her palms moistened at the thought of it all. Her flashbacks of the dreaded reptiles were slowly reoccurring, almost as though she was there again.

Snakes! How Loretta hated them. She wished they would all disappear from the face of the earth! Her attitude certainly wasn't environmentally correct, particularly in today's nature-friendly world. Yet, she just couldn't help herself. Snakes, with their slimy looks, the coldness about them, and of course, their killing fangs and poison were something she had grown to detest.

Indeed, one of her earliest nightmares, at age six, had centered on being stalked by a gigantic snake. It was a childish fairytale of a dream in which she, the beautiful princess, was being chased by a big, floating serpent sent to kill her by an evil ruler and his soldiers. Loretta had experienced this nightmare many times during her youth. It was always the same snake in the dream with the same childish ending. The slithering reptile chased her around for miles, continuously trying to slay her. But always, Loretta's hero, a mystical white knight with a great silver sword, appeared just in the nick of time. Her hero then killed the serpent and the evil men who had sent it. She and the handsome knight then rode off into the sunset and lived 'happily ever after.'

Young Loretta had dreamt this childish fantasy repeatedly, and each time it had the same happy ending; all except once. She trembled while recalling that one nightmare exception. In this particular terrifying version of her fantasy, the recurring dream had a very different conclusion. This time, her white knight had been too late and the serpent had finally caught up with Princess Loretta, sinking its deadly fangs repeatedly into her while she screamed. When the handsome knight hero finally arrived he sadly clutched her dying body, vowing to avenge her by killing the snake and the evil men. But alas, his poor princess was gone forever!

It was this singular version of the dream that Loretta always remembered most. Even now, some twenty-five years later, she recalled abruptly awakening, terrified, with sweat-soaked pajamas and sheets.

It was one of the first times she had ever experienced her *inner feelings* of doom. That's how real and terrifying the nightmare had seemed back then. Six-year-old Loretta had immediately run into her parent's room and told them about the dream, but they merely chuckled at their daughter's childish imagination.

Recalling the nightmare now, she again shivered. And to think, Dr. Klaus Braun single-handedly faced and captured these hideous creatures nearly every day at his afternoon extraction shows. No wonder the place was a *must see* for tourists.

Still trembling, her thoughts returned to Dr. Braun and his bizarre welcoming of her to the snake center. She recalled his mesmerizing voice and the details of his unique appearance. Klaus Braun was tall, well over six feet, with odd, yellowish skin. His unusual, almost evil eyes looked a bit like a modern-day vampire, with the shadowy Dracula gaze of *Bella Lugosi,* the old black-and-white horror film actor. To Loretta, the doctor seemed to be a combination of an emotionless undertaker and psychopathic dentist, the type who would smile caringly while inflicting great pain and discomfort upon his patients. Reluctantly, Loretta now admitted that the snake man had kept her in a trancelike stupor, mesmerizing her into being strangely ineffective around him. As they strolled past the various snake habitats, each more frightening than the next, Dr. Braun knowledgeably informed her about each reptile.

"This enclosure holds the giant anaconda. Miss Swanson, a snake so large it's capable of killing and eating an extremely large cow. Hence its name." Loretta could see the massive animal plainly as they strolled past. "And here we have the Puff Adder, *Bitis arietans*, with haemotoxic venom so potent and painful that the flesh of its victim begins to rot a few minutes after the excruciating bite has taken place. This snake virtually digests its victim's body from the inside out, in a necrosis style." He happily watched his guest cringe and then went on, "The cage next to it houses the Gaboon Viper from Africa; *Bitis gabonica*, known for possessing the world's longest fangs." Dr. Braun then pointed across the way. "Over there we have the most venomous snake in the world, the inland Taipan, *Oxyuranus microlepidotus,* better known as the Fierce Snake. It's native to Central Australia. One bite from that serpent could conceivably deliver enough venom to kill fifty people."

They next came to one of Braun's favorite creatures, a long and muscular grayish snake. "And this, my dear, is the dreaded Black Mamba of Africa. The *Dendroaspis polylepis* is by far the quickest of the neurotoxin serpents. One of these beauties once crawled into a small tent in which a native African family was living. They were all asleep one night, when their youngest boy accidentally rolled over the snake. The enraged serpent bit him, and then, in a lightning fast attack, it also bit the other three members of his family. The following morning, neighbors found all of them dead in their small tented abode. Quite a creature this one!" Klaus Braun smiled proudly, seemingly more impressed with the reptile than sad for the unfortunate family.

Before she could respond to the tragic account, her mind momentarily went blank due to a bizarre surprise. Because of the heat of the day, the doctor took off his suit jacket. The dark, short-sleeve shirt he wore revealed his scaly, almost pure yellow arms. Loretta stared transfixed at him, but then to her horror she became embarrassingly aware that Dr. Braun had noticed what she was looking at. Smiling coldly he chided, "I see that you've noticed my unusual skin tone."

"No, I - I mean," she gasped incoherently, too ashamed to continue.

"Please don't feel badly," he assured her sympathetically. "Everyone stares at first. Actually I'm quite proud of it. You see, Miss Swanson, the yellow nature, as well as the flakiness of my epidermis, comes primarily from being bitten numerous times by various venomous snakes. I've been bitten by some of the most lethal reptiles in the world. I also purposefully injected many other types of venom into my body."

"Injected? You mean putting that poison into your body was by *choice*?" Loretta was astonished, yet also fascinated.

"Had to, my dear," Braun explained. "I knew from the start that no matter how good you are at grabbing a snake by hand, there's bound to be a fast one that will ultimately catch you off guard. So, with hypodermic needles, I purposely began injecting small amounts of venom into my system to help give me stronger immunity. These shots, coupled with the many accidental bites I've received over the years, have served their purpose. I dare say, Miss Swanson, that I have more snake venom in my system than any other living being!" As their walk ended, her shadowy host allowed her a very cursory glance at his private laboratories, where he nebulously informed her that *'around the clock research'* took place.

"Thanks for the personal tour, Dr. Braun. I know you're a very busy man and I truly appreciate your time." Loretta then got down to the business at hand. "Your work is very impressive, as well as the facility itself. How about recordkeeping? I would assume you keep detailed files on your reptiles and their whereabouts?"

Dr. Braun's ears perked as he responded with obvious annoyance. This inquisitive FBI agent had suddenly changed from a simple tourist to an official interrogator and Braun seemed irritated by her transformation. "Yes, Miss Swanson, we keep comprehensive records of each and every animal, both here and at my estate. My personal secretary, Miss Kent, handles all that. In addition to those records being invaluable to the pharmaceutical side it's also like having a reptilian census bureau, a complete file on each and every reptile. Why do you ask?"

"Just a routine question, Doctor. I'm simply looking into the possibility of missing snakes. That is, if there are any. I was wondering if you had confirmation of every serpent here."

Braun growled his reply. "I've already addressed that question and that's all I'm going to say about it!"

Loretta persisted politely but firmly, and insisted on talking to Dr. Braun's recordkeeping assistant. The few moments Braun had reluctantly granted with his private secretary, a strikingly gorgeous brunette in her late twenties, had proven interesting yet futile at the same time. "It would be next to impossible to give you an inventory of each and every snake at this very moment," Miss Kent had civilly, yet firmly, informed, all the while displaying a lovely and seemingly never-ending smile. This false demeanor was one that Loretta knew quite well from her own experience as a high school cheerleader.

"I might eventually be able to work on a list if it really is that important," Sandra pointed out, but then added, "although I don't see why it would be. As I'm sure Dr. Braun has told you, we're not in the animal retail business. Not one of our snakes has ever escaped and none are currently missing! I would swear to that in court."

Loretta had been forewarned about Sandra Kent's fanatical loyalty to Dr. Braun. Upon hearing the rest of the pretty girl's spiel, Agent Swanson couldn't actually say that Sandra was knowingly part of anything illegal. Yet it was quite obvious that Braun's beautiful assistant had swallowed the snake doctor's *helper of the masses* Kool Aid, and couldn't be swayed to reveal anything of substance. Loretta Swanson had seen this type before, the charming secretarial mute who could defuse any issue, dodge any question, or quell any scandal, all with a beautiful and disarming smile. Given more time, Loretta was sure she could have gotten through to Miss Kent. She had perceived integrity in Sandra during their brief moments together, despite the woman's blind devotion to Dr. Braun.

Her drive home from Braun's Miami Reptile Center was mixed with a swirl of emotions. The whole afternoon had been frustrating, and yes, even terrifying at times. Worst of all, Loretta had left the Center without one piece of productive information or data. *Yet what was there really to find?* Klaus Braun might have been a bit off kilter, but he certainly didn't seem to be a knife-wielding serial killer. The doctor was too polished and too private for any of that. He was most likely only interested in protecting his billion-dollar empire, his top secret formulas, and of course, his snakes. Yet somehow the FBI operative instinctively knew that this mysterious snake man was hiding something; something very important and perhaps even dangerous.

Loretta Swanson had pretty much written off Dr. Klaus Braun until tonight. Her new satanic theories on snakes as a cult instrument of vengeance unexpectedly brought him back into the picture. Suddenly, as a loud boom of thunder sounded, Loretta got another chilling thought. *What if Dr. Braun himself was a cult member?* He had the sinister, mysterious quality of one, and heaven knows he was quiet and secretive. It could just be. *First thing tomorrow I'm going to look into the personal lives of Dr. Braun and Sandra Kent. Perhaps one or even both were serving a higher cause. The cause of the devil!*

Checking her watch, Loretta was astonished to find that it was after two in the morning. While putting away her files she reflectively thought of her dad, feeling somewhat guilty about the half-finished letter to him now over in the sofa's end table. Removing it from the thin drawer, Loretta reread the few sentences she'd penned earlier, but then quickly returned it to the drawer, finally admitting she was just too fatigued to finish. Maybe before breakfast she'd give it a try. She walked over and locked the front door. Then, for some odd reason, one she couldn't put her finger on, perhaps those 'inner feelings' again, she double bolted the door. This was something she had never done at the beach house before.

Finished with that task, she strolled over to the small hall closet and carefully hung up her holster and GLOCK pistol just outside the master bedroom. This was where her gun was always stored when it wasn't on her person, although she now fought off a rather curious urge to keep it with her for the night. Entering her bedroom, decorated smartly in light blue and white colors, she removed her slightly sweaty clothes and retired to the bathroom for a soothing shower.

Just outside Loretta Swanson's small beach home, two sinister characters crouched in the sand, now soaked by the steady rain. Waiting silently in hidden subterfuge, like two sand-covered chameleons, they watched for the lights in the house to finally be turned off. One man carried a black case with air holes and a demonic red skull painted on its side. The other man gently fondled an ominous looking carving knife and fantasized about the FBI girl's pretty neck.

B ehind their sand dune hiding place, topped by a lone, tall palm tree, the two Mid-Eastern henchmen continued to hole up in silence, unprotected from the light rainfall. One of the men, aided by a pair of excellent binoculars, carefully watched the movements of the fine looking woman through the small picture window of the beach house. He had learned from several reconnaissance forays here that whenever the living room lights went out, the FBI girl would immediately shower and retire to bed.

The shorter of the two stalkers, a bearded thug named Rahmad, looked over and whispered to his partner, "Amir, the woman is at last finished working. Soon, she will sleep."

Amir, dressed in black coveralls, as was his sidekick, was still not certain if the actual moment had arrived. There had already been two false alarms tonight. Nonetheless, he was stirred by his partner's words. "That is good, Rahmad. Hopefully, we can move in soon." As Rahmad nodded back, the living room turned dark as if on cue.

Fifteen minutes later, the two men, stooping low, hurried across the sand, serpentine style. Amir led the way carrying the ominous black case, moving as light footed as possible. Rahmad quickly followed, careful to place his feet precisely in the footsteps of his partner. If the diminishing rain didn't wash away all the footprints at least it would appear that only one person had been there. After coming to a stop they crouched beneath the picture window of the woman's cottage and momentarily waited, still staying very low to the ground. Anticipating the violence of their upcoming task, Rahmad nervously laced and unlaced his black-gloved fingers. He next placed his ear against the exterior wall. As of yet, no sounds were coming from inside the house. Rahmad again dropped to the ground near his partner and waited.

For Amir and Rahmad, waiting was an important part of their preparation. Both men were overcautious to a fault. Their methodical training at a secluded desert combat camp in Afghanistan, as well as the vigilant nature of their fastidious new leader, had made them so. These assassins were true experts, killers who never made foolish assumptions or mistakes. They wouldn't now.

Ten more minutes passed. Rahmad rose and again put his ear against the wall. He heard water running through the pipes, indicating that the woman was bathing before sleep. Nodding to his partner, Rahmad licked his lips at the thought of the shapely lady in the shower.

Next, it was Amir's turn to stand up and glance into the house. The view through the picture window of the interior of the home was pitch black, except for a tiny crack of light coming from under the door of the girl's bedroom. He knew that this would be the telltale sign. When the bedroom light went off, the FBI agent would soon be asleep. They could then proceed!

Inside her bedroom, oblivious to the terror lurking outside, Loretta Swanson turned on the small TV atop the dresser and dried herself with a white bath towel. The soothing shower had left her totally relaxed. She watched part of a late night repeat of a local newscast, the lead story of which was, *Would the Ripper strike again, and where?* Loretta frowned and quickly switched the channel to an old Bogart film. Patting on some lilac body powder, she watched Bogie shoot a bad guy, and then slipped on a short, pink nightshirt.

As Loretta stretched out between the smooth, cool sheets, she briefly worried about having nightmares on devils and snakes. "Darn that Jack Hanover for trying to put scary images into my mind," the drowsy agent mused, though smiling at the thought of him. She then turned off her bedside lamp, closed her eyes, and was almost instantly asleep.

~

When the two thugs lying outside the living room window noticed the thin ray of light disappear from under the master bedroom door, their senses came alive with fervent anticipation. "We'll wait one hour more," whispered Amir with a sinister grin.

Rahmad nodded and glanced at the luminous dial of his wristwatch. The purple numbers indicated it was 2:44 a.m. The rain had finally stopped and all was quiet and serene. With a contented sigh, he looked over at his partner who was gazing intently into the dark living room. How they both loved this part of the 'hunt'. The prelude before the kill! The fact that they were soon going to eliminate an important official of the evil American government only intensified the satisfaction. Rahmad reflectively recalled past memories of similar nights back in Afghanistan, when the two partners had eliminated other Mideast enemies; mostly foes of al-Qaeda, and later on ISIS K. There had been so many assassinations back then that after a while these political slayings became a matter of dull routine for them. True, they'd had honed their skills as trained assassins, but the thrill of carrying out those political executions had gradually waned.

Rahmad remembered discussing this emptiness in their lives with Amir, and they soon jumped at the chance to journey to the hated land of America. This in order to join a North American terrorist cell. It was at this point that fate intervened. Shortly after arriving in America they had been introduced to *Him*, their present leader; and more importantly captivated with the dark powers of Lucifer. Now their killing would be for a greater purpose, not just for some government or political agenda. It would be used to further the glorious cause of Satan and to elevate the Fallen Prince back to the heights that were rightly his! Rahmad smiled widely as his partner quietly informed, "The time has come. The bedroom light has been off long enough."

With a precision glasscutter taken from the leather bag he carried, Rahmad rose up and noiselessly and deftly cut out a sizable piece of glass from the picture window, just large enough through which they'd be able to enter. Access into the female agent's darkened home was now assured.

Careful not to make even the faintest sound, the two stalkers skillfully removed the piece of cut glass and silently slipped through the new opening, pulling the black case and their other implements with them. Inside the home it was very dark, and the faint, lingering aroma of the woman's perfume still drifted in the air. Stimulated by the scent, both men immediately directed their attention to the closed bedroom door. Killing the woman would not be a problem, but making the deed look as if it were the work of a deranged serial killer might prove tricky. Nonetheless, this part of the assignment had been carefully rehearsed and successfully carried out seven times before, succeeding beyond their wildest dreams. The fools of the *West* had bought it all, panicking frantically at a so-called new Ripper. They and their satanic leader had laughed heartily at each Ripper headline and news story.

Rahmad felt Amir tap his shoulder softly. He was then handed one of the two humanlike facemasks; masks his partner had been carrying in a small bag. These supple skeletal faces, very detailed and heinous, seemed to scowl with a devil's visage. Repulsive was the only word to describe them. The masks, called *Yucids*, had been expertly made from a combination of a thin latex substance and actual human skin; skin that had been flayed from non-believing victims. The satanic high priest himself had blessed the masks before giving them to Amir and Rahmad, and the duo always wore these demonic face coverings during a kill as a tribute to Lucifer.

Now clad in their hideous devil faces, Amir and Rahmad bowed to each other, a signal that they were ready for their mission. One held an ornately designed knife with a razor sharp blade, and the other, the black carrying case. Tiptoeing silently to the bedroom door, they were almost certain that the woman would now be in a deep sleep. Yet they couldn't count on it. If she was awake, or awoke suddenly and saw them, they would just have to rush her. After all, as an FBI operative, she undoubtedly owned a gun and was probably well trained in its use.

Rahmad reached the bedroom door first, and for good reason. He had earned the nickname, *'the ferret'* by his peers because of his innate talent for entering any space, any entry, and indeed any door, completely undetected. He could almost will a door to open without as much as a squeak or a groan. The ferret felt the door with expert precision, using only his left hand, much like a fine-tuned violin. The door opened smoothly and soundlessly, providing a space that was just wide enough for them to quietly slip into the woman's room.

The two stalkers now stood inside the bedroom, frozen in absolute silence. With their eyes acclimated to the darkness, the small amount of light through the window shade, emanating from a hazy half-moon, allowed them to clearly see that their target was indeed soundly sleeping. As they noiselessly approached the girl's bed, anticipation of the events to come stirred their senses like an erotic elixir. Amir carefully opened the black carrying case, smirked cruelly, and slowly emptied its content upon the bed. The black case with the tiny air holes housed only one thing; a six-foot-long Egyptian cobra, one of the world's deadliest snakes!

The serpent lay completely still on the mattress for a moment, assessing its new environment. Then, cautiously and deliberately, the reptile flicked out its forked tongue and slowly edged away from the men toward the woman's pillow. Satisfied, the now excited stalkers eased to the floor, knelt below the foot of the bed, and waited for the inevitable.

The cobra crawled a few more inches and then stopped. It again flicked its tongue, and almost simultaneously the woman stirred. The snake became nervous with her sudden movement, and within seconds, reared its head in the classic flat-necked cobra pose.

Something, perhaps the slight vibration caused by the rearing reptile, or perhaps its noise on the sheets, brought Loretta Swanson out of her slumber. As she yawned, widely, the agitated snake stiffened and readied its defenses.

Loretta's eyes slowly opened. She was surprised to find herself drenched in a cold sweat. *What woke me?* she wondered. *A sound? A dream that has already left my memory?* Still a bit groggy, the startled FBI agent lay in the darkness, completely unaware that a large and deadly snake was only inches from her body. She was likewise oblivious to the hideously masked men waiting silently below the foot of her bed.

Wiping the sweat from her brow, Loretta listened for what might have awakened her, while Rahmad and Amir waited in silence below her footboard, ready to spring if necessary. The cobra, perceiving danger, also lay perfectly still. With that *inner feeling* of hers suddenly sending out a warning, Loretta began to sense another presence in the room. Her body stiffened and she was immediately wary and alert. Hearing only the whir of the air conditioner, and unable to see anything in the darkness, she decided to turn on the bedside lamp. It was a bad decision!

The movement of switching on the lamp startled the cobra, causing it to rear up even higher in the now well-lit bedroom. The snake's hood spread wide as it poised, now standing a full four-feet tall and looking straight down at Loretta! The serpent's black, beady eyes zeroed in on hers. As it became ready to strike, Loretta froze in abject terror. For a brief moment she thought she was simply having a terrible nightmare and that it would all end with her waking up. However, reality quickly set in as she realized this was *not* a dream. The deadly reptile was real and poised to attack!

If she hadn't been terrorized by her lifelong phobia of snakes, Loretta might have shown more bravery. Perhaps, had she been able to think more clearly, she would have frozen until the snake backed away. But there was absolutely no chance of that now. The terrified agent's right hand went to her mouth, almost as if she was trying to hide her face from the beast, and this added movement immediately brought a vicious, lightning fast attack from the cobra.

"Noooo!" Loretta let out a blood-curdling scream just as the snake bit her on the forehead. It reared back and inflicted two more bites on her neck, causing her to scream again. Horrified, she placed her hands on the front of her head where the first bite had occurred and immediately felt the warm stickiness of blood. As Loretta grasped her predicament, the cobra, now just as frightened as she was, slithered off the bed, and curled up in a corner of the room, well away from the encounter.

Almost immediately after the snake's strike, a new horror, perhaps more terrifying than that of the reptile, confronted the quivering woman. Two hideous, devilish faces rose up from the foot of her bed! One of the devils held a huge knife that glistened in the light. She stared, transfixed in utter disbelief. The sight of the skeletal faces was more frightening than the shock and bites of the cobra. *Is this nightmare ever going to end*?

The horrified girl, with the look of a terrified deer, panted in anguish. Trembling, and literally unable to move, she started to find it hard to breathe. Her thoughts grew cloudy and unclear, and as the lethal venom rushed through her body she was unable to fully concentrate on the situation. Loretta's previously strong mind slowly drifted to visions of the gruesome crime scene videos she had studied so many times, followed by the sad realization that the next one could be of her own dismembered body. There was absolutely no resistance left in her now, only raw terror. She was literally frozen with fear, dazed from the continual effects of the venom; a helpless rag doll, waiting for the next horror to occur.

The deadly toxin injected by the cobra's needle-like fangs was methodically working its way through her body. Her skin tingled, and her neck, already swollen, was turning darker. Totally engulfed with fright, the onset of complete shock rapidly began to sweep over Loretta. The snake had done its job well. The panic it induced, as well as its poison, had rendered the FBI operative totally incapacitated. Her expression showed only the fear and loathing of a vulnerable human puppet, waiting to be hurt again.

The two skeletal faces calmly approached the stunned woman. One stuffed a rag in her mouth, silencing what little cries of helplessness she had mustered. The rag tasted of salt and dirt. Now fading fast into a trance of nightmarish trepidation, Loretta Swanson continued to stare at her unknown assailants in total repulsion and disbelief. Underneath the masks she could see the teeth of their cruel smiles as they snatched her arms and legs. Holding the woman spread-eagle for a short while, and leering at her shapely body, the two men fought the momentary urge to sexually invade her. Rahmad and Amir knew well that if their leader ever became aware of even the thought of such an act, they would meet a similarly cruel fate themselves. Instead, they chose to tightly hold her down and patiently wait for the snake's venom to complete its deadly work.

While she grew flaccid, the two assassins began to howl and chant. It was a dreadful rhythm that started as a low guttural hum and grew louder with each fading beat of her heart. Loretta hardly heard it now as she began to fade into final shock, although she did make out the words *Lucifer*, *Blood*, and *Death to America*. In detached revulsion, her eyes were open just long and wide enough to see the taller of the two devils raise a large knife over his head and hold it there while continuing the terrifying chant. What was left of Loretta's fleeting mind instinctively instructed her body to struggle in defense, to kick out at this man, but she could not. She began saying to herself, *Please not this way*, when suddenly the thought of her father and the unfinished letter swept through her mind. She now felt terrible about not completing it.

With a perverted flash of inspiration, Amir lowered his arm, casually laid the knife on the bed, and walked over to the corner of the room. He carefully picked up the cobra by the back of the neck just the way the leader had taught him to handle dangerous snakes. Brandishing a malicious grin, Amir returned to the bedside with the horrifying serpent. His cohort roughly jerked the rag out of the agent's mouth and forced it open, making sure that his heavily gloved fingers were well away from the approaching efforts of his accomplice guiding the reptile. Both men began chanting loudly, "Prepare to taste the serpent of Lucifer." Carefully guiding the wriggling cobra down the woman's pried open mouth, Amir watched with sadistic glee.

Apathetic now from the snake venom and from being in total shock, Loretta was mercifully oblivious to the snake, which was being forced down inside her. Unable to breathe, she continued to weaken, drifting away in a whirl of colors and dizziness. Her last semiconscious thoughts were that snakes weren't really that slimy, and sadness that the rescuing hero knight of her childhood dream was nowhere to be found. In a matter of seconds, Loretta no longer felt the snake crawling down her throat, or anything else for that matter.

The two killers, sensing her impending death and feeling a bit disappointed that their perverted fun had come to an end, simply set the woman free. Amir carefully pulled the snake out of the girl's throat and then placed the reptile into its black carrying case. Loretta Swanson moaned softly and breathed her last.

Rahmad felt the woman's wrist. There was no pulse. Cause of death was from one of three things he surmised; the venom, suffocation, or shock. His partner, Amir, made a long cut on the girl's leg and dipped a thin paintbrush into the oozing blood. He then wrote a short note on a white piece of heavy paper. It was the very specific message that his leader had dictated to him earlier, words he now retrieved from memory.

It read: *This policewoman said in the newspaper that I would eventually be caught. She was foolish enough to say where she lived, as if to dare me to come to her! So I came, you impudent policewoman! No one can ever catch me and I dare you all to try. I am too clever for everyone, and I will surely kill again! The blood and flesh keeps me going. April Fools! — Until the first day of May — Your slashing friend!*

After finishing his note, Amir pinned it on one of the pillows and turned toward Rahmad. "Lucifer's work is almost complete. I must now prepare the body so it will be nearly unrecognizable as a human form. Afterward, we can take care of her blasphemous eyes."

Amir had absolutely no remorse about the gruesome task left for him to perform on the woman's body. It was simply part of the assignment and he alone would have to do the work. Their leader had told them that they must keep up this New Ripper charade at all costs.

Taking a large hatchet from his partner's leather bag, the masked assassin began his ghastly handiwork of mutilating the body. He saved the dead woman's still-beautiful face for last. Then, in a sick finale, he took a small surgical instrument, one with a finely honed blade, and commenced to slowly and methodically perform the perverted eye surgery.

Watching off to the side, Rahmad walked over and took the woman's eyes from his partner, carefully placing them in a small wooden box. He faced upward and began chanting, "These eyes, which saw only the falsehoods of nonbelievers, will be brought back to feed Satan's dragon. *Vioanos,* oh Lucifer, son of the morning star." With those intoning words, their appalling satanic handiwork was at last complete.

An hour or so later, on the eastern horizon, the initial light of morning slowly broke over the Atlantic Ocean. It was the first day of April. To an awakening world it would appear that the New Ripper had struck again.

Chapter 7

Bitter Thoughts in New York

F ive days after the hideously mutilated body of FBI Special Agent Loretta Swanson had been discovered at a lonely beach house in south Florida, the entire country was still in shock. It seemed that everyone was talking about the brutal murder and the media in most markets was having a field day with it.

The reaction in New York City, on this unseasonably cold and rainy April 5th, Tuesday morning, was typical of the frenzy. All of the major New York newspapers and TV stations were leading with the Ripper story and the Big Apple's dreary weather, which felt more like January than April, seemed morbidly appropriate.

Sitting alone in his office in a tall New York City office building on Madison Avenue, the raw climate outside was of little concern to Colonel Peter M. McPhail. Colonel McPhail, Acting Director of G5, a hybrid, top secret federal agency headquartered in Manhattan, had more important things to worry about; his agency for one thing. McPhail's secret department, known only to a very small and select group of government officials, answered *solely* to the President of the United States. That alone made it unique and Peter McPhail, the agency's charismatic leader, was as atypical as the clandestine bureau he headed.

The organization's early roots actually extend back to the OSS' famous G2 Bureau of World War II, used extensively by the President for covert wartime operations. Once the war ended however, it ceased operating, primarily for budgetary reasons. Then, in 1979, the Bureau had once again been created, reestablished really, during the Carter Administration, immediately following the onset of the Iranian hostage crisis. The agency was reborn and today still operates as a top secret, special executive branch of the intelligence department; one that can only be called upon by the President himself.

Over the years G5 has been, and still is, situated in the same location in which it originated, on the top three floors of a nondescript high-rise government building on Madison Avenue. The department has served every US President since Carter, with involvement in classified domestic investigative work, overseas espionage, antiterrorism, and more recently, homeland security. No mention or listing of G5 can be found anywhere in government records, since its effectiveness lies strictly in its shielded anonymity. This top secret agency takes no credit or blame for anything it does, and reports to just one person on the President's staff, usually a high-ranking White House official designated by the Commander-in-Chief himself. Only the President can request G5 involvement, albeit with one sworn restriction; absolutely *nothing* of a political nature can *ever* be endeavored by the agency. Specifically, G5 cannot be used against any administration's political opponents. Over the years, G5's non-political Directors have made certain that this Presidential pledge is scrupulously honored.

G5 has links to *five* separate intelligence groups: the FBI, CIA, NSA, Military Intelligence, and the Secret Service. G5's Director is fully authorized to recruit from any and all of these agencies. Colonel McPhail, US Army (retired), and his predecessor, Major Gordon Matheson, carefully selected their unique mixture of operative *all-stars*, recruiting and drafting some of the best agents and brightest minds from these *five* bureaus; hence the name, G5.

Today, on this chilly April morning in New York City, McPhail was not worried about any political misuse of power. In fact his concern was quite the opposite. His apprehension centered on a hastily scheduled and rare visit to his office from two US Senators. The President himself had called earlier on the secure green-line phone to inform the director that two senatorial VIPs from *each* major party were coming in. He had instructed Colonel McPhail to brief the senators on the impending participation of G5 in the New Ripper serial killings in Florida. "Enough is enough," the President had forcefully exclaimed, "especially with the brutal murder of a senator's daughter." The Commander-in-Chief wanted action, and he wanted it immediately!

Colonel McPhail's main worry this morning was just how much he should actually reveal regarding G5, and how far he could trust the visiting senators in keeping this top secret information to themselves. The colonel was always concerned about his agents, and with protecting their cover and security. Nonetheless, these two senators had been given the highest clearance classification and that was good enough for McPhail. He would act accordingly and obey his orders. The tricky part however, was that the President had left the decision up to McPhail regarding how *much* to actually tell the visitors, and that responsibility now weighed heavily. While the Colonel again pondered the senatorial visit, his interoffice phone rang. He picked it up on the first ring. "McPhail here."

"Hi, Pete, it's Hank," greeted Henry Carson, Colonel McPhail's number-two man and the second link in the chain of command at G5. "Just got back from London, but I'll be available for your briefing with the senators if you need me."

"Thank goodness, Hank. You couldn't have arrived at a better time. I can really use your help today. Political correctness is not usually my cup of tea."

Hank Carson chuckled into the phone. "Don't worry Colonel, I'll be there."

"Presumably, the President wants me to inform the senators that G5 has a viable plan on this Ripper thing," McPhail explained. "Well, we do, but I may need your help in selling it."

"You've got it, Pete."

Colonel McPhail rubbed his forehead and sighed. "This whole Ripper business is an unsightly mess, Hank. Especially with the outrage fueled by the latest killing. If a senator's daughter, and an FBI agent at that, can be brutally attacked and murdered, who then is safe? Everyone, here and abroad, is calling for America to catch the killer without delay, and to show her teeth, if she has any left."

"I fear the effect this fiend is creating has been greatly underestimated, Colonel. We look weak and helpless and that always increases the chances of some sort of terrorist activity."

"Exactly, Hank."

" And there's one other thing, Colonel. With this Ripper maniac still at large, what if copycat killings start happening? It could become a real mess, like the pins and needles we were sitting on during the early stages of the COVID pandemic. Some of us felt it could be a terrorist plot, most likely from China, to be followed by more virus strikes."

Hank Carson took a small drink of his bottled water and continued, "Back then you and I were similarly worried. Worried that international repercussions, or even possible terrorist plots, could be heightened due to America's perceived vulnerability. There's always that chance when the country appears weak. Panic spreads everywhere and public confidence wanes as well."

Carson shook his head irately and further exclaimed, "I also remember those two DC sniper punks, acting alone, when I first got here. Back then they had the cops and the feds running around in circles for weeks. The police might still be hunting two white guys in a van if G5 hadn't been called in."

Colonel McPhail beamed inwardly while recalling the details of his unit's involvement in solving of that infamous DC sniper case. G5 had helped crack it, though nobody would ever know. Working behind the scenes, after being called upon by the President, two of McPhail's agents had connected some out-of-state robberies with the sniper's weapon of choice. Then, with inside help from two of Malvo's former mistresses, we got perfect descriptions of the killers and their car; a 1990 Chevy Caprice. That led authorities from other law enforcement agencies and ultimately to the killers themselves. Only the President, a few trusted aides, and the top echelon of the FBI, knew of G5's undercover work, and that's the way Peter McPhail wanted it. His agents had simply faded into thin air.

Carson's voice interrupted his chief's memories. "The problem is, Colonel, where do we *begin* on this Ripper thing? There's precious little to go on. After eight killings, the FBI doesn't have one suspect, and the first day of May is not that far away."

McPhail tapped his fingers on the desk and then gave his reply. "Loretta Swanson's final notes, her new theory about the snake thing, and this mysterious Dr. Klaus Braun, are, in my opinion, the only place to start. And even that information is vague and has its own serious political complications." McPhail frowned. "There's that lousy P-word again, Hank."

"Are you going to tell the senators about the *Studs*, Colonel?"

"Don't know yet, Hank. I've been wrestling with that all morning. Right now I'm planning to give them a quick briefing on it, although in a very vague manner."

"Well, your plan for our agent, from what I've seen of it earlier this morning, looks to be a darn good start", said Carson. "G5 might be able to help in certain areas where other agencies can't. It's high time we got involved."

Their conversation was cut short by the buzz of the intercom. "Sorry to disturb you, sir," announced the secretary's voice through the intercom. "The senators have just arrived downstairs. They should be coming up with Branson any minute."

"Very good, Miss Gallo," McPhail replied. "Oh, and, Nancy, We could use some coffee, tea, donuts, bagels, or whatever the heck it is you feed a senator."

"She smiled. I'll see to it, sir."

Colonel McPhail quickly hung up with Carson and then rose from his desk He could feel the dry mouth and the nervous perspiration begin. With a quick glance around the room he made certain everything was neat and orderly. It was. The Colonel then pulled back the pale gold drapes and glanced out his large window overlooking Madison Avenue. It revealed a picturesque view of Manhattan, although the view wasn't quite the same as it had been before September 11, 2001. For though the newer single tower building was magnificent, Peter McPhail still missed the towering twin buildings of the World Trade Center that had once dominated the skyline. Their absence was a constant reminder for him and his agents to be diligent.

Continuing the scrutiny of his office, McPhail walked over to the two high-back, brown leather chairs opposite his desk. He removed a tiny green feather from one of them and dropped it into the decorative wooden trashcan beside his desk. Confident his office was in order, he strolled over to the large antique mirror on the far wall and decided to check out his personal appearance.

His gaunt, weathered face stared back at him. It was that of a man who had lived sixty-eight hard and anxiety ridden years. G5's director had thinning gray hair and blue eyes, and many friends said that he looked a bit like Henry Fonda in the actor's later years. For some reason McPhail had always disliked the comparison, although he admired the actor. He straightened his trademark bowtie, now for the third time, and sat down behind the desk. Satisfied that he and his office looked fine, his only worry now was Quack.

Quack was Colonel McPhail's beloved pet, an Amazon Yellow Nape parrot. The bird, a large green beauty, was brilliantly colored with yellow spots on the back of its neck. The perky and feisty parrot lived by day in a large ornate cage directly behind the colonel's desk. Being devoted to the bird, McPhail lovingly brought him back and forth every morning in a special transport cage from his Connecticut home. He had owned the parrot for over fifteen years and would not hear of working or living without him, even though Quack had occasionally blurted out embarrassing spoken words and noises as was a common personality trait of the extroverted Amazons.

As McPhail took one last look around, his heart begin to race. Just at that moment, the intercom buzzed again. Nancy Gallo nervously announced, "The senators have arrived, sir."

Chapter 8

Top Secrets

T he two politicians walked into the room guided by McPhail's thin, attractive secretary, Nancy Gallo. Colonel McPhail smiled courteously to the easily recognizable VIPs as they shook hands and sat down in the leather chairs directly in front of his desk. After the required social introductions and pleasantries, and several friendly grins directed toward Quack the parrot, Nancy politely left the room. Her boss pressed the black *Privacy* button under his desk. From this point on there would be no interruptions.

While the senators continued playfully speaking to the bird, Colonel McPhail sized them up with a professional eye. Senator Diane Bowman, a Democrat from California, leaned to the left politically. Nonetheless, she'd always been tough on crime, and surprisingly, had often supported additional military funding. Well respected by both parties, she had served on many bipartisan committees over the years, including the powerful *Senate Intelligence Commission.*

Senator John 'Tank' Philips, McPhail's other visitor, was short and stocky, hence the *Tank* nickname. His flowing, silver-lined hair gave him a distinguished, mature attractiveness. With a reputation for being savvy on the economy, and having vehemently opposed most of the stimulus and national healthcare packages as complete wastes of money, he was someone from the minority party to be reckoned with in the future. A fifty-six-year-old Republican from Michigan, he'd twice run in his party's presidential primaries, coming in a distant third both times.

With two of the most influential politicians of both parties seated before him, Colonel McPhail was extremely careful with his opening words. "Senators, it's an honor to have you here today. I know you must be just as concerned about the Florida serial killings as we are. I was told this was the reason for your visit today."

Senator Phillips, nearly foaming at the mouth, couldn't hold back his comments. "Colonel, let's cut to the chase. We know you're in charge of some type of special security branch. We've been briefed a bit, and frankly, I don't really care what it is. The President said that for national security reasons we shouldn't dwell too much on that anyway. Regardless, we need practical answers fast. How do you plan to catch this Ripper guy when everyone else, including some of the finest law enforcement organizations in the country, have failed so far?"

McPhail was actually appreciative for Senator Philips candor. He was even happier that both these politicians appeared to be letting him off the hook as far as his having to go into the full background of his covert agency. The Colonel looked up at Tank Philips and answered, "As of yet, sir, we here at G5 haven't been involved in the Ripper case. But when we start, there's one lead we'll immediately pursue." Colonel McPhail leaned back in his swivel chair and explained, "Before she was murdered, Senator Swanson's late daughter, FBI Special Agent Loretta Swanson, was apparently focusing on a possible link to Dr. Klaus Braun's Miami Reptile Center."

"Klaus Braun?" Diane Bowman asked incredulously. "The wealthy pharmaceutical mogul?"

"That's right," replied Colonel McPhail, mindful that one, or possibly both, of his guests might have received considerable financial support from Dr. Braun for their senatorial campaigns. McPhail nonetheless forged on. "You see, a couple of hours before she was killed, Agent Swanson informed an FBI colleague that she suspected one of Dr. Braun's rare reptiles could have been involved in the murders. Perhaps some type of cult group that had somehow gotten their hands on one. Loretta Swanson didn't come right out and accuse Klaus Braun of anything unlawful, but she didn't rule him out either. More likely though, someone within Braun's organization, and not the doctor himself, might be indirectly involved. The fact that Agent Swanson was discussing Dr. Braun and his snakes on the night of her death was doubtless just a coincidence. Then again, she did become the Ripper's last victim, so it's a contingency we're now going to delve into."

Senator Bowman and Senator Phillips looked at each other with genuine concern. Klaus Braun was a character they both wanted to avoid angering, for obvious political and financial reasons. They listened in nervous silence as Colonel McPhail explained more. "There are still a lot of unanswered questions about the rare, venomous snake being selectively utilized by this Ripper fiend. The kind of atypical serpent that only a Klaus Braun, or some other dedicated herpetologist or large zoo might have. True, there's a small but thriving black market for poisonous reptiles. But we'd still like to know how a lone killer could even obtain one. It would have to be purchased or stolen from *somewhere*."

The senators nodded their heads as McPhail went on, "For some reason, Dr. Braun steadfastly refuses to even *talk* about that possibility. Therefore, our first move will be to covertly infiltrate his operation in order to see if any of his reptiles have been sold or stolen."

Senator John Philips quickly voiced what both politicians were thinking. "Tread easily with Klaus Braun, McPhail," Senator Phillips angrily insisted. "That man gave a heck of a lot of money to both of our campaigns, as well as over two million dollars to my charities last year. Moreover, he's practically a god to senior citizens all over the country with his arthritis medicine."

Diane Bowman looked over at Tank Philips and grinned sardonically.

"Not to mention those erectile dysfunction pills of Braun's, huh, John?"

A red-faced Senator Philips ignored the remark as well as McPhail's smile and stridently continued his tirade. "You better be one hundred percent *certain* when the time comes to arrest Klaus Braun, Colonel. Why, it could cost me a million senior citizen votes if word ever got out that I knew about any of this!"

Colonel McPhail was taken aback and immediately set the senator straight. "Hold on there, Senator Phillips. I never said *anybody* was going to arrest him. And I can assure you that nobody here believes the doctor is the serial killer. That being said though, Dr. Braun steadfastly refuses to reveal anything at all about his snakes or their whereabouts. And he won't reveal the names of *any* herpetologists to whom he has sold rare snakes. The only thing he keeps saying is that he'd never sell or give a snake to anyone but a qualified expert." McPhail shrugged his shoulders and finished his thoughts. "Still, Klaus Braun has a lot of employees who work with his reptiles on a daily basis, and any one of them could have made a fast buck selling a hard-to-get snake to some loner. Whether Braun wants to admit it or not."

"I'm still worried about ruffling his feathers," voiced Philips.

McPhail looked John Philips directly in the eyes. "I can promise you this, Senator. As far as our plan goes, Klaus Braun won't even know we're there. My people are very good at what they do, sir, so you can both count on total confidentiality. We simply want to see if anyone in Braun's organization might be involved, or if further investigation of his reptile center is even warranted. Naturally, any connection between Dr. Braun's place and the Ripper is a long shot. Yet, I'm sure you'll both agree that everything and everyone must be checked out after that brutal murder of Miss Swanson."

"But how do you propose to get into Dr. Braun's inner loop?" Senator Bowman inquired. "It's a very tight-knit group."

Colonel McPhail took a long breath. *This next part isn't going to be easy*, he thought. *I better bring Hank Carson into it now*. He pushed the intercom button. "Miss Gallo."

"Yes, sir."

"Send in Mr. Carson, please."

In less than a minute, Henry Carson entered the room smiling at the visitors. McPhail quickly made the introductions. "Senators, this is Henry Carson. Mr. Carson personally helped inaugurate the department we're about to tell you about."

Carson nodded his head, as the Colonel continued with the explanations. "Klaus Braun's entire empire is protected by a wall of absolute secrecy, one that the Pentagon would be proud of. I guess that's due to those top secret drug formulas of his, the ones that make him all the money."

Everyone nodded, as McPhail looked at the senators conspiratorially and further informed, "Yet there could be one potential weak link down there; one we just may be able to penetrate. Dr. Braun has a beautiful and trusted personal secretary, a Miss Sandra Kent. I believe you both know her, as she's been to Washington many times on public relations matters for the doctor."

The two senators, still uneasy, nodded affirmatively as McPhail added, "Miss Kent is devoted to Braun. Not in any personal relationship or manner, but to the doctor's work itself. It's said that this pretty assistant of his is the *only* person whom Braun really trusts with his important inside organizational secrets. Including, or so the FBI says, some private reports involving Dr. Braun's snakes. If anyone should know who and what we'd be interested in, I believe it's this Sandra Kent."

"Has anyone tried with point blank questions to her?" asked Diane Bowman. "I've only met her two or three times in DC, but she seemed like an upright and talented young lady."

Hank Carson nodded his head. "As a matter of fact, yes, Senator. Shortly before her tragic death, FBI Agent Loretta Swanson had tried. Only to be cut off and reprimanded by Klaus Braun himself before any definitive answers were provided. Not that Sandra Kent would have spilled anything anyway. She's supposedly as loyal and tightlipped as they come."

"Conventional questioning of Miss Kent would never work anyway", McPhail added. "You see, from the little we've uncovered about her, Sandra Kent is probably more protective of her boss and his empire than anyone else down there. She's already stated that she'd rather go to jail than reveal anything that could possibly hinder or delay what she terms Braun's great work for mankind. Sort of like Susan McDougal to the Clintons."

Both senators smiled their savvy political understanding as Hank Carson forged on. "Over the past few years, whenever a government department, such as the IRS or the Treasury Department, wanted to look into some of Braun Industries' activities, they were usually referred to Sandra Kent. Dr. Braun simply smiles and says '*Sandra has all the details.*' Yet, this Miss Kent seemingly never divulges any of them. Dr. Braun's beautiful assistant is polite and civil, but only vague facts ever get revealed. She's a trained master at stonewalling.

Carson shook his head and exclaimed, "Nonetheless, after studying the entire situation, we're now firmly convinced that the doctor's steadfast assistant is still an excellent, untapped source into Braun's secretive world. In fact, she's the *only* one as far as we can see. Hence, the key is to keep Sandra Kent working there while stealthily getting her to spill whatever she knows."

"But you just said she would never willingly reveal anything," said Senator John Phillips. "So, how are you going to get her to talk? Torture?

Scopolamine?"

McPhail chuckled. "No, Senator, those techniques went out with the Civil War and the Inquisition. We plan to use a newer technique, equally effective and much less messy."

"What's that?" asked Diane Bowman.

"We're going to use one of our best men from a unique, top secret department," the Colonel replied.

Pausing a moment, Colonel McPhail again glanced over at his assistant director for reassurance. Then, for the first time ever, McPhail revealed the name of this ultra-secret unit to someone outside of G5. "Code name, *Super Studs*."

T he senators glanced at one another and then looked back at McPhail
with confused expressions. It was Senator John Philips who broke the
awkward silence. "Code name *Super Studs?* What's that? Another one of
our secret weapons that nobody's told me about?"

Colonel McPhail simply smiled and patiently began to explain.
"The Super Studs make up a unit of six men, hand-picked for their
amazing good looks and their sheer magnetism to women. These agents,
specifically trained to be irresistible to females, are sent out to procure
vital information from unsuspecting women. This assignment should be a
perfect fit for their, ah, special talents."

Diane Bowman responded with a sarcastic grin. "Oh, come on now,
Colonel. We didn't just come to the big city from the backwoods, you know.
Do you expect us to believe that these types of guys actually exist and that
this tactic works?"

McPhail looked over at Hank Carson. Promptly taking the cue, G5's
second in command confidently assured, "They definitely exist and the
system works amazingly well, Senator."

After opening the top drawer of his desk, Colonel McPhail handed
each senator a thin file folder containing the words *Top Secret* stamped
in red on the covers. "I've provided you both with a short file on various
cases in which the Super Studs have been involved. This information is
classified, so please treat it accordingly. The significance of some of it will
surprise you, including an assignment involving one of our Studs who's
code-named *Charming*. He's our only Middle-Eastern stud, by the way, and
he was used to infiltrate one of Saddam Hussein's regal palaces through
a tryst with Hussein's niece. That particular affair was instrumental in
locating Saddam's bunker hiding place and in his ultimate arrest."

"We didn't know anything about that aspect of the capture," said
Senator Bowman incredulously and also a bit angrily. "Perhaps, we should
have been informed!"

"Ma'am, complete anonymity is paramount around here," answered
Colonel McPhail softly, but with a slight hint of admonition. "Obviously
everybody couldn't be told the details. You see, G5, and particularly our
Super Stud department, has to work in complete obscurity in order to be
effective. That's why both the President and I trust you'll keep all of what
you've just heard here to yourselves. The existence of the Super Studs, as
well as its anonymity, is truly a matter of national security."

Surprisingly, both senators were quickly mollified, partly because
they were being let in on an unusual top secret program. "Of course,"

said the placated Senator Bowman. "And we thank the President and yourself for your confidence in us." Senator Philips awkwardly echoed his agreement. McPhail smiled inwardly at them, knowing now that he'd made the right decision and was safe in revealing the existence of the Studs.

With a slight grin on her face, Diane Bowman exclaimed, "Gentlemen, let us please get back to these gorgeous men and their effect on unsuspecting women."

"Well," continued Hank Carson, "our Super Stud concept works far better than anyone first imagined. In fact, I'd say that at times, it works better than most anything we've tried."

Now, much more intrigued, Tank Philips further inquired, "Just how *does* it work, Carson?"

"It's an offshoot of the female Swan unit used by the United States during World War II; great looking women coaxing info out of unsuspecting male targets. Except we've changed it from women to men." Hank Carson leaned back in his chair and added, "You see, Senator, using beautiful ladies to extract information from powerful men is a tactic as old as time itself. The most famous was the alluring Mata Hari. When America joined the war we utilized and perfected this age-old idea against the Nazis. From what I heared, we and the Brits trained attractive females as covert agents to obtain inside information from male enemies. These alluring agents traveled in the best European circles, met Nazi VIPs, and garnered many important secrets. After the war, the gals went their separate ways. Two of them wrote books about their experiences. Sensationalized a bit, but it was interesting reading all the same."

"I'll bet," smirked Senator Philips.

Carson grinned back and expounded further. "During the past few decades many of our standard intelligence channels had been drying up. Even so, there were many fronts to infiltrate.

Colonel McPhail interrupted, "Of course, we and all the other government agencies sent out spies. A few were effective but not enough reliable information was coming back. The only halfway effective method of getting good information was bribery, and that's never totally trustworthy. People will tell you anything just to get paid. And as for getting crucial data from the men who controlled the international scene, such as Castro, Hussein, Gotti, and even bin Laden, they had all played the game too long and knew our methods. But you go on, Henry. Sorry to have butted in."

"Our G5 studies revealed that, in many instances, the women and mistresses of powerful male leaders were an untapped part of the chain. That's the one vulnerable link these otherwise extremely cautious men have. Details they occasionally reveal to their secretaries, wives, lovers, or female confidants. As new players, the ladies surrounding our targets are not as perceptive about security as their men are. Yet there was still one question. How could we persuade these women to come over or reveal anything of importance? Females don't react to bribes the same way men do, and beating up or torturing some secretary or girlfriend is not the image or the method we wanted."

"That's all we'd need after those GITMO water-boarding years!" barked McPhail.

"That type of rough stuff is usually ineffective anyway," admitted Carson. "But our Super Studs were quietly effective right from the start. They usually got what we wanted."

Senator John Philips nodded his agreement, but feisty Diane Bowman wasn't so sure. She had a high regard for her fellow females and remained skeptical as Hank Carson continued explaining. "Our analytical studies showed that most women only blurt out important facts when they're in a sound and trusting relationship. Consequently, we had a dilemma. We recognized that there were females around the world who knew or overheard valuable info. Women such as secretaries to the Soviet armament commissioners, or wives, or lovers of some of them. And there were other potential targets as well. Female couriers for the terrorist buyers and leaders, for instance. Or even the *moll* girlfriends of organized crime bosses right here in America. The problem was how to persuade them to spill their information."

It was now McPhail's turn to fill in the gaps. "G5 felt that many of these women could become great sources for us if we could just find a way to captivate them and gain their confidence. We knew that if we could exploit women in certain VIP circles, instead of their powerful and usually unapproachable male chieftains, perhaps we'd get some of the answers needed."

"That makes sense," Senator Bowman admitted, suddenly impressed with the soundness of the whole thing.

"Some years back," continued McPhail, "just before the creation of our Super Stud program, we were trying to squeeze some info out of a local gangster's attractive, but uncooperative maid. Specifically, facts about this Mafia man's schedule and the names of associates who met at his home. One of our G5 underlings commented in jest that it was too bad we didn't have any *male* Swans to turn this maid. Everyone laughed at his statement at the time, but the more I thought on it, I realized he might just be on to something. The next day I kicked the idea around with Hank here and a few other trusted confidants. We all agreed that a group of handsome male operatives like that might indeed be useful. A week later we came up with the basic concept of the Super Studs."

"G5 realized that we had to search scientifically for these men," Henry Carson explained. "We just couldn't put an advertisement in the classifieds that read, *WANTED: World's best looking males*. Everyone recognized the potential obstacles and difficulties in finding some of the country's most attractive men. But fortunately, and unlike the OSS back in 1941, with their search for beautiful female agents, we had the use of modern technology; computers, electronic media, and other advanced tools. Remember, back then there was no Internet or Facebook. We, however, were in the computer age and that was a huge advantage."

"There were also other ways to help find the best looking men in America, if not the world," added Colonel McPhail. "We checked with modeling agencies and Hollywood talent scouts. Thousands of yearbooks were searched. Advertising agencies were discreetly hired to painstakingly look through websites and fashion magazines of every type. Hank and I also set up screening committees, some men, but mostly a sizable group of savvy women. They acted as *handsomeness* judges, so to speak."

"Initially, we just wanted to find the best looking men in the world," Carson informed. "Astonishing looks along with pure magnetism to women. We knew that once you had that, you could then teach these handsome hunks all about etiquette, fine wines, personal hygiene, and grooming. But incredible looks is the one thing you *can't* teach."

The senators, particularly Diane Bowman, sat fascinated as Colonel McPhail explained more. "After our initial hunt, a special computer program designed by experts at MIT, with input from us and our panel of female experts, helped even further. This new software program utilized all the data. Information from several sources, as well as many knowledgeable people, guided us as well. Everyone from psychologists and movie agents, to teenage debutantes and international beauties."

"This is amazing!" Tank Philips exclaimed. "Did it work?"

"Yes," Carson replied. "After extensive and meticulous searches, we eventually found what was without a doubt twenty of the best looking males in the world. This great looking group was then narrowed down even further. So you can imagine just how attractive the six men we actually *did* keep turned out to be!"

"Did you have to tell them what role they would eventually be required to play?" asked Senator Bowman. "How did you even motivate them for an interview?"

"That was one of the hardest parts," Henry Carson acknowledged. "Members of our staff tactfully interviewed each of them, at first under the guise of a possible movie deal. Then, after they had passed our initial entry level background investigation, we gradually let them in on some of our plans. Even so, the finalists were put on a strict 'need-to-know' basis."

"How about money?" asked John Philips, notorious in the senate for wanting the ballooning deficit as low as possible. "I bet it cost a pretty penny, with you guys going Hollywood and all!"

"Well," admitted Carson, "we did have to offer some real incentives to get them to even respond to our initial queries. A generous salary was indeed proposed to each man. You see, Senator Philips, fabulous looking men such as these just don't come that easily, or cheaply. We were competing with Hollywood and Madison Avenue in many cases. But by then the concept had the blessing of the White House and some top level security committees as well. Our project was quickly granted sizable funding to obtain prospective agents."

Hank Carson noticed Philips's frown and quickly added, "The Super Stud budget was admittedly high, but if you compare that cost to one nuclear submarine, a Stud's lifetime costs would be a fraction of that. And our agents have proven themselves to be every bit as effective." His comment brought a positive grunt from Senator Philips.

Colonel McPhail decided it was time to wrap things up. He passed two manila folders filled with several printed pages and numerous color photos to the senators. The Colonel watched them open the files and then proudly announced, "Senators, you now have in front of you our Super Stud team. The folders I just gave you contain photographs of all six men. Please, have a look."

"You look at them, Diane," said Tank Philips. "I'm not into incredibly handsome men. But if you have any pictures of those Swan girls around, McPhail, I'll look at them!"

Everyone shared a laugh as the photographs began shifting through Senator Bowman's smallish hands. The effect on her was instantaneous! The moment Diane Bowman began studying the astonishing portraits she seemed truly stunned, virtually hypnotized by the great looks of these agents. There were six implausibly gorgeous males in their late twenties or early thirties, each one better looking than the next. As hard as it was to fathom, every one of these men was infinitely better looking than say, a young Elvis Presley, a youthful Sean Connery, or Pierce Brosnan in his prime. Even Brad Pitt or George Clooney at their best couldn't come close to these guys. Senator Bowman thought about those famous celebrities and their well-known faces. As good looking as she had once thought those personalities to be, these agents of McPhail's were in a much different league. They were far better looking; *striking* was a better word for it. Diane Bowman hadn't thought it possible. There wasn't one man in this Stud group who wasn't easily the best looking male she'd ever seen. There was none of that *neatly nice looking* or *ruggedly handsome* stuff. No facial hair or manly beards. These men were simply drop-dead gorgeous!

Yes, thought the lady senator. *These Super Stud agents were indeed irresistible!* She could clearly see Colonel McPhail's point. How these men enthralled women, and how they could easily gather intelligence from swooning females. "I never knew men this handsome even existed," Diane Bowman stammered. "It's as if they were each chiseled into individual Adonises. Much better looking than any movie star or fashion model." She shook her head. "It's a good thing my Gary isn't here to see me going gaga!"

"Don't feel strange about it," Colonel McPhail consoled. "Every woman who has seen those photos, or better yet, has seen the actual men themselves, has reacted the exact same way. The hardest part is keeping my secretarial staff away from them."

"I'll say!" Senator Bowman exclaimed loudly, continuing to gape at the photographs, and still unable to believe her eyes or the incredible looks of the men. Suddenly she stopped cold. For a brief moment, Diane Bowman just couldn't take her eyes off one individual's picture in particular. This man somehow stood out from all the other hunks, the '*pick of the litter*' so to speak. "Who is *that*?" she blurted. "Without question, he's got to be the handsomest man in the whole world!"

Colonel McPhail smiled widely at her and answered, "That, Senator Bowman, is Agent Christopher Seven. And he just happens to be the Super Stud whom we have in mind for this particular assignment."

Chapter 10
The Handsomest Man in the World

D iane Bowman looked at McPhail with a confused expression. "Did you say Christopher *Seven*? Like the number?"

"Yes."

"Is that his *real* name?"

"Well, yes, and no, Senator. You see, the actual family name when his great-grandfather, Giuseppe, first came over from Italy, was Sevenetti. Years later, this very Italian last name was shortened out of necessity."

"What do you mean by *necessity*?" asked Senator John Philips.

McPhail promptly explained. "You see, when his grand-father, Albert, opened an auto dealership in 1949, the last name was shortened because of pressure from the business world. This was only a few years after World War II, a time when it was not very popular to have an Italian last name. You were automatically perceived to be a fascist or a gangster. Unjust, but that's the way things were back then. Political correctness was still a long way off."

"Actually this particular Super Stud agent has mixed lineage," Henry Carson informed. "His father was Italian, while his mother was of Swedish ancestry.

That mixed lineage explains his extraordinary face, Diane Bowman mused. *Being part Italian and part Swede gives him the chiseled features of an Italian Adonis, coupled with the natural beauty of a Swede.* Her daydreaming was interrupted by Carson.

"Seven's grandparents, Albert and Anne Sevenetti, opened their car dealership in New Jersey under the required shortened last name, 'Seven', and the dealership opened as *Seven Motor Sales.* Some of the relatives back in the old country never forgave them for abandoning the Italian moniker, the new, mandatory name stuck. Actually it turned out to be a catchy name, one that customers easily remembered."

"The dealership did quite well", Colonel McPhail informed, "and like most family businesses, it was eventually turned over to Agent Seven's father, Albert Jr. He was able to send his two sons to expensive private schools where they not only excelled academically, but were also outstanding athletes. Life was good, but, tragically, all good things must come to an end as they say."

After clearing his throat, Hank Carson again took over. "Albert and his wife were returning from a vacation in Italy. School was in session and the kids had stayed home with relatives. According to FBI confidential sources, the mob had been trying to worm their way into the Seven auto business for some time. In those days a car dealership was one of the best industries for the top mobs to get their claws into. A great place to skim or hide cash. It still occasionally happens today."

The two senators nodded as Carson continued, "Anyway, Albert Seven was a no-nonsense guy, and he played it straight and tough with the gangsters. He wasn't afraid to tell them where to go, and probably did. Twenty minutes after his chartered plane to Rome took off from Salerno, it exploded in mid-air somewhere over the Mediterranean. The airplane was never recovered and the cause of the explosion is still unknown. Those same FBI sources suspect a 'hit' was carried out by one of the Sicilian families as a favor to their American gangster cousins. We'll probably never know for sure."

Both senators shook their heads as Carson gave them more bio. "At the time of the tragedy, young Christopher was fourteen, and his brother, Timothy, was twelve. Their parent's death was quite a shock but the brothers made the best of it. From insurance money, sale of the dealership, and the large New Jersey house they inherited, the boys were pretty well set financially. As per a guardian clause in their parents' will, their Aunt Mary, a truly amazing and loving woman, moved in with them. She, along with the loyal family housekeeper, stayed on at the house until both boys finished college. Seven still lives there, but his brother moved to LA. "

Almost simultaneously the two politicians looked at Seven's picture again. Hank Carson used the opportunity to sip a glass of water from a pitcher on the desk before resuming. "We found Chris fresh out of NYU just as we were beginning our search for the Super Stud program. He was a journalism major, which, by the way, has often helped us immensely with past 'cover' assignments and will again on this Ripper mission. Other than his great looks, what grabbed our attention was the fact that not only was Christopher Seven a gifted athlete, best performer on his college tennis and fencing teams, he also excelled in chess. Seven was one of the better chess players in the school's history, with a great aptitude for anticipating what move an opponent was going to make. A natural skill like that can't be taught and is invaluable in our line of work."

"Makes sense," said John Philips as Carson explained more, "Of course, with his incredible looks, it wasn't long before Hollywood came calling. But after going through the screen test process and dealing with some of those West Coast types, Seven decided it wasn't for him. We thought we had him then, but the next thing we knew, several top modeling agencies were making him offers."

"His face couldn't miss," Diane Bowman exclaimed.

"That was the problem," agreed Colonel McPhail. "This guy was so good looking we couldn't compete with the opportunities that were coming his way. We persevered however, and since Seven was once interested in law enforcement, and still had a burning desire to find out exactly what had happened to his parents, we finally got him. Christopher

Seven has been with us ever since, and I must say he's performed admirably."

"Do these stud guys carry guns?" asked Tank Philips. "Are they licensed to kill like those spies I read about in the thrillers?"

Diane Bowman chuckled. "You've been watching too many movies, John."

Colonel McPhail smiled and patiently clarified. "Actually, Senators, it's quite the contrary. Our Super Studs hardly ever carry weapons or gadgets. They're trained to depend solely on their looks and their guile. We want them to blend in, not stand out like some Samurai. Their main mission is to gather information, not to kill."

"The Super Studs are usually either disguised as vacationing jet set playboys, or in some other *cover* occupation that fits their mission," Henry Carson further informed. "Of course, they're all physically fit, and are regularly trained in basic martial arts. We insist on that, but only for self-defense purposes. Just enough to protect themselves." Carson grinned. "You never know when a jealous husband or lover might unexpectedly appear." Both Senators grinned back. "But we want anonymity here, so our guys are first and foremost trained ladies men. They're not Robocops, and they have no tricky weapons, clever devices, or exploding cars. We'll leave that kind of stuff up to our paramilitary friends."

Senator Philips nodded. "I get it. No guns, no Rambos."

"They're certainly great looking enough," Diane Bowman interjected, "but what about brains? Some of the pretty boys I've seen couldn't spell cat if you spotted them the C and the T."

Colonel McPhail laughed as he replied. "I hear you. And we ran across a few of those types. If they were completely brainless they were quickly eliminated. But not Seven. His IQ is way up there. For that matter, all the guys we have are pretty clever. Regarding their techniques with the ladies, the Super Studs have all been schooled on just about everything concerning the opposite sex. They've been meticulously instructed regarding hygiene, grooming, table manners, connoisseur food, top-shelf liquor recognition and wine appreciation. Basically, all the gentlemanly skills required to mingle comfortably in the circles of upper crust society anywhere in the world. *Most* importantly, they've been thoroughly educated in the fine art of being irresistible. And believe me, there definitely is such a thing."

Colonel McPhail's last statement brought a smirk from Senator Philips and a giggle from Diane Bowman. She then asked the obvious. "And just who is your authority on *that*, Colonel?"

"We use the services of some of the country's top female psychologists, Senator. As well as input from beautiful women in all walks of life. A lot of research, time and money have been spent on it, I can assure you."

Everyone nodded except Senator John Philips. With a stern face, he inquired, "So, let me get this straight. These handsome guys, on a taxpayer-footed payroll, are simply hopping from one bedroom to another, huh?"

"Not really," argued Hank Carson.

McDonald frowned. "Why not, Carson? What, are they, *gay*?"

"No, Senator, none of the Super Studs are gay. Nothing discriminatory in that. It's just that according to our experts most women can sense if a man is showing genuine animal attraction toward her. As for actual physical relations, just how far an agent goes with a prospective female informant is strictly up to him, though none of them are keen on becoming *call guys* for flag and king. The Swans of World War II never had to go that far to be effective and neither do our men. Besides, our extensive scientific studies showed that pure sex only complicates things. We've found that pent-up anticipation works far better."

Both Senators chuckled.

"To clarify that further," Colonel McPhail added, "our precise sociological research shows that a female target is much more likely to give information during the *early* stages of a relationship, the *flirting stage*, so to speak. We use science and human reaction tables in just about everything the Studs do. Our agents are taught to bring the relationship along slowly and tantalizingly, and this technique has paid off royally. Simply hopping into boudoirs or the back seat of a sports car wouldn't be nearly as effective." McPhail frowned. "Or as sanitary in this day and age."

"Sounds a bit clinical, if you ask me," said John Philips.

"And how about the new love of my life, this Christopher Seven?" asked Diane Bowman, still holding Seven's picture in her hand. "You've said he's one of your most effective studs, Colonel. Is he one of the more celibate ones?"

"Interestingly enough, he is. At least when he's on the job. The biggest obstacle we had in recruiting Seven was his rather conservative religious beliefs and upbringing. He expressed some strong objections about going *too far* with the target relationships."

"Our argument to recruit him was twofold," Hank Carson expounded. "First of all, most of Seven's assigned targets wouldn't exactly be saints. Furthermore, he'd never be ordered or forced to deflower anyone. Seven was assured that he'd really only be doing what initially comes natural in dating any woman. There'd be some kissing and petting of course, but had he become an actor, he'd certainly have steamy, romantic scenes to play."

"He definitely had some strong moral reservations," recalled McPhail, shaking his head at the memories.

Senator John Philips then asked the big question. "But, how will this, er, super chap help us on the New Ripper case?"

McPhail was ready with his answer. "As we discussed, our best lead, in fact the *only* promising lead, really, centers on Klaus Braun's Miami Reptile Center. It's one of the few places in Florida that still houses rare, deadly serpents. But like I've told you. So far, Dr. Braun adamantly refuses to tell us anything. So that's where our agent Seven will come in. Dr. Braun's attractive young secretary, Sandra Kent, just might be able to tell us what we need to know, with a little romancing and coaxing from a Super Stud of course."

Diane Bowman gushed. "I'd bet on him."

"Of course, this Sandra Kent woman may know nothing at all about missing snakes", admitted McPhail. "But that's the chance you take." He shook his head, angrily. "If only these Braun fools would see we're not after them; just the Ripper." McPhail frowned. "Unless they really *do* have something to hide down there."

"But," Senator Bowman interrupted, "you told us that Sandra Kent seems to be the tightest lipped of all. And that Braun's entire organization is apparently shielded tighter than our national space program. So, how do you guys plan to break through it?"

Henry Carson pointed to Seven's photo. "The answer is right there in your hand, Senator. If Christopher Seven can gain access to top secrets in Europe by captivating some of the most sophisticated women in the world, it stands to reason he can persuade Dr. Braun's young assistant to spill."

"Well, you and your super guy have my vote," exclaimed John Philips, without hesitation.

Senator Bowman looked at the G5 Director with a somber expression on her face. She wasn't about to give her approval instantaneously, not without a bit of political speechmaking. "Colonel McPhail, I have to admit that this meeting today has been simply fascinating. Yet even after all you've told us, I still find it hard to believe that our government is sponsoring a program that breaks most of the rules of proper social behavior. To top that off, you also expect us to believe that these admittedly extraordinarily handsome faces can actually obtain state and military secrets by romancing the wives or lovers of the world's most powerful men." Her stern gaze went from Colonel McPhail and Hank Carson back down to the photograph in her hand. It momentarily worried the men in the room.

But then Diane Bowman's serious expression turned into a mischievous grin and they all breathed easier. "Yet, I've got to hand it to you G5 gentlemen," she declared. "If we could figure out a way to settle differences between global enemies in some romantic restaurant or cocktail lounge, instead of on the battlefield, then this old world just might survive." She smiled widely. "You've got my vote as well."

It was now going on four o'clock. Colonel McPhail's VIP visitors had left a few hours earlier, and he now sat alone in his office. The meeting with the senators had gone as well as could be expected. G5's director had covered his tracks to infiltrate Dr. Klaus Braun's Reptile hub and the doctor's mysterious pharmaceutical center. And more importantly, McPhail had gained the senators personal go-ahead to use the studs. It was therefore time to bring in Super Stud Christopher Seven and get his thoughts on the assignment. The Colonel glanced at his watch, hoping Seven would for once, be on time. The young man was a good agent but punctuality was not always his strong suit.

"Hello, Colonel McPhail, how are you?" Quack the parrot unexpectedly screeched. McPhail grinned at the cage behind him. No matter how many years he'd owned the bird, the parrot's talking always amused him. He smiled at his feathered friend just as the intercom buzzer brought him back to the work at hand. "Christopher Seven's here, sir," the pleasant voice announced.

"Send him right in, Miss Gallo."

"Go on in, Chris, he's expecting you," a smiling Nancy informed Seven. She watched dreamily as he walked away. It was always that way with the Studs, particularly this one. For like Senator Diane Bowman of California, G5's executive secretary, Nancy Gallo, felt that this good looking hunk was either *the handsomest man in the world*, or darn close to it. To Nancy, Christopher Seven was pure perfection, the stuff of which dreams were made. In fact, all the Super Studs were and she frequently reflected on how lucky she was just to be around them. It was truly special to work with six of the best looking men on the planet and she often felt her job was much like being a kid in the proverbial candy store. Still, Colonel McPhail's secretary knew that this was candy she could never have, on direct orders from the boss. The Studs were strictly 'off limits' to her and to the rest of the female personnel. And since Nancy Gallo loved and needed her job, she wasn't willing to chance it. Therefore, instead of dating any of them, she did the next best thing. Nancy mothered them all, anxiously worrying when one of *her boys* was off on a dangerous assignment. Still, she had her private moments in which to fantasize as she did now, as the lean, magnificent looking agent walked into the Colonel's office.

"Sit down, Chris," McPhail welcomed, looking up at Seven.

"Thank you, sir."

"By the way, congratulations on your mission in Greece. You did quite well. How'd you like Athens?

"Athens was great, sir. Wish I could have seen more of it."

"I saw from your report that General Molzov wasn't so clever. He probably thought he was too well hidden. Didn't figure on that Deleon woman giving him away."

"He sure didn't, sir. And your hunch turned out to be correct. Molzov was, and still is, working with Iran. The countess finally blurted this out to me after dinner at the Grande Bretagne. A few of Ahmadinejad's remaining loyalists are hiding him in Zagros."

"Yes, I thought so. Those old Russians are still easy to read. I guess they've never heard *you can't teach an old dog new tricks*. Oh well, now that we've located Molzov, he's the CIA's problem. Hopefully they'll take care of him before he helps the Iranians get their hands on any more of those missing Russian missiles."

"I hope so, Colonel," replied Seven, with delicious, lingering thoughts of the beautiful Countess Maria Deleon, the general's mistress. The Super Stud silently wondered what Maria was doing at the moment. It had been a pleasure getting *that* gorgeous lady to talk. A vision of her bikini-clad body, tanning on her yacht somewhere in Mykonos, brought a grin to his handsome face.

Colonel McPhail tapped his fingers on the desk and leaned forward to get his agent's full attention. "I know you've just returned from Greece, but have you been following any of this New Ripper stuff? Those serial killings in Florida?"

Christopher Seven was surprised by the question, one that seemed to come out of left field. He had to think a moment. "I've followed it in bits and pieces, sir. Mainly just from what I've seen on TV. I know it's a big story. Even the foreign papers are covering it. Do they have any suspects?"

McPhail shook his head. "No. But that's where we come in."

Seven should have seen it coming, but didn't. Not with a domestic murder case. He looked over dubiously as his chief asked, "Ever hear of Dr. Klaus Braun?"

Again it was a question the Super Stud agent hadn't expected. "Sure, Colonel. He's the millionaire who's made all that money with those controversial drugs of his, right?"

"That's the guy. And try billionaire. At least everyone at *Fortune Magazine* believes he's one. In addition to his pharmaceutical empire, Braun's got a big research and tourist operation in Florida; some zoo type park called the Miami Reptile Center. That's where he gets the snake venom needed for his drugs and experiments. Don't ask me how the whole thing works. It just does. And while many people think Dr. Braun is merely an eccentric quack, he's actually made some real medicinal inroads over the years. Primarily through his use of minute parts of snake venom. Braun even experimented with a new venom based drug that seemed to halt the COVID virus. You can read all about it in here." McPhail slid a thin folder across the desk.

Seven's face showed a doubting expression. "If you say so, sir. About the use of snake venom, that is." He shook his head. "It's just hard for me to imagine deadly snakes being good for *anything.*"

"Well, evidently they are. However, that's not our concern. This fiendish serial killer is. By order of the President. The tie-in is that some of the Ripper's victims, including his last one, a female FBI agent by the way, were found with traces of cobra venom inside their bodies."

"Are you suggesting that Dr. Braun is somehow involved in these serial murders, Colonel?"

"Good heavens, no! Klaus Braun may be a lot of things, but a serial killing psycho isn't one of them. Yet it may be possible that the killer's snake could have come from Braun's Reptile Center. Most likely without the doctor's knowledge. That being said, not many people would have access to such a rare serpent. Other than a zoo or a small handful of noted collectors."

"Why doesn't the FBI just ask Dr. Braun, sir? Surely he'd know if one of his snakes were missing?"

"Apparently they've tried to talk to him about it. The problem is Braun has everybody on his staff completely paranoid about being closed down for *any* length of time due to an embarrassing ongoing investigation. I guess he's worried about adverse publicity to his Center. Can't blame him. That retile hub of his is a huge profit maker."

"Yes, sir."

Colonel McPhail scratched his forehead. "It seems Klaus Braun doesn't want *anyone* poking around his place, Chris. First off, there are those top secret formulas of his, which he obviously wants to protect. And, secondly, it's home to his beloved reptiles. The doctor has a rather curious devotion to the creatures. Guess he'd rather accept the existence of a few dead humans before admitting that one of his precious serpents could be involved. Even if it was involved without his knowledge."

McPhail shrugged his shoulders, took a sip of water, and continued, "Dr. Braun is quite adamant about it, and apparently won't let any law enforcement agents near his Center again. Not without warrants and a full-fledged 'show trial' investigation. One he knows would be potentially very awkward to the government."

"Sounds like a political sticky wicket, Colonel."

"It is. But that murdered FBI girl believed there might be a connection between the Ripper and a Braun snake. In fact, she'd actually visited Dr. Braun shortly before she was murdered." McPhail frowned. "Just a coincidence? Well, you know how I feel about that."

Seven looked up as he responded. "Yes sir. You've told us to never believe in coincidences."

"Exactly. And Dade County Police say that Klaus Braun employs some pretty unsavory characters from time to time. So there could have indeed been foul play or thievery of one of Braun's reptiles."

"You mean someone Braun employs could be the killer or a snake thief Colonel?"

"Yes. Though most likely it's just an illegal trying to make some quick cash. You see Chris, it seems the doctor needs a lot of menial workers at his Miami reptile hub. Lowlife transients who don't mind being around those slimy creatures of his. These types of uncomplaining employees are not easy to find, so Braun probably takes whatever he can get by way of unskilled help. A lot of the big Florida conglomerates work that way. They don't ask too many questions when hiring people, and some of their workers are roughneck illegals, taken right off the boats."

Seven nodded as his chief explained more. "It could be that some sleazy employee at Braun's place sold a rare snake to an unknown buyer, doing so behind Dr. Braun's back. Who knows? But with all of the secrecy and stonewalling down there, neither Klaus Braun nor any of his people are talking. So, that's going to be *our* concern now."

The Colonel leaned back in his chair. "From what I've learned from the FBI's report, and from the Treasury Department, I think there could be a lot more to this Dr. Braun than meets the eye. Even without a Ripper connection. The FBI, along with other government bureaus, has been trying to get some bona fide info about Klaus Braun for years. Maybe this assignment of yours will give them that chance."

McPhail looked over at Seven with a dour gaze. "But, we've got to be very tactful in what we say and do. Top level politics play a role as well. Seems Braun contributes a great deal to both parties."

Seven, still wondering where he, himself would fit in, listened intently."

"Dr. Braun has understandably gone to extreme lengths to keep his lucrative pharmaceutical work going 24/7. Maybe that's why he's so hesitant to admit even the possibility of his Center's connection to the Ripper's snake, fearing it might bring an investigative ton of bricks down on him. And a lot of meddling people marching around the place."

"Could be something like that, Colonel. If forced to close for even a short while, Braun would most likely lose a ton of money. As well as prestige with the public if he was shut down by the authorities. The press would be all over him. Quite natural that he'd clam up."

Quack, the parrot unexpectedly let out a high-pitched squeal, momentarily startling both men. A smiling Colonel McPhail then resumed, "G5, specifically the Super Stud section, has been officially called upon to penetrate Klaus Braun's inner realm. This, in an effort to possibly get clues about the serial killer. Like I've said though, we'll have to use extreme discretion in order to avoid angering the DC politicians that are someway connected to Dr. Braun. He donates tons of money to some of the most powerful names in Washington. Two of them were just here to see me."

Christopher Seven was still confused as to how the Super Stud section was going to be utilized. As if reading his mind, the Colonel finally gave him the answer. "Since Klaus Braun himself, as well as the inner lair of his empire, have both remained inaccessible without a lot of awkward red tape and search warrants, the idea is to get to him through his beautiful young secretary. And that's where you come in. The full plan, along with your cover story and background information, are in this dossier."

The Colonel slid another much thicker file across the desk. "For cover, I thought we'd go with your being an independent journalist, since it's worked so well before. Our plan, which is already in the works, by the way, is for you to go down there to ostensibly do a flattering magazine story on Dr. Braun and his Reptile hub." McPhail grinned. "They say there's one thing about Klaus Braun. As long as someone is feeding his huge ego, the doctor usually goes along with it. He's a sucker for *any* publicity for his Center."

Seven smiled back and continued listening.

"I've already spoken with Ben Hoffman from *Global Magazine*, and Ben's now onboard for a Klaus Braun story. Since your own articles have occasionally appeared in Hoffman's magazine before, and will again, no one should get suspicious as to why you're down there asking questions."

Seven was still amazed by the fact that even the most secretive of men would let their guard down when it came to their egos. More interested now, he looked up while Colonel McPhail, G5's *old man*, explained further. "To get any bona fide information on Dr. Braun, you'll most likely have to go through Miss Sandra Kent. She's Braun's private secretary and his main PR liaison. FBI sources say that she's the key. So that's why your, ah, *stud* qualities have been called upon. Miss Kent's picture is on the inside cover of the file. She's quite a stunning woman."

"She certainly is," Seven agreed, looking at the photo, his vision of the Mykonos countess quickly becoming ancient history.

"Klaus Braun has already agreed to your doing the magazine piece on him. Just an hour ago in fact, after Ben Hoffman called him personally on it. Braun told Ben, that providing the doctor himself is able to have the final say as to the story's content, restrictions and questions, and as long as all interviews are directed through him, it should be fine. So, it's all set. You're expected the day after tomorrow, but I actually want you in Florida tomorrow. Being the stickler he is for security, Braun will undoubtedly have you tailed from the moment he knows you're down there. My way you'll have a day on your own."

"I understand, Colonel."

"I want you to check in with FBI Special Agent Jack Hanover at the North Miami Field Office once you've landed tomorrow. He was the original lead agent on this Ripper case and he's now been reassigned to it. Best to meet up with Hanover somewhere outside his office."

McPhail looked up and added, "The FBI has been very helpful and forthcoming with us, Chris, especially since one of their own is now on the victim list. Keep in mind, though, that they're also discreetly looking into the murders and will eventually want to check out Klaus Braun themselves. I've spoken to my opposite number at the FBI. In exchange for your providing them with some inside tidbits from time to time, they've agreed to temporarily stay away from Klaus Braun while you're doing your thing with the girl. But I won't be able to keep the FBI sitting on their thumbs forever."

"Naturally, Colonel."

"There's also talk that the FBI already has a paid mole in place down there" McPhail added. "Don't know much about that. Guess you'll have to ask this fellow, Hanover. Just don't step on the FBI's toes. It's their territory you'll be operating in so I expect you to be deferential and to check in with them whenever it's practicable."

"Certainly, sir."

"Of course, with the exception of their director, the FBI doesn't know much about our little operation here, especially your stud branch. And I'd like to keep it that way. So be respectful without saying too much about the Super Studs. From what I hear this Jack Hanover is a good man."

"I'm sure he'll be helpful, Colonel."

"Apropos your assignment, Seven, while you're supposedly following Dr. Braun around for the magazine feature, your *real* target will be this gal, Sandra Kent. To convince her to tell you what she *really* knows. This girl is apparently the main keeper of the Braun operation, so she should have some of the answers we and the FBI need. Mainly details about any illegal sales or recent thefts of the Center's venomous snakes. As for your seeing her, it would only be natural for any reporter worth his salt to want to meet and talk with some of Braun's key people, including Ms. Kent."

Seven nodded his agreement.

"Regarding the magazine article itself, Chris, you're the journalist major. So write it however you want. Just so long as you get to this Kent girl and ultimately persuade her to tell you what we need to know. Mainly names of confidential reptile buyers or the possibility of any missing cobras."

While Christopher Seven began getting the drift of his role, Colonel McPhail glanced over at him contritely. "Lastly, Chris, try to observe if anyone working at Braun's place is known for being involved with cults or strange religious groups, that sort of thing."

"Cults, sir?"

"That's right. Loretta Swanson thought that could be a possibility." The colonel raised up his hand. "I know it sounds a bit farfetched but I guess we'll have to follow up on it." McPhail shrugged his shoulders. "Anyway, I'm sure that once you've won over this gal, the snake info will be fairly easy to procure. After that, you can quietly leave the scene, write your story, and let the feds do their thing."

"I think I have it, Colonel. I can get the rest from the dossier."

"Best be on your toes, Seven. There could be some danger in all this. Loretta Swanson was the last person to actually concentrate on Klaus Braun and we know what happened to her."

"Yes, sir."

"Of course, Klaus Braun's attractive secretary might be a hard nut to crack. Some of the doctor's biggest competitors have already tried. She'll be very wary of telling you anything, other than what her boss has authorized. So you'll just have to use your, er...charms on her. Hopefully, she'll come around like all the others."

Seven smiled sheepishly. "I'll do my best, Colonel. But are we sure that Dr. Braun doesn't mind me coming?"

"Ben Hoffman says Braun's actually looking forward to it," McPhail informed. "Practically foaming at the bit. Like I've said, the doctor has an enormous ego. And he's always been willing to talk to the media when he thinks it's in his best interest."

"Sounds like there shouldn't be any problem with Braun then," Seven asserted. "But this closed-mouthed secretary of his might be a different matter. I just hope I can win her over."

The Colonel stood and pushed his chair back, indicating that the meeting had ended. A bit of irritation, most likely triggered by Seven's sudden hint at negativity, showed on McPhail's weathered face. Glaring at his young agent, he heatedly addressed the good looking Super Stud. "You're supposed to be *Mr. Dream Boat*, and you've been trained extensively for this type of thing. Just bring the Kent woman around. And that's an order!"

Chapter 12

Invisible Shadows

United Flight 1613, destination Fort Lauderdale, Florida, was only half-filled with passengers, which suited Christopher Seven fine. Now airborne, the Super Stud agent sat in a row all by himself near the deserted rear of the plane. He was thus free to peruse the few classified Klaus Braun notes he'd brought along that were encoded in the standard G5 code of the month. The rest of the data, mainly Klaus Braun bio information, could easily be explained away as necessary background for Seven's magazine article if spotted or lost.

Sitting alone now in row 36, the G5 operative still habitually covered his notes with a newspaper, particularly each time the same two teenage girls made one of their frequent trips to the rear ladies' room. It was quite obvious that they were doing so purposely in order to swoon at him, and these two silly teens became bolder with each pass. With years of experiences such as this one, obviously due to his looks, Christopher Seven was accustomed to women, especially younger girls, gawking at him. He knew it came with the territory and simply smiled each time the two teenagers walked by. They, in turn, just stared and giggled.

Over time, Seven had become immune to this type of attention, much like celebrities do when they are stared at for more than a minute or two. The blessing and curse of his extreme good looks was, of course, always with him. It was usually this way, girls or women with whom he came into contact forever gawking. There was really little he could do about it, except to smile back at them. Shrugging his shoulders he turned his attention to the Ripper assignment.

Having perused three newspapers while waiting in the Newark Liberty Airport terminal, Seven found that the *New York Times,* the *Daily News,* nor the *New York Post* had any hard news stories about the Florida serial killer. *The Times* did have a short op-ed piece criticizing the federal government for not doing more to catch the killer, surprisingly placing some of the blame directly at the feet of the President. Aside from that, there wasn't much coverage.

Of course it was only the beginning of the month. If the Ripper's killing patterns continued, the Florida fiend wouldn't strike for at least three more weeks. Then the harsh criticism would begin all over again. The feds, and even the President in some circles, would be excoriated for not doing enough, as no one would know that Seven, a special agent from one of the government's most elite and secretive units, had been assigned to the case; ironically by direct order of that same Commander-in-Chief.

Regarding his assignment, the Super Stud would first be meeting Special Agent Jack Hanover, the FBI man who probably knew more about the New Ripper case than anybody else. As for the shadowy Dr. Klaus Braun, Seven planned to initially play on Braun's enormous ego in order to gain his confidence. Hopefully, by saying the right things to the doctor, especially in the beginning of their relationship, he'd perhaps get the green light to accompany Braun on one of his upcoming lecture tours. If so, it might then be an excellent forum to try and pursue his *real* objective, the lovely but guarded Sandra Kent; since the file notes mentioned that Sandra usually accompanies Dr. Braun on most of his trips.

Seven knew he'd have to impress Sandra right off the bat, since in just a few weeks another brutal serial murder would most likely occur. There would be little time for *playing the game*, but that was no problem. One of the most important traits that women love, as he had been told repeatedly during his Super Stud training, was confidence; not conceit, but confidence. And, other than his looks, confidence was probably Christopher Seven's strongest asset. One he attributed to athletics, in which he excelled at a very early age in nearly every sport he attempted.

The G5 agent closed his eyes a moment and began concentrating on his target's pretty face, the face he'd studied last night via several FBI file photos. Miss Kent was indeed a gorgeous woman, one with an outward air of intelligence and mystery. Her gaze seemed self assured, as if she knew how truly lovely she was. Being a natural beauty might make the task of captivating her a bit tougher. Despite that, Seven felt he could eventually overcome any obstacle that stood between them and ultimately get what he needed from his stunning quarry. Experience had shown that the potent combination of his looks and trained sophistication usually made women do pretty much what he wanted. Thus, his confidence was literally sky high as the airplane flew steadily south.

Seven quickly covered his files as the two teenagers strolled past again, once more giggling and gawking. For what seemed like the millionth time, the Super Stud thought about how people were constantly commenting on how handsome he was. Over time, this had become a rather shallow compliment. He often wondered if he was simply wasting his talents, and maybe even his life, by being a glorified dating service for the good of his country. His mind often wrestled with that question, although he was certainly aware that his under-cover efforts for G5 had yielded vital information. At times, lifesaving information.

Reflecting on this, a Super Stud mission he'd worked in Baltimore a few years earlier came to mind. This one had involved a brief affair with an attractive Syrian exchange student. Through a purely contrived social and romantic relationship with this young lady, cleverly orchestrated by Colonel McPhail, Seven had extracted several critical details; inside information which had helped thwart the infamous Maryland Harbor Tunnel bombing plot at the very last moment. The public had never known how near the tunnel had come to catastrophe, though Seven had always felt a bit sorry for the Syrian girl. She'd merely supplied the terrorists with a safe house, probably not even knowing their actual mission. Nevertheless, she was now locked away in a federal prison.

His next thoughts were of a similar assignment in Buffalo, New York, organized by G5's Hank Carson. There, he had befriended, captivated really, a female doctor who originally hailed from Pakistan. She was suspected of somehow being involved with a terrorist group. This lady doctor, not exactly a beauty queen, had succumbed quite easily to Seven's charms and had literally melted in his arms. Swayed by his accepting her bizarre marriage proposal, the woman revealed that she had been hiding several al-Qaeda operatives in a large apartment she owned. Homeland Security agents, armed with the address and info, soon raided the apartment building, captured five members of a potentially deadly terrorist cell, and then arrested the woman. Super Stud Seven simply faded away in all the confusion.

"Sir. Sir," a stewardess's voice called out some twenty minutes later. The G5 agent looked up and saw an attractive redheaded flight attendant standing at the end of his row. "We'll be starting our descent shortly, sir. You'll need to put on your seat belt." The shapely stewardess smiled seductively.

Watching the redhead reluctantly retreat, Seven opened the window shade, as his mind immediately began to focus on Florida. He was excited about traveling to the Sunshine State, with its fine beaches, luxurious hotels, and most especially its top restaurants. The G5 agent always loved to frequent the best eating spots around the world, one of his very few personal self-indulgences. Gourmet and fine wine courses during Stud training had thus come easy.

These gastronome skills, like all of the required Super Stud classes, had been invaluable. The various courses had stressed what women liked best in a man. Sophisticated and knowledgeable female instructors who educated the Super Stud agents constantly
trained them to utilize perfect hygiene and grooming habits; practices that soon became automatic. The men had been taught everything that a woman might appreciate, stressing personal appearance, neatness, and most especially cleanliness. The agents had been indoctrinated repeatedly as to the best bar soaps to use when showering, the most effective colognes and after-shaves, as well as just the right amounts of these products to use. *Never be overpowering with a scent*, one beautiful Australian lecturer had told the class.

In the beginning, almost all of the Super Stud trainees had privately scoffed at these personal hygiene courses, joking about them continuously. Eventually however, the agents realized how beneficial this knowledge could be. They quickly learned to trust in these instructions as valuable tools. Nonetheless, at first it had seemed somewhat ridiculous and sometimes still did. Things like the fastidious Super Stud *preferred list*, a list of tried and tested personal hygiene products that the trainees were practically ordered to use exclusively while in the field. These were very definitive choices such as *Dial's* 'Tropical Escape' and 'Spring Water' bar soaps. Or *Colgate's* 'Baking Soda and Peroxide mint toothpaste'. Or to only use *Listerine's* 'Advanced Artic Mint mouthwash'. Seven and the other Studs had been assured that each and every item on this select list had been thoroughly tested and approved; accepted only after conferring with young, attractive *test* women who knew what they liked in a man.

Agents were provided everything. They were given pocket-sized after-meal tooth-care kits, consisting of a thin toothbrush, a tiny tube of toothpaste, and a small mouthwash bottle, along with several brushing strips that could be used in a pinch. All Studs were taught to brush and gargle often, especially after each meal, regardless of *where* they were at the time. "There's always a deserted men's room around, so brush after *every* meal, no matter *where* you're located," a savvy brunette mentor had coached.

The Studs even had a wardrobe provided to them for all occasions. Clothes expertly coordinated and updated by an exacting London fashion authority now working in New York City. As inane as some of these tips, precautions and provisions had first sounded, they soon became important tools of the Super Stud trade; the trade of being irresistible.

A somewhat younger flight attendant, a shapely blonde, soon joined her redheaded colleague. The two stewardesses then hovered around Seven's seat awhile, as the antsy agent tried to gather his belongings and put up his seat for the final approach into Lauderdale.

The attendants smiled solicitously and then slowly made their way to the front for landing duties. After finishing, the blonde whispered excitedly, "Is he the best looking human being you've ever seen, or what? I'm going to try and get his phone number."

"Hands off, gal," the redhead replied. "I saw him first."

~

Twenty minutes after landing at Ft. Lauderdale's International Airport, Christopher Seven was driving a Hertz-rented Mustang GT convertible to Boca Raton. Enjoying the oceanfront scenery on A1A, a longer but more attractive route from the airport, he turned onto Camino Real, perhaps Florida's prettiest road. He pulled up to the front of the world famous *Boca Raton Inn and Resort* where he'd procured a mini suite. The sight of this pink castle-like oasis, originated in the 1920s by the famed Florida realty pioneers Addison Mizner, never failed to impress. The magnificent resort hotel was surrounded by numerous palm trees and brilliantly colored flowers, beckoning serenely.

Following a flawless check-in, Seven was shown to his room and, after a quick shower, changed and sat down at the suite's small writing desk. He opened and studied the file folder on Sandra Kent for the final time. After taking one last look at her photo, he took a match to the dossier and flushed the ashes down the toilet. The notes on Braun he did not destroy. If unexpectedly seen or found, these could be explained away as a reporter's normal research files. But Sandra's photo and dossier would be impossible to defend.

At exactly 4:30 p.m., as arranged by their two agencies, the Super Stud grabbed his cell phone and dialed the number of the North Miami Beach FBI office. Special Agent Jack Hanover was soon on the line. Seven, trying to recall the prearranged opening remarks, began the conversation. "Hello, Jack. Christopher Seven of *Global Magazine*. Just arrived at the Boca Resort Inn. Thought we could get together on my media piece. Are you free for dinner?"

"As a matter of fact, I am, Chris. I live in Delray, which is quite near to Boca Raton. Perhaps we can dine somewhere around there."

Seven thought a minute and then responded. "Fine. How about *La Maison* on Palmetto Park Road?"

Jack Hanover was taken aback. The dinner part of the meeting had been formulated by their two chiefs, but the place, especially one that fancy, hadn't been in the plan. *"La Maison?"* Jack asked hesitantly. "It's the most lavish restaurant in Boca. I hope your expense account will cover that, Mr. Seven. Mine certainly won't!"

"No worries," Seven chuckled, "it's my magazine's treat.

"Then you're on, Chris. See you at eight o'clock."

~

A short distance away, at nearly the exact same moment, a nattily dressed gentleman, the same man who had coldly decreed the murder of Loretta Swanson, addressed the two assassins who'd carried out that gruesome order. As always, Amir and Rahmad sat in respectful silence while their superior spoke.

"A magazine correspondent from New York will be arriving tomorrow. I have no reason to believe that this man is anything other than what he purports to be. However, we must be vigilant and wary. Our enemies are not always fools. When this journalist arrives, he'll come directly here from the airport before going on to his hotel. After he leaves my offices I want to know *what* he does, *who* he sees, and *where* he goes. Understand?"

The two thugs nodded their affirmation. Starting tomorrow they'd become this magazine reporter's invisible shadows.

"This arriving journalist must *not* be approached or harmed in any way, unless by direct order from me," ordered the chief. "Right now, he serves my purpose. But if his visit turns out to be some trickery of the Western dogs, I promise in Lucifer's name that I will allow the two of you complete freedom to make his death an excruciatingly slow and violent one!"

The two killers simultaneously licked their lips in sadistic anticipation, mentally planning the torment they could inflict upon this visitor should he be an imposter.

"Here is this journalist's name and some admittedly minor background information on him and his publication," added the leader. He passed two thin envelopes across the desk. "I will try to get more for you later on, including some photos if possible. For now, this was all my sources could obtain. We only recently learned that this man was coming. But just remember. If the arriving journalist is indeed who he claims to be, he will not be your next victim. But if he is *not* what he claims, then I want this fool so tortured, and so butchered, that he will be unrecognizable!"

"We understand," his henchmen replied in unison,

"Excellent," proclaimed Dr. Klaus Braun.

Rahmad and Amir bowed reverently and then reached out for the sparse folders. The outside of each file was embossed with a familiar insignia, the ancient satanic symbol depicting a bizarre looking bird with horns standing on an ornate vase. It was the *Lucifer Crest*, an emblem they all knew well. Directly underneath the unusual bird crest, penned in large red letters, was a singular name, the name of their potential next victim.

That name was *CHRISTOPHER SEVEN.*

Chapter 13

Dinner amongst the Trees

The dining experience at Boca Raton's *La Maison* is unlike that of any other five-star restaurant in the country, with its fabulous European setting, divine gourmet food, and breathtaking environment.

Christopher Seven arrived at the elegant eatery at precisely eight o'clock and left his car with the valet attendant. Inside, a tuxedoed maître d' smartly greeted him and led him up an ornate, circular staircase. They soon arrived at the lone table set for two outside on a quaint, tree-lined balcony. Seven had specifically reserved this particular alfresco table, akin to feasting in an elegant tree house, and knowing that dining without any other neighboring tables would be more private for discussing the Ripper case.

A few minutes later the maître d' returned, accompanied by a muscular man who appeared to be in his mid-thirties. Seven immediately recognized the FBI agent from the file photo he'd seen the day before in New York. It wasn't hard to place him. Jack Hanover was an impressive figure, with the build of a pro athlete. He was close to six-feet tall, and he filled his two hundred pounds with what appeared to be solid muscle. Jack had striking green eyes, and short, blonde hair. Sizing his dinner guest up quickly, Seven guessed the FBI man had played college football, probably as a middle linebacker. The Super Stud stood and stuck out his hand. "Hello, Jack. Welcome to one of Florida's best restaurants."

"Nice to meet you, Chris." Hanover smiled warmly, and with a very strong grip shook Seven's hand. "The way the parking lot valet looked at me I'm not sure he's ever parked a Ford before. Nothing but BMWs and Jaguars outside."

Seven laughed and motioned to the open seat. A waiter soon arrived and took their drink orders, a glass of champagne for Seven, and a simple chardonnay for Jack. Both men then waited for the waiter to move inside. Hanover spoke first. "My boss told me to assist you in any way I can, Chris." Then, with a sly grin he added, "By the way, you don't look like any ghost or invisible man I've ever met, yet they told me you're someone who officially doesn't exist. I know the Company's domestic policy, so you're not CIA, or FBI. Should I ask, or just leave it at that?"

Seven replied discreetly, "Wish I could tell you more, Jack. But let's just stick to the magazine reporter thing for a while."

Hanover nodded and replied, "Understood. Anyway, I'm ready to do whatever it takes to get this New Ripper creep. Agent Loretta Swanson was a very good friend of mine."

"Don't worry, Jack, we'll nail him. And I'm terribly sorry about your friend, Loretta. She seemed like a fine agent." Hanover lowered his head sadly as Seven declared, "As you've hopefully been informed, my cover for being here is to do a flattering magazine story on Dr. Klaus Braun. They say the man has a huge ego."

"That I can *definitely* confirm, Chris."

"But my *real* assignment," Seven continued, "is to get one of his top staff people, some secretary of his, to spill what she knows. And then hopefully, with her help, get an opportunity to pick her brains on all things Braun, and hopefully look through a few of Dr. Braun's private files. We might get lucky and find something on Braun himself, or on the snake connection to the serial killings. Something that hopefully leads your people to the Ripper. By the way, what do you know about the doctor's private secretary, Sandra Kent? Think she might possibly be turned?"

"Good luck on that piece of dreaming," Hanover answered candidly. "All of Braun's people are secretive, and every one of them is on a very tight leash. But Sandra Kent seems to be the most close-mouthed of all. Anyway, that's what our agent, Loretta Swanson, discovered. I haven't met Miss Kent, though I'd like to. She's quite the looker from what I hear."

The conversation paused when the waiter arrived with their drink order. Crusty bread and a crock of creamy white butter were then placed on the table. "Boy, I'm starved," Hanover announced, taking a piece of bread and buttering it.

Seven likewise helped himself to the delicious freshly baked loaf. "Jack, did you ever notice that the finest restaurants in the world also have the best breads and butter? You see, if an establishment goes through the time, trouble, and expense of baking great bread, and then provides only the finest, creamy *unsalted* butter, that's usually a sign of a first-rate meal to come."

"Wouldn't know, but obviously you're at a higher pay grade than me."

"No, it's true," insisted Seven, trying not to sound too preachy. "Go into any restaurant, order a glass of their house wine, try a piece of the bread they put on the table, and sample their butter. You'll be able to instantly determine if it's a good place or not." The Super Stud laughed loudly. "Sorry. Didn't mean to bore you. Good food and fine restaurants have become an obsession of mine. It probably comes from having too much free time on my hands."

"I understand, Chris. And I'll try to remember that about the butter, although I'm a devout hamburger guy myself." Hanover stared down at the lengthy menu with a perplexed expression. "Looks like I'm going to need your help with this as well. Most of it's in French, except for the prices." He glanced at the right side of the menu. "Wow!" Jack winced playfully. "Incidentally, I didn't actually expect you to pick up the entire bill. It'll cost you a small fortune."

"Like I said earlier, it's my treat, Jack. You can get the next one. And by the way, I love a good hamburger too. Now let's see what looks good here." Seven perused the menu choices and decided to choose something classical and uncomplicated rather than some way-out nouveau dish. "This chateaubriand for two with béarnaise sauce looks delicious. That is if you like beef. With the fabulous French chef they have here, I would wager that the chateaubriand is spectacular."

Hanover nodded in agreement. "Let's go with that then."

"Done. By the way, I hope you like your beef medium rare?"

"Of course. I'm certainly not an expert like you, but one thing I do know. It's the only way to cook good beef!"

"Excellent selection, gentlemen," the now hovering maître d' complimented. "You won't be disappointed. We serve the finest certified prime beef in the country. I'll start you out with a small house salad as well. Now, how about the wine?"

"We'll try the Jordan Cabernet," Seven suggested after studying the huge wine list.

"One of California's best," commented the sommelier, also standing by. Both servers bowed politely and left for the kitchen.

As soon as they departed, the business at hand resumed between the two agents, started by Seven. "I've studied the file notes on this case thoroughly, Jack. I understand that Agent Swanson visited Klaus Braun not long before she was killed. Most everyone thinks that was merely a coincidence. Tell me if I'm wrong, but the predominant theory is that the Ripper saw Loretta's address in a local paper. He then attacked her, perhaps assuming that she was mocking him in that unfortunate newspaper story." Seven shook his head. "I guess that's typical of these serial killers. They either want to contact or speak with the police chief or negotiator involved in their case, or they want to kill them. Usually there's no in-between."

"Absolutely," agreed Hanover, "although our profile experts certainly know there's no cookie-cutter, one-size-fits-all serial killers, like Hollywood loves to portray." Jack frowned, "I warned Loretta it was dangerous to live alone. Especially after her name and address had been leaked by the press. Even I have two bodyguards at the beach house now." Hanover sighed. "Yet it is a bit odd that Loretta had just recently spoken with Dr. Braun about the case before she was murdered. She never liked Braun at all."

Seven nodded and asked, "Is there anything more you can tell me about this Klaus Braun himself? Have you guys been able to find out anything yourselves from the inside?"

Hanover, now sporting a sly grin, informed, "After Loretta's death, the FBI began taking this Braun guy a bit more seriously. After all, Loretta had just seen the man, coincidence or not. Three days ago, through a very reliable contact, we learned that one of Braun's daytime maintenance managers, a fellow named Ken Fusco, had a significant gambling problem. Fusco is a trained sanitation worker at Dr. Braun's lab. These cleanup specialists are very important with all of the hazardous waste they have to meticulously dispose of over there. Anyway, we heard the guy owed the wrong people and figured it would make him ripe for the take. We figured right. Fusco readily accepted our bribe and has begun doing a bit of inside spying for us. Nothing yet, but he could be a good source." Hanover drank some of his wine and then gave Seven a few more details. "Right now, Fusco's only doing some general snooping. You know, peeking into open offices or file cabinets. He's come up with a few tidbits but no smoking gun yet. At least he's confirmed that most all of the suspected illegal aliens over there are assigned to Braun's nightshift where they don't have to come into contact with the public."

"Nightshift?"

"Yes. Klaus Braun divides his workers into two distinct shifts, completely separate from each other. The dayshift runs the zoo, tours, and the public relations work. They also deal with the more mundane pharmaceutical products. But at six o'clock every evening that daytime group is quickly ushered out. Then, at exactly eight o'clock, Braun's secretive nightshift files in. This night stint is supposedly the time when the top secret experiments take place."

Seven nodded as Jack went on, "Over the years we've heard bits and pieces about the nightshift, but unfortunately we've never really been able to penetrate it in any way. Klaus Braun has a concrete rule. Only those on the official nightshift payroll are allowed on the grounds during the hours of darkness." Hanover shrugged his shoulders. "Whatever's going on during the night ends promptly at sunrise. Then the security guards usher the night staff out at exactly 6:00 a.m. A few hours later, the entire process reverses itself and starts again when the daytime workers arrive at eight in the morning. Sounds crazy, I know, but Dr. Braun must have his reasons. And after all, it is a billion-dollar industry." Jack reached for another piece of bread and then resumed, "We'd dearly love to know more about this mysterious nightshift. I've heard there are some pretty unsavory characters attached to it." Hanover looked over at Seven. "I don't know where your girl Sandra fits in, but I'd bet she's only connected to the daytime staff."

The waiter arrived with their salads, which were dressed with a delicious vinaigrette, one that had a hint of lemon and tarragon. The men ate in contented silence for a few moments until Seven picked up the dialogue. "This daytime/nighttime divide of Dr. Braun's is interesting. Maybe I can somehow check it out. There could be a lot more to the nightshift thing than meets the eye."

Jack Hanover quickly agreed. "I'll say. With his two shifts, Braun can do pretty much what he wants under the cover of darkness. And there's one other interesting twist. During the night security increases and the place is guarded as if it were a prison compound." Hanover frowned. "One thing our mole Fusco did manage to find out was that a lot of these nighttime people come from foreign countries: Haiti, Cuba, Eastern Europe, and the poorer Caribbean locales. It's also rumored that these foreigners occasionally volunteer, and I use that term loosely, for human experimentation. Guinea pigs for the snake venom drugs, that sort of thing. I guess those poor souls will do anything for a bit of extra cash."

The FBI operative rubbed his forehead. "If you do get in the loop, Chris, be very careful. Those Braun security guys look pretty shady and dangerous from the little we have on file. They're apt to shoot first and ask questions later."

Seven was taken aback by all this new information. He had thought the Braun assignment was merely going to be a pleasant interlude in the sun trying to probe some beautiful secretary. Now, he was being told of security thugs and strange nighttime shifts. Infiltrating a target that was surrounded by a dangerous security squad was more a mission for the main line units of G5. Even so, Christopher Seven had to admit that this new element of potential danger was somehow thrilling and appealing. "Any chance of your man Fusco checking out that nighttime shift himself?" he asked.

Jack smiled, deviously. "We almost gave up on the idea, as he was only on the daytime payroll. That is until yesterday."

"What happened yesterday?"

"We caught a real break", grinned Hanover. "The main overnight sanitation manager got sick and had to leave with a serious kidney problem. They needed a trained replacement immediately, one who knew the complicated ropes of correctly disposing hazardous materials. There weren't any around on the spur of the moment and Ken Fusco had all the right qualifications. He quickly became the obvious choice. Even at that, it took the sworn assurances of two of Fusco's buddies in security, after sizable bribes to them both, to get Fusco into the nightshift. With the personal guarantees and recommendations of those two nighttime security workers behind him, Fusco was approached yesterday and accepted instantly. He began working the nightshift last night. Hopefully, we'll start getting some *real* info soon!"

Just then their entrée and a bevy of waiters arrived. Hanover and Seven immediately ceased discussion of the case and began contemplating the delicious looking beef which was now being expertly hand-carved by the maître d'. He did so on a small wooden platter atop a rolling cart. Juicy, perfectly pink, and literally mouthwatering, the delectable aroma of the steaming Chateaubriand slowly wafted its way toward them. The two agents watched in eager anticipation as the headwaiter plated their meal, and then poured a bit of the creamy yellow béarnaise sauce on the side of their dishes. He finished the plate by adding buttery asparagus spears and some scrumptious oven-baked fingerling potatoes.

After they finished, Jack couldn't stop talking about the food. "It'll be tough eating at my regular coffee shop now and it's all your fault!"

"Excellent," said Seven. The Super Stud waited till the plates were taken away and made sure that only he and Hanover were present. He then resumed, "I'll keep my eyes and ears open Jack. We can trade info via our cell phones. Mine's secured and I know all FBI cell phones are too." Seven frowned. "Guess we won't be able to meet together any longer. I imagine that after I appear on the scene tomorrow, our friend, Klaus Braun, will have me under constant surveillance while I'm down here."

"You can count on that, Chris. It's standard operational practice in their world. These pharmaceutical giants are all spying on each other. In Dr. Braun's eyes, you might be in cahoots with some shrewd industrial spies. People who could later sell Braun's inside secrets to the competition. Hence, Klaus Braun will undoubtedly have you tailed from tomorrow on." Hanover grinned. "But if this Sandra Kent doll gets lonely while you're with her boss, just send her to me."

As Seven laughed loudly, Jack again glanced around to make certain that no one else was nearby. The FBI man then purposely lowered his voice and spoke with a seriousness he hadn't shown before. "Now listen carefully, Chris. And I'm telling you this on the QT. Two suspected Middle-Eastern terrorists, assassins who slipped past us a while ago, are now thought to be in the South Florida area. These guys are professional killers. Not brainless suicide bombers, but trained executioners. I wouldn't put it past them to hide out in some secretive setting, like Dr. Braun's nightshift environment. I doubt Braun would even know who they are. And I'm sure he wouldn't hire or house them if he did. Then again, he apparently isn't picky when it comes to getting cheap help or hiring his security watchdogs.

Jack Hanover looked around once more and quickly finished his thoughts. "These strong-arm goons of Braun's have got to come from somewhere." He paused for emphasis and then gave Seven a somber warning. "All I'm saying is, be on your toes!"

Chapter 14

Coincidence or Murder

After saying goodnight to Hanover, Christopher Seven left the restaurant shortly after 10:00 p.m. and decided to take a ride up A1A before returning to his hotel. With the convertible top down, and some early Beatles' music on the radio, the leisurely drive through the mansion-laden, oceanfront neighborhoods of Delray and West Palm Beach was soothing and idyllic. At one point, however, near panic occurred! The Super Stud had the distinct feeling he was being followed, and instant chills ran up and down his spine. If true, this would mean there was a mole somewhere in the chain, since only a few agency people were supposed to know that he was actually in Florida the day *before* his announced arrival date. Then, to his immense relief, the imagined tail turned out to be an unmarked Palm Beach Police vehicle, one that had been routinely keeping an eye on the neighborhood's posh homes.

Seven got back to his room around midnight. Fatigue had finally set in, as was usually the case at the end of any travel day. While preparing a hot bath in the suite's Jacuzzi, and thinking about how a good night's sleep in the luxurious pillow-top bed would feel, his cell phone rang. It was Jack Hanover.

"Hey Jack. What's the matter? Still hungry?"

"I wish it was just that."

Seven sensed from the tone of the FBI agent's voice that the news might be of a serious nature. "What's up, Jack?"

"Trouble at Braun's place. It concerns our mole, Ken Fusco, that maintenance guy we discussed. Afraid he won't be able to tell us anything now. He's in the hospital. In a coma from a snakebite."

"What!" Seven exclaimed, his mind racing with all sorts of scenarios, including a revenge strike ordered by Braun's people.

"Hold the phone before you jump to any conclusions like I did when I first got the news," Hanover cautioned. "Let me give you all the details and then you can judge for yourself. Believe it or not, it appears to have been a legitimate accident. And by the way, Dr. Braun wasn't even in Florida when it happened."

Seven cradled the phone near his ear and listened closely.

"It occurred about eleven thirty tonight, Chris. An Australian Taipan, one of the world's deadliest snakes, nailed our mole Fusco. Most likely buoyed on by our offer of more bucks for more info, Fusco was admittedly keen to snoop around places he shouldn't have. He could have simply made a fatal mistake or had a severe lapse of judgment in his zeal to snoop. Amateurs sometimes do, you know. And obviously, a place crawling with deadly reptiles is a bad place to make an error."

That makes sense, thought Seven on one hand, while at the same time remembering what Colonel McPhail steadfastly preached. *In this business, there's no such thing as coincidence.* The Super Stud continued listening, trying to do so with an open mind.

"The details are still a bit sketchy. They come from the police report and a statement from the nighttime security manager at the Reptile Center." Seven heard the rustling of papers as Jack went on, "Fusco began his nighttime cleanup rounds at nine o'clock. At roughly ten-fifteen, he apparently made his way into an unattended *restricted* file zone. There were warning signs posted all over the place, but it sounds as if our man wanted to get in there no matter what. Apparently no one was around, and, as I've said, we were paying substantial bonus money for anything really juicy."

"I understand, Jack," affirmed Seven, as Hanover gave more specifics.

"Braun's nighttime security people believe that Ken Fusco accidentally walked into a large storage closet in the Center's '*restricted files*' area. They can't figure out why he did so, obviously unaware that Fusco was spying for us. The guards told the cops that a snake was inside one of the walk-in closets. That's not as unusual as it sounds. Though it's not common knowledge, some of the larger serpents are occasionally allowed to roam around in closed-in areas like this closet. Just so long as it's in a totally restricted area. It's a way to get the larger reptiles some much-needed exercise. And since only trained herpetologists are allowed to enter these restricted vicinities to corral them, there's usually no danger." Hanover sighed. "Poor Fusco. Evidently only the professional snake keepers know when a serpent is loose inside, and Ken Fusco never asked."

Seven shook his head, still not buying the story. "Weren't there any warning signs posted, Jack?"

"Like I've said, large 'keep out' signs were clearly displayed, and the Miami police have confirmed that. According to Dr. Braun's security head, a guy named Rosier, Fusco was bitten twice on the arm. In a matter of minutes he began having trouble breathing, but was able to get to a house phone, called for help, and then collapsed. The Reptile Center's nighttime operator, a Ms. Josie Ramos, immediately paged the guards who then rushed to the area. The snake was coiled in the far corner, and they found Ken Fusco passed out on the floor. The Center's security team immediately called an ambulance, which for some inexplicable reason took nearly thirty minutes to arrive. Fusco was then rushed to Miami General Hospital where he went into a coma and is not expected to live. We don't know why it took the ambulance so long to get there. An investigation has been launched into that. But I guess we can't blame that one on Braun's people."

Seven didn't agree. This thirty-minute delay sounded very dubious indeed, as did the whole story told by Klaus Braun's security squad. He held his thoughts, not wanting to interrupt Jack.

"Klaus Braun was in Atlanta for a longstanding lecture date.   The Miami police chief who talked to him on the phone said that Dr. Braun seemed genuinely shocked and saddened, and that he was furious with both his security people and his snake handlers after hearing about the unattended reptile. Threatened to fire them all. In fact, he's on his way to Miami right now in his private jet in order to donate his own blood for a transfusion."

"Did you say *his* Blood, Jack?" asked the slightly confused Seven.

"Yes. With all that venom in Braun's body, a transfusion of the doctor's blood often works better than any antivenin. Provided the blood types match, of course. Unfortunately though, for this transfusion to work properly, it usually has to be done quickly. Yet you have to give Dr. Braun credit for trying. He told the police he'd start for Miami General as soon as he landed, and to let him, or his secretary, Sandra Kent, know if there was anything further they could do." Hanover sighed into the phone. "So, what was it? An unfortunate accident or murder by snake? Believe it or not, it actually sounds like the former to me. But you can add that question to your 'to-do' list."

Christopher Seven thought a moment before replying, "Fusco's not dead yet, Jack. He just might answer that question himself. I hope you have his hospital room guarded."

"Taken care of. But there's one last thing you should take into account, Chris. This isn't a singular tragedy. These snake accidents definitely happen from time to time at the Reptile Center. After all, they're working with some of the deadliest creatures on the planet. It's an occupational hazard, one that the employees know and fully accept. In fact, they're required to sign a release prior to working there. And although most of Dr. Braun's people are well trained in safety procedures, there have still been several fatalities over the last ten years. Each incident was checked out by the police and ruled accidental. There's also been numerous non-lethal bites and several narrow escapes."

Seven's instincts and his keen, logical chess player's mind told him that Fusco's case was different. This was no mishap. There was definite danger about and something ominous surrounding Klaus Braun and his reptilian and pharmaceutical empires. Whether it concerned the Ripper murders or not, the G5 agent wasn't sure. Yet at this point, he was even more intent on learning the truth.

"So, there you have it, Mr. Seven. And since you'll be arriving on the scene tomorrow, you'll obviously be walking into quite a buzz saw of activity. I'll be extremely interested to see just how Dr. Braun tries to downplay this Fusco episode to you, a reporter."

"It should be an interesting day indeed, Jack. I'll tell you one thing, though. Since I'm really not a big fan of snakes, I think I'll stay away from those *off-limit* areas. Snakes kind of spook me."

"Me too," Hanover replied, now thinking of poor Loretta.

"Did your people talk to the ambulance attendants, Jack?"

"As a matter of fact, a fax is coming in right now on that." Seven again heard the rustle of papers being gathered on Hanover's end, followed by Jack's voice. "There's a whole bunch of medical stuff, Chris. Hang on. Let me skip through all that."

The Super Stud could hear Jack thumbing through the sheets. "All right, here's the important data, Chris. It says, 'together with his unintelligible babbling, the patient kept screaming out the same three things over and over again. That is, until he passed out shortly after arriving at the emergency room. ER worker, Samuel Newman, has confirmed this, as did the police officers working security at Miami General." Jack paused briefly again, silently read a bit more of the report, and then exclaimed in disbelief, "Aw, man, this stuff doesn't make any sense at all, Chris. Fusco must have *really* been out of his mind."

"What is it?"

"This is just nuts, but the faxed report says that Fusco wasn't just mumbling. According to the witnesses the three things he was clearly screaming were *venom, old age,* and *Martin Bormann.*"

"Martin Bormann?" Seven asked, incredulously. "Wasn't he one of Hitler's cronies back in World War II?"

"I believe so. But that would make no sense at all. The word *venom* does though. As for old age, and this Martin Bormann guy, what the heck is *that* all about?"

~

An hour later, Christopher Seven sat alone in his room, searching the Internet on his pre-coded laptop computer. Although feeling a bit foolish, he nonetheless typed the name *Martin Bormann* into the word search. As far as Seven knew, Bormann had died several decades earlier.

When he plugged in Bormann's name, the Internet keyword steered him to a website on World War II. Once there, he again clicked on the name Bormann, which was near the top of the list.

- Bormann, Martin—Born 1907, date of death unknown. One of Hitler's most trusted personal aides. It is believed that Martin Bormann might have had a secret hand in planning some of the sordid death camp experiments, though this was never confirmed.
- It is further believed that Martin Bormann was the last Nazi to speak with Hitler, although shortly before Adolf Hitler's death, and the morbid cremation of Hitler's body that followed, Bormann mysteriously left the scene and

was never seen or heard of since. Details of that final day in Hitler's underground bunker are sketchy, at best. However, most historians claim that Martin Bormann was already on his way out of Berlin, most likely on the way to Argentina.

• Bormann was the highest ranking Nazi official to elude the allied powers, despite extensive searches. Particularly those conducted by the Russians. Rumors of his whereabouts and activities continued to surface until well into the 1970s. To this day, Martin Bormann is still worshipped as a hero by many of the hardcore neo-Nazi groups. For more information, please see Nazis, World War II war criminals, and Hitler, last days of.

Seven stared at his computer screen and wondered what on earth this Bormann character had to do with snakes, venom, old age, or, most importantly, with the New Ripper case. He rubbed his forehead and glanced at his watch. It was well after 1 AM.

After taking a long, hot shower, and brushing his teeth for the sixth time that day, he climbed into bed. As was his custom, he then said a meaningful nighttime prayer. Christopher Seven, by no means a saint, took great comfort in the fact that he could pray to God for guidance, protection, and forgiveness. A very spiritual person, he took his Christian faith seriously. His prayer tonight seemed to have a bit more urgency, for Seven was somehow certain that he was going to need a large amount of God's protection.

Chapter 15

The Merchant of Venom

A t exactly 7:45 a.m., the electronic beeping of his travel alarm clock brought Christopher Seven out of a deep, dreamless sleep. Yawning and stretching he lazily got out of bed, walked over to the window, and threw open the floor-length curtains. The room was immediately flooded with golden Florida sunlight.

From his vantage point, high on the twelfth floor of the hotel's famous *pink tower*, he could see much of Lake Boca Raton, and the stunning cove that led out to the Atlantic. For a full five minutes he stood in the bath of warm sunshine, taking in the serene Boca beachfront. The white sandy beaches dotted with lavish condominiums, the magnificent oceanfront mansions, the meandering Intercostal, and the tranquil turquoise ocean itself.

With a long sigh, Seven reluctantly turned away from the dazzling view below and made his way to the suite's marble bathroom. Here he showered and shaved, using all of the required Super Stud products. While drying his thick head of hair, he propped up his well-used Bible on the vanity and read some verses. Today's prose was from the book of Job. After reading it, the agent hoped he wouldn't need Job's patience on this assignment. Finished with his daily Bible reading, Seven bowed his head and said his brief yet heartfelt morning prayer.

At five past eight he called the tennis shop and confirmed his 10:00 a.m. playing lesson with the hotel's pro Eric Gold, an old friend from their teenage days of competitive tennis on the national junior circuit. He next phoned and scheduled a one-hour private martial arts session at the *Tiger Pro Karate Center* in Pompano Beach. Regular martial arts workouts were mandatory for all Super Stud agents, helping them maintain sharpness, physique, and stamina.

The subsequent tennis and martial workout proved quite vigorous, particularly the latter. The instructor, more correctly called the *Sensei,* had worked him on the basic *Gochen Sho* defensive techniques. These moves centered on the principle that a less experienced karate fighter could keep a more expert martial arts combatant at bay with a reflex shielding strategy. The central tactic was to always deflect a more skilled adversary and never rush in to attack him. This suited Seven well, as neither he nor any of the other Studs were black belt masters. Colonel McPhail's theory was that, though they should be able to skillfully defend themselves, their main job was to simply gather information. Instead of fisticuffs, they should first try to avoid a fight whenever possible. Use their looks and charms, rather than brawn. Besides, if they were *too* proficient in elite hand-to-hand combat, it might draw undue attention from the wrong people, ruining both their individual covers, and quite possibly the anonymity of the whole Stud section.

Nonetheless, Christopher Seven was grateful for his weekly martial arts training. It had come in handy on several occasions and had even saved his life a few times in the field. One such occasion was a dangerous mission he'd undertaken in Columbia, the first of only two times he'd been forced to kill a man. A crazed drug lord from one of the major cartels had come at him with a pistol, after spotting Seven and the man's mistress talking in a deserted alley. Seven instinctively relied on his martial training, kicking the weapon out of the attacker's hand and then grabbing it off the ground. As the druggie whipped out another gun from his back pocket and aimed it at Seven's chest, the G5 agent had no choice but to fire, killing the man instantly. Even though it was pure self-defense and had prevented his own death, as well as saving the life of the woman, Seven's conscience had bothered him for months. He shrugged his shoulders at the memory, stripped off his workout clothes and hopped into the suite's opulent shower.

For this initial meeting with Klaus Braun, Seven had carefully chosen one of Godfrey's (the Super Stud clothing guru) more recent ensembles, a pale yellow Italian sports coat and *Callenia* black dress pants. He felt that these casually elegant clothes would befit his role as a nattily attired magazine journalist. "Tools of the trade," he murmured, standing for a final personal inspection in the mirror.

To anyone seeing him now, particularly women, Christopher Seven knew he would surely turn heads. That was just the way it was and had been for almost all of his life. He'd learned to simply appreciate the God-given gift of his extraordinary looks, and felt no need to boast about it. His calling as a Super Stud agent dictated that he was to be as attractive and desirable as possible to the opposite sex. Satisfied he now met those requirements, he picked up his briefcase and was soon off for his meeting with the enigmatic Dr. Braun. Despite the complications and possible dangers, Seven welcomed the challenge and hoped this initial encounter would be the needed entrée toward his *real* target, Sandra Kent.

~

Driving toward the Miami Reptile Center, the G5 operative knew the starting gate of his mission had officially opened. He smiled confidently, turned right onto Hillsboro Boulevard, and headed south on I-95. Exiting near the old Orange Bowl section, Seven soon found himself driving through the underbelly of the City of Miami. These squalid backstreets housed a mixture of dilapidated warehouses, vacant parking lots and several deserted office buildings. Noting the seediness of the area, Seven was glad he'd kept the convertible's top up.

According to his *Waze* navigation tool, the Reptile Center was located between Miami and Miami Beach, just off of Route 1 and Atlantic.

After a few minutes of stop-and-go traffic he came to a giant cobra statue towering over a sign that read: *Welcome to the World Famous Miami Reptile Center.* This was it, the jumping-off point!

Seven pulled the blue Mustang GT into a front space in the spacious parking lot. Being late in the afternoon on a slow weekday, the lot was only half-filled. With his leather attaché case in hand, and looking every bit the magazine scribe, he made his way over to the entrance gate booth where an attractive young worker named Donna eyed him longingly. She checked his name off the pass list, and directed him toward the smallish welcome center building.

"May I help you, sir?" inquired the melodious voice of the welcome center's receptionist from behind a large polished desk. A gold nameplate informed visitors that her name was Glenda Ellis.

"Yes, Glenda; I'm Christopher Seven." He gave her a friendly smile. "From *Global Magazine.* I'm here to see Dr. Braun."

"Oh yes, we've been expecting you Mr. Seven. I hope you had a pleasant flight?"

"No problems at all. For once today's plane was right on time."

"Wonderful. And how do you like our beautiful weather?"

"Couldn't be better. Makes one wonder why they'd live anywhere else."

"That's what I've been telling my sister. She lives in North Dakota and the snow is still falling there. By the way, would you like a cup of coffee or perhaps something cold?"

"No thanks." He casually surveyed the surroundings. "What a lovely office you have here, Glenda." Seven's trained eye immediately spotted the hidden camera that was recessed into the ceiling, cleverly disguised as a fire sprinkler. It was situated behind her desk and he wondered if she even knew it was there.

"Thank you, Mr. Seven. It's a nice place to work. I'll buzz the doctor and let him know you've arrived. His office is over in the main building, just a short stroll from here." She smiled sweetly, picked up the phone, and after a few moments of conversation hung up.

"You're cleared to go, sir. I'll have one of the staff take you over to the executive offices."

A few moments later a young man in his early twenties strode into the reception area. Glenda introduced him as one of the college interns working there part time. "Thomas will walk you to the main building," Glenda explained. "Since some sections of the Center can be potentially dangerous, with the snakes and all, visitors must be accompanied by a staff member at all times. We have a very strict safety shadow code."

"Of course," Seven agreed, suspecting that Dr. Braun probably had other self-serving reasons for this policy. "Never can be too careful,

Glenda." His thoughts quickly turned to the unfortunate FBI informant, Ken Fusco.

"This way, sir," Thomas guided, leading the way out the back door located at the end of a narrow hallway.

A very impressive structure soon loomed before them, Klaus Braun's massive executive building. It was beautifully landscaped and had the look of a large southern plantation home rather than a working business hub. Its tall white columns and huge, elaborate double front doors resembled Elvis' Graceland. The entire place reeked of money and power. "Here you are, sir," Thomas proudly announced. "Dr. Braun's executive office suites. Just go right in. One of the secretaries will take you from here on."

Seven walked through the entrance doors, where another secretary greeted him, this one a short, harsh looking redhead with a cold demeanor. This inhospitable woman was almost the exact opposite of the personable Glenda, and the G5 operative didn't like the looks of her. He nonetheless smiled politely.

"Yes?" she asked in a detached manner, as if confronting an unwelcome salesman.

"Hello. I'm Christopher Seven of *Global Magazine*. I believe Dr. Braun is expecting me."

"Oh," she said, a bit startled. "That stupid kid. He should have walked you in here. Oh well. Just one moment." Slightly flustered, she picked up her phone. "Sandy? There's a Mr. Seven here to see the chief." The redhead listened for a moment before hanging up. Her tone immediately became more agreeable, though her forced friendliness was obviously strained. "Dr. Braun is expecting you. I'll take you to his office."

"Thank you. Miss Elsa Dykstra, is it?" Seven asked, eyeing the nameplate on her desk.

The woman said nothing except, "Follow me."

Miss Dykstra and Seven walked together in silence down yet another long and spotlessly clean corridor. There were offices and small laboratories on either side. Unfortunately there were no glass windows to peer through, so the G5 agent could only guess what was happening behind the walls. He tried, unsuccessfully, to nonchalantly glance into the one or two offices, those that had their doors ajar.

Finally, at the very end of this seemingly never-ending hall, loomed a large mahogany double door. A decorative brass plaque on the outside of it read: *Dr. Klaus A. Braun – Founder and President.* The redheaded secretary knocked on it gently.

"Proceed," a baritone voice from inside boomed. It had the slightest trace of an accent, one that the G5 operative couldn't place. When the boorish red-haired secretary opened one of the big doors, Christopher Seven looked into perhaps the plushest private office he had ever seen, and he'd seen some of the finest in the world. The room was pure, unabashed opulence! It was furnished extravagantly, with a floor of beautiful beige marble, some of it covered by expensive Oriental area rugs. Fresh flowers were abundant, and there was a stunning, saltwater aquarium behind the main desk. Yet one particular item more than anything else in the lavish office immediately caught Seven's attention; the very large orange-and-brown spotted snake curled up on the end of Dr. Braun's desk. The Super Stud was taken aback by the sight of such a large reptile, which lay quietly and completely free near the hands of its master.

There it is, my first Braun snake, the G5 operative thought to himself. *I sure hope it's the last.* It took all of Seven's willpower to pretend not to be nervous near the serpent, hoping his eyes wouldn't give away his apprehension. A smiling Klaus Braun stood up and extended his hand directly over the reptile. *Is this snake gambit some sort of test,* Seven wondered. Still nervous, the Super Stud nonetheless reached out, all the while keeping a wary eye on the snake, which seemed to be lazily looking up at him. As he shook hands with the doctor, Seven tried hard not to show his surprise from the unnatural feel of the man's fingers. Braun's yellowish skin was ice cold to the touch.

"My good man," Klaus Braun welcomed, "so nice to meet you. Please don't be alarmed by Alice. She's a rainbow boa from Argentina, *Epicrates canchria*, to be precise, and as tame as a kitten. Not at all like some of the other residents we have here at the Center." Braun grinned at his last remark. "I house many snakes that possess some of the most toxic venoms known to man. But Alice here is one of our non-venomous inhabitants. We study all types of reptiles although we primarily depend upon the venomous variety for the basis of my research. Our products and venoms are sold to researchers and clinics worldwide. I guess that's why I'm sometimes referred to as the Merchant of Venom."

Braun laughed loudly at his little joke. Seven dutifully grinned as Dr. Braun continued. "But please forgive me for talking shop. I know you're not here to be bored with my lecturing." He then brusquely dismissed his secretary. "That'll be all, Miss Dykstra."

Seven nodded to the exiting redhead as Klaus Braun began again, "I trust everyone here has made you feel at home?"

"Absolutely. They've been most kind."

"*Global* Magazine," uttered Braun. "I've seen your publication from time to time. Can't say I'm a regular reader though. My work keeps me far too busy, practically 24 hours a day. No time for leisurely reading with all the scientific periodicals I must digest."

"I understand, Doctor. As for our circulation, *Global* is distributed every Sunday in thousands of newspapers around the country. From Maine to California. I'm actually a freelance journalist, meaning I don't work directly for *Global.* Every so often, I accept assignments from them.

Mainly unusual stories that I think might be of interest to the public. I took this assignment because the beneficial work you do here is very appealing to me, as I'm sure it will be for our many readers. I'm hoping to give you and your fine pharmaceutical work the credit it truly deserves."

Seven hoped he wasn't laying it on too thick. It was hard to tell by Braun's reaction. The doctor showed no change in expression. He appeared to be sizing up his visitor with the probing antennae that most scientists seem to possess.

"Would you care for a cigar, Mr. Seven?"

"No thanks, I'm not a smoker."

"Do you mind if I smoke then?" Dr. Braun asked although already taking out a cigar from his top drawer. "It's one of my few vices, but I do love a good cigar."

"Go right ahead, sir. I'm on your turf."

The doctor went through a ritual of snipping off the end of the cigar, lightly wetting it with his tongue. He held the flame from the gold lighter just below the tip, careful not to let the fire actually touch the tobacco. As Braun lit the cigar, Christopher Seven silently took inventory of what he had learned thus far.

Klaus Braun had the appearance of a very robust man in his early fifties, though Seven knew this wasn't so. According to the FBI file, Braun's exact age was unknown, but it was estimated that he was at least sixty-five. Braun's thinning black hair was combed back and his steel grey eyes seemed to have a malevolent look to them, despite the fairly ordinary reading glasses resting on the bridge of his nose. Impeccably attired, it was obvious he loved to dress to impress, with unabashed vanity spewing from every inch.

There was one feature however, that was in direct contrast with Dr. Braun's flawless appearance; his unusual skin tone. The skin on his hands, and from what the G5 agent could see of the doctor's arms, was quite yellow in color. Seven tried hard not to let on how strange the bright yellow skin looked. It was bizarre and startling. *Was this man sick with some disease?* Seven wondered. *Or was the jaundiced look from years of experimenting with venom?*

On closer inspection, the Super Stud determined that the doctor's face and nose had a definite European look. Yet when Dr. Braun spoke, Seven's ear sensed a slight accent that he couldn't quite pinpoint. Perhaps it was Cuban or South American. Klaus Braun was a man who was tough to figure in every way, as if he had parts made up from several cultures, countries, time periods, and perhaps even from several other species. It might be ironic, but to Seven, this snake guru had definite *reptilian* characteristics.

One thing was eminently clear, however. Dr. Klaus Braun appeared to be a confident and formidable figure, a tough looking character indeed. After taking a long puff on his cigar and blowing out a thick cloud of smoke, the doctor leaned back in his chair and menacingly stared at Seven. "And just what exactly do you have in mind, Mr. Seven? What's all this about, this supposed story of yours? What's your *real* angle?"

Upon hearing Dr. Braun's frank and direct question, and the cold, calculated way in which it was asked, the shocked Super Stud instantly began to worry that he and his journalist camouflage might have already been compromised. Had someone along the line betrayed him? Perhaps a mole in the FBI or even someone from his own agency? Beads of sweat began forming on Seven's forehead, as the suddenly worried agent wondered if his cover had somehow been blown. It seemed inconceivable, but judging by Klaus Braun's present demeanor and his evident suspicion, maybe the jig was up before Seven's assignment had even begun!

Klaus Braun's tone of voice, as well as his troubling inference, threw Christopher Seven into near panic. He wondered if Braun's query was more than just a simple question, perhaps even an accusation. Yet, with nerves of steel, which most secret agents seem to possess, Seven merely looked around calmly and remained silent; as if he hadn't a care in the world. Inwardly, however, the Super Stud wondered if this was yet another Braun evaluation gambit, like shaking hands near the snake.

Before Seven could respond, the doctor explained himself. "I didn't mean to imply anything derogatory, Mr. Seven, and I certainly don't want you to take offense. Perhaps my words were a bit callous." The snake man grinned sheepishly. "Diplomacy is not one of my strong suits. What I merely meant was, do you think your magazine, and you personally, will likewise benefit from the article on me? I've learned over the years that everyone has a private agenda in this capitalistic world. I was simply wondering about yours."

The G5 agent relaxed immediately. Klaus Braun, though somewhat direct and crude, was apparently still onboard with the magazine piece, and continued to view Seven as simply a harmless journalist. The relieved Super Stud smiled politely and replied, "I think I understand what you meant, Doctor. I've found that personal agenda philosophy of yours to be true enough. And there's nothing really wrong with it in most cases. As to your question, however, yes, the magazine will certainly benefit. Both financially and in esteem. Hopefully, so will I."

Seven leaned forward for emphasis "You see, Dr. Braun, extremely private people like yourself are not easy to access for featured articles. Circulation and publicity always goes up when we do a piece on anyone who is viewed as somewhat secretive or aloof. Particularly when the subject himself agrees to cooperate. The harder they are to nab, the better. And though *Global* has a duty to report accurately, fairly, and entertainingly, the magazine is, after all, still a business venture. As such, it does what it can to increase readership and revenue."

"Well said," Braun acknowledged, staring directly at his young visitor. "But what about you, Mr. Seven? What do you yourself gain, other than a standard salary?"

Having rehearsed this part of his cover, Seven's reply was ready and confident. "From what I've learned in my preliminary research, Doctor, you've brought healing and hope to people all over the world. Yet most articles written about you have merely focused on your wealth, your rather hazy persona, and, at times, your provocative personality. As interesting as those things are, no one has really pointed out the healing benefits your pharmaceuticals have made. My editor tells me that folks suffering from many diseases, ranging from arthritis to cancer, have sworn that your formulas have cured or helped them."

Klaus Braun took another puff of his cigar, listening intently as his handsome visitor continued.

"And that's primarily what I want to write about, Dr. Braun. Though the salary for this project is quite decent, part of my personal agenda, as you've called it, is getting that seldom cited message across. For me, it's additional motivation." Seven nodded politely. "So that's my *angle*, sir. As per the actual storyline, I'm certainly aware there's been controversy and mystery surrounding you over the years. I may even mention some of it in my article. But in general, I'd like to dwell on the *positive*. The man behind the cures. You're a very interesting and fascinating character, Dr. Braun, one whom the public will enjoy learning more about."

Braun's head bowed slightly, posturing in false modesty. This was music to the doctor's ears. He was therefore pleased when Seven continued talking shop.

"As you know, Doctor Braun, there's been quite a few hatchet pieces on you and your domain. Frankly, I think they've been unfair, especially those aimed at you personally. Then again, I guess that comes with the territory of being one of the country's wealthiest individuals. In any event, and as I see it, it's time America sees another side. My article could also be helpful down the road when the Senate committee votes on several lucrative pharmaceutical grants in two months. Seeing this type of story *before* they vote could eventually help sway some senators, and indirectly aid a lot of sick people."

Seven thus ended his speech, again hoping that he hadn't overplayed his hand. He also hoped the mouse sitting across from him would swallow the cheese. Dr. Braun's immediate response was a big egotistical grin, one which told the Super Stud all he wanted to know. This particular mouse literally jumped at the bait.

Klaus Braun leaped to his feet somewhat startling his pet snake. "Well, Mr. Seven, if you and your fine publication think so. Frankly, if I do say so myself, I agree that my story and my successes *should* be featured." Holding up his right hand in counterfeit modesty he bragged, "For the good of science of course, not mine. And as long as nothing about my early past or my secret formulas is included, I'm always happy to help the press."

"Fine, Doctor. And I know it will make a great story, sir."

Seven was now completely at ease, thankful that his fears about a potential leak were unfounded. It had obviously just been an innocent, though alarming, choice of words by Braun, followed by Seven perhaps overreacting to them. Maybe it was the large snake that was lying within striking distance that had made the G5 operative overly nervous.

Christopher Seven leaned back in his chair, at this point cocky and confident.

But then, just as the G5 operative was beginning to relax, it appeared that Klaus Braun's antenna was up once more. As Seven glanced over at his host, the doctor's friendly demeanor abruptly changed again. Braun's body seemed to stiffen, and the previously smiling face took on a harsh expression. Glowering at the pseudo reporter with menacing eyes, it was almost as if the enigmatic doctor was trying to probe Seven's mind. And for a few discomforting moments Seven felt an uncanny sensation that this bizarre snake man could!

Braun's steel-gray eyes stared directly at the young journalist, as if he was looking through him, rather than at him. It seemed that this man was trying to read his visitor's thoughts. *Is Braun reconsidering?* Seven wondered. *Or worse, had he been tipped off by something I've said or done?* After what seemed like an eternity the doctor finally began to loosen up. Calmly taking a finishing puff on his cigar he appeared to be satisfied. He slowly exhaled the smoke, smiled thinly and spoke. "I have just now decided. You have my provisional cooperation and approval for your magazine project. You may proceed, so long as you stay within certain parameters that I will now delineate."

Seven was somewhat amused by the tone of Braun's response. It was as if the billionaire was speaking to an underling about some trivial business matter. The doctor looked at him and explained. "You see, Mr. Seven, we have certain rules here at the Reptile Center. Strict regulations that I must insist you adhere to if we go forward with this. First of all, many areas at the Center are strictly off limits, for your protection as well as ours. Second, nighttime researchers cannot be disturbed at all. And thirdly, there's to be no questioning of my daytime scientists or workers without my express permission. As you've undoubtedly surmised, my secret formulas are very valuable."

"Sounds reasonable, Doctor."

Klaus Braun forced another thin smile. "Please understand, Mr. Seven, that security and safety are our number-one priorities here at the Center. Obviously, we can't have you wandering about with hundreds of the world's deadliest reptiles in residence. Why just yesterday, we had a little mishap with one of my most experienced maintenance workers. Poor chap was in an unfortunate mix-up and I'm afraid he was bitten. While that's an extremely rare occurrence here, it does happen. We were all truly saddened. However, accidents crop up in every industry, including ours. We must therefore learn from our mistakes and go forward."

Seven gave Braun a solemn look. "I'm sorry to hear that. I hope your man is alright?"

Dr. Braun ignored the journalist's concern without elaboration and continued, "Of course, there's also corporate security. Many unscrupulous businessmen would love to steal details concerning my secret pharmaceutical experiments and formulas. So naturally, any mention of these formulas or experimental theories is completely forbidden. Accordingly, your contacts with my workers must therefore be limited. All interview requests must first go through me, or my secretary, Sandra Kent, should I be away." Dr. Braun again held up his hand. "Not that I mistrust you, Mr. Seven. It's just that an innocent answer from a scientist who wants to be cooperative, or some naive slip of the tongue by you, could inadvertently lead to a security breach. I'm sure you can appreciate that."

"Absolutely, sir. I'd never want to accidentally upset your fine work here." Seven's reply felt somewhat lame as he gave it.

The doctor seemed okay with it however. He simply completed his set of rules, in a friendlier, though still authoritative tone. "Additionally, while I'll try to be available whenever I can spare you some time, my secretaries and office staff are *never* to be approached without my express consent. For any further background needed for your story, feel free to contact our public relations department. They can provide a corporate press kit, which I think will be of great help to you."

Seven nodded as Dr. Braun finished up, "I expect you'll want to interview others who know and work with me here. To a degree, I'll allow that. I can certainly have some of these people available from time to time. Those of my choosing, of course, but nevertheless those who know the score." Klaus Braun then looked up and again smiled widely. "But if you can live within those boundaries, Mr. Seven, I'm very confident that we can give you and your readers a first-rate article."

Seven wasn't sure what to say. He knew he had no choice but to go along with this restrictive nonsense, hoping that Sandra Kent would be one of the key people whom Braun would pick. He also knew that if he wanted to stick around for a while he couldn't be a nuisance or a security threat. Yet, this eccentric snake man was very crafty and obviously quite perceptive. If Seven, as a supposedly aggressive reporter, agreed too quickly to all of these restraining regulations it might arouse reverse suspicion. With a slight frown, the Super Stud replied to Braun's edict.

"Well, Dr. Braun, I'm not so sure about a few of those rules. Some of them are quite restrictive. Yet, most of what you've said shouldn't be a problem. As long as I can speak with some key people. Naturally, I'm not thrilled about being told who I can and can't interview. I've never worked that way before, and most of the time we journalists won't agree to that." Seven pretended to be seriously contemplating something for a moment. "But of course, this is a very unusual situation, with your formulas and all. Like the time I did that piece on NASA. They had similar confining guidelines." Seven looked up to the ceiling as if fighting a tough battle within. After appearing to be wrangling with himself, he slowly nodded. "But yes, I think I can work around it. Though I dare say, you certainly have some very rigid parameters."

The G5 agent hoped his frankness, and his not being overjoyed with the strict conditions laid down by Dr. Braun, had at least showed a realistic side. As well as a small amount of a journalist's self-dignity. Seven also hoped the mentioning of his wish to interview Dr. Braun's key associates would pave the way for his meeting up with Sandra Kent. He ended his protests on a friendlier note. "As for roaming around your Center alone, believe me, Doctor. I'm the *last* person to go wandering around this place." He gave a nod toward the boa on the desk. "In case you haven't noticed, though I'm sure you have, snakes scare the bejeebers out of me."

Klaus Braun said nothing. He seemed relieved that this influential magazine's finished product would be a media piece that he himself could control. Do so nearly every step of the way. This shallow Mr. Christopher Seven, for all his smart clothing and pretty-boy looks, would be easy to work around and manipulate. *The arrangement is going to be perfect*, Braun thought greedily, not knowing he'd arrived at the exact conclusion the G5 agent had wanted of him.

To Braun, the journalist's agreement had turned him into a simple pawn; one that could easily be molded and persuaded by a superior mind. Perhaps this shallow writer might even be swayed to take a little *economic inducement* in exchange for other helpful messages that Dr. Braun wanted relayed in a family publication.

Looking at the correspondent, and beaming as he spoke, Klaus Braun could hardly contain his obvious delight. "Then it's all settled, my boy. It will be a grand story, of that I can assure you. And who knows? If it's beneficial to my work and to my Center, it might lead to even more valuable opportunities for you." Braun winked. "If you know what I mean."

With a sly grin the doctor paused intentionally to let his words sink in. Seven likewise grinned to himself, well aware of the obvious hint at a bribe. It was not only an unmistakable suggestion of enticement, but to the Super Stud it also confirmed that the mouse had indeed taken *all* the cheese. Dr. Braun spoke again, now more friendly than ever. "We should celebrate this with a drink. Unfortunately, I have a pressing business matter tonight. But why don't you come to my home tomorrow evening? I'll also invite a few of my key personnel for dinner. You can meet them socially and we can discuss your assignment a bit more informally then."

"Thank you for the invitation, sir. I'd be delighted."

"By the way, we always dress for dinner, Mr. Seven. Your present attire would be perfect. Dinner is served promptly at 7PM. If you can be there by six, I'd be happy to show you around."

"Wonderful. I've read a lot about your beautiful home in *Architectural Digest*, Doctor. It sounds fascinating."

Now all Seven wanted to do was to simply get out of there before he made any blunders. He stood up to leave and shook Braun's hand. Then, just as he reached the door, Klaus Braun called out to him, "Miss Dykstra is waiting to escort you out. She'll have printed directions to my home. See you tomorrow at six."

"I'm looking forward to it."

With that Klaus Braun gave him a mischievous grin. "One last thing, Mr. Seven. No need for alarm, but many of the world's most deadly snakes also live at my home. Some folks find it a bit disconcerting. Just thought I'd mention it. Have a nice evening."

Several hours after Seven's initial meeting with Dr. Braun, lights still burned at the sprawling Reptile Center, both in the main office and in the two cavernous research buildings. The Center's morning and afternoon activities, along with its zoo and snake exhibitions, had ended hours earlier. All of the daytime employees were long gone, having exited promptly at 6:00 p.m. Though it was nearly midnight now, and though the facility had long since closed to the public, the reptile hub had almost magically been transformed into a beehive of clandestine activity. It was now occupied by the doctor's secretive nighttime force, and, as always, when the nightshift clan took over, security tripled.

In accordance with Braun's strict routine, sixty or so of his covert satanic army, an assemblage of his most trusted employees, had replaced the daytime workers. Dr. Braun aptly and affectionately called these nighttime employees his *nightshift inner circle*. This tight-knit group consisted of scientists, lab technicians, herpetologists, security staff, general and menial workers, four secretaries, and the doctor's two top assassins, Amir and Rahmad. These hand-picked employees, all experts in their respective professions, had been meticulously recruited with two very important qualities in common; unswerving loyalty to Klaus Braun, and fanatical devotion to Lucifer and the Yozem satanic cause.

Dr. Braun was certainly not naïve enough to believe that cult devotion alone would guarantee unwavering obedience and longevity. His nightshift employees had therefore been given extremely generous salaries, far more than they could ever expect from any other employer in their particular fields. Additional benefits included the unique perk of Braun's devil-worshipping *celebration nights*; lascivious debauchery during midnight orgies of lovemaking, ritualistic animal slayings, and even the occasional sadistic spectacle of the torture and slow death of doomed *human* prisoners during satanic 'punishments sessions'. Braun's devil-worshipping nightshift assemblage had steadily grown into a strong and secure group of loyal cultist workers. They shared a special bond of unity, a bond that was literally soaked in blood!

Of course, there was hard work to be done here as well, efforts to ensure that Lucifer would soon rule the Earth. To help bring this mantra about, their esteemed leader, Dr. Klaus Braun, needed to have the manpower and wherewithal necessary to punish an unsuspecting and unbelieving world. For Klaus Braun was the selected instrument of Satan himself, the *'chosen one'*. Or as the Black Mass proclaims, *the exalted facilitator.*

Consequently, Braun needed a continual flow of loyal nighttime employees. This to enable his various satanic campaigns. As such, getting additional Satanist workers was always on his mind. Yet, despite this crucial need of talented pharmacological professionals, becoming a full-fledged member of the doctor's shadowy nightshift clan was extremely difficult. All prospects, who showed intense interest in the occult, had to first be nominated by at least *two* current Braun workers. And, after that was verified, closely observed in a stringently controlled setting. As per the in-house sponsorship, woe to any guarantors who foolishly nominated or even recommended an unworthy candidate. Dr. Braun had made it very clear that to submit a new worker for membership into the sacred nighttime clan was also to pledge one's own life as security of this candidate's worth.

And though this 'endorsement pledge' came with the risk of torture and execution for promoting an undeserving applicant, the prize for bringing in a capable new *believer* who made the nightshift team was equally great. Rewards consisted of huge monetary bonuses and other fabulous perks, such as cars, homes, and even women. Talented satanic workers were hard to find, and Klaus Braun handsomely rewarded those who brought them to him.

In the rare event a new candidate was pressed into *immediate* emergency service, Dr. Braun was forced to rely solely on the solemn word and life-pledge of that candidate's two sponsors. If the results were good, there was lavish remuneration to the sponsors. If *negative,* however, swift and horrific punishment to the candidate and his two promoters was quickly administered. And this was what was to take place tonight, due to the recent debacle of the maintenance man turned FBI spy, Kenneth Fusco.

For that reason, this night at the Reptile Center was going to be different than most. Tonight there would be a violent reckoning for the blatant indiscretion of Ken Fusco's two unfortunate sponsors. A satanic *punishment session* had been hastily scheduled, the ancient, euphemistic term for the terrible public retribution that Lucifer demanded when someone failed him.

Normally, these vindictive punishment sessions were carefully orchestrated and announced well in advance. With everyone in the nighttime *inner circle* required to witness the torment and death of a disloyal victim. But on this occasion, Dr. Braun's punishment gathering had been hurriedly called, due to the necessity of Braun wanting to slay this particular offender as soon as possible. Tonight's satanic retribution event would therefore be witnessed by a much smaller audience.

Only twelve of the nightshift's most important members, eleven men and one woman, stood at attention in the doctor's office, waiting in sadistic anticipation to witness the execution. Along with the 10 others who were an integral part of the ceremony.

Sitting behind his desk, Klaus Braun, chosen '*enabler*' of Satan, spoke to none of them. He stared straight ahead, acknowledging no one, until the room's tense silence was finally broken by the chiming tones of a large Swiss-made wall clock. The twelfth chime was still echoing when all of the overhead lights dimmed and a single orange spotlight was somehow magically illuminated. It lit up the entire area in a ghostly amber glow.

As the illumination slowly grew brighter, a piercing, wolf-like howl reverberated from outside, and eerie flute music began sounding through a large pair of speakers in Braun's office. Six scantily dressed dancing figures, with revolting black and white skeletons tattooed over their nearly nude bodies, danced out onto the floor; three men and three women. They were howling madly, digging their long pointed fingernails into their exposed bodies, and then eagerly licking the blood from their fingers which had emanated from the scratching. After five minutes of this bizarre ballet, the human skeletons promptly exited the room, still howling loudly toward the sky. This decadent dance was called the *Gessem,* Satan's musical prelude to death.

Next, a sliding door off to the side slowly opened. All eyes watched as a hideously masked and robed figure entered, carrying a ceremonial ax in his left hand. This robed figure, a practicing Yozem disciple, was called '*the Carver*', or more accurately, the *Mesop*. He was accompanied by three beefy security guards who were dragging in another man. One who'd obviously been worked over. The moaning prisoner soon became the center of attention. His swollen face showed traces of blood and bruising, and both his socks and shoes had been removed. With his pant legs rolled up well over his knees, the barefoot man was made to stand in front of Dr. Braun's desk. The captive's terrified eyes now glanced from side to side around the room, as if looking for someone who might come to his aid. No one did. Other than the man's frightened breathing, the entire office was eerily silent. Klaus Braun let the prisoner squirm for a few minutes and then spoke.

"The condemned man, who stands before us tonight, is the worthless Cuban, Santos Alverez. This former nightshift security man has disgraced us all. So has his still missing partner, also a long-term security guard, Frank Stevens. These men have brought shame and a major breach in security to our cause. And potentially to our sacred Operation D as well. More importantly, Alverez and his missing accomplice have disgraced the hallowed name of Lucifer."

Dr. Braun glared at the prisoner with disgust, and then went on, "It has been determined by me, with concurrence from the Yozem council, that these two nighttime workers are guilty of endorsing an unreliable candidate for inclusion into our sacred nightshift brotherhood. To compound their crime, they did so simply for money. They took a common bribe, an unforgivable and reprehensible offense!"

The others in the room sneered at the trembling captive as Braun continued. "The person they sponsored, a maintenance specialist named Kenneth Fusco, turned out to be an industrial spy. Fusco himself has been punished via a Taipan snake, though he still awaits his final fate of death. Hopefully, Lucifer will deem that this Ken Fusco *never* awakens. But if not, our hospital operatives will make sure he doesn't. The traitorous Fusco has thus been punished, but the pathetic worm who stands before us now, as well as his AWOL partner, Frank Stevens, have not." Braun frowned. "Stevens, for the time being, has eluded his inevitable fate. Yet I can assure you. He, like all who defy me, will soon be found. And when he is, Mr. Frank Stevens will *likewise* face his consequence. For now, the man who stands before us shall be dealt with tonight. This is appropriate, for it was he who initially recommended Fusco."

"No", screamed Santos Alverez. "It was Stevens. I had nothing to do with it!"

His plea was quickly silenced by one of Braun's three security men, who violently pummeled the prisoner in the face with a pair of brass knuckles.

Klaus Braun's beady snake-like stare zeroed in on the now bleeding prisoner and angrily addressed him. "Lies, Alverez! Ken Fusco, the maintenance man turned spy, whom you and your accomplice Stevens both heartily recommended, was found in a restricted area looking through my father's personal files. We suspect that *Arnett Pharmaceuticals* might have hired Fusco for this clumsy attempt to steal some of our formulas." Braun shook his head. "We're lucky this Ken Fusco was simply an industrial mole. He could have been working for the police."

The doctor groaned disgustedly and then finished his diatribe.

"Satan will not stand for failure, or for the hindering of his sacred work. And neither will I!" Braun pointed towards an unusually dressed man to his right. "As always in these maters, our high priest has conferred with the forces of darkness below. So I ask you, Cleric Yezid. Do you agree with the verdict?"

The cleric smiled cruelly through the mouth slit of his skeletal mask. He quickly concurred. "Yes, Doctor. A slow and painful death is indeed called for. Let Lucifer's retribution commence!"

The eyes of the accused man grew wide in abject terror. He began screaming uncontrollably as the three guards dragged him over to the far corner of the room where a white-jacketed lab technician was standing. The technician, wearing boots and heavy rubber gloves, was holding a large basket. He motioned for the assembled audience to move away from his immediate area and then dumped the basket's contents onto the floor. Then, he likewise moved back as six very plump snakes fell to the ground. The reptiles remained perfectly still even as they hit the floor. Then, ever so slowly, they gradually began to intertwine with one another.

Dr. Braun nodded toward the snakes and began speaking to his assembled audience as if he was giving a lecture. He was now oblivious to the weeping prisoner. "Lady and Gentlemen. The large snakes on the floor are puff adders, more specifically *Bitis arietans*, from Africa. The most interesting aspect about them is their unique venom. Oh, it's quite toxic, but what makes it stand out from all the other venoms is the truly *excruciating* pain it causes. No one knows why this particular toxin is so agonizing, but the bite from a puff adder has been described as one of nature's most unbearable sources of pain. Some people have gone mad from the pain alone, trying to actually cut off the affected area or limb from their bodies."

Braun shook his head in obvious admiration and expounded further, "The agony of this snake's bite has been compared to a constant 800-degree branding iron held on one's skin. Or a white-hot piece of coal continuously lying on one's body. An interesting description, but I would think the pain is more akin to being skinned alive. Having your skin cruelly torn off your flesh. For after a puff adder bite has been inflicted, venom circulating through the body soon begins eating and digesting the victim's flesh from the inside out. It causes tissue to deteriorate and rot. Quite unbearable, I would think. As I've said, just like being skinned alive."

Klaus Braun then nodded to the four security men who were holding their barefoot prisoner. The husky guards, wearing thigh-high, thick leather leggings, lifted the accused off the ground and held the wailing man directly over the pile of snakes. Alverez attempted to pull free from the grip of his captors, but to no avail. At this point, the wide-eyed onlookers collectively held their breath. Only the lone woman among them, receptionist Elsa Dykstra, was sadistically smiling, erotically aroused by the impending torture. The rest of the assembled group nervously waited for the inevitable. It came quickly.

The screaming man was slowly lowered onto the snakes, his bare legs and feet forced in and amongst the suddenly agitated serpents. In their fury the adders bit him at least nine or ten times, striking angrily at his bare toes and exposed legs! Several more bites drew blood as the snakes sunk their huge fangs into the man's uncovered ankles.

Dr. Braun waited a moment while the horrific events continued. Satisfied that ample punishment had been administered, he coldly nodded again. The security men lifted the sobbing prisoner up and carried him to another corner of the room. Blood was now copiously oozing from the numerous bite sites.

While Santos Alverez moaned uncontrollably, half in pain, and half in shock, they threw him roughly to the floor in a heap of blood and tears. The three guards then dispassionately watched over him, though it was an unnecessary precaution. For the unfortunate Alverez was going nowhere. He was a helpless lump, now screaming loudly, while his body uncontrollably jerked and twitched. The excruciating pain Braun had described was rapidly beginning to take hold.

Klaus Braun watched him for a moment and then calmly directed a few final commands to the guards, having to speak loudly over the now deafening screams of agony from the victim. "Take him to the holding room and keep an eye on him. The pain will get much worse every ten minutes or so. He'll be in constant torment until the Dark One's will is done. I predict three, four hours, tops, before all that venom finally kills him. When the moment comes, I want his body thrown into the crocodile pit. That way no further cleanup will be required." Braun looked over at one of the security guards. "I assume no one will miss him?"

"No, sir," answered the heaviest of the guards, trying to speak over the earsplitting wails of the dying man. "He's here from Cuba. No family, few friends. We'll put the word out that Immigration caught up with him and that he was quickly deported." Dr. Braun nodded as the guards picked up the half-dead Alvarez and carried him out.

For a moment, there was nothing but stunned silence in the room. The malicious snake man then looked over at his shocked audience, taking care to make eye contact with each and every one of them. "Well, Madame and gentlemen. Two down and one to go." Braun stood up from his chair and smiled. "Now then, any questions?"

T he following morning, Christopher Seven awoke in his hotel mini-suite to yet another day of bright Florida sunshine. He wolfed down a light room service breakfast of fruit and Wheaties cereal, along with his favored *fresh squeezed* orange juice. He then prepared himself for the day ahead, using all the Super Stud hygiene requirements.

Two hours later, Seven again played three sets of grueling tennis with the hotel's pro, worked out vigorously in the resort's cavernous gym, and followed it all with another hot, soapy shower back in his room.

After resting awhile in his luxurious mini-suite, he visited the resort's huge pool and swam several laps. While relaxing poolside in a lounge chair, the Super Stud was eyed by several leggy beauties, politely returning their gorgeous smiles. He never noticed the two nondescript men in hats and sunglasses who were mingling with the other camera-toting tourists by the hotel's famous flower gardens. Amir and Rahmad, however, were paying very close attention to him.

Once back in his room, Seven emailed headquarters from his laptop and requested more information on Klaus Braun's attractive secretary, Sandra Kent, plus anything they might have on the doctor's private estate, *Mi Casa.* The return message, via his secured and coded email, advised him to expect the information shortly.

Maintaining his journalist cover, the G5 agent next sent a second email to Jonathan Dale, feature editor at *Global Magazine.* The message simply stated that Seven had arrived in Florida, met with Dr. Klaus Braun, and would be seeing the doctor again later that evening at Braun's home. It also noted that, in Seven's opinion, the Klaus Braun article should be of great interest to *Global* readers.

Still parched from tennis in the hot sun, he strolled over to the room's mini-fridge, quenched his thirst with a Perrier, and returned to the laptop computer. As promised, there was a new email from G5 headquarters, this one with more info on Sandra Kent.

<u>Memo To</u>: Christopher Seven
<u>From</u>: New York Headquarters
<u>Subject</u>: Kent, Sandra E.
[Info shared from current FBI compilation:]
<u>Personal</u>: Kent, Sandra: Age 28; single
<u>Education</u>: Stanford University: Bachelor's degree in Marketing
Dean's list: four years

Associations: Member of MENSA

Pertinent Info: As a college senior, Ms. Kent interned for the Governor of California on his public relations staff, where she served with distinction. She quickly advanced and became the Governor's number one 'go to' person for PR and damage control assignments. Upon graduation from Stanford, Miss Kent left California for Washington, DC with highest recommendation of the governor. Was promptly hired onto the White House public relations staff. Served skillfully in their PR department for two years, working almost exclusively with the President's press secretary, and often with the chief executive himself. Two years later Miss Kent took a top position with *Braun Industries and Pharmaceuticals.*

Tie-in: Dr. Klaus Braun, who had supported the former President financially, was a frequent visitor to the White House. He knew of Miss Kent from attending White House social functions and from her occasionally sitting in on several tough negotiating sessions between Braun and the President's staff. Soon after, Dr. Braun personally and tenaciously recruited her for his own company. After several such attempts Sandra Kent finally signed on with Braun. This was facilitated, in part, by the fact that Kent's mother was a recipient of Dr. Braun's controversial cancer drug, *Cobraison* (a formula made with minute amounts of venom from the African Spitting Cobra). The girl's mother, Mrs. Susanne Kent, had been diagnosed with terminal lung cancer, with a prognosis of four to six months to live at best. Following the Cobraison treatment, Mrs. Kent lived three years longer than expected. Sandra Kent thus became, and still is, a staunch, almost fanatical supporter of Dr. Klaus Braun, with steadfast loyalty and allegiance to him; and most especially to his pharmaceutical research endeavors.

Current Employment: Miss Sandra Kent has been employed by Braun Industries for almost five years, as both Klaus Braun's executive secretary and his trusted confidential assistant. Though she may well be an excellent, untapped source to unlocking many of Dr. Braun's corporate secrets, no person or investigative organization has ever been able to garner *any* inside or meaningful information from her whatsoever. Her resolute loyalty and appreciation of Braun, due in large part to Braun's help to her late mother, remains unwavering. (See FBI attempts, Freeman report.)

Additional Personal: Miss Kent lives alone in a large condo complex in Ft. Lauderdale, Florida. She is described as 'stunning' in appearance; brunette, excellent figure, unmarried. Has never been involved in any serious long-term relationships.

Nonsmoker, drug free, occasional social drinker; no known vices. Sandra Kent has never been arrested; no major traffic citations.

Hobbies: Avid jogger, crossword puzzles.

Note: Miami Dade PD records show a report of an attempted robbery, and/or assault on her in a Miami parking garage, a little over a year ago, by three men. It's not certain if she was molested in any way, but report states she was 'severely shaken' by the incident.
Should any further information be added to her file, you will be immediately notified.
NG—From G5, via FBI database

While reflecting on both the information and its bearing on his assignment, Christopher Seven began to realize that this Kent woman might be a bit more complicated and difficult than he'd first surmised. Particularly with the attempted assault on her by the three thugs. Due to the girl's possible emotional state, the ideal plan would have been to proceed slowly and cautiously, but Seven wasn't sure there was the luxury of time. With this Ripper serial killer striking on the first of every month, time might already be starting to run out for him should the FBI or any other agencies want to take over. Sandra Kent's personal indebtedness to Dr. Braun, via her mother, might also complicate matters.

Seven rubbed his forehead and thought on it for a moment. A traumatic experience like that parking garage incident could change Sandra's, or any woman's mind about men. Might the incident have led her to swear off men for good, or to completely distrust or rule out any new relationships? Again the Super Stud mulled it over. Perhaps there were other reasons. As for her still being single at twenty-eight? Maybe she had a thing against men even *before* the incident occurred. According to the memo, she's never had a male love interest. *Hmmm.*

Seven cautioned himself about reading too much into the report, knowing these types of dossiers were usually quite superficial. Anyway, he was probably going way too fast, perhaps psychologically trying to give himself a readymade excuse for failure. A confrontation, similar to the one Sandra Kent experienced with those thugs, could shake up anybody. Certainly she wasn't to blame, and it would have been a truly frightening experience for any young lady. Still, people can get over anything. He himself had eventually gotten over the tragic experience of his parents' death. Seven shrugged his shoulders, knowing he'd just have to meet this girl and do what he was trained to do. If things didn't work out he wasn't going to blame anything or anybody but himself.

Thinking more positively, he searched the memo for any helpful hints, making a mental note of Sandra's love of jogging. That could conceivably be an entrée for a social encounter down the road. He stood up a second or two, stretched his legs, and then sat back at the computer. Glancing at his incoming emails, which were not as copious as usual, he noticed that while he'd been reading and analyzing the Kent memo, a new email had arrived from Global Magazine:

*FYI and eyes only.- A Ms. Sandra Kent from Braun Industries
called twice to confirm how often you've worked for us in the past,
and if we were fully backing your assignment on Klaus Braun. I
assured her that you've indeed worked with us several times in the
last four years, are an excellent reporter, and that we eagerly await
your feature story on Dr. Braun. - Dale*

The Super Stud grinned and exclaimed aloud, "So, that clever mouse, Braun, is checking up on the cat, huh? Figures!"

Seven reread the messages and notes, and then, laying down on his comfortable bed, perused a few back issues of *Architectural Digest* he'd packed. Articles that featured exposés on Klaus Braun's magnificent home, *Mi Casa*. The G5 agent was fascinated to note that Braun's mansion had a secured backyard snake habitat, protected by a deep moat and several powerful electrocution beams so that no wandering snakes could ever escape alive. Here, in this enclosed *snake garden*, deadly reptiles could roam freely, ostensibly to be observed by Dr. Braun and his fellow herpetologists. That must have been what Braun had meant by deadly snakes living with him. Seven shook his head. He couldn't picture a worse place to reside. Yawning, he decided to take a brief nap, setting his travel alarm clock for four o'clock.

The agent awoke to its familiar ring, refreshed and raring to go. After a short, but strenuous series of calisthenics, he followed these with a shower and the familiar Super Stud hygiene routines. As Seven contemplated his wardrobe, an elegant, lightweight Armani beige suit, his cell phone rang. Nancy Gallo, Colonel McPhail's secretary, spoke in her usual sensual tone. "Hi, Chris. How's sunny Florida?"

"Just fine, blue eyes. Wish *you* were here."

Immune to his flirting manner, Nancy merely grinned. "Okay, lover boy, listen up. Mr. Carson has arranged for you to meet with a man named Benjamin Greenfield. Mr. Greenfield lives in Vero Beach, about an hour and a half ride from Boca. He's one of the foremost authorities on the Nazi regime and on Nazis who escaped the allies. Greenfield used to be a professor at Lynn University and he frequently lectures on the subject. It says here that he used to work for Simon Wiesenthal. I wasn't sure who that was. Do you know?"

"Yes. Simon Wiesenthal was the famous Israeli Nazi hunter. A brilliant man who tracked down several top war criminals." A smug Seven conveniently neglected to tell her that he had just read about Wiesenthal's exploits the night before on the Internet.

"Oh, wow. Look at you, Mr. Jeopardy," Nancy responded with a laugh. "Anyway, I'm trying to set up an appointment for you to meet with him tomorrow. When I have all the details, I'll shoot you an email or phone you back. Mr. Carson says that if anyone would know about Martin Bormann,

Greenfield would."

"I appreciate it, Nance, but I still think this Martin Bormann slant, or meeting with Greenfield, is a waste of time. Bormann croaked years ago"

"Sorry, Chris. Both the Colonel and Mr. Carson insist on it."

"Yes ma'am," Seven replied with mock formality, still wondering how a long-dead Nazi could be relevant now. "And you can tell the big bosses I'll email them the details of my dinner at Braun's."

"Okay, Chris, but listen. Please be careful down there. I don't know why, but I've got a funny feeling about your present assignment."

Seven grinned as he answered. "You know, Nance, the two things that keep resurfacing on this case are deadly snakes and female intuition warnings. Do you suppose there's a connection?"

"If anybody would know, it would be you, Romeo. And just remember. We women don't always rattle before we strike. Maybe that girl you're after won't either. So like I've said, be careful."

"Don't worry, I'll take care. Have to if I want to take you to *La Goulue* for your birthday next month."

"It's a date," Nancy replied, surprised and thrilled that he'd remembered her birthday. "And that sound you hear is me chiseling it in stone. Seriously though, promise me you'll take this whole snake thing more seriously than you usually do." As she clicked off, her uneasiness suddenly got to him.

A few minutes after Nancy's call, the cell phone rang again. It was FBI agent Jack Hanover. "Hi Chris, Jack."

"Hey, big guy, what's up?"

"Just got a call from the hospital. Ken Fusco, our informant, is dead. Apparently he never regained consciousness."

"That's too bad, Jack. He would have had plenty to tell us."

"It would seem so, Chris. Especially about Braun's night crew. Wish we could somehow check out that nightshift and see what's *really* happening there. But without a messy court order or search warrant, that's impossible . . . Unless -"

Both men simultaneously thought the same thing. This *closer* covert look might have to fall on Seven. Jack Hanover didn't come right out and say it but Christopher Seven did. "Just what I'm thinking, Jack." And, with that, the two agents simply let it go.

"By the way," informed Seven, "I'm due at Braun's home at six. Any suggestions?"

"Not really. Except don't step on any Taipans."

They both laughed. Seven promised to keep the FBI abreast of his findings, while Jack let the grateful Super Stud know that the FBI would still be taking an arm's length approach to Klaus Braun. At least for the time being.

Although this was certainly welcome news, the G5 operative knew the FBI would probably only do so for as long as Seven was reciprocating with important inside details. In essence, Seven had now taken the place of the dead informant, Fusco.

Christopher Seven grinned, resignedly, said goodbye to Jack, and made his way toward the elevator.

*M*i Casa, Dr. Braun's beautiful estate home, sat inland, halfway between West Palm Beach and Palm Beach itself. A dwelling this magnificent should have been situated on or near the ocean, but Klaus Braun longed for space and privacy above all else. He therefore chose twenty isolated acres in a plush and fertile location atop a short hillside.

As Seven pulled up to the front doors of the incredible mansion, after first going through a rather strict security check at the entrance gate, he was struck by the sheer majesty of the place. *Mi Casa* looked like an elegant castle fortress, perhaps a junior Buckingham Palace or a scaled down Versailles. The agent surmised there were probably twenty or more bedrooms inside. From what he could see of the compound's magnificent grounds and gardens, they too were quite impressive.

After leaving his car with the uniformed driveway attendant, he walked up to the massive mahogany doors and rang the bell. A distinctive, tubular clang sounded and a pretty young maid dressed in Victorian black lace instantly appeared. Seven nodded and introduced himself.

The maid gave him a lovely smile of welcome. "Yes, Mr. Seven. Dr. Braun is expecting you. Please follow me."

Following her through the passageway, the Super Stud found himself in the foyer of the most beautiful private home he'd ever seen. The place seemed like a fantasy setting, with its high ceilings, massive crystal chandeliers, finely polished wood surfaces, and beautiful antiques throughout. Several medieval flags of the roundtable were draped from the rafters and there were lavish fixtures everywhere one looked. Two gleaming knights in silver armor topped it all off, their perfectly polished bodies standing tall on either side of the doorway. The entire scene was straight out of Camelot, and for the first time in a long while the G5 operative was speechless. The maid's voice snapped him back to reality. "The doctor is waiting for you in the great room. This way, please."

They walked through a wide corridor that smelled of polished wood with a slight scent of lemon oil, and continued on through another large door, the entrance to Mi Casa's great room. This area, an immense circular expanse, was even more spectacular than the front foyer. The massive room was great alright, with a high cathedral ceiling that seemed to reach to the stars. And there, sitting all alone in a large chair, as if a tiny speck in a large auditorium was his host, Dr. Klaus Braun.

The doctor was dressed in a smart looking smoking jacket, black pants, white shirt and a striped tie. He appeared to be simply relaxing in a high-back, red-velvet Victorian chair, one of two situated in front of an enormous stone fireplace. Dr. Braun rose immediately, extended his hand,

and spoke. "Ah, there you are, my boy. Welcome to my humble abode. Good of you to come. What do you think of my little bungalow?"

"Spectacular, Doctor! As impressive as anything I've seen."

"Glad you approve. This home, if I do say so myself, is considered one of the finest examples of European architecture in all of North America. Come, sit down and join me. Let's have a drink, shall we? What'll it be? Brandy? Or perhaps some wine?"

"A glass of white wine would be fine."

Dr. Braun smiled and turned to yet another servant, a tall, dignified man who had somehow magically appeared. "Garrett, please bring a glass of our finest white Bordeaux for our young friend here. And I'd like a glass of champagne. Make it the Tattinger. I feel like celebrating tonight."

"Very good, sir," Garrett confirmed, rotating smartly as he walked away.

Turning back to his guest, Klaus Braun bragged, "No good having a lot of money if you don't appreciate the joys it will buy. You see, Mr. Seven, I've worked hard over the years, sacrificing most of my time for science. I've gone through a lot in order to produce several pharmaceutical breakthroughs; breakthroughs that have greatly benefited mankind. True, I've made a tidy profit in doing so, but that's the way it is in this society. Those who provide much, make much."

"Nothing wrong with that," Seven purposely agreed. "There's a definite need and market for your services. Why shouldn't you capitalize on it and make what you deserve? I fully believe in that credo as well."

Braun looked at the reporter with a curious expression. *Was there a message here? Has this magazine journalist picked up on my hint of a 'personal incentive'? Perhaps so. But I'll have to tread lightly for a while. Wait till I have this naïve young reporter in the palm of my hand, like so many of the other fools I've used over the years.*

Dr. Braun nodded and replied, "It's a good credo, Mr. Seven. Supplying something that's needed usually has its rewards."

Now it was Braun's inference that couldn't have been plainer, and Seven grinned inwardly. A few moments later, Garrett returned with the drinks. The wine was excellent and the Super Stud made sure to say so.

"Glad you're enjoying it. Please, have another glass if you like. But we shouldn't really drink too much before dinner. Excessive drinking dulls the palate and we wouldn't want that. Cook has prepared a fine meal for us." Dr. Braun took him by the arm. "Come. Allow me to give you a tour."

What followed was an impressive thirty-minute excursion. Many of the breathtaking highlights of Braun's castle home were shown and explained in egotistical detail. First was the library, where volume after volume of leather bound books lined the walls of the multi-level library and study. Wheeled ladders leaned against the expanse, bridging gaps of knowledge between the highest tomes and the literary adventurer.

Stunningly furnished bedrooms on the second and third floors afforded luxuries intended to impress. Such as full marble baths with bidets and whirlpools, and private balconies overlooking the picturesque grounds. The pleasant aroma of food being prepared tickled the stomach and lured the two men down the breathtaking stairway. They walked through a spacious and busy kitchen, and then strolled on through to the great dining hall, which held the longest dining room table Seven had ever seen.

Yet it was on the way to Dr. Braun's private office, near the end of the tour, that the most noteworthy part of their walk took place. Seven and his host came to a medium sized alcove, which Braun identified as his 'Sword Room'. Here, one of the finest private collections of swords and cutlasses anywhere in the United States was exhibited, with antique weapons displayed in elegant trophy cases. Several of them were mounted on the walls. As a top-notch fencer in college, Seven's knowledge of these ancient swords was substantial, and allowed him to fully appreciate Braun's incredible collection.

Back in their university days, Seven and his brother Tim toyed with their own small collection of cutlasses, reading and studying everything they could on the subject of antique swords. Eventually, they gave up on the hobby, when the time and expense needed to collect the old-fashioned armaments proved too prohibitive. Even so, he and his sibling had always retained their love of swords, as well as the sport of fencing, having been state champions on their college and prep school teams. Over the years Seven had seen many exceptional private sword collections, but the quality and multitude of Dr. Braun's was on an altogether different level. The doctor's assemblage was world class and of rare museum quality. Certainly valued in the millions. The spectacular cutlasses caused the G5 operative to reflect with a bit of envy upon his own meager personal assortment at home.

Christopher Seven eyed each sword in Braun's remarkable collection with true admiration. Yet one particular cutlass caught his eye almost immediately. It wasn't the most expensive rapier by a long shot, but it was certainly one of the most beautiful. The sword was a large ornate silver blade, circa 1812, which had been briefly owned by the famous buccaneer, Jean Lafitte. As with the others, there was a letter of authenticity at its side. Seven was very familiar with it, as he and his brother had tried to buy one just like it several years back. That is, until they learned the asking price was in excess of ninety thousand dollars, well beyond the budget of two college lads. Knowing that only a few of these swords even existed, Seven couldn't help but be impressed. Klaus Braun perceptively noticed this and quickly spoke. "I see you're particularly enthralled with the Lafitte."

The Super Stud beamed at it as he answered, "Yes, it's a beauty. At one time, my brother and I were novice sword collectors, and we once had a shot at a similar Lafitte cutlass. But it proved to be way too costly at the time. Too bad we passed on it. I've heard they've appreciated quite a bit."

Braun looked his young guest over for a moment, his intricate brain seeming to spin rapidly. He then spoke, slowly and deliberately. "Mr. Seven, I'll be frank with you. I would admit that a favorable article by someone such as you, dwelling on the specific message I'd wish to convey, would be most welcome to me at this time. In fact, it would be very beneficial when my request for additional government funding comes up for consideration. *Before* the senate committee meets next month. Your story in a trusted family publication, if worded properly, and exactly as I'd instruct, could be extremely beneficial to my efforts. And to me as well. What's more, since my work is so meaningful to many ailing people around the world, it would be safe to say that you'd also be doing a valuable service for mankind." Dr. Braun looked at the journalist with a somber, businesslike expression. "Mr. Seven, I'm a man who speaks plainly. I need your help."

Braun paused, took a sip from the last of his champagne, and continued. "If I can be assured of your, ah, cooperation, all things are possible. Perhaps even your owning that pirate sword, which I can assure you is now valued at well over a hundredthousand dollars."

The doctor glanced over at the Lafitte cutlass and went on, "All I ask is that you think it over and let me know your feelings on the matter by next week. If favorable, some type of arrangement can easily be arranged. A quid pro quo, so to speak. Of course, if you don't feel comfortable with the idea, we can simply forget that it was ever mentioned. I would then trust it would go no further than this room."

Christopher Seven was absolutely dumbfounded! He had expected something akin to bribery to possibly come from Klaus Braun or his people. But not this quickly, not this directly, and certainly not on this scale. Yet, how should he play it? If he jumped at it immediately, Braun might smell a rat. Yet, if he flat out refused, he might lose a golden opportunity to get closer to Klaus Braun himself. There was only one way to handle it. String the snake man along, and bait the hook a little more.

With a softer voice than normal, the pseudo reporter cautiously responded. "Dr. Braun, what you've just proposed creates an ethical dilemma for me. My relationship with the magazine is certainly very important to me, and could be permanently compromised by, shall we say, an economic *inducement?* One must also consider the possibility of this thing leaking out. That would not only harm my professional reputation, but there's the chance that you also could be implicated negatively as well. These are all serious considerations." Seven wiped a bit of sweat from his brow in fake astonishment. "Yet, I must admit that it's a very tempting offer. One that I'm not about to simply dismiss out of hand. As a former sword collector, I realize it's one in a million!"

Pretending to be wrestling with his conscience, the G5 agent whispered, "Of course, and as you've rightly pointed out, helping you get that government grant might indirectly benefit a lot of sick people." Rubbing his chin, as if still pondering his position, Seven added, "Perhaps something might be worked out between us." The Super Stud held up his hand. "I'm not promising anything yet, of course. You'll have to allow me time to think on it. However, I solemnly vow to give it my full consideration. And, if for some reason I decide against it, you most definitely have my word that *none* of this will ever be mentioned. Is that satisfactory to you?"

To a pragmatic but forceful man like Dr. Klaus Braun, Seven's response was more than satisfactory. The doctor was accustomed to buying things and buying people just as easily. The mere fact that this journalist had not flatly rejected him out of hand was, in his mind, tantamount to a definite agreement. This reporter chap would most assuredly come around and take the bribe. Braun was certain of it. The envy and longing was plain to see in the younger man's eyes, and Braun could hardly conceal his self-satisfaction as he smiled his reply.

"Fine, my boy. Take some time on it. But just to assure you of my sincerity, I'll now write up a tentative promissory note giving you full ownership of the Lafitte sword." Braun grinned craftily. "It'll simply be a little enticement, knowing the receipt's already written. Just waiting for your okay. We won't date it of course, and I'll keep it safely locked up until such time you come to a favorable decision."

Braun quickly corrected himself, not trying to sound too self-confident. "What I mean is *should* you decide to accept my offer, the sword will be yours."

Seven smirked to himself at Braun's final piece of crafty gamesmanship. This pre-written receipt, or whatever it was, would be meant simply to whet Seven's appetite. The tempting and elusive carrot on the stick. Just out of reach, only to be grabbed *after* he'd gone along with his host's wishes. Seven's thoughts were cut short by Dr. Braun's deep voice. "Come into my private office. We can draw up the papers in there."

The two men walked through another vestibule and then down a small ornamental staircase, stopping in front of a heavily built mahogany door. Seven noticed a tiny video monitoring camera above it. The door was locked tightly and marked with a large brass sign: *Dr. Klaus A. Braun - Private Office: Absolutely No Admittance. - Mortal Danger.*

As Klaus Braun quickly unlocked the office door, using two of the keys from a large ring he took from his pocket, Christopher Seven nervously wondered what the '*mortal danger* 'would be once they got inside!

Chapter 20

King of Death

As expected, Klaus Braun's sizeable home office was decorated to lavish perfection, just like *Mi Casa's* other luxurious areas. There was fine imported wood paneling on the walls, expensive *Caledonia* marble on the floor, and an exquisite antique rolltop desk in front of a beautiful stone fireplace.

Yet, no matter how stunning the room's furnishings were, they were quickly eclipsed by an even more unusual piece that drew Seven's instant attention. In the center of Dr. Braun's spacious office was a large glass cage, about ten feet in diameter. Its thick glass walls were at least four feet high. Atop the enclosure, a removable sliding glass lid, now tightly closed, provided an opening for the ornate enclosure. Both the sides and heavy glass top of the cage were perforated with numerous air holes, and the structure was supported off the ground by four curved mahogany legs, making it look much like a dining room table. Seven's first thought was that it was some sort of beautiful antique pen, big enough to house several small pets. Perhaps an opulent home for rabbits or hamsters. That was until he saw a huge King Cobra curled up in the corner of the enclosure!

The forked tongue of the deadliest creature on earth probed the air as if sensing the sudden presence of the two men. Seven was thunderstruck, never expecting the world's largest venomous snake to be living inside someone's exquisite home. Although the reptile was housed safely within this glass habitat, the Super Stud still stood well away from it. Klaus Braun, however, did not.

Casually approaching the reptile's cage, the doctor began to animatedly speak, as if he was giving a business speech. "The remarkable serpent in front of us, living in this beautiful handmade enclosure from Burma, is the celebrated King Cobra. This creature is the *hamadryad*, or properly speaking, *Ophiophagus Hannah*. It is both feared and revered in many circles and even considered a *god* to some worshippers in India. The King is the largest venomous snake in the world and generally regarded as the most dangerous living thing on the planet. It can reach lengths of almost eighteen feet, although the one before us is just shy of fourteen. Drop for drop, the King Cobra's venom may not be nature's most potent, although it's certainly lethal enough to do the job. The astonishing thing about this serpent, and indeed the source of its well-deserved reputation of being nature's most deadly creature, is the enormous *amount* of venom it can inject with just one bite. A truly massive dose."

Braun smiled, glanced from the King Cobra to Seven, and continued his self-imposed lecture. "While one drop, to a drop and a half, of any cobra venom is usually capable of killing a man, some cobra bites aren't always fatal. A bitten victim could get lucky and only be injected with say, a half-drop, or in rare cases, no venom at all. But not so with this big fellow! No sir. The King Cobra is *never* stingy and always envenomates. Just one of his strikes can contain as much as *thirty* drops, theoretically enough to kill *twenty* men. In fact, one bite from this creature can kill *any* living thing. Even a huge bull elephant if bitten on its trunk." Dr. Braun beamed, proudly. "No second chances when this beast gets you. Even I must be very wary of him, Mr. Seven. I'm not at all sure that the precautions I've taken over the years, nor the protection of the lifesaving blood that now flows through my veins, would prevent my own death should I ever be bitten by this species."

Klaus Braun stared at the huge creature with veneration for a while, as if in a momentary trance. He quickly came out of it and then inquired, "Now, where were we? Oh yes. I was about to write that receipt for the Lafitte sword." Taking an ivory colored sheet of paper from the desk's top drawer, and a beautiful fountain pen from a gold holder, Braun sat down at his desk. He looked up at Seven, muttered something, and began to write. "Let's see, this should do . . . The following legal form is a receipt of *'payment in full'* from Mr. Christopher Seven to me, Dr. Klaus Braun, of . . . shall we say, one hundred and twenty thousand dollars? That figure is about right."

Braun continued writing as he pronounced, "This sum, paid to me by Mr. Seven, is full and final payment for the Jean Lafitte pirate cutlass, item number 103. With this legal document in hand, Mr. Christopher Seven is now the new and rightful owner of said Lafitte pirate sword, circa early 1800. - Signed, *former* owner, Klaus Braun.

" The doctor nodded. "That should take care of it legally, don't you agree, Mr. Seven?"

Seven sighed, and again tried to state that he was still not sure he'd actually be able to comply.

"Yes, yes," answered Klaus Braun, becoming a bit irritated. "We've been all through that. Let's just say this receipt exists if you *do* agree. I'll merely keep it in a safe place in the event you come around."

Glaring menacingly at the young journalist, Braun then warned, "But don't go getting any foolish ideas about this receipt. Neither you, nor anyone else, will *ever* get at it should we *not* reach an agreement. Of that I can assure you. For the spot where I'm now about to place this Laffite document is safer and more secure than Fort Knox! Also, please remember, Mr. Seven. You'll *never* get this receipt, or the sword, if you don't, as they say, 'play ball.'" Braun barked out a short laugh, and got up from his desk.

Seven laughed as well, though only inwardly to himself. For the wily Dr. Braun had just swallowed his own bait, hooked by his own greed. Now the two men would become co-conspirators, linked together in a bond of unsavory action. This bribery deal, if played right, not only indicated a leap of trust on the part of Klaus Braun. It might also allow the G5 agent to penetrate deeper into the doctor's secretive world. Even so, the Super Stud still didn't want to appear over eager to take the offer.

Braun folded the receipt and returned to the snake enclosure. Then, turning his full attention to the huge serpent inside the glass table, Klaus Braun's face showed a strange look of both contempt and admiration. Was it also a look of fear?

Christopher Seven couldn't tell for sure. He watched closely as his host continued to glare at the reptile. The snake man's voice then began rising in volume and intensity. "The King Cobra is indeed a shrewd and dangerous adversary, Mr. Seven. It's no wonder they call him the 'King of Death' in herpetology circles."

Seven looked over at Dr. Braun, fascinated, as the snake guru bellowed, "Many of my fellow reptile authorities have good-naturedly warned me that this particular serpent will be the one living creature that finally brings me down. They continually remind me about an old Malaysian legend concerning the King Cobra. How this species can actually exact revenge on its enemies even without its fatal bite. That a King Cobra can somehow take on human qualities, including calculated vindictiveness." Braun seemed to stare blankly for a long moment before finally asking, "Who knows if the legend is true? But if it is, I, Dr. Klaus Braun, the man who has mastered the entire reptilian world, will *always* prove to be the stronger! Neither this serpent nor anything else can defeat me!"

The tone and volume of Braun's words momentarily startled Christopher Seven. The doctor's face turned red, and his expression showed a trace of madness. Sensing he'd gone too far, Klaus Braun quickly composed himself, wiped the sweat from his brow with an embroidered silk handkerchief, and forced a smile.

Slowly calming down, he pushed a small button on the right side of his desk. "I want to show you something, Seven. I've just rung for one of my top snake handlers who will be here in exactly six minutes. At least that's the way we've planned it in our many emergency drills." Dr. Braun pointed toward the cobra enclosure. "I'm about to open this snake cage so you can be properly introduced to my friend, the King. When, and if I've captured him, I'll put the cobra into his new holding box." Braun pointed toward the fireplace. "That large wooden crate on the floor over there."

At first, Seven laughed, thinking his host was merely pulling his leg to frighten him. "No need for you to go to all that trouble, Dr. Braun. I can see the snake fine from here."

Klaus Braun completely ignored him, and as the doctor slowly approached the glass snake enclosure, it soon became quite apparent that he was deadly serious. Seven gulped and tried to summon his courage, speculating that perhaps this was some sort of manhood test. Or worse, if Dr. Braun was planning another 'accident'. For a brief and terrifying moment, Christopher Seven wondered if Braun had found him out!

Continuing to disregard his visitor, Braun's attention was now fully focused on the top of the glass cage. "Don't worry, Mr. Seven. You'll have plenty of time to escape should I be struck. If so, just calmly walk out of my office and shut the door tightly behind you. I'll be fine and coherent for at least three or four minutes, no matter how much venom this reptile injects into me. And by that time, my associate, Dr. Wilcox, should be here. We've practiced this procedure many times. It's like a well-rehearsed fire drill. Do you have any problems with it?"

Again, Seven had the definite impression that his courage and worth were now being tested. "It seems pretty straightforward, Doctor. If you're bitten, I should get the heck out of here and tightly shut the door behind me. I've got it."

Braun nodded.

The Super Stud, still close to the exit door, watched intensely as Dr. Braun inserted a small metal key into the lock of the cage's sliding glass lid. *What on earth is this all about? Some sort of show trial, with Klaus Braun trying to size up my bravery?* Whatever it was, Seven was determined to pass. He took a deep breath and waited.

Braun slowly slid the glass top off of the pen, his eyes glued on the serpent. At first, nothing occurred. Then, in a startling instant, the massive body of the great reptile, similar to a thick rubber hose, reared straight up in the air with astonishing speed!

Gosh, thought Seven. *The thing is huge! I hope it doesn't hop out of that enclosure toward me.*

The beast's fearsome head was now well above the wall of the cage. Hissing loudly, it had risen up menacingly, eyeball-to-eyeball with Klaus Braun! As it did so, the doctor's total absorption was apparent. Braun noticed nothing around him, save for the hissing reptile. He was truly immersed in the moment. It was just Braun and the snake now, staring each other down, face-to-face. Christopher Seven wondered who would blink first.

Slowly and deliberately, Dr. Braun moved his left hand in a circular motion, directly in front of the reptile's face. The huge serpent seemed mesmerized by it, as if the hand and not the man was the enemy. This dance of death took several seconds, the cobra intent on watching the moving hand, its deadly fangs only inches away. But while the snake's attention was riveted on the slowly rotating left hand, the creature seemed unaware that Braun's right hand was inching up behind its slender neck.

Then, in a flash, it all ended! In one fell swoop, Braun's right hand deftly grabbed the snake from behind just below its head. It was a flawless slight of hand trick, one that had worked perfectly. A grinning Klaus Braun safely held the world's deadliest creature in his right hand. "It's quite alright now," he calmly assured, as the snake squirmed harmlessly within his secure grasp. "I've got him. In fact, you can come closer if you'd like. Not many people can come near a King Cobra and live to tell about it."

Though naturally hesitant, Christopher Seven did so, still awestruck. After Braun put the snake safely away in its wooden holding crate, Seven exclaimed, "Dr. Braun, that was truly amazing!"

"Thanks, my boy. You see, the trick is all in the *left* hand. You must keep the reptile's eyes focused on *that* hand while you capture him with the other. It's actually simple. A child could do it. I could teach you or anyone else this technique in a few minutes. Anybody can make the capture if they stayed calm and duplicated what I just did."

Seven shook his head. "You're just being modest, Doctor."

"No," Braun protested, "it's true. Just remember. The secret is in the fact that the circling left hand distracts the snake, while the right hand actually makes the capture." Seven nodded, as Braun added, "In any case, I'm sure you were wondering what this was all about; why I went to all the trouble of taking the King Cobra out of its home."

With a slight smirk on his face, Klaus Braun reached down into the King Cobra's now empty glass enclosure. He brushed away some of the sand covering the floor of the reptile's habitat, revealing several small drawers secured with a combination lock. Braun appeared to fiddle with a bright red button on the left side and then quickly unlocked and opened one of the drawers. Next, he took the Lafitte sword receipt and casually placed the folded document into it. After locking the draw again, the snake guru reversed the opening process. Though he had just revealed a unique secret lockbox to a virtual stranger, Klaus Braun wasn't at all concerned.

"You see, Mr. Seven, this is as good a home safe or bank deposit box as one could ever have. And it doesn't matter who knows about it, you or anybody else. If anyone unauthorized ever tried to get into these drawers they'd have the small problem of getting past my King Cobra friend who lives on top of the files. There are a few other unpleasant surprises we've planned as well. And of course my office area is monitored by video cameras back in the security hut twenty-four-seven." Braun then made a show of innocently explaining why he needed this type of security. "You'd be surprised at the lengths some of our competitors have gone to in order to steal my pharmaceutical formulas. And I might add they've failed in most every attempt."

Klaus Braun put the keys back into his pocket, and proudly exclaimed, "I also get great pleasure in knowing that a snake stands guard over my private files. You see, Mr. Seven, I would trust this snake, or any other reptile for that matter, with my life. And with my most valuable secrets too. Certainly much more than I would entrust any human. Ever since I was a lad, I've often said that if I had a really big secret to hide from the world, a world by the way that I genuinely distrust, I'd leave it with these incredible and beautiful creatures. To me, snakes are the most dependable comrades of all!"

This bizarre dissertation was suddenly interrupted by a loud knock on the door. Dr. Kevin Wilcox, Klaus Braun's top snake handler, was responding to the call buzzer.

Seven hardly noticed Braun's colleague enter. In fact, he hadn't noticed much of anything. His secret agent's mind was now focused on only two things. First, his mounting suspicion that the famous Dr. Klaus Braun was obviously a bit psychotic and paranoid; perhaps dangerously so. The details of everything Seven just witnessed and heard had revealed that. Along with this troubling fact, came the second and much more important part of the Super Stud's thoughts. Seven now wondered what other vital secrets might be stored inside the unique reptilian lockbox, the one Braun had just willingly shown him. Was the demonstration simply a display of pompous braggadocio? Or was this bizarre 'home safe' actually where Dr. Braun hid some of his top secrets?

Either way, Christopher Seven would just have to get into Klaus Braun's unique lockbox. King Cobra and all!

Chapter 21

Supper with the Rest of the Snakes

"**A**h, there you are, Wilcox," boomed Klaus Braun. "And right on time." Braun glanced at his wristwatch. "Six minutes on the button. I guess when it comes to our little King Cobra fire drills, practice makes perfect!"

Christopher Seven looked over at the worker who had just entered the room, a short, balding man wearing a white smock, and what seemed to be a permanent frown. The associate's nametag read: *Kevin Wilcox – Head Herpetologist*. After Braun introduced him to Seven, the doctor's eyes widened with inspiration. "Say, I've got an idea, Wilcox! Let's bring this snake out to the patio after dinner. I haven't extracted venom from a King in quite a while. Perhaps my dinner guests would enjoy a private showing after supper." Braun grinned widely. "As long as I still have my wits about me, this King Cobra and I should continue to have our little battles. That is, until one of us retires the other. Permanently!"

Seven tried to force a smile, but all of this absurd madness about serpents and death was starting to get to him. *What a nut house*, he thought, as Dr. Braun took him by the arm. "Come along now, Seven. My other guests will soon be arriving for cocktails. Let's go meet them."

Despite the mild climate outside, a showy gas-log fire burned brightly in the great room's massive fireplace, adding an air of formality and beauty to the setting. Only three dinner guests had arrived thus far. Two of them were already socializing, laughing happily with drinks in hand. The other, seated alone, showed absolutely no sign of life. He was a very frail old man, serenely watching the glow of the fireplace flames. Klaus Braun looked at the three men and clapped his hands for attention. "Gentlemen, allow me to introduce our new friend, Mr. Christopher Seven."

Seven was first introduced to the two men standing; an overweight spectacled scientist named Peter Von Brunner, and Dr. Braun's head of nighttime security; a muscular Haitian named Alvin Rosier. This second character was particularly sinister looking and seemed quite unfriendly. After those introductions, Dr. Braun turned his attention to the old man sitting in the chair.

"And this, Seven, is my father, Mr. Floda Braun. The name Floda is really an Austrian nickname. Sort of the equivalent of *Freddy*, or as close as they can get to it. Father is originally from Vienna." Klaus Braun smiled at his elderly father with noticeable admiration.

Seven nodded courteously to the oldster while the doctor continued, "Believe it or not, my father is in much better shape than it might appear. And while he doesn't like to talk about his actual age, you'd be shocked if I told you. He's quite remarkable, and still has all his faculties. Father's health, longevity and well-being are due in part to the effects of some of my pharmaceuticals." Dr. Braun beamed with pride at his last statement. "Some experts have scoffed at my claims over the years, Mr. Seven. But as many folks will attest, including my own father, the results of my scientific work have improved and extended the lives of seniors who would otherwise be in an invalid state. Or perhaps even dead by that age. So please tell your readers *that!*"

Dr. Braun bent down and spoke directly into the old man's ear. "Father, this is Christopher Seven. He's here to do a magazine article on me and the Center." The elder Braun didn't reply, merely staring up at the journalist as if with x-ray eyes. Seven found the man's glare a bit disconcerting.

"Well," Klaus continued, "Now that we've met, what do we have to do to get a drink around here?" He called for one of the servants. "Brimley. Be a good man and bring me a sherry. And bring Mr. Seven whatever he desires."

Soon, more guests began arriving, loudly filing into the great room. As Christopher Seven was politely introduced to them, he was careful to remember their names and faces, using the Luca Memory System, which had been drilled into him during Super Stud training.

Although most of the guests were men, there was one woman in the group. To Seven's disappointment, it wasn't Sandra Kent, whom he had hoped had been invited. Instead, and to his utter consternation, it was the horrid Miss Dykstra; Miss Elsa Dykstra to be exact, the unfriendly and unattractive red-haired secretary whom he'd met at the Reptile Center. Yet, on this particular evening, Elsa appeared to be quite different from that initial meeting. She was barely contained in a red, clinging v-neck tank, covered by a sheer red chemise blouse. All this, over an outdated black leather mini-skirt. Elsa Dykstra was unquestionably dressed to kill, and annoyingly shadowed Christopher Seven around with a torrent of constant chatter. Wearing tons of makeup and far too much perfume, her intentions were obvious; she was out to *conquer.*

This nauseating Dykstra woman was gracelessly pushy toward Seven, never leaving him alone for even a minute, and dominating the entire cocktail hour with her flirtations. *Thank goodness Elsa Dykstra is not my Super Stud target,* the frustrated G5 agent mused. *The snake factor is bad enough, but this woman? I'd rather be spending time with the King Cobra!*

To his immense relief, a loud dinner gong rang out from behind him. *Saved by the bell,* Seven quietly sighed.

"Dinner is served," Miles Hoffman, Braun's head butler, proudly announced. Everyone then headed toward the huge dining hall.

As two more white-gloved servants slid open the massive dining room doors, the G5 agent could hardly believe his eyes. The most lavishly set dining table he'd ever witnessed had been arranged beautifully for the feast. The stunning thirty-foot long table had been laid out with gold leafed Rosenthal china, expensive Baccarat crystal, and a magnificent pink floral arrangement at its center. In front of each dining chair, small gold nametags sat in front of the chairs.

Seven quickly found his place card, and was annoyed to learn that he'd been seated right next to Elsa Dykstra. However, with a glance at the empty chair directly in front of him, his displeasure faded immediately. The nametag opposite him read: *Miss Sandra Kent.* But where was she? Had she begged out of the evening? His questions were immediately answered when he saw Hoffman, the butler, escorting one of the most beautiful women the Super Stud had ever seen over to the empty chair. It was indeed Sandra Kent, the target of his top secret mission, and none of the file pictures had come close to capturing her real beauty. For a brief moment, the G5 operative was speechless. This young woman was truly stunning.

Sandra Kent was a gorgeous brunette with piercing brown eyes. Her shapely figure and five-foot-eight-inch frame held everything in perfect proportion. She had a beautiful face, a cute nose, and an attractive, sensual mouth. The girl reminded Seven of a famous movie star currently starring in a box office hit, yet the air of beauty about her was tempered with a girl-next-door quality. The lovely, tight-fitting pale yellow dress she wore showed off her voluptuous curves to a tee. In short, Sandra Kent was a genuine knockout, with looks of which male fantasies were made.

"Sorry I'm late, Dr. Braun," Sandra apologized. "I had to finish giving our report to that congressman from Tallahassee back at the office. He insisted we have a drink before I left, and I didn't want to appear rude. Hope I haven't caused any inconvenience."

"My dear Miss Kent," a gushing Klaus Braun gently replied from his position at the head of the table. "As you know, I always demand punctuality. But how could I possibly be angry with someone as dutiful and beautiful as you? Please be seated." Braun snapped his fingers. "Miles. Get Miss Kent a glass of wine, please."

Dr. Braun then nodded toward Seven. "Forgive me, my dear Sandra. You haven't met tonight's guest of honor. Miss Kent, this is Mr. Christopher Seven. He's the reporter we've been expecting. The journalist who's going to tell the whole world what a benevolent genius I am." The entire group of guests, including Seven, laughed. Klaus Braun, clearly enjoying himself, and basking in the dazzling glow of his gorgeous associate, then finished the introductions. "And Mr. Seven. This is Sandra Kent, the one I truly couldn't do without. Aside from my snakes of course."

Sandra held out her hand to shake and smiled warmly. "Sandy's fine, Mr. Seven. That's what my friends call me. I keep telling Klaus that Sandra is a bit too formal. Anyway, I'm very glad to meet you." They then shook hands.

"Nice meeting you too, Sandy. And, likewise, please call me Chris. Mr. Seven was my father." He smiled back while holding her soft warm hand in his, actually getting a tingle out of her touch. His momentary pleasure was interrupted by Braun's booming voice.

"Ladies and gentlemen," Dr. Braun began announcing pompously. "Chef has prepared another masterpiece for us tonight. One I'm sure you'll enjoy. After the tasty starters, and a special cream-of-tomato soup, he'll be serving prime rib of beef, the very *finest* Midwest prime. It will come with sides of creamed spinach, oven roasted potatoes, and his excellent Yorkshire pudding."

The guests oohed and ahhed, a bit like trained seals, as their proud host continued, "For dessert, we have Chef's specialty. His vanilla bean crème brûlé, served with a dab of handmade mocha ice cream, all finished with Belgian chocolates and fine coffees. And for those of you who prefer a vegetarian meal, like my father and me, the Chef has also prepared a fabulous cheese soufflé, with a spinach casserole. Lastly, the wines served tonight will be a choice of select French reds and whites, some of the finest from my cellars."

The table erupted into light applause. Seven awkwardly joined in with the others, wondering if this type of ritual went on every night at *Mi Casa*. Directly after Dr. Braun's menu announcement, there was so much loud chatter that Seven was barely able to hear himself think. Unfortunately it was likewise impossible to truly engage Sandy Kent in conversation, although he did offer polite comments across the table to her from time to time. This was made even more difficult by the unwanted attention he was still getting from the bothersome, almost smothering, Elsa Dykstra. She was boring him silly with some blather about the affect of the weather on certain reptiles.

Each time Seven glanced over at Sandy, he noticed that she too seemed politely bored with the incessant chatter of the nerdy chemist sitting to her right.

The meal that followed was indeed delicious. Dr. Braun hadn't misled about the cooking. It was truly first class. The fabulous wines that accompanied each course were likewise some of the world's best, including a fine *Poligny Montrochet* and a spectacular *Chateau La Fleur-Petrus Pomerol*, the latter being served with the excellent medium rare prime rib. With dessert, Dr. Braun provided them with a memorable *Château Yquem*, one of France's best.

Near the end of the dinner, Seven excused himself and ducked into the beautiful marble bathroom located down the hall, taking advantage of the solitude to collect his thoughts and plan his strategy on how to engage Miss Kent. After using his travel toothbrush kit, he returned to the dining table just in time to hear Klaus Braun launching another announcement.

"Ladies and gentlemen. In exactly fifteen minutes, we'll all retire to the patio where you will be treated to a thrilling King Cobra venom extraction starring yours truly." There were a few gasps and then more applause. Some was genuine, but most of it was merely a nauseating example of *kissing up* to the boss.

Seven, who had already seen Dr. Braun battle this particular reptile, was far more interested in making some type of personal contact with Sandra Kent. As the Super Stud contemplated on how he'd do so, Klaus Braun tapped his empty wine glass with a spoon. Much like a ringmaster he announced, "There'll be a brief interlude while I prepare for the show. In the meantime, brandy and cigars will be served back in the great room." He then left the dining hall.

Once Braun had exited, his guests rose from the table and followed the servants into the great room. Here, various rare brandies were set up on an elegant rolling bar. The plump servant, who'd just rolled the bar in, then made a short announcement. "Those of you who smoke cigars, please do so by the bar here as a courtesy to the non-smokers. Those refraining may retire to the fireplace area, where air purifiers will keep away any fumes."

Most everyone seemed to stay near the bar, selecting a brandy and an expensive cigar, including the awful Elsa Dykstra. She looked masculine and unattractive as she puffed away with the rest of the boys. Elsa quickly became the center of attention, loving every moment of it, as she told one off-color joke after another. Her captive audience howled at the stories. It seemed that only Christopher Seven and the octogenarian, Mr. Floda Braun, who was now being pushed toward the fireplace in a wheel chair, didn't partake of a smoke.

Seven slowly strolled over to one of the two red chairs by the fireplace and sat down. As he did, a sensuous, soft voice, coming from a person whom he hadn't seen sitting in the other red chair, startled him. "Have a seat, Mr. Seven. I'm glad you're not a cigar smoker. I suppose that you, I, and Mr. Braun senior are the only ones who avoid that unhealthy habit." Sandra Kent smiled up at him, her beauty literally breathtaking. She appeared totally relaxed.

The G5 agent returned her smile and replied, "I deplore cigars and cigarettes of all types. Hate even being around them as a matter of fact. But some men do enjoy them after a fine meal. Apparently some women do as well, judging by Miss Dykstra. I guess we'll just have to respect their silly ritual. And by the way, I thought we had agreed that I would call you Sandy and you'd call me Chris?"

Her smile widened, showing her perfect teeth. "Okay, *Chris.*"

Seven, equally at ease, pulled his chair a bit closer. "That was some great meal, wasn't it, Sandy? The wines were spectacular."

"It's always that way at formal dinners here at *Mi Casa*," she responded. "Dr. Braun really puts on a royal spread, especially when he entertains his night staff. Usually I'm not invited to those meals, as I work primarily with the daytime folks. But the few times I *have* been invited to a nightshift function, I've noticed that the wines are particularly excellent and rare."

"Oh," Seven said, indifferently. "Are all of these folks from the nightshift?"

"Yes. All except Elsa and me. Then again, she actually works both shifts. As for myself, I really don't have much to do with the night people. That's an entirely different world."

The Super Stud made a mental note of this fact, to go along with the names and faces he'd later pass on to Jack Hanover. *All of these dinner guests are apparently from Braun's mysterious nightshift. That might be important to the FBI. From what Ms. Kent is now saying, she's not part of it, though she could be intentionally misleading me.*

"Do you live close by, Sandy?" Seven asked, although knowing from the FBI file her exact address in Ft. Lauderdale.

"Not far. I'm over at the *Gault Commons*, in Lauderdale. Some forty minutes or so from here. How about you? Where are you from, Chris?"

"New Jersey. Rutherford to be more specific. No one's ever heard of it, except for maybe the Meadowlands. You know, the football stadium and sports complex."

"I've heard of it," she said. "I used to fly into Newark quite often while working on the President's staff, before I relocated to the *Sunshine State.*"

Seven nodded. "Do you enjoy being a Florida resident, Sandy? I like the area a lot, but don't know if I could actually live here full time. For one thing, I like a change of seasons. And no offense, but I've heard the average age down here is deceased."

She laughed loudly. "It does take some getting used to. I'm originally a California girl. Love the beach. So for me, the weather here is truly terrific. Especially for an avid jogger like myself. And, of course, we have the ocean."

Christopher Seven quickly sensed an opening. "Oh, so you love jogging, too? I try to run most every day. Maybe if there's time, perhaps you and I could jog together while I'm here. You probably know some of the better places to run. Don't know much about where to jog here myself."

She looked over at him rather intensely. Was it a look of encouragement, or one of suspicion? The G5 agent couldn't tell.

"Yes, that might be fun," Sandy responded, with an air of polite non-commitment.

Ever the positive thinker, Seven took it as a sign that the glass was half full, rather than half empty. He then added, "I just hope I actually have some time for jogging. My responsibilities to the magazine article will be very time consuming. Incidentally, sooner or later, I guess I'll be asking you some questions about Dr. Braun and the pharmaceutical side of things."

It was the wrong tactic, and the Super Stud knew it almost instantly. He could have kicked himself for blurting out the comment. At the mere mention of having to answer some questions about her employer, Sandy Kent stiffened and quickly got her back up.

"I'm probably the *last* person you should question about that, Mr. Seven." Sandy's tone was cold and businesslike. "I simply don't know as much as everyone seems to think I do, and I don't usually like speaking about our work." She then stood up and the heel of her shoe could be heard scraping against the floor. It was evident she was nervous and quickly losing composure. "I think I'll go get a brandy," she informed, tersely.

As Sandy grabbed her purse, Seven politely said he'd be happy to walk over to the bar and get her the drink, but she flatly refused his offer. "That's all right," she said. "I don't mind. I have to speak to Dr. Phillips about a staff meeting they're having next week anyway." Braun's gorgeous assistant then turned sharply and walked away.

Knowing he'd misplayed it, Christopher Seven angrily gripped the arms of his chair.

Little did he know, however, that he might not have blown it quite as completely as he imagined. For as Sandy Kent strolled over to get a drink, she couldn't get her mind off of him. True, he had raised her interest by hinting at a social get-together. Only to ruin the moment with an attempt to selfishly use her for his magazine work. Nonetheless, as she dwelled on it a bit more calmly, Braun's lovely assistant admitted it was merely vanity getting the best of her. Here, at last, was someone her own age. And there was certainly no one else around Dr. Braun's empire of similar age and interests; no one at all with whom to really socialize. As Sandy approached the ornate brandy setup, she now wondered how she could still get this striking young journalist to go jogging with her. Or even just call her, without acting too forward.

Twenty minutes later, Klaus Braun's King Cobra extraction show was in full swing. Seeing Braun subdue the snake for a second time, Seven now agreed with him that anyone with nerves of steel could indeed capture a cobra by the back of the neck. Yet there was no denying that one small slipup would bring about rapid death.

Following the reptile demonstration, the party quickly began to wind down. Seven soon left without seeing Sandy Kent again, as she had apparently gone home earlier.

As the Super Stud drove back to his hotel, he pictured Sandy's beautiful face again and said aloud, "In spite of all the snakes, Elsa Dykstra included, I think I'm going to like this assignment."

Chapter 22

A Mysterious Tale from the Past

The following morning, a gloomy and windy Saturday, was totally uncharacteristic of the fine south Florida weather that Christopher Seven had been enjoying. It was gray and overcast outside, with a good chance of rain. After a hard workout in the hotel's weight room, followed by a fast shower, Seven hopped into the Mustang. He then made his way up I-95 North for the ninety minute trip to Vero Beach. This for his afternoon appointment with Ben Greenfield, the celebrated Nazi hunter. Two hours later the G5 agent was sitting in Greenfield's comfortable living room.

Benjamin Greenfield, now in his eighties, was a thin, diminutive man. He wore khaki trousers and an old blue shirt. Despite his years, he proved to be exceptionally productive and alert, with quick and keen faculties. The man was a walking encyclopedia on the Nazi regime and World War II, a subject of which Seven never grew tired. The Super Stud had always found the Second World War the most interesting of all wars, with the American Civil War a close second.

Mr. Greenfield proudly showed him the medals he'd received, tracking down many of the Nazi war criminals with Simon Wiesenthal, mostly back in the 1950s and 60s. The mention of this historic work brought a satisfied look to Christopher Seven's face. In his opinion, international criminals of all types, particularly the butchers of Hitler's SS and Gestapo, should *never* be allowed to go free, no matter how ancient their crimes. Seven felt that the so-called 'live-and-let-live' philosophy, now prevalent in Europe, was an insult to the holocaust's millions of dead victims. The G5 agent was a firm proponent of *'never forget'*. And he deplored those morons around the world who denied the atrocities, and even the very existence of the holocaust itself. Seven accordingly thanked Greenfield for his fine work.

"I thank you for humoring an old man with your kind words, Christopher. But what exactly did you come here to find out?"

"To tell you the truth, Mr. Greenfield, I'm not sure myself. I guess you could start by telling me all about Martin Bormann."

Greenfield sighed and his face showed frustration and suppressed anger. It was evident that the very mention of Martin Bormann had struck a nerve. The old man stared into space a moment and then began speaking in a slow, resigned manner. "Bormann, Bormann, and more Bormann. For years that's all I heard about. All I dreamed about, really. Oh how we wanted to get him! Martin Bormann was really the first of the big Nazis to escape us."

Ben Greenfield took a sip of his black coffee, looked up at the ceiling a moment, and then resumed. "Martin Bormann was born in Halberstadt, in 1900. He was an agriculturist by trade until 1924, when he joined the NSDAP, the Nazis, and eventually rose to head of the Deputy Fuhrer's office in 1933. From 1938 on, Bormann served on Hitler's personal staff, and in 1941 he was appointed head of the Nazi Party Chancellery. One of the top positions in all of Germany, and one with unlimited power. He was instrumental in just about everything, including mass murder, and was said to have Hitler's ear more than any other Nazi. With the possible exception of Albert Speer."

Pausing to take a second sip of his coffee, the elderly Greenfield shared more. "But those are merely surface facts. Now, let me tell you the *real* story. Martin Bormann spearheaded the top secret Strasser Experiments. Those were the horrible medical experiments performed on concentration camp inmates. This butchery was mainly performed in the Nazi's so-called *insane asylums*, which in reality, were experimental torture chambers. The victims were primarily Russian prisoners from the Eastern Front, although women and children from the other camps were used as well. The Nazis did all sorts of terrible things, such as trying to impregnate women with animal semen. They also experimented to see how long a person could survive exposure to freezing temperatures, and likewise tested to see how many days people could go without water. Near the end of the war those butchers tried even more bizarre medical experiments that they hoped would serve their self-proclaimed master race."

Ben Greenfield looked away a minute, obviously thinking about the unfortunate victims. His eyes began to tear and it took him a moment to compose himself. He then continued. "One of the main aspects of these experiments centered on trying to find the key to controlling the aging process; a so-called *fountain of youth*. Martin Bormann was especially obsessed with it. You see, Christopher, the Nazis had a theory that toxins, in just the right, sub lethal quantities, might actually slow down aging. Particularly poisons such as strychnine and cyanide. Obviously this would only be useful if the patient survived."

Seven nodded, listening intensely to Greenfield's every word.

"Dr. Frederick Huffman, a noted Austrian scientist, wrote about this theory in the years leading up to the war," Greenfield informed. "Of course Huffman's problem was getting volunteers to be injected with the different poison concoctions in order to try his hypothesis."

Mr. Greenfield placed his empty coffee cup in the saucer and then went on, "But the Nazis had no such problems with *volunteers*. Their prison camps were filled with an inexhaustible supply of human guinea pigs. Prisoners, who were indeed forcefully injected with various poisons. After a while, more scientists were recruited for the project and their hideous work was expanded. The Nazi doctors even tried injecting cancer cells and various overdoses of hormones to see what would happen. They frequently experimented with this method on twin children, under the direction of the notorious Dr. Joseph Mengele. One twin was injected, the other was not."

Benjamin Greenfield sighed sadly. "Horrible things they did to those kids, usually without anesthetics. The Nazis also tried to determine just how much continual pain the human body could endure. Some of these butchers theorized, that pain, combined with poison, might send a message to the brain to slow down the aging process. Like I said, Martin Bormann was fixated with finding a medical fountain of youth. Thousands of innocent men, women, and children lost their lives for the cause of this perverted science, much of which was encouraged by Bormann himself."

"Was he the main catalyst?" Seven asked.

"Yes. Other Nazis also kept at it, but Bormann was the unquestioned leader of this perverted anti-aging program. And he somehow convinced Hitler to give the Strasser Experiments top priority."

"Did they have any known successes, Mr. Greenfield? Or was it like always. That they murdered thousands for no reason?"

"Now you've hit on a gray area, Christopher. There were rumors claiming some of their work was vaguely successful. At least successful in their twisted way of thinking. I'm sure a few tainted inroads were made. When you can kill thousands of people freely, in order to find out a little something, you most likely will. At any rate, we heard there were volumes of notes the Nazis kept regarding their alleged age inhibiting successes. Unfortunately, none of those notebooks have ever been found. Someone either escaped with them or they were intentionally destroyed. Too bad. They would have been helpful evidence at the war criminal trials. The scuttlebutt at the time was that all of these medical journals, as well as other data on the anti-aging experiments, escaped to South America with Joseph Mengele."

Seven was still a bit puzzled. *What could this, as tragic as it was, have to do with a Florida serial killer? Or a dying FBI informant's murmurings on the way to the hospital?* He decided to ask the big question. "Mr. Greenfield, what *really* became of Martin Bormann, in your expert opinion? Most historians claim he just *disappeared*."

"That's another good question, Christopher." Greenfield's eyes seemed to gaze off into the distance. "There are many theories. Some say he died in Berlin at the very end of the war. The Russians don't believe this, nor do I. I think Bormann escaped, probably to Brazil. Concerning his last days in Germany, they're definitely some of the most unusual in the entire sordid history of the Nazi regime. It's quite a bizarre tale."

"I'd like to hear about it, Mr. Greenfield, if you don't mind."

"Don't mind at all." Greenfield grinned widely. "Talking about this takes me back to my old lecture days. Back when I was a professor at the university." Seven smiled back as Greenfield began the story.

"Near the end of the war Hitler and his staff were holed up in an underground bunker in Berlin. The Soviet invaders were steadily making their way toward his lair and Hitler knew the end was near. He couldn't take the heat and decided to commit suicide. He and Bormann hastily drew up plans for a huge funeral pyre, one in which the Fuhrer's lifeless body would burn. Hitler didn't want his mummified remains hanging in some exhibit or museum."

Christopher Seven shook his head, as Ben Greenfield restarted.

"After Hitler shot himself, his corpse was wrapped tightly in heavy black sheets, and then dutifully burned in the outside courtyard. As I've said, this was supposedly done so that no one could disrespect Hitler's body by hanging it up somewhere, as Mussolini's had been. No telling what the Russians would have done if they'd found the Fuhrer's body. Might have hung it from the Reichstadt building and taken potshots at it."

Greenfield's animated voice suddenly grew louder and more forceful. "Now here's where the story becomes very strange and confusing, Christopher. Hitler's corpse, covered in a thick black sheet and then doused with gasoline, was to be ceremonially carried to the funeral pyre by six of his most exalted lieutenants; the Circle or *Kreis,* as it was called back then. It was comprised of Goebbels, Axmann, Hewel, Kempka, Gunsche, and, of course, Martin Bormann. As members of the Fuehrer's *Kreis*, it was their sworn duty to stand at attention and give the Nazi salute while Hitler's lifeless body was consumed by the flames. ."

Greenfield momentarily closed his eyes in deliberation, trying to recall all the details. "The story then becomes even more bizarre. One of the eyewitnesses, a chauffeur, later questioned and imprisoned by the Russians, claims that for some inexplicable reason Martin Bormann was definitely *not* there. With Bormann's high position in the party, he should have stood directly to the right of the Fuehrer's body. This, in accordance with Nazi funeral tradition. Yet, this chauffeur witness swore Bormann was absent. The witness also claimed that someone *else* suddenly appeared. Some mysterious figure wearing a bizarre devil's mask. Or as he described it, a ghastly satanic skeletal face, of all things."

Ben Greenfield paused, looked over at the captivated Seven, and quickly resumed. "This shadowy figure walked with the other VIP funeral marchers, wearing his macabre devil mask the entire time. The skeletal face was later described as looking a bit like the skull on the black SS uniforms, with definite demonic features. So, now we wonder. Could that masked figure indeed have been Martin Bormann? If not, then who *was* the man in the mask?"

Greenfield shrugged his shoulders and acknowledged, "Simon and I could never find out. But, if this chauffeur's story is accurate; and remember, we got to methodically grill him after he escaped from the Russians. Then the masked stranger had to be someone of great importance. Must have been, since he was included in the funeral ceremony. So we now have to ask. Was this demonic-faced character even there, as the witness insists? Or is the whole thing a fairytale?"

"What do you think, Mr. Greenfield?"

The oldster gently shook his head. "I'm not sure. But why would this chauffeur fellow lie? Even when tortured by the Russians the chauffer stuck to his story. Thus the masked demonic figure could indeed have been Martin Bormann. Bormann was said to be a devotee of cults and astrology, just like Hitler was. And both men dabbled in devil worship near the end of the war. Particularly Bormann. So the account might be true. Then again, many stories were fabricated the last days of the Reich, to throw off soldiers hunting the Nazi escapees."

Ben Greenfield reflected a moment before concluding. "Yet if it wasn't Bormann in that skeletal mask, where did Martin Bormann go? Why *wasn't* he there? And what was the significance of the homage to the devil? In any event, after Hitler's funeral, no one sees or hears from Martin Bormann again. Some say he got out of Berlin and escaped to South America, along with several other top Nazis. British historians claim Bormann was simply killed fighting in the streets. A bunch of questionable dental records turned up in Berlin years later, claiming that Bormann died in Germany. Most likely, we'll never know for certain. And we'll never know if the puzzling devil part of the story, the lone masked figure, is factual or not."

Greenfield sighed again. "But what is sadly true is that we didn't catch Martin Bormann, and he didn't pay for his crimes."

"Don't worry, sir. You and Simon Wiesenthal got most of them, and for that the world is forever grateful." Seven got up from his chair, shook Greenfield's hand and prepared to leave. Yet there was one seemingly ridiculous question still on the agent's mind; something, although absurd, that nevertheless had to be asked.

"One last thing, Mr. Greenfield. I know this sounds preposterous, but do you feel it might be possible that Martin Bormann could still be alive? I mean, if the history books were wrong about his actual age?"

Greenfield, a bit startled by the query nonetheless tried to answer it. "Of course, anything's conceivable. But I'm afraid that possibility is pretty well out of the question. First of all, Bormann would be well over one hundred years of age. And secondly, we would undoubtedly have heard something about him."

"Yes, I suppose it's impossible," Seven replied, though now thinking about the frail old man with the unusual name of *Floda* whom he'd met the night before at Klaus Braun's *Mi Casa*. "But you did mention those Nazi anti-aging experiments. In your estimation, could they have ever succeeded in any of that?"

"Like I said, anything is feasible, Christopher. But in my opinion, those Nazi fountain-of-youth experiments were much too dangerous and radical to succeed." Ben Greenfield thought on it a moment. "Still, if they had achieved any breakthroughs, Martin Bormann certainly would have been the one to know about them. Even so, I doubt they could have actually been successful with their ridiculous *anti-aging* formulas."

"Why's that?"

"Mainly because of the extremely risky methods and their insane toxin ideas. Remember, they were injecting people with massive doses of the worst types of poisons. Everything from cyanide to arsenic was used. No human being could have survived it." Greenfield suddenly laughed out loud. "Can you imagine those quacks and their crazy theories?" He laughed again, this time even louder. "Why those fools even tried using snake venom."

Christopher Seven instantly froze, his body shuddering in a cold chill. Staggered, he again shook hands with Mr. Greenfield, silently exited, and then slowly made his way to the Mustang.

"I should have seen it coming," Seven grumbled through clinched teeth, as he walked to his car. "Snakes!"

"In a few weeks, that maniac Ripper will be slashing apart the body of another victim!" the youthful parking attendant at the Boca Inn angrily opined to his even younger valet assistant. "And nobody's doing a blasted thing about it! I blame that weak-kneed politician in the White House. Instead of his stimulus packages, free healthcare, vaccines and bailouts, he ought to concentrate on law enforcement!" With this parking employee's youthful energy focused entirely on the conversation with his coworker, he hadn't noticed that Christopher Seven, a hotel guest, was standing right behind him, patiently waiting for his car to appear.

Despite the lad's lack of professionalism, the Super Stud didn't mind the young man's tirade. He knew that the serial killings were on the worried minds of most Floridians. Seven smiled inwardly at the irony of his being the principle government agent sent to ferret out information about the killings. Sanctioned by the very president the kid had just castigated.

When the Mustang finally drove up, Seven over-tipped the attendant, got into his car, and headed north for the short stretch down Federal Highway to Palmetto Park Road. His destination was the City of Boca Community Church, an interdenominational place of worship ten minutes from his hotel.

It was Seven's practice to attend church every Sunday, whether he was at home or on the road. The sermon, delivered by a thin, red-haired minister, had dwelled on both the book of Mark in the New Testament, and also on David's writing in the book of Psalms. Both scriptures covered the subject of 'having faith no matter what', and this was a soothing tonic to the secret agent's troubled mind. Like always, Christopher Seven felt blessed after attending the service.

He next drove to his martial arts workout at the *Tai Chi Karate Center* in Deerfield. Then, returning to his hotel suite for a relaxing shower, and a delicious room service club sandwich for lunch, the Super Stud placed a coded cell phone call to FBI Agent Jack Hanover. Seven was aware that this particular conversation might prove to be a bit awkward. Earlier that morning, Colonel McPhail had cautioned him, via a private text, to continually be '*discreet*' when speaking with the FBI.

Yet, just exactly what was there to tell them, anyway? the Super Stud now asked himself. Confused and troubled, particularly by the new Martin Bormann fountain-of-youth angle, and the possible connection to Braun's octogenarian father, he realized he couldn't mention much of this to Jack yet. The last thing Seven wanted now was for the Feds to come barging in, guns 'a blazing', looking for missing snakes and old Nazis. Especially before Seven had even begun tackling his beautiful target. Sighing, he waited for Jack to answer.

"Hanover here."

"Hey, Jack. It's Seven. You busy?"

"Not at all. How's it going so far? Did you make contact with your gal at Braun's dinner party?"

"Only for a minute or two. Some old hag kept getting in the way. But at least I finally met Sandra Kent. And I don't mind telling you, Jack. This is *one* assignment I'm looking forward to."

Hanover chuckled. "So what's your next move?"

"I'll be at Braun's Pharmaceutical Center bright and early tomorrow. I'll see what happens then. Anything new on your end, Jack?"

"Not really. We thought we had a good Ripper lead yesterday. Some voodoo nut over in Boynton Beach who owned a few snakes. Turned out to be a false alarm. Nothing else to tell you."

The G5 agent suspected that Hanover was being just as discreet as Seven was, probably on similar orders from his own FBI bosses. "Oh well, keep in touch, Jack."

~

The next morning Seven was out of bed early and ready to go at eight o'clock. His plan was to get to Sandra Kent's office at Braun's Reptile and Pharmaceutical Center before she arrived. And then, to meet up with her without Klaus Braun's advanced approval. Surely, Dr. Braun would know that any astute reporter would privately try to pump some of the company's essential workers for background, and wouldn't always wait for permission. Nodding determinedly, Seven pulled his car onto I-95 and headed toward Miami.

Thirty minutes later, Sandy Kent was likewise readying herself to leave for the office. While examining her face in the bathroom mirror, she found herself thinking about Christopher Seven again, dwelling on thoughts of this amazingly good looking man. He'd been on her mind ever since Klaus' dinner party. Why was this? she wondered. Was it simply his unbelievable looks? No, there was something more to it, something she couldn't quite get a handle on. Perhaps it was the fact that lately almost all of her time was spent with people twice her age; doctors, pharmaceutical geniuses, reptile experts, and a bevy of dull scientists. None of these colleagues were close friends, particularly her male coworkers.

Admittedly, she was still very wary of men, and of course that was quite understandable. Constantly in the back of her mind was her terrifying encounter with the three thugs who'd accosted her in that Miami parking garage. The nightmare still haunted her, being pushed and threatened by those animals. Fortunately, two brave souls had come onto the scene just in the nick of time and quickly chased the hoods away. Still, the whole experience caused her to swear off men for a while, and Sandy had only recently considered dating again.

Somehow, though, this Christopher Seven appeared to be different from most of the men she knew or had met. Either before or after the incident. The ones who simply tried to impress or conquer every decent looking woman they came across. Of course this was only a first and superficial impression of the handsome reporter. Yet somehow she was almost sure of it. Seven seemed decent and unassuming. And with his great looks he certainly didn't have to prove anything with the opposite sex. His easygoing friendliness and cool, controlled manner had also impressed her.

Sandy sighed. This last year and a half with Dr. Braun had been all work and absolutely no play. Oh there were the glamorous business trips, with their fine hotels and restaurants. But those had simply been part of the job. Up until the dinner party, she hadn't really dwelled on it too much. But seeing and meeting this attractive young writer seemed to open her eyes and her senses. Perhaps he had liked her too. After all, he'd invited her jogging.

"Oh, who am I kidding?" Sandy asked the girl in the mirror. "With his looks, he's either married, engaged, or has dozens of women at his beck and call."

In any case, what did she really know about him? Klaus had merely told her that this Mr. Seven was an important journalist, and advised her to make sure that everyone was courteous but very discreet with him. Dr. Braun had even coached her a bit on what and what not to say, advising her that she herself would most likely be approached for Seven's story. That was probably the only reason this suave reporter had even reached out and spoke to her, Sandy now surmised. In all likelihood, this handsome hunk just wanted to use her for his silly magazine article. "Men. They're all the same!"

Oh, she would undoubtedly see him again, maybe even today. He would naturally be charming and polite, but only as a means to an end. That would almost certainly be his only motive for contacting her. She sighed resignedly. "What's the use in dreaming? What would a man such as him see in me anyway? Surely, he'd find me dull and old fashioned."

Yet, as Sandy started out her front door, she suddenly got an urge to go back and check if her hair and makeup were just right. While looking in the mirror, her reflection gazed back into her eyes. It was as if a woman in another dimension was searching for the real Sandra Kent. Gently, she straightened her back and raised an eyebrow intently, trying to see herself as a total stranger might. Vanity lights highlighted the mahogany glints in her brown locks. Hair that was swept up into a cascade from the top of her head down her long, elegant white neck. The brown of her eyes showed depth and turned up at the edges in a cat-shaped setting. A slightly irregular nose, making her beauty natural and believable for its slight imperfection, offset her high cheekbones. Her lips glistened alluringly as her tongue unconsciously moistened them. Sandy knew she was pretty, but wondered if looks alone could ever attract a man such as Seven.

Her clothes were the next thing she checked. A shiny crimson blouse added a touch of brightness to her conservative navy suit, and the plunge of its neckline accentuated the soft swell of her breasts without being immodestly revealing. Turning away from the mirror, Sandy laughed at herself for acting like a teenage girl trying to get the attention of the new boy in school. Tucking her purse under her arm, she strolled to her car as if walking on air.

Forty-five minutes later, a still beaming Sandy Kent walked through the ornate front doors of the Miami Reptile Center's 'Welcome Building' and its main executive offices. The stern face of Elsa Dykstra greeted her. "Good morning, Elsa," Sandy greeted cheerfully.

"Morning, Miss Kent," came the unsmiling reply.

So, Sandy reflected to herself. For some reason, Elsa is mad at me. Or in a bad mood again. Sandy knew instinctively that whenever she was referred to as Miss Kent instead of Sandy, she could be sure that Elsa was on the warpath. However, on this day, with her happy, romantic fantasies, Sandy Kent just didn't care. Even the often obnoxious Elsa Dykstra couldn't inspire her to frown.

Sandy made her way down the long hall, courteously nodding to a few passing workers, and soon arrived at her office. Opening the unlocked door labeled - Miss Sandra Kent - Executive Secretary to the President - Senior Public Relations Manager - she immediately checked to see if the red message light on her office phone was blinking. Thankfully, it wasn't. Then, just as she was about to sit down at her desk, a voice from behind startled her.

"You didn't have any messages, and so far, your phone hasn't rung at all this morning," Christopher Seven informed with a wide grin on his face. "By the way, I like the way you keep your desk so clean and organized. Mine is somewhat neat but not like yours."

Abruptly, Sandy froze in her tracks. She couldn't believe it. Here was the very man about whom she'd been daydreaming all morning. What was he doing here, and who let him in? Did Klaus know? Her boss had a very strict rule regarding unannounced visitors, and she was certain that Dr. Braun would never have approved. Her initial instinct was to scold this brash reporter. However, his infectious smile and gorgeous face made it impossible. She decided instead to adopt a businesslike attitude, praying he didn't sense her excited trembling.

"Really, Mr. Seven, I usually have my appointments planned and visitors announced," she stated firmly with a stern look on her face that quickly melted. "As for my desk, it's usually a mess. I clean it up every Friday just before leaving for the weekend. That way it doesn't look so daunting when Monday rolls around. But please tell me. How on earth did you get in here? Security is very strict."

"Okay, but first of all, you promised to call me Chris, not Mr. Seven. Moreover, if you must know, I noticed on today's reception appointment calendar that you and I were supposed to meet this afternoon anyway. We're scheduled to go over my prospective interview subjects a bit later. So I figured, why wait? I was here early, hence I merely told a little white lie to our friend Miss Dykstra. She most certainly had some doubts, but for some reason didn't stop me."

Seven grinned mischievously before continuing. "I told our pal, Elsa, that you and I drove in together this morning, and that you wanted me to go right to your office while you were parking the car. That was nearly twenty minutes ago, so I guess Elsa's caught on by now. Hope she isn't too angry."

Sandy frowned. "She's livid. I can always tell. Thanks to your shenanigans, she probably won't speak civilly to me for weeks. Yet now that you're here, would you like some coffee?"

"No thanks. But if you have a few moments, I'd like to follow up on a few things."

"Okay," she replied, disappointed that he would get right down to business so quickly. He then pleasantly surprised her.

"Listen, Sandy, I was serious when I spoke to you about jogging together. I haven't been down this way in a long time. Thought you could show me a few areas where it's fun and safe to run. You know, somewhere near the beach or even a nice park."

Sandy was delighted and cheerfully responded. "Sure, Chris." Her spine tingled slightly as she called him by his first name. "There are some really great places, especially in Fort Lauderdale. Near where I live." Maybe he does like me a little, she thought.

"Sounds great," said Seven. "Just tell me when."

Sandy smiled, sweetly. "I'll let you know before the day is over. Promise. It'll be fun to run with someone again." She couldn't believe how easy it was to talk with him, and even the prospect of a casual get-together like jogging genuinely thrilled her.

Christopher Seven was also pleased. He knew instinctively that he was making headway with her. But for some curious reason, unlike on previous assignments with other beautiful targets around the world, this one seemed different. There was innocence about this girl, a wholesomeness that made him want to protect and embrace her. For a moment he felt a strange twinge of guilt, knowing he'd have to use their relationship as nothing more than a fact-finding tool. Yet the thought of the Ripper murders transformed him back to a trained Super Stud, sent to conquer a prey no matter what the human cost.

"You know, Sandy, I see you're not married. At least I hope not, as there's no ring. Of course, I don't know if you have a steady guy or something of that sort. Wouldn't want to foist myself on you in that case." He smiled gently, "It's just that I'll be alone down here for the next few weeks. I'm not trying to be brash, just simply looking for some company. I've been thinking about it ever since we met. Would you be free for dinner tonight?" He playfully put his hand across his heart in mock fear. "If not, it would have to be Miss Dykstra. So please don't leave me with that daunting prospect."

Though she giggled with pleasure at his humor, Seven felt a genuine pang of guilt as he mouthed the now familiar refrain. Those words, or something like them, that he'd uttered so many times before, to so many women, in so many parts of the globe. This was the standard first invitation, issued solely for the purpose of getting closer to an unsuspecting target. It was always the same. Nevertheless, it had to be done, in order to begin the well-practiced Super Stud process. Inexplicably, however, he felt like a heel doing so with this girl.

"Unfortunately I have a staff conference tonight," Sandy replied. Then a smile she couldn't quite hide told him she was overjoyed with his invitation. "But I'm free as a bird tomorrow evening. If that's alright with you, of course."

Seven was instantly taken by her obvious trust and innocence. From his training on interpreting body language and facial expressions, the G5 agent knew that she was sincere in her response. Yet inwardly he felt another touch of unexpected remorse. I'll probably have to use her, he thought. Still, there's one thing I hope I'll never have to do. Take hurtful advantage of this girl, or permanently scar her in any way.

With resolution, he looked up at her beautiful dimpled face. "Tomorrow it is then, Sandy. I'll surprise you with a new restaurant I recently heard about. One I'm hoping you'll like."

Sandy beamed with excitement. "I love surprises. Just so long as you tell me how to dress."

A buzz from her desk intercom ended their pleasant conversation. It was an angry Elsa Dykstra. Her tone, deliberately cold and annoyed, sounded even more menacing through the metallic twang of the speaker "Miss Kent?"

Yes."

"Dr. Braun arrived a few moments ago. He wants to see you and Mr. Seven in his office. Immediately!"

"**O**h dear," exclaimed Sandy Kent. "We could be in for a bit of trouble."
Seven looked at her encouragingly and replied, "Don't worry. I'll
take full blame. I'll just tell him I didn't understand the rules."

"I'm afraid it's not as simple as that," Sandy informed. "First of
all, you should have checked in properly. We have a strict policy about
unescorted visitors in the offices. Of course, I should have sent you back
immediately."

Sandy seemed to be scolding herself with a mixture of fear and
self-flagellation, leaving Christopher Seven concerned by the genuine
anxiety she showed for breaking some silly rule. Had he gotten her into
permanent trouble with the boss? The G5 operative certainly didn't want
to cause problems at this point. He also didn't want to disrupt the chummy
relationship he now enjoyed with Klaus Braun. Most of all, Seven didn't
want to arouse Braun's suspicion or anger.

Yet, Seven knew that any first-rate investigative reporter would be
expected to bend some of the rules, in order to get to the heart of a story,
and he felt confident in that defense. Perhaps it might even strengthen his
hand with the big chief. Seven shrugged his shoulders and followed Sandra
up the hall as they walked toward. Braun's office. Much like two guilty
school kids on their way to the principal.

Sandy nervously knocked on the big double doors and waited for a
response. "Enter," said the cold, slightly irritated voice of her boss. They
walked in slowly, she with trepidation, and Seven with detached curiosity.

"Sit down, Miss Kent," ordered Braun. "You too, Mr. Seven."

Christopher Seven, still unconcerned, was inwardly amused by
the calculated gravity that Klaus Braun was trying to convey. After a few
moments of chilly silence, the doctor spoke again. "Mr. Seven, I asked
you the other day to respect the policies and privacy of my staff. Yet, you
deliberately lied to my receptionist. Afterward, you waltzed right in to
Miss Kent's office, without clearance, I might add." Glancing over at Sandy,
Dr. Braun continued, "And you, young lady. When you saw that a visitor
had entered your office unannounced, why did you not send him back to
Miss Dykstra so he could sign in properly?"

Seven immediately spoke up, without giving Sandy a chance to
speak, or Braun the chance to further chastise them. "If I may, sir, the
oversight was all mine. Miss Kent was indeed very upset with me and
she gave me a stern lecture on it. She was about to send me back to the
reception area when you summoned us. As for my going directly to her
office, I saw that she and I were scheduled to meet this afternoon. But
earlier this morning, I learned I might be needed for a conference call with

Global's editors that same time. So I took it upon myself to try and see Miss Kent *earlier* rather than later. I foolishly assumed that since I was cleared to see Miss Kent anyhow, I didn't have to be cleared again. My mistake. It won't happen again. As for barging into her office, I really need to get going with my research. So I changed things a bit. I'm sorry if it upset you, Miss Kent, or Miss Dykstra. But I've got an article to write. One which, unfortunately, is subject to a deadline."

Christopher Seven had spoken with authority, firmness, and conviction, three qualities Dr. Braun admired; whether exhibited by a peer or rival. Braun looked directly at the handsome journalist. When he did, Seven thought he detected an air of grudging respect in Klaus Braun's eyes. The doctor's scowl slowly disappeared as he addressed them. "I'll accept your explanation, this *one* time only, Mr. Seven. But from now on, no more little pranks. And certainly no violating the parameters I laid down, and to which you agreed. Is that clear?"

"Absolutely, Doctor."

"Good." Dr. Braun then turned toward his secretary. "Miss Kent, I'm sorry if I was angry with you, Sandra. I can see now that it was none of your doing." He smiled gently at her. "Now. Would you please excuse us so that Mr. Seven and I can chat privately for a moment?"

"Certainly, sir." Braun's stunning assistant stood up, looked over at Seven, and addressed him with a professional demeanor. "That list of names you asked for, Mr. Seven, I can have it for you in an hour or so. You can then make your interview requests and appointments accordingly, through Miss Dykstra or me."

"Sounds fine, Miss Kent," Seven answered, in an equally businesslike tone. He glanced at her shapely body as she walked out of the room. A brief silence was then broken by Braun's pining voice. "She's quite a woman, in many ways. Exemplary worker as well. Tell me, Seven. Do you find her attractive?"

Braun's question took the agent by surprise. It had an air of suspicion to it, one that put the G5 agent on high alert. Was Klaus Braun testing him again? Seven decided to answer guardedly. "She's certainly very beautiful. I'd have to be blind not to see that. I also admire her intellect, from the little time we've had to chat."

"Tell me then," Dr. Braun asked pointedly. "Are you thinking of, how do you say, *seeing* her?"

Seven stiffened, deciding that he'd better answer this one truthfully. It was quite possible that Dr. Braun had all of the offices, including Sandy's, bugged. Perhaps he already knew of their dinner date. Even if he didn't, the crafty snake man was sure to find out anyway. Still, it would be perfectly natural for any young male to be interested in such an eye-catching woman. Looking up, Seven spoke candidly. "The thought had crossed my mind, Doctor. She's quite lovely." He quickly added a lie for

Braun's benefit. "Of course, I already have a steady girl at home. In fact, we're discussing engagement. So, I can assure you, sir, there'd be nothing very serious between Miss Kent and me."

Making up his mind to at least mention the date, the Super Stud continued, "That being said, I *was* thinking of asking Sandra out for dinner. For purely platonic, social reasons, of course. That is, unless you have any objections?" Seven shrugged, innocently. "You know, two young people, lonely new city for me. That sort of thing. But rest assured, I'm definitely not looking for anything meaningful with her, if that's what you were wondering."

The doctor forced another thin smile as he spoke. "I see. Of course we do have a very firm rule about fraternization among the staff. But you're not technically in that group, so I guess I have no real objections. Still, I'd prefer it if you'd be discreet. These social things have a way of growing into a life of their own. I must insist, however, that there be absolutely *no* shop talk when you're with her."

Braun looked straight at the reporter. "That's *also* a firm rule, and I do have ways of finding out if you ignore my request." He paused for affect and then finished his warning. "Sandra knows this, and it could mean serious consequences to her career if she violates my security directives. I'm sure you understand, with my confidential formulas and all. Even an innocent question, or a careless answer, could bring about troubling repercussions."

"Oh, I quite understand, Doctor. And you have nothing to worry about on that score. I'm just glad that you have no problem with me seeing your assistant socially."

Suddenly, the G5 operative got an idea, a way to both test and tweak the snake guru. Seven quickly proceeded with his ploy. "I almost felt for a while there that you had your *own* eye on her, Dr. Braun."
Seven gave a short chuckle. "Couldn't blame you if you did. She's a real beauty. Must make working with her quite nice."

The ploy worked. For just a second, Braun's face flushed beet-red. His whole body seemed to twitch with an embarrassed nervousness. *Got you, Braun!* Seven thought, feeling a winner's joy. *You secretly long for this young girl yourself, you dirty old man.*

A visibly shaken Klaus Braun slowly regained his composure and spoke again, almost as if no one else was in the room with him. "No," he said softly, gazing up at the ceiling. "I'm a bit too old for that, I suppose." He stared into space with a bizarre expression.

After returning from his private thoughts, he quickly came back to his usual self-assured manner. "By the way, have you given any further thought to that Lafitte sword and our agreement? The senate committee's first funding meeting is coming up soon."

Seven nodded. "I assure you, it's definitely on my mind, Doctor. But I still need a bit more time to decide. Naturally that Lafitte cutlass is very tempting. But my career and reputation are likewise important to me if word ever got out."

Dr. Braun's face showed irritation. "Well, see to it that you don't take too long in deciding, Seven. My deal won't be on the table forever." With that, he abruptly reached down to his Bluetooth intercom and called Elsa Dykstra. "Miss Dykstra, Christopher Seven is in here with me. He'll be stopping by your desk later to get a list that Miss Kent is drawing up concerning his interview requests. See that he's only shown the workers *I've* designated. No one else."

"Very good, sir."

Satisfied that he had fired back at this brash journalist, Braun stood up, indicating that the meeting between the two of them was over. "Now, if you'll excuse me, Mr. Seven. I have work to do."

Christopher Seven quickly made his exit, still basking in the undeniable knowledge that he'd scored a few points. Having stood up for himself over the Sandra Kent office incident, he skillfully paved the way for taking her out socially. More importantly, he'd struck Klaus Braun where it would hurt most. Into the older man's vanity!

The remainder of the morning passed without incident. Seven received a list of *approved* workers available for interview in a memo from Sandra Kent, along with her home phone number. A bit later on, he began the mundane process of interviewing these obvious Braun shills. The bothersome Elsa Dykstra sat in on most of the talks, making sure the journalist didn't probe too thoroughly. Miss Dykstra told Seven she'd try to schedule three or four interviews per week and they both agreed that his magazine research would take the better part of a month, or longer.

Later that afternoon, after first telling Elsa that his 2PM *Global* teleconference had been cancelled, the G5 operative did manage to do a bit of minor snooping on his own. Doing so whenever and wherever he could. Randomly speaking to a few workers who were *not* on Dr. Braun's approved list, these impromptu chats with scientists or chemists were mostly met with icy stonewalling, usually in foreign accents. The few daytime workers who did speak with him wouldn't discuss Braun's secretive nightshift at all. Their nervous, tightlipped reactions confirmed that Braun's late shift was truly a *separate* and self-contained entity.

One thing was becoming evident. Klaus Braun's nighttime operation could very well be bonded by some unusual, cult-like allegiance. From the little Seven could gather, Braun's nightshift had more than just an air of a close-knit team. There was something else linking them; something forceful. Could it be something unlawful as well? The G5 agent wasn't sure. Yet he knew he'd need concrete evidence before Colonel McPhail would recommend any further action. Even so, Seven's professional instincts told him that there was definitely something abnormal and perhaps even ominous happening at the Reptile Center during the night.

While interviewing Braun's approved workers, Seven heard them talking about some 3:30 p.m. coffee break. Apparently this was *never* to be missed. A mid-afternoon break in which *all* daytime workers dutifully filed into the commissary across the street. Here, in addition to coffee and pastries, corporate announcements and awards were given out. Accordingly, Dr. Braun insisted that *all* day workers, save the main phone receptionist, attend the half-hour coffee session. Knowing that the place would apparently be deserted at half past 3PM, Seven decided that this might be the ideal time to do a bit of secret reconnaissance. That is if he could fine a covert way of staying in the building when most all the other occupants were across the street.

Sure enough, at exactly 3:30 p.m., a loud bell rang out and Dr. Braun's entire daytime staff marched out toward the commissary. Braun's cavernous executive building would soon be completely abandoned and the Super Stud knew he'd now have a full thirty minutes to do some quiet spying. Yet how could he stay put in the main building without being spotted? He decided to feign walking out with the horde, and then double back after making some innocuous excuse to the new switchboard receptionist.

Waiting until he saw the ever-vigilant Miss Dykstra stroll out of the main building with Dr. Braun, Seven casually wandered up to the front switchboard and reception area. Here the remaining workers were all filing out, on their way to the dining hall across the street. A younger blonde woman with large horn-rimmed glasses had temporarily replaced Elsa at the reception desk. She was on the phone, most likely chatting with her boyfriend, and she seemed far more interested in filing her nails than in any security procedures. Seven grinned inwardly as he approached her, knowing he'd probably found the one weak link in Braun's tight security chain.

"Hi," he said amicably, hoping not to disturb her phone chatter. "Left my laptop in one of the back offices. I'll just run back and get them before I walk to the commissary."

As he hoped, blondie brusquely waved him back in, while continuing her phone conversation. Giggling loudly into the receiver, she was oblivious to the actions of the handsome visitor.

That's a break, Seven reflected. *Even the ever cautious Klaus Braun has a few slipshod underlings. He'd probably fire her instantly had he seen her carelessness.* The G5 agent then guardedly made his way up the empty hallway.

No one seemed to be in any of the offices or labs. *Good. Here's my chance,* he mused. *Perhaps a few of the rooms or cubicles might be unlocked.*

Cautiously walking into a few offices, he hurriedly opened several drawers and cabinets. Disappointingly, nothing unusual or revealing was found. After trying a few more doors, all of which were bolted, Seven spotted the partially opened door of a large conference room. Not expecting much classified information to be hidden there, he shrugged his shoulders and strolled into it nonetheless. As the Super Stud began looking through a few of the drawers in the room's oversized desk, he suddenly heard male voices. One of them was Klaus Braun's, emanating from not too far down the hall.

"We can talk in the conference room, Alvin," Braun ordered, his voice and footsteps definitely getting closer. "No one will be back for half an hour. Even so, have your two security men check it out."

Trying not to panic, Seven hastily glanced around for some type of hiding place. The only possibility was the conference room's supply closet located to his right. He quickly made it to the closet and leaped in, closing the door softly behind him. When he did so, he spotted a smaller, half sized door on the floor. It was obviously the entrance to some type of additional storage space. Its door was fairly large, so there could be room to hide inside, in case Braun's goons checked the larger supply closet itself.

Seven, now crawling on the floor, somehow squeezed his lean body into this smaller, though surprisingly ample pigeonhole. It was tight but workable. Somehow managing to sit up once inside it, he silently prayed that this wasn't the same area in which the FBI's deceased informant had stumbled upon a deadly Taipan!

A fter quickly diving into the supply closet's diminutive crawlspace, which provided just enough room to uncomfortably scrunch up inside it, Seven pulled its small door closed and took out a pocket-size penlight. Shining it around the area, with visions of poisonous reptiles swarming about, he hastily inspected the cubical. Thankfully nothing stirred. Now sitting uneasily, he waited for Braun's group to enter the room. It didn't take long.

A few moments later the G5 operative heard them march in. Braun closed the conference room's large, single door, and walked down to the far end of the room - Seven's end. Chairs were heard moving on the parquet floor as four men sat down at the long conference table. Dr. Braun was the first to speak, addressing Alvin Rosier, his head of security.

"Before we begin our brief discussion, Rosier, please have your two security men check out the area for any electronic bugs. I know it was done earlier, but you never know. Those rival pharmaceutical companies are quite devious. And as you're all aware, aside from that single hidden security-cam in the Welcome Center, we have no security cameras anywhere else. I simply can't afford videos of our nighttime efforts falling into the wrong hands. We must therefore rely solely on human reconnaissance. Accordingly, please have your men do a quick, second inspection."

So, thought Seven, *this is it. Dr. Braun's security duo will now begin checking out the entire conference room area. I knew something like this might be coming. They're not going to have a meeting without precautions, no matter how certain they are that no one would be foolish enough to spy on them.* Holding his breath, the agent waited, hoping his crammed hiding place would be secure.

"Let's start with the table, Hank," one of the guards said to the other. Seven could hear them moving a few things around, obviously searching for hidden wires. He next heard windows and drawers being opened and shut, and then the inevitable words he was dreading, "Main room's clean, Hank. Let's check the supply closet."

The Super Stud could hear the heavy-booted footsteps approaching his tiny hideout. He worriedly asked himself, *Will they check out the cubbyhole crawlspace where I'm hiding, or merely be content to have a cursory glance in the closet itself?* Seven quickly decided that if he was discovered, his only excuse would be the *zeal* of an investigative reporter. Yet he had no illusions that Braun and his beefy security squad would believe him. Or even care about niceties if they did. What would follow then? At best his mission would be scrubbed. *And at worst?* Seven didn't want to think about it.

Yet, *would* they find him? Why should they even look in this small crawlspace? All that had been in here was a single package of inkjet paper, and some unopened printing cartridges. It was the main closet where most of the supplies were now stacked. Even so, Dr. Braun's security men were probably very thorough in their tasks, and Seven knew his odds were slim. Oh well, in a few more seconds he'd certainly have his answer!

The supply closet door squeaked opened and the overhead light was switched on by one of the security guards. The two men then began looking around, roughly moving a few supply boxes. Seven could see an occasional arm or foot through the tiny door cracks.

Suddenly, one of the men's burly arms inched closer toward the crawlspace's handle and Seven's heart nearly stopped! As the hairy arm came nearer, the G5 operative had half a mind to leap out, surprise them, and then try a wild run down the hall. But then, just at that moment, the guard's partner exclaimed, "Hey, Brian. Maybe we should throw a few snakes in here like the one that nailed that Fusco guy."

Both men laughed heartily, and, miraculously, this jocular distraction made the first man relax and pull his hand away from the crawlspace door. "Come on, let's get going, Bri." He gestured toward the crawlspace. "Ain't nothing in that tiny closet, anyway. The other security squad checked out this whole area earlier and said everything was fine." With that he turned off the closet light and made his way back to the table where Braun and Alvin Rosier were waiting patiently. The security duo sat down, and Dr. Braun began.

"We'll have to be quick in here, gentlemen. My daytime workers will be returning from coffee break in twenty-five minutes. No worries, though. My comments and suggestions should only take a moment or two." Klaus Braun cleared his throat and explained, "I just wanted to go over a few concerns I have about security as it pertains to Operation D. Like I mentioned last night, my father and I have selected the twenty regions targeted for possible action. I alone will choose the *actual* ten locations, and naturally I'll keep that knowledge to myself."

His men nodded in unison as Braun went on, "Some of the choices were obvious. The populace in most of these areas has bought into our '*controversial*' pharmaceutical promotions for years" The doctor laughed at the terminology "In fact, some of these same targeted cities were similarly chosen when we unveiled that bogus headache powder. You remember; the phony headache medication that made us a blooming fortune." Braun chuckled. "They should likewise get a big headache from Operation D."

Hearty laughter followed his statement. Seven listened intently as Dr. Braun resumed, "New York, Los Angeles, Chicago, and Washington DC are all logical choices. However, I think you'll agree that Orlando and Las Vegas could be interesting possibilities as well. So could Boston, Toronto and Dallas. Like I've said, I can't tell you my *actual* ten choices for obvious reasons. Suffice to say, they will be chosen for maximum impact and economic significance. Once they're finally selected, it will be up to you three men, along with the rest of your nightshift security team, to make sure none of the details get out. Secrecy in this matter is of paramount importance!" There were again murmurs of agreement around the table. "Before I continue, are there any questions as to the areas themselves?"

"Dr. Braun," said Alvin Rosier, in his heavy Haitian accent, "Some of our most important and loyal people are working in these locales. Will they be informed?"

"Arrangements will be made," answered Braun. "No one worthy shall be neglected. Additionally, a week or two before the operation actually begins, my financial planners will transfer most of our assets in these and other areas to my new bank accounts in Zurich. Of course, some funds and stocks must be left where they are for cosmetic reasons. A required precaution. But the bulk of my assets will be relocated, and by then, we should also have the cash funds of a very sizable pharmaceutical grant from the United States Senate in our coffers. Think of it, gentlemen. Millions of dollars given to us by the US Government *itself*. It couldn't be any better!"

There was a smattering of applause along with some more derisive laughter. Klaus Braun also laughed, and Christopher Seven wondered what the heck was going on here. Dr. Braun's next words disrupted Seven's worried thoughts.

"The senate committee will vote on the hopeful funding of our grant sometime the middle of June. June 9th, I believe is the actual date. My Washington sources are fairly confident that I'll receive the funding, via a huge cashier's check by the way, and I think they're correct. The US Senate is very much enamored with our work here and many senators will greedily try to cash in on the benefits of being associated with it. It's always good for their individual poll numbers. To seemingly be helping those in need of health enhancements; particularly senior citizens."

Once again, impressed murmurs of approval could be heard when the doctor informed, "As some additional assurance for convincing these annoying and unreliable politicians to give us the grant money, I myself have personally been working with a young journalist from *Global Magazine*. Pushing to see that he conveys *exactly* what I want in his story. His forthcoming propaganda piece about me, orchestrated by our gifted public relations department and myself, should work wonders in Washington. We'll see to it that some of his flattering magazine story is leaked to key senators *ahead* of time. That will most assuredly help us obtain this huge financial grant. The politicos won't want to buck the opinions of a prestigious, popular family publication." Braun sneered. "And a financial windfall of this size from those Washington fools will have *particular* meaning to father and me. It will be sweet revenge!"

Another voice at the table nervously asked Klaus Braun a question. "Doctor, what about Operation D's exact timing?"

"So far, the target date is still July 4th, as planned," Braun replied. He chuckled, slyly. "A great way for America to kick off its national holiday, is it not, gentlemen?"

There was immediate, roaring laughter around the table as Dr. Braun added, "If necessary, of course, the target date can always be changed. Quickly, easily, and timing wise. As you know, *all* my ventures allow for rapid rescheduling. That's part of my brilliance. In Operation D's case, a lot of the supplies are already here. The other truck drivers can simply leave ahead of time, if needed, and implementation can commence earlier or later at a moment's notice. I've planned these precautions, in the event there are any complications. We accordingly have two tentative *back-up* dates; July 24th and August 14th. For now, though, the target date is still July 4th."

Once again there were murmurs of agreement as Braun finished up. "Keep in mind, though, that the success of Operation D greatly depends on the obedient loyalty of each of you. It's your sacred responsibility to the Dark Prince himself!"

Christopher Seven froze in total bewilderment. *What's this nonsense all about? And who in heaven's name is the Dark Prince?*

Braun's voice boomed out again, "Operation D will be successful no matter *when* it takes place. And unless there's something unforeseeable, it will indeed take place on July 4th." Klaus Braun stood up from the table. "That's all, gentlemen. This meeting is now adjourned." Glancing at his watch he informed, "I'm running late for my appointment in Lauderdale. Tell my chauffer I'll be right out, Alvin."

"Yes, sir."

With that, there was again the noise of chairs being moved as the four men exited the conference room.

Still scrunched in stunned silence, and with his muscles beginning to ache from the constant squatting, Christopher Seven remained perfectly still. His discomfort was of no concern now. Klaus Braun's puzzling operation was. *What in the world did any of this mean?*

Seven's analytical mind raced with several different scenarios as he tried to calmly reason it out. It definitely sounded as if Klaus Braun was planning some sort of nationwide pharmaceutical scam. It would begin sometime in early July, with a June or August alternate date, and total secrecy was required. The operation would take place in at least ten major US and Canadian markets, and for some reason Dr. Braun was also planning to transfer most of his assets to Swiss banks shortly before it commenced. *Did Braun suspect major law suits?* Possibly, for he likewise wanted the US Government's grant money *before* he unleashed his scam. Apparently, Klaus Braun had done something similarly deceitful with a bogus headache remedy a while back, for he'd specifically referred to that swindle as well.

The Super Stud scratched his head in bewilderment and again silently asked himself, *why is this snake guru suddenly putting his assets into overseas banks? Was he planning to disastrously bilk the public with some risky new wonder drug and then move out of the country before there were 'Bernie Madoff' type consequences?*

Seven thought on it again. Perhaps Dr. Braun's crooked lawyers had already warned him to expect trouble, because someone had mentioned protecting the Braun employees who were headquartered in many of these targeted areas. It sounded as if the thing could easily turn into a potential Enron or Tyco type scandal; some large-scale pharmaceutical fiasco with heaps of lawsuits. Possibly countless victims would be seriously burned, a la Madoff.

Yet wouldn't Klaus Braun himself still be around to face the music, like those Enron honchos? Christopher Seven shook his head. Still confused, he tried to decipher how his magazine piece was going to be utilized by the crafty snake man. Evidently, Seven's article was significant in obtaining the huge government grants; much more money than Klaus Braun had casually mentioned back at *Mi Casa.* No wonder Braun had approached him with such a hefty bribe.

The baffled agent shook his head again, silently wondering what Braun and his cronies were *really* up to? Oh well, at least he had heard this much of the plan. It was now time to escape without being discovered.

Seven glanced at his watch. Five minutes to four. He'd wait until Braun's horde of workers began streaming back from coffee break, merge in with them, and then calmly leave the building.

The G5 operative waited three more minutes and then cautiously exited the supply closet. He next walked up to the partially closed conference room door, and hid behind it. A minute later, forty or so harried employees rushed up the long hallway, anxious to get back to their offices and labs. As they did so, Seven calmly edged out into their crowded mass, completely unnoticed, and amicably began chatting with a few of the chemists he'd interviewed earlier. No one paid him the slightest mind, and the few workers who did recognize him merely thought he was doing more of his magazine research.

A few minutes later, Christopher Seven calmly approached the reception desk. Seated behind it was the same inexperienced blonde gal, still chatting animatedly on the phone. Seven casually grabbed the sign-out pad, and holding it away from her view, wrote in the false exit time of *3:30 PM* as his final departure hour. It hardly mattered; Blondie seemed completely disinterested, still blabbing away with her beau.

Careful to avoid making eye contact with this fill-in receptionist, Seven then walked straight out of the building, strolled past the guard at the gate, an unfamiliar Korean gent who didn't give him so much as a second look, and got into his Mustang. Thankful that there wasn't as much scrutiny for people leaving the building as there was for those entering, the relieved Super Stud was soon driving home, finally breathing normally again.

Completely spent, the exhausted agent arrived back at his hotel wanting nothing more than a hot shower, followed by a good meal. As he turned on his laptop to send a detailed report to headquarters, his mind kept dwelling on two troubling questions. First, what was this Operation D of Braun's *really* all about? And secondly, who or what was this *Dark Prince* to whom Klaus Braun had referred?

Christopher Seven knew he needed answers quickly. He was also well aware that he'd now have to step up his spying, starting tomorrow evening via his dinner date with Sandy Kent. And he'd better be *super* if he was going to get her to open up about the shadowy world of her enigmatic boss.

Chapter 26

Passion Please

O n the evening of her eagerly anticipated dinner date with Christopher Seven, Sandy Kent felt like a silly schoolgirl again, giddy with expectation. To her, the idea of a relationship with this incredibly handsome journalist seemed a thrilling prospect, and she'd had been looking forward to his *surprise restaurant* all day.

Seven, on the other hand, was inexplicably feeling a bit of a cad, knowing his mission was to use Sandy as quickly and as forcefully as he could. He knew his Super Stud assignment was to pursue her as just another target, and after a few moments of scolding himself for any personal feelings about it, he realized she was strictly business.

The G5 agent arrived precisely on time at Sandy's condo in the exclusive Gault Ocean section of Ft. Lauderdale. As he entered her well-appointed living room, Seven complimented the fantastic 14th floor oceanfront vista it afforded.

"Thanks," she replied. "Klaus found this place for me. The first thing I do every morning is have a cup of coffee while enjoying the ocean view. I never get tired of it."

Seven, glancing at her appealing, tight-fitting dress, remarked, "One could get accustomed to *that* view too. You look absolutely stunning, Sandy."

"Why thank you, Mr. Seven. You look pretty swell yourself."

"I bet you say that to all the reporters."

"Most of the reporters I speak to are balding old men who aren't impeccably dressed." She looked at him reflectively. *It's still incredible,* she thought. *He's got to be the best looking man I've ever seen!*

"We'd better get going, Sandy. My surprise begins promptly at eight o'clock."

Christopher Seven waited until they were exiting the elevator and then took her arm. She hesitated for just the slightest moment, but then smiled and put her arm in his as the two of them made their way out to the parking lot. There was something about her touch, her gentle mannerisms, and the way their eyes met that aroused genuine excitement in him. Although he'd been with some of the most beautiful and sophisticated women in the world, Seven now felt a rather strange and new sensation, one that was hard to explain. Being with the vivacious and friendly Sandy was akin to college dating again.

"I don't know where you're taking me, but I hope the food is good," she exclaimed, sliding into the passenger seat of the convertible as Seven held and then closed her door. "I'm starved."

"You'll just have to trust me, Sandy. Or at least trust the food critic who touted it." With that he hopped in, pushed the convertible roof button, and the Mustang GT dutifully opened to the beautiful night above.

Twenty minutes later they pulled into the valet parking area of a stunning new Polynesian restaurant called *Hawaii Mai*. Seven had chosen the place thanks to a tip from a restaurant reviewer he knew at the *New York Times*. He'd been assured that this was one of the most decadently beautiful restaurants in the country, with supposedly first-rate food as well.

When Seven and his gorgeous date entered the dazzling eatery, neither was disappointed. The soft, seductive Hawaiian guitar music, coming from the flower-shirted trio, added perfect ambiance and romance to the glorious atmosphere. As did the fresh orchids and flora everywhere, along with a striking tree-lined waterfall.

"It's lovely," Sandy gushed. "Absolutely stunning!"

"Let's hope the food is as good as the setting," Seven replied.

A smart looking Hawaiian Maitre D, clad in a white dinner jacket over a bright red shirt, greeted the couple warmly. He then guided them to a cozy booth nicely situated in the main dining room. Smiling widely, he asked them if they'd like a drink.

"I suppose we should order one of the fancy Polynesian concoctions," Christopher Seven said with a slight smirk.

"Oh yes, let's do, Chris. I feel like celebrating."

Seven looked up at the Maitre D. "What do you suggest?"

"Our most requested house drink is the *Passion Please*. It's a mixture of coconut, dark rum, a bit of cream, and several delicious freshly squeezed fruit juices. I heartily recommend it."

"Sounds good to me," Sandy said with a gorgeous smile.

"Fine, make it two," Seven agreed. He then turned and looked at her, undoubtedly one of the most natural beauties he'd ever met. "Hmm, *Passion Please*," he grinned. "Sounds like fun. I just hope it doesn't have one of those little umbrellas sticking out of it."

Her response came with a giggle; "Oh, don't be an old fuddy duddy. Just go with the flow."

"If you say so, Miss Kent. At any rate, I certainly approve of the drink's name." She blushed endearingly without responding. "By the way, Sandy, did you think of any good places to jog?"

"I sure did. But maybe I'll surprise you, just like you did me with this beautiful restaurant. How about this Saturday?"

"Saturday's fine, Sandy. Say around eleven o'clock?"

"Perfect," she beamed. "Gives me the morning to sleep in."

A waiter soon returned with the drinks showcased in tall, frosted Lalique glasses. The tasty concoctions were ice cold and delicious, much like a perfectly made smoothie with a bit of a kick. "There goes my figure," Sandy protested. "These things are delicious. Deadly as well, I should think."

Seven shook his head. "The *last* thing you have to worry about is your figure." He clinked his glass against hers. "Here's to a wonderful evening. And to one of the nicest figures I've seen."

Sandy blushed again, her innocence once more charming him.

"Thanks," she said softly.

After ten minutes of affable chatter, along with their drinks, the waiter again resurfaced and took their food order. Seven watched him as he march toward the kitchen. He then looked over at Sandy resignedly, knowing it was time to get to work. Hoping it wouldn't wreck the cheerful mood between them, he began, "I spoke with Klaus today. He said he won't have much time for me this week because of something he's doing with the nightshift. I suppose supervising both shifts keeps him quite busy."

The expression on her face told him that though Sandy was happy to be with him, she was still somewhat reluctant to talk shop. Nonetheless, she accepted his query as merely one of an innocent observer and answered it affably. "Klaus runs the two shifts as if they're separate companies. I don't have much to do with the nighttime activity, other than occasionally scheduling a few things for them. I really don't want to. Got enough on my plate as it is with the daytime doings. Besides, the overnight side of the pharmaceutical operation is a bit more intricate." She didn't elaborate.

After taking a small sip from her drink, Sandy continued, albeit unenthusiastically. "Still, I fully understand that the doctor's nightshift work and experiments are far more important than his reptile displays, daily shows, and normal daytime activities at the Center. So don't be dismayed if Klaus can't see you this week, and please don't be offended if he doesn't discuss his nightshift projects with you. He doesn't share much with me about them either." She looked over at him. "But enough about my workplace. I want to know more about you. Like how you got into journalism?"

Knowing she had deftly rebuffed his probing, and not wanting to push any further for now, Seven cordially answered, "Journalism, huh? Well, I guess I've always loved it. Had a knack for it in college. You know, school paper, various periodicals, things like that. When I realized I couldn't make a living playing tennis or fencing, I found that writing was also a passion of mine. So, after graduating, I worked freelance for various publications. In fact, I still do. I like it better that way. No particular boss or inexperienced kid editors looking over my shoulder every day. And the job choices are my own."

With a practiced vagueness that he'd used many times and in many places, the G5 operative expertly parried her inquires. After this polite exchange of give-and-take sidestepping, both were relieved when their appetizer arrived. The vegetable spring rolls were crisp and delicate, perhaps the best they'd ever eaten.

Following a bit more small talk, mostly about the excellent food, Seven again attempted to steer the conversation back to the probing for which he'd come. "I've been wondering, Sandy. Aren't you nervous working amongst all those deadly snakes? I know I'd be."

"Not really." It was an obvious question, one she got all the time. "There are strict safety procedures and firm rules for all employees. Besides, I'm in the office most of the day so I hardly ever see a snake."

Seven persevered, knowing he was approaching some potentially tricky ground. "But couldn't one of them escape from its cage? Has Klaus ever lost one for instance?"

Sandy Kent stared at him a bit suspiciously for a moment. Then she shrugged her shoulders and said, "Not that I recall."

Her brusque response was followed by a brief but awkward silence. Seven felt he'd better conclude his attempt at spying. "Well, I'm only asking because I'll be spending some time around the place. Don't know about you, but I'm terrified of being bitten."

"You'd have to be pretty careless to get bitten," she said without emotion. "Like I said, there are firm safety rules in place and warning signs posted everywhere. Although we've obviously had a few mishaps."

"Like that poor maintenance guy I read about in the papers?"

"Listen," she affirmed, somewhat sternly. "Accidents can happen in *any* workplace. Ours are just a bit more dramatic."

It was obvious that Sandy was uncomfortable speaking about her work. She again changed the subject. "Tell me, Chris. How long will you need to complete your magazine research for the article?"

Now it was the dutiful secretary rather than the social butterfly that was doing some investigative legwork of her own. Seven sensed it immediately and decided to be vague. In truth, he wasn't actually sure how long he'd need for his *real* assignment. Her! It all depended on how much time it would take to exploit the very girl who was asking.
Looking up at her, he spoke with contrived ambiguity.

"Hard to say, Sandy. I can see already that there's a lot more to Dr. Braun's Center and his fine work. More than either I, or my editor, had first envisioned. So you'll probably have me on your hands for at least six to eight weeks."

Sandy smiled, genuinely pleased with his answer and excited at the prospect of having him around for a while. After a brief silence she once again steered the conversation in another direction; doing so when the restaurant's island musicians began playing a pleasing version of *Yellow Bird.* "I love that song, Chris. From now on, every time I hear it I'll think of you and this evening."

As Seven commented on how he too enjoyed the song, two waiters abruptly arrived with their steaming entrees. The moist, tasty Peking duck had a delectable flavor, with a slight smoked essence. And the excellent moo shoo pork, wrapped in its thin oriental pancake, was equally delicious.

Shortly after they finished dinner, they stood and walked away from the table. Sandy excused herself to the ladies' room and Seven likewise paid a quick visit to a nearby men's room. Once there, he discreetly performed the ingrained Super Stud tooth brushing routine in the silence of the deserted washroom.

As Seven stepped out of the lavatory his date also emerged. Winking at each other, neither one noticed the tall MiddleEastern man wearing dark sunglasses, quietly sitting at the restaurant's crowded bar. The tall man watched carefully as the attractive couple strolled to the valet stand and soon pulled away from the *Hawaii Mai.* Continuing to observe them from the bar window, Amir's mind fantasized with several malicious thoughts.

Taking the long way back on A1A, Sandy and Seven unhurriedly cruised to her apartment with the top down. Listening to soft rock music on the radio, the two talked freely about whatever popped into their minds. They had crossed the barrier of tense sociability into new friendship, and there was now no shoptalk. Twenty minutes later they arrived at Sandy's condo.

Seven accompanied her into the building and onto the elevator. Nothing much was said as they rode to the 14th floor in polite silence. After exiting the lift, and making the lengthy walk down the hall to her door, the Super Stud noticed that Sandy's knuckles were turning white as she gripped the handle of her small handbag. *This woman is frightened* he thought. *Perhaps the lingering effects of that incident in the parking garage? Or maybe she's worried that I'm expecting a 'payoff' for a night of wining and dining. How should I play this? Careful now, Seven. Don't rush it. You absolutely need this girl for your assignment. Don't risk losing her goodwill by being too aggressive. Play it cool. Just escort her to her door and say a courteous goodnight.*

"Would you like to come in for a minute? Coffee, or a nightcap?" she asked in an unsuccessful attempt to hide her anxiety. Seven again noticed the trembling hands.

"I'd better not, Sandy. I've got a really early wakeup call and a full day tomorrow. Thanks, though." His soft smile seemed to put her at ease and her face showed instant relief, as if an awkward weight had just been lifted from her shoulders.

She looked at him and spoke with gentleness and affection. "Thanks for a lovely evening, Chris. And thanks for being a gentleman. They're hard to find nowadays." Then, to his complete surprise, she put her arm around his neck, pulled him close, and kissed him passionately on the lips. The affection may have been impulsive, but the kiss was a curious combination of thanks, fear, and incredible sensuality. "Good night, Chris," she said and quickly closed the door.

Caught totally off guard, Seven tried to stammer out a hasty response but none came. He knew he should have expressed something, but before he could, she had vanished.

As he awkwardly stood facing the closed door, the stunned Super Stud could only whisper, "Good night, Sandy."

The following morning Christopher Seven arrived at the Miami Reptile Center for his first formal interview session with Klaus Braun. The smiling snake man greeted his young visitor cheerfully, informing him that he was delighted Seven would be with them for the next month or two. The Super Stud grinned inwardly, knowing it must have been Sandy who'd apprised her boss about it. He silently wondered if it had been an early morning or a late night phone call. Either way, Sandy Kent's duty as the ever loyal secretary was obviously still paramount to her.

Seven shrugged his shoulders. At least the positive thing was that Braun knew the journalist would be around awhile and apparently didn't seem to mind. "Yes," Seven confirmed. "Afraid I'm going to need more time than I thought on this thing. Hope you don't mind my being here longer than we all expected?"

"Not at all."

"Thanks, Doctor. And now, let's start, shall we?"

The counterfeit magazine writer took out his notepad and began with a line of simple yet proficient background questions. Forty minutes later, the session was brought to a sudden halt with the loud buzzing of Dr. Braun's intercom. The businesslike voice of Elsa Dykstra informed her boss that his two guests, scientists from Norway, had arrived and were waiting in the conference room. "Thank you, Miss Dykstra." Braun looked up, apologetically. "Sorry, my boy, but duty calls. I've got to get to my meeting."

Suddenly Seven had a thought. It was a long shot, and rather bold, but worth a try. "Dr. Braun, would it be possible for me to sit in on some of your meeting? It would make great copy for the article. Your conferences with some of the world's top scientific minds."

Although Seven's request was logical for any diligent reporter, Braun looked at him rather suspiciously for a moment. He then relaxed. "Afraid not, my boy. We'll be discussing some confidential data and formulas, and my guests might be uncomfortable with an outsider in the room taking notes. I'm sure you understand?"

"Of course. Just thought it would make for interesting copy. Sorry I asked."

"Don't worry about it. You're just trying to do your job." Klaus Braun suddenly beamed with inspiration. "Hey, maybe you've got something there! Perhaps it would indeed be helpful if you observe and write about some of my various roles. You know my outside lectures and business trips. I think my public should read about those as well."

My public, Seven mused, silently. *This snake guru actually thinks he's a celebrity playing to an adoring audience. What an ego!*

"Tell you what," said Braun, "In two weeks I leave on a ten-day lecture trip to Nassau. Paradise Island, more specifically. It's not really a pleasure trip or vacation, although it will be held at the renowned *Atlantic Club*, perhaps the world's most exclusive resort. I'm scheduled to give several talks there on how certain venoms can reduce pain. I've done lectures at this hotel for the past six years. They're a good way to drum up publicity for the Reptile Center and also a good means of getting large contributions to my various charities. Since the resort's clientele are mostly millionaires. My appearances, and the subsequent publicity about them, are likewise advantageous to the hotel, of which I happen to be part owner."

Braun forced a brief smile before continuing, "We do this Paradise Island exhibition every year. And right after my week of lectures in Nassau, I always host our annual employee *'Thank you weekend'* in the Bahamas. We alternate between the day and the nighttime employees, and this year it's the nightshift's turn to come. Our corporate weekend party is held on my own private island. A small isle I purchased in the Bahamas called Royal Keys. It's one of those tiny, deserted 'out-islands' located in the Exuma Sound. I acquired it from the Bahamian government five years ago and built it up primarily for these types of company get-togethers. Although we also keep a small staff there year round for research work."

Dr. Braun shrugged his shoulders apologetically. "Afraid I can't invite you to our corporate weekend party, but we have a very firm rule about 'employees only'. Absolutely *no* exceptions. Yet I'm sure you'd enjoy my lecture week on Paradise Island, and also get some good background for your magazine piece." Braun smirked, derisively. "And since Miss Kent is also coming along for my secretarial needs, you could continue her companionship as well. So, what do you say?"

Seven was inwardly elated. This was an opportunity too good to miss. An excellent means to keep tabs on Klaus Braun, and likewise, a perfect opening to mingle with his Super Stud target, Sandy Kent. The private island outing for Braun's nightshift might also prove important if the G5 agent could somehow find a way to sneak into it. Mindful of not appearing overanxious, Seven seemed to carefully weigh his decision. "Well, my editors might have some questions about it. But if you need a quick answer, I'd say, yes, count me in, doctor."

"Fine then," Braun replied, doing so in his usual bullying manner of assuming things were settled. "Now if you'll excuse me, I really must get to that meeting." He paused a moment, then added, "And, Mr. Seven. Please give some final thought to our proposed arrangement. Like I've been telling you, the Lafitte sword deal won't be on the table much longer. I'll need a flattering magazine piece ASAP if it's going to do me any good."

"I'll give it my immediate attention", Seven assured, now thinking of what he'd overheard hiding in the closet."

And with that, the two men shook hands and parted company.

~

The next morning was a picture perfect Florida Saturday, and Seven and Sandy's jogging date turned out to be really special. Like Seven, Sandy was a skilled and tireless runner, and he laughingly joked about not being able to keep up with her. Later that evening they enjoyed an intimate meal at a romantic Italian eatery in Delray, where the homemade *spaghetti carbonara* was divine. No cream at all, and not overly eggy or sauced too thick. And with just enough pancetta.

After another convertible ride along the beach, the couple returned to her place for a nightcap. This time, it was Seven who kissed her first, doing so gently over a cognac in her apartment. Sandy showed none of the nervousness of their previous date, and the long kisses that followed were romantic, sensual and warmly affectionate.

Although it easily could have, nothing more physical happened. This was partly due to the Super Stud's practiced strategy of *teasing a target*. Holding back' to gain the trust and longing of an assigned female quarry. This teasing technique had been taught to all of the Studs by a brilliant female psychologist from Quebec. Seven grudgingly admitted, however, that perhaps this time it was *he* who was feeling teased, as his growing desire for Sandy was hard to ignore.

~

The next two weeks seemed to fly by, and Seven and Sandy spent a great deal of time together as their relationship grew in leaps and bounds. Throughout all of it, the G5 operative knew instinctively that his target was falling for him. Yet he had to admit that he was likewise falling for her. And, though these encounters with Sandy were personally pleasurable, they were nonetheless professionally disappointing. Nothing really substantive had been learned about Klaus Braun, any missing snakes, or Braun's operation. The doctor's attractive assistant was still proving to be ever faithful and discreet, especially whenever Seven asked about Dr. Braun. The frustrated Super Stud realized tomorrow's upcoming trip to Nassau might be his final chance to *turn* her, well aware that he'd *really* have to initiate the charm there.

While packing his suitcases on this foggy Thursday, May 5th evening, in preparation for tomorrow's flight to Nassau, Seven felt deep personal guilt. He was mainly depressed by his failure to garner any helpful leads on the New Ripper serial killer. His remorse had actually begun four days earlier, after another hideous murder had taken place during the May 1st night. This one near a deserted parking lot in Dania, a mile or so from the Fort Lauderdale airport.

The Ripper's latest victim, a white male from Ohio, had been butchered beyond recognition as he made his way back to his rented car. This, after a visit to an all-night strip club. The victim's head had been decapitated from the rest of the mutilated body, and his fingers and ears were viciously sawed off and stuffed into the mouth of the detached head. Like all of the other victims, his eyes had been surgically removed from their sockets.

The details of this horrific crime, relayed to Seven by FBI agent Jack Hanover, had been ghastly. While he listened to them on his security coded Smartphone, Seven felt genuine shame at not coming up with any clues that might have somehow prevented the butchery.

Despite nothing of real substance to report, the Super Stud was still keeping in constant communication with his own headquarters as well as with the FBI through Hanover. He supplied both bureaus detailed, though superficial written reports, playing down most of what he had heard while hiding in Dr. Braun's conference room closet. Casually summarizing his wide-ranging thoughts, Seven averted any premature dramatics by low keying the same subdued 'pharmaceutical scam' story. Now, as he neatly placed the final items into his two suitcases, he silently wondered if he'd been too cavalier about the whole thing.

Finished with his packing, thoughts of Klaus Braun soon flooded his brain, and the secret agent began speculating about sneaking onto the doctor's private Bahamian island party for this upcoming nightshift gathering. *Perhaps it might be doable*, Seven reflected, wondering what Dr. Braun was up to at the moment.

Had Christopher Seven known Braun's actual plans for this dark, murky night, he would have been thoroughly repulsed. For the malevolent snake man, along with fifty or so of his nightshift Satanists, were about to commence with one of their brutal ceremonial midnight punishment sessions.

Braun's security department had finally caught up with the second half of the guilty employee duo, the pair who had foolishly taken a bribe to recommend industrial spy, Ken Fusco. Tonight, the second guilty man, Frank J. Stevens, would pay dearly for that indiscretion, just like his late partner in crime, Santos Alverez, had. Pay for it with his life via an excruciating and terrifying death!

At exactly 11:45 p.m. all the lights of the Reptile Center dimmed slowly. Gas-lit poles were then simultaneously lit by six robed satanic disciples, illuminating the immediate area in an eerie amber hue. As a lone human howl was heard baying at the moon, the six robed figures, dressed in ghoulish black and white skeleton outfits, slowly made their way out to a large platform that had been hastily constructed for tonight's ceremony. This temporary staging platform, which would be completely disassembled before Braun's daytime workers arrived the following morning, had been put up in the Center's Croc Garden; a separate zoo section where Dr. Braun's largest reptiles were housed. It was in this area that the biggest and most ferocious beasts of the doctor's reptilian empire lived; the huge saltwater crocodiles from Australia, several massive Florida alligators, and the most venerated and dreaded of them all, the sinister Komodo dragon! It was directly over the dragon's enclosure where the six satanic disciples now stood, glancing down at the monster's pen and the sizable audience gathered in front of it.

All of them were intensely observing the Komodo, a prehistoric looking beast that was the most feared and savage creature in the entire park. The Komodo dragon was also the most revered in the realm of Satanist culture and worship, the 'sacred dragon of Lucifer'. In fact, it was to this very beast that the severed eyes of each new Ripper victim were usually fed, in the hopes of gaining a special blessing from the Satan's *Dark World*.

Weighing in at nearly 300 pounds, the mighty Komodo was a virtual killing machine, a powerful creature armed with huge razor-sharp claws and piercing, serrated teeth, which it used to rip apart prey with amazing tenacity. These teeth also injected a virulent, poisonous saliva and venom, making the creature's bite particularly dangerous. The attack of this fearless and deadly beast was nearly unstoppable, especially when it went into its legendary 'feeding mode'. Once in that agitated state, it was said to eat anything and everything that came near it in the wild, including the occasional human.

Accordingly, at special nightshift inner-circle sacrifice ceremonies, Dr. Braun and his Yozem high priests sometimes fed it human body parts, mainly legs and arms they had obtained from unscrupulous medical centers or old-age homes via sizable bribes. At times, when the debauchery sunk to horrific depths, live human sacrifices were likewise fed to it in hopes of getting a special satanic blessing. These unfortunate screaming victims were generally homeless vagrants, found for the occasion in back alleys by Braun's roving henchmen.

A few moments later, a terrified naked prisoner was being dragged onto the stage by three armed guards. Klaus Braun and his satanic High Priest of the Yozem, a menacing looking cleric clad in black leather and a demonic mask, also walked out onto the podium. At the sight of them, the fifty devil worshippers below started singing a strange, melancholy hymn in callous anticipation. Upon hearing the familiar death song, the trembling captive began crying in fear. It was a scene straight out of hell and Braun and his cleric reveled in all of it.

Grinning widely, Braun yelled out, "Fellow Satanists of the Yozem, may I please have your attention?" The audience instantly grew silent. "Please direct your concentration on the sacred beast below. This creature is the great Komodo dragon, specifically, *Varanus Komodoensis*, the largest of the monitor lizards. More importantly, it is the revered dragon of Lucifer, the Dark One's noble assassin described in our ancient scrolls."

Abruptly, and with a particularly cold and vicious glare, Klaus Braun and his bizarre high priest then turned their attention to the quivering prisoner. The robed Priest of the Yozem, looking much like the grim reaper in his heinous facial mask, walked over toward the captive, and loudly announced through his wireless microphone.

"This worthless specimen of a human being in front of you is Frank Stevens. Our security people caught up with Mr. Stevens right before he was set to flee the country. This fool dared to betray us and he will now be dealt with." The cleric again glared at the prisoner and gave the final order. "Prepare the prisoner's body!"

Next, in one last preparatory task, the security men primed their pleading prisoner for his punishment. They reached for a small bucket containing a mushy, reddish substance. This gooey concoction was a mixture of blood and offal from several recently slaughtered chickens, and its pungent odor permeated the air, greatly exciting the giant reptile that waited in the pen below. The beast's senses were now awakened, as an aroused Komodo could literally smell blood a mile away. Using paint brushes dipped into the chicken offal, not unlike preparing a turkey for Thanksgiving dinner, the guards basted Stevens' naked body liberally with it.

Seeing the preparation was finished, the cleric slowly nodded his head to the guards. With sadistic grins on their faces they hoisted and flung the thrashing body of Frank Stevens into the dragon's compound below.

The victim hit the ground hard with a hollow sound, the fall bringing fresh blood from his body. Almost instantly the huge lizard began pacing wildly in small circles knowing there was food about. The snorting reptile was now fully into feeding mode, its brain commanding the creature to seek and devour the prey. Stevens, lying prone, and facing the beast, was a terrified front-row spectator to the dragon's newfound excitement.

With a force much like that of a great shark, the powerful reptile grabbed its victim and sunk its huge teeth into Stevens' right side! In one vicious maneuver it violently began ripping and tearing flesh and body parts from the prisoner's naked body. The crowd roared with perverted glee! Now, not even the cheers of the throng could cover up the wails of the dying man. His piercing screams of agony, along with the sight of the dragon's attack, whipped the satanic mob into even greater frenzy!

Moments later, the savagery was over. The Komodo had eaten most of Steven's body in just three horrific minutes, swallowing the victim via several huge gulps.

As the nightshift audience reluctantly dispersed, one of the most violent and bloody satanic punishment sessions ever witnessed was complete. The iniquitous Dr. Klaus Braun smiled satisfactorily, knowing he'd exacted a cruel triple play. His just completed revenge on Frank Stevens, his past killing of Steven's guilty partner, Alverez, and the death of the snooping spy, Ken Fusco. Braun had orchestrated all three of these horrific deeds with the help of his beloved reptiles, utilizing the deadly Taipan, the agonizing puff adders, and tonight, the ferocious attack of the Komodo dragon. These creatures had not disappointed him. They had indeed been his noble assassins.

Chapter 28

Welcome to Paradise

The gleaming white 757 slowly made its way across the tarmac and rolled to a stop at American Airlines Gate 14. Happy to be back on the ground again, Christopher Seven made his way through the terminal at Nassau's International Airport in New Providence. Approaching the baggage area, he saw a sign that read, *Welcome to Paradise* and hoped it was prophetic.

Klaus Braun's sizeable contingent, mainly scientists and security men, had taken nearly all of the airplane's first-class section, making Seven wonder why so many people were required for a simple week of lectures. Dr. Braun's elderly father was also onboard, something that also seemed a bit puzzling. As for all of the other nightshift workers still in Florida, Sandy had casually mentioned that they'd be transported to *Royal Keys,* Braun's private Bahamian island, in just a few more days. Getting there via chartered seaplanes from Miami.

Along with the usual hassles of the flight itself, the morning had already been a busy one for Seven. An hour before his 8:00 a.m. airport limo arrived, he received a phone call from Jack Hanover. Jack had given him the name of a Cuban fisherman, a part-time FBI operative currently living in the outskirts of Nassau.

"Eduardo Valdez is a good man and could be of use to you in Nassau, Chris," Hanover had informed. "He's semi-retired now, and from what I hear, it's been tough going for Eduardo lately. Troubles with his daughter and a few financial setbacks as well. Despite all that, Ed's always willing to help, so I phoned him. Mentioned a bit about you and said you might be in touch. Valdez currently runs a small charter fishing boat near the pier, so using him should still allow you to stay within your cover. Look him up. You never know. A willing ally might be useful down there. He knows the area like the back of his hand."

After retrieving his luggage from the carousel, Seven politely informed the waiting Klaus Braun that he preferred to ride to the hotel alone rather than in one of Braun's six rented limousines. "If you don't mind, Doctor, I'd like to see some of the island on my own this afternoon. I'll catch up with you at the resort a bit later."

"See to it that you do," Braun gruffly ordered. "I'm throwing a welcome party in my penthouse at three o'clock sharp. There'll be a few VIPs there and some other people you should meet. They'll be able to give you more background for your story."

Great, thought Seven. *More propaganda from Braun's trained shills. Oh well, it's got to be done.* And with that the Super Stud made his way to the outside taxi stand.

~

Seven's leisurely sightseeing ride on the way to the elegant Atlantic Club Hotel was calm and relaxing. The driver, a friendly and informative Nassau native, pointed out the sights, doing so in his charismatic accent. They toured Front Street and Cable Beach, observed the straw market by the cruise ship pier, and then rode up Bay and Shirley Streets. Eventually making their way toward the hotel, they drove over a long elevated bridge, one of the two one-way structures that were the only way to and from Paradise Island. After paying the toll, the taxi passed several stylish hotels, the most impressive being an enormous canal lined pink resort.

"Dat's dah *Landis* Hotel," said the cabby. "All dah celebrities stays in their famous bridge suite. Dat costs em eight grand a night."

"Bit out of my league," grinned Seven. "Tell me. What do you hear about a private Bahamian out-island called *Royal Keys*?"

The cabby showed the whites of his eyes and his face reflected genuine fear. He replied guardedly. "Me hears all sorts of tings 'bout Royal Keys. But I don't knows if dey's true or not. Dat's a place peoples shouldn't go." After that the driver clammed up and they rode the rest of the way in silence.

Ten minutes later, they pulled up to the beautiful *Atlantic Club*, considered to be one of the most lavish hotels in the world. Seven thanked and paid the taxi driver and then made his way to the welcome desk.

"Yes, sir, Mr. Seven," said the amicable young brunette from behind the reception counter. She eyed him, unabashedly. "I see you're with Dr. Braun's party. We've got you in bungalow 18."

As Seven and the bellman entered the exquisite 'bungalow', which in reality was a small private home, the impressed agent was truly awed by its opulent luxury. After a soothing shower in the cavernous marble bathroom, followed by his required Super Stud hygiene routines, he dressed for the party, choosing a stylish light blue double-breasted blazer and white slacks. With it he wore an open-collared white shirt, knowing that ties were never worn on the island. It was now going on three o'clock, time to make his way to Braun's penthouse, cottage number 1, for the welcome festivities.

Upon entering Dr. Braun's enormous chalet, the agent was amazed at both its size and extravagance. It had to be five times the space of Seven's. As the Super Stud tried to observe some of the party guests, a booming voice, accompanied by a hard slap on his back, startled him. "Ah, there you are, Seven" greeted Klaus Braun. "Glad you're here. I trust your accommodation is satisfactory?"

"Absolutely fantastic, Doctor. You've got a fine little palace here yourself. This chalet is absolutely incredible."

Braun grinned pompously. "Rank does have its privileges, as they say." He then called out to a waitress who was passing by with a tray filled with glasses of chilled champagne. "One second, young lady. A glass of *Dom Perignon* for my friend here, if you please." Dr. Braun handed a glass to Seven, took one himself, and continued his welcome. "There's caviar, lobster, shrimp, and hot filet mignon. Enjoy yourself, Mr. Seven. I'll send a few folks over to you later who'll tell you and your magazine what a great guy I am." Braun barked out a laugh. "Now, if you'll excuse me, there are some guests I must say hello to." With that, he nimbly made his way to the other side of the massive suite, greeting everyone he passed.

Seven took a sip of the Dom and found it ice-cold and truly superb. Casually strolling to the edge of the living room to get a clearer view of the guests, the G5 agent observed everything with a professional eye. He was about to contemplate the huge food table set up along the far wall, when Sandy Kent entered the room, arm-in-arm with the senior Mr. Braun. She carefully guided the frail old Floda to a chair near the back of the living room.

Sandy looked magnificent in a tight fitting red dress. Her hair was alluringly parted to the side, and her radiant face looked exceptionally beautiful. Seven noted that many of the men, particularly the hotel executives, couldn't help but stare at Dr. Braun's stunning assistant. For a brief moment a wave of jealousy came over him.

From his vantage point against the wall, the Super Stud took it all in, including Klaus Braun's aged father, Floda, who was now sitting on a plush sofa in the back of the room. Seven wasn't sure what to think about the old man or the secrecy surrounding him. Just where in the scheme of things did this octogenarian fit in? And then there was the Martin Bormann thing. Could this feeble old coot, via some type of experimental drug, really be the celebrated war criminal? Could the Nazis actually have found an age inhibitor, and was this elderly man, Floda, proof of it? If so, what about Klaus? Did any of this relate to the snake man's schemes or was it merely just coincidence? Before he could consider all the possibilities Seven's brainstorming was ended by the sexy, pleasing voice of Sandy Kent.

"Hi, Chris. Glad you made it."

"Wouldn't miss it for the world, Sandy. Good food, expensive champagne, and now a beautiful gal greeting me on a tropical island. What could be better?" She reacted to his playful question with a sardonic grin as they clinked glasses. Seven then commented, "I must say, Klaus is in rare form. Quite the perfect host. Who are those two men he and his father are talking to?"

Sandy looked over at them. "Oh, that's Dr. Neil Gustaff and Dr. Walter Schilling from Norway. They're two of the foremost nuclear physicists in the world. About six months ago, they began a working relationship with Dr. Braun. Something to do with nuclear medicine. I've only met them a couple of times. Seem like nice fellows. Apparently, we're going to be working with them on an upcoming project. That's why they're here. Klaus has scheduled several working conferences with people he's invited on this lecture trip. Including you. Dr. Braun is like that, you know. Combines business with pleasure whenever possible and always picks up the tab when doing so. He's a very generous and thoughtful man."

"He certainly is," smiled Seven, desperately trying to discern what possible connection there could be between nuclear science and deadly snakes. He also wondered if the involvement of these two scientists had anything at all to do with Braun's Operation D. *Better get all this off to headquarters as soon as I can. Perhaps they can check out those Norwegians through Interpol.*

Sandy took him by the arm. "Like to meet them, Chris?"

"Sure. Might get an angle or two for my article."

They walked over to the scientists who had left Braun and were now standing alone. Sandy introduced them. "Christopher Seven, this is Dr. Walter Schilling and Dr. Neil Gustaff."

Walter Schilling grinned a cheery hello. "So you're the young reporter who's going to make Klaus a star."

Seven grinned back. "Oh, he's *already* a star, Dr. Shilling. My job is to make him an even *bigger* star."

Everyone laughed, just as a waitress approached and offered them all a hot hors d'oeuvre. The Super Stud then gently began probing the two doctors under the guise of a mild interest in science. "Tell me, gentlemen. It's quite interesting, your working with Dr. Braun. Although I can't fathom what nuclear physics has in common with cobras or coral snakes?"

"Oh, you'd be surprised, my good man," Dr. Schilling quickly answered, as if he'd been expecting the question. "Nuclear science actually plays quite a large role in many areas of our daily lives. Take medicine and pharmaceuticals for instance, Dr. Braun's field." Walter Schilling smiled politely. "I'll try to explain it in layman's terms so I don't lose you." He smiled again. "Without revealing any top secrets, I can tell you that Klaus is working on something with us right now. You see, in today's medicinal world, doctors frequently prescribe radioactive medication, things like radioiodine for instance. That's been used for certain thyroid problems, specifically, Graves' Disease."

Seven nodded his head as the Norwegian further explained, "Dr. Braun is currently experimenting with a new radioactive formula for the thyroid, one which contains minute quantities of certain snake venoms. We're hoping that his new formula will do the same thing as present medications, that is, shrink any problems. But if Klaus' theories are correct, his venom-based radioactive derivative could be cheaper and safer in the long run. If Dr. Braun is successful, it will be of huge benefit to all. And Neil and I would be proud to be part of it."

Christopher Seven had to admit that this Norwegian nuclear

scientist had just given a very sound and innocuous reason for his connection with Braun. *Could this be all there was to it?* Seven's musing was cut short by a beaming Sandy Kent. "That's Dr. Braun for you. Always doing things for the benefit of mankind."

"Absolutely," echoed Dr. Gustaff. "Our firm in Oslo has already started working with him, using some of the radioactive characteristics we've isolated from present thyroid medication. Hopefully, this will help Dr. Braun with his venom derivative."

"There are also a few other exciting prospects that Klaus has in the hopper," added Dr. Schilling. "Things he'd like us to contribute to as well. Cancer-fighting drugs, better nuclear-stress testing, and other potential venom radioactive cures, to name a few. Of course most of the details are classified so I can't really elaborate. Yet, as you can see. Nuclear science and venomous reptiles could indeed work hand in hand for many exciting advances."

"That is," added his colleague, Dr. Gustaff, "If Klaus can get that additional funding he needs from the US Senate."

Seven grinned inwardly at this obviously rehearsed attempt at pandering, just as the two Norwegian scientists waved to someone across the room and politely took their leave. Sandy grabbed Seven by the arm again and led him toward the rear of the penthouse. "Come on, Chris. Let's go out on the patio."

Once outside, the Super Stud looked at his beautiful target and began concentrating on the mission. "You know, Sandy, Mr. Braun senior seems like a nice old man, but isn't it a bit risky for Klaus' father to be making a trip like this?"

Sandy shrugged her shoulders and replied, "I guess Klaus feels his dad doesn't have too many more years left. So why not let him enjoy one nice vacation before it's too late? The old man's personal physician was brought along as a precaution as well."

"I don't know, Sandy. If he were my father, I wouldn't let him come, even *with* his private physician here. It just seems careless. I wonder if Klaus knows what he's doing."

The ploy worked, hitting Sandy square in her resolute loyalty to her boss. "Listen, Chris, Dr. Braun knows his father better than anyone. Along with constant medical care, Klaus has been treating his dad with a special vitamin formula called *Vitas M*. The old guy's been taking it for years. It's done wonders for him, increasing his movement and energy a great deal. I'm sure Floda will be just fine during his stay on Paradise Island. So, despite what you apparently think, Dr. Braun knows *exactly* what he's doing."

"Vitas M?" Seven asked, quizzically. "Never heard of that one. And I've researched almost all of Klaus's products for my story."

"The Vitas M treatment I mentioned is not for general sale. It's one of Klaus' *private* formulas. Apparently the therapy isn't for everyone. And please, what I've just told you is *not* for publication."

"I understand, Sandy. But I'd surmise from your answer that this Vitas M thing is still in the experimental stage." Seven shook his head. "So Klaus' old man is sort of a human guinea pig, huh?" Seven knew he was pushing her hard and she indeed responded irately.

"Dr. Braun doesn't *use* human guinea pigs! The treatment obviously helps Mr. Braun senior. And for your information, it also helped keep my mother alive an extra two years." She glared at him, crossly. "I think I need some more champagne." Retreating back inside, the fuming secretary made her way to the rolling bar, where the waiter promptly served her another. Hastily grabbing it, she then stomped out of the party.

Christopher Seven should have been troubled by her reaction, but instead he was justly satisfied with what he'd uncovered. Information on Klaus Braun's private vitamin treatment might be significant, particularly as it pertained to the old man, Floda. As Seven watched Sandy angrily exit Dr. Braun's penthouse chalet, he made a mental note to try and find out more about this mysterious Vitas M formula. It just could be a secret *fountain-of-youth* formula developed during World War II by a group of Nazi butchers!

Chapter 30

Decisions on the Beach

The following morning, a gloriously sunny Sunday, Seven attended the 9:00 a.m. church service at the *Paradise Island Calvary Chapel* located just down the road from the resort. The congregation was made up mostly of native islanders, with very few tourists in it. As always, Christopher Seven could never figure out why so many blessed vacationers, especially those affluent enough to afford the top hotels, didn't bother to spend a few moments in church or synagogue to thank God for their good fortune. *Oh well,* he mused. *His was not to judge.*

Buoyed by post-worship joy, and by the beautiful morning outside, Seven's step was lively and swift as he walked back to the hotel. Upon entering his bungalow he sent a quick email to headquarters, and then phoned the resort's front desk to procure a taxi to the *Tako Karate Center* on Front Street, Nassau's only martial arts academy. Here he spent the next hour practicing defensive moves with the muscular black belt instructor, and was back in his hotel room at 12:30, knowing he was scheduled to pick up Sandy at 1:00 p.m. for a day at the beach.

Quickly showering again, he changed and called Sandy's cottage. Her excited voice thrilled him. A bit embarrassed by her outspoken, alcohol-induced confession of love from last night, she now awkwardly tried to make light of it.

"Listen, Chris, last night I had a few troubling things on my mind. I also had way too much to drink and I might have . . ."

"Forget it, Sandy. The entire evening was grand. We were *both* a bit 'tipsy", he fibbed. "Anyway, I'm on my way to your place to pick you up for our swim."

Thirty minutes later, their dilapidated, old Pontiac taxicab, driven by a rotund character who called himself 'Big Pants', pulled up to *Secret Cove,* a secluded beach Seven had read about in *Travel & Leisure.* Sandy and Seven loved it immediately. It had white, powdery sand, sparkling turquoise water, and a superb private setting. The cabby informed them it was the best beach in all of Nassau.

"I can't wait to finally get into the water," Sandy exclaimed. "I've been waiting three days to swim in it."

"The water in the Bahamas is some of my favorite anywhere," Seven replied. "It's such a bright turquoise and crystal clear. Far better than Hawaii. Of course, the true Caribbean, particularly the British Virgin Islands along with St. John's Trunk Bay and St. Maarten's Mullet Bay are great too." He grinned. "And even without the name, I also like *Seven* Mile Beach in the Caymans. I've never been to Tahiti, but some people think that's the best."

Sandy shook her head. "Can't see how it can be any bluer or nicer than this, Chris." She waved him on to follow her into the sea.

The rest of the afternoon was absolute bliss. They swam, sunned, and occasionally kissed, sandwiching all three things in between some delicious piña coladas purchased at the tiny beach bar which had just opened. An hour before they were scheduled to leave, the Super Stud agent knew he'd have to get down to business. While he and Sandy sat side by side in rented beach chairs, Seven casually rolled over to face her.

"You know Sandy, it's hard to imagine that while we're here safely enjoying ourselves, people in south Florida are still coping with a vicious serial killer. It seems so unfair."

"I guess," Sandy answered, still uneasy with that topic after overhearing Dr. Braun's revelation regarding the Ripper's snake.

"To tell you the truth," Seven continued, "I was hoping they'd have caught him by now. But the *USA Today* claims the authorities are still baffled. Apropos, I just received a call on my cell phone this morning from a good friend in the FBI's media relations department. He said, off the record, that the Feds are desperately trying to make some type of Ripper connection with that poisonous snake." Again repositioning his body, Seven casually asked, "I wonder what Klaus thinks about it? His being a noted authority on reptiles and all."

The G5 operative watched her expression with a professional eye. She seemed deep in thought. *What's going on in that mind,* Seven silently asked himself. *Does her thinking concern me at all?*

Yet for once, Sandy wasn't thinking about Christopher Seven, the good looking man with whom she now shared the beach. At the moment, her thoughts were squarely on her employer, Dr. Klaus Braun, and the troubling cobra statement she'd heard him make.

Sandy sighed, thinking on it again. Dr. Braun's shocking cobra declaration, coupled with the curious termination of her 'snake logging' duties. Duties that had suspiciously ended almost *exactly* when the Ripper murders began. It now had her extremely worried. Could there be a menacing connection between the two? The cobra and the snake logs? If so, she'd have critical decisions to make, both about her boss and her career. Yesterday, when she overheard Braun say, 'No one will connect my cobra to the Ripper', whatever that meant, had made her put the two issues together. And when she did, a chilling sensation shuddered through her shapely body.

Obviously her secretive boss knew more about the serial murders than he was letting on. The Ripper had almost certainly gotten hold of one of Dr. Braun's snakes, and in all likelihood, the doctor was now trying to cover that fact up. Most likely to protect those repugnant reptiles of his. Yet Klaus Braun's incriminating cobra statement had been definite and clear, and Sandy couldn't dismiss her fears about it.

Christopher Seven instinctively sensed Sandy's growing uneasiness and knew it was time to act. There was no longer any way around it. Seven needed her help and some quick answers. He glanced over at the beautiful woman he'd been sent to captivate. Ironically the woman with whom he might be falling in love. He knew in his heart that there was integrity and goodness inside her, and the G5 operative now hoped his heart was correct. Yet this time, unlike all the others, it wasn't the suave Super Stud who finally decided, *now's the time.* It was simply a tender man praying his instincts were accurate.

"Sandy," he said in a tone she'd never heard him use before. "I'm going to ask you something now. And if I'm off base, just tell me and we won't speak of it again." She reached for his hand and held it tenderly, likewise knowing that a significant change was about to take place in their relationship. Something that transcended mere romance or physicality. She also knew that whatever he was going to ask of her would be coming from his heart and that she would unquestioningly help him if possible.

"Yes, darling?" Sandy asked, softly.

"I want you to trust me about something and it may not be easy for you. Yet it's very important Sandy, and it's simply got to be done."

"It's about Klaus, isn't it?"

Yes," he replied, somewhat surprised that she knew. "But how could you -"

"Never mind, Chris, I just do. As a matter of fact, I've had some private concerns about him myself. I've been meaning to speak to someone, but haven't been able to find the right person."

Confused, Seven gazed at her for a moment and then asked, "You remember my mentioning this FBI friend of mine?"

"Yes."

"Well, he knows I'm down here working with Dr. Braun and Braun's staff for my magazine. So, just this morning, he phoned, and asked a big favor of me. He wants me to somehow have a peek at that snake tracking file you mentioned last night, and then pass the information on to him." Seven held up a hand. "Not to hurt Klaus in any way, or anyone in Braun's employ. Simply to see if it could pertain to that Florida serial killer."

Sandy stared at him without expression. There was no trace of anger, suspicion, or even betrayal for what he'd just said to her, so the Super Stud slowly continued. "If the killing pattern stays the same, this Ripper maniac is going to strike again very soon. And despite what Klaus might have said to you, it almost certainly has to be one of Braun's snakes that the Ripper is utilizing. Quite possibly without Dr. Braun's knowledge. My FBI friend said that the venom found at several of the crime scenes was from a very rare cobra. Too unusual for some amateur pet owner to have hanging around."

"Go on," she said, still without emotion.

"If we could somehow check the dates in question from Dr. Braun's snake tracking log, and then get that data to the FBI, it might be of great help. Specifically any cobra information. Dr. Braun has adamantly refused to talk about his snakes with the authorities, which I believe is a terrible mistake on his part. So there seems to be no other way to check it out, other than someone doing it on the sly. I'd do it myself but Braun would never let me near the logbooks."

Sandy nodded. "Of course, Klaus certainly isn't suspected of being the killer. The Feds' only concern is where the snake is *now*. As of yet, they don't want to close down or arrest Dr. Braun."

Seven felt slightly guilty with some of his spiel, knowing full well that several agencies, including his own, were now gunning for her enigmatic boss; on several levels. "Anyhow, Sandy, I've been asked to help if I can and the only one I can trust around here is you." He looked directly at her, half of him as the blunt secret agent who merely wanted to use her. And the other half as someone who cared deeply for her. Either way, he hoped the decency within her might trump any overzealous loyalty to Klaus Braun.

After what seemed like an unending silence, Sandy finally responded. "If anyone else had asked me to help with something like this, I'd have been deeply offended. I'd quickly tell them where to get off. But somehow I know your concerns are genuine, Chris. To tell you the truth, I'm greatly troubled myself."

Sandy paused and glanced at Seven. She had recently begun to wonder if this handsome enigma of a man was indeed *'just a reporter'*. Possibly he was some type of police agent. One who could indeed cause problems or delays for Dr. Braun and the Reptile Center. Despite that, she now knew she'd do anything Seven asked of her.

"I trust you with all my heart, Chris." Holding his hand tighter, she looked at him longingly. "Whatever happens, I'm not afraid of the consequences or the future. That is, as long as you'll be with me through it. So I'll do whatever you ask."

Christopher Seven knew instinctively that this was the 'turn' moment for which his training had taught him to watch for. The critical instant when a Super Stud agent should begin to lay it on thicker in order to get a target's full compliance and admissions. Do so without remorse, using contrived, well-rehearsed fabrications. Like a phony marriage proposal. Or some exciting, yet bogus, talk about vacationing around the world together.

Seven silently asked himself, *should I try this now with Sandy? Convince this emotionally confused girl that I love her and then promise to take her away if she helps me?* Seven recalled similar cock-and-bull stories he'd told to other female targets around the globe. *No*, he decided. He wouldn't lie, for several reasons. *Real* love being one.

"Listen, Sandy, I care for you more than you'll ever know. But I can't honestly promise you that we'll always be together just because you might help me with this." As he heard himself speak these straightforward words, the Super Stud couldn't believe he'd mouthed them. "It's just that innocent people are being slaughtered every month and I think we should help if we can. There might not be anything at all in what we find. But if there is, and it leads to apprehending a crazed killer, it'll be well worth it."

Sandy smiled at his candor. "Let's hope so, Chris. But I honestly don't know if I can be of much help to you. You see, right around the time these Ripper murders began I was taken off my snake-monitoring duties. For some reason they were given to Elsa Dykstra. As a matter of fact, this job function change had me quite upset. It now has me extremely suspicious. I was thinking about it just a short while ago."

She shook her head and Seven keenly observed her while she spoke. "With regard to the New Ripper, Chris, or any connection to one of our snakes. I truly wanted to help Miss Swanson, that FBI girl. As well as all the other police officials who've asked me things. But Klaus was adamant that I shouldn't say much. He claimed that if I told them anything at all, the Center would be closed down for a long investigation. Something that would hinder our work and hurt a lot of ailing people. And I'd never want to do that."

Seven nodded his understanding, as Sandy added, "Yet I'm now certain that one of our cobras is somehow in the Ripper mix." She paused a moment, took a deep breath, and then admitted, "I – I overheard a few things yesterday. Maybe I should have told somebody about it, but I didn't." She again shook her head, this time in frustration. "I don't think Klaus understands how important it is to come clean if one of our snakes was illegally sold or stolen. Surely the police would understand if he just told them the truth." She looked up, hoping he'd empathize. "Perhaps Klaus is merely concerned about being shut down a while, with all this Ripper paranoia."

"Perhaps," replied Seven, knowing there was a lot more to it than that. "Is there any way you might be able to look at Elsa's most recent log sheets, Sandy? Say the last six months or so?"

She thought on it a moment. "Well, Dr. Braun always brings the snake logs with him whenever he travels. He likes to study them in his spare time. Although he almost always keeps those records locked up securely when he's not reviewing them."

Sandy reflected on it a bit more. "Klaus undoubtedly has the logbooks here in Nassau with him. I'd bet they're somewhere in our makeshift office over in his chalet. I might be able to have a quick look, should the opportunity present itself. The Doctor and I will be working together several times this trip. And he occasionally leaves me alone in the office. But I'd have to try peeking at the logbooks here in Nassau. *Before* he heads out to his island for this weekend's nightshift party. For Dr. Braun will undoubtedly take his files with him to Royal Keys as well." She frowned. "But Chris, I feel like such a Judas even thinking about it. It's like spying on your parents."

"I know it's awkward, Sandy. But it could lead the authorities to a vicious murderer. Obviously Klaus doesn't understand the gravity of it, so we'll have to do the thinking for him."

"I suppose so," she replied, apprehensively.

Just then they were interrupted by the loud exclamations of their stout taxi driver. "Times to go, folks."

As she got up off her beach chair, Sandy Kent wondered if anything in her suddenly mixed up world would ever be the same.

Chapter 31
The Plot Thickens

Christopher Seven spent the next few days dutifully writing his magazine piece and showing much of it to Klaus Braun for approval. The Super Stud had finally informed the snake man that he'd accept Braun's offer of the Lafitte sword, in exchange for a *'puff piece'* article. Accordingly Seven put in a few flattering paragraphs that Dr. Braun personally dictated. The G5 agent had come to the conclusion that *'being on the take'* would make his presence much more welcome, and might also allow him to stick around longer.

Wednesday evening, a balmy May 11th, Seven and Sandy enjoyed a relaxing candlelit dinner in a small Bahamian bistro near West Hill Street. Sandy gave him a friendly kiss of thanks when he dropped her off at her cottage around ten.

"Thank you for another beautiful dinner, Chris. And for again not bringing up my, uh, little alcohol-induced scene of a few nights ago." She giggled, girlishly. "Now that you've turned me into Mata Hari, I'd better stay sober. Speaking of that, I think I'm going to take my shot at spying sometime tomorrow afternoon. Klaus and I have one more dictation session left before he leaves for Royal Keys on Friday night. So this may be my last chance."

"Just be careful," said the anxious Super Stud, with genuine concern. He then made his way back to his own bungalow with a strange feeling of trepidation inside him.

~

The next afternoon, while Seven was playing three vigorous sets of tennis with the hotel's talented pro, Marv, Sandy Kent was in Dr. Braun's massive suite dutifully working with her boss. The makeshift office in which they labored was in the far corner of Braun's spacious bungalow, where she and the doctor had been toiling for almost two hours now. Braun had demanded two desks and a load of office equipment be brought there by his staff shortly after Braun's arrival on Paradise Island. The doctor's security squad had placed Braun's *personal* files in there as well, where it now remained under lock and key. This specially designed file cabinet was with Klaus Braun or one his henchmen, at *all* times, no matter *where* Braun traveled. Accordingly it had arrived on Paradise Island via private seaplanes, tightly guarded by four members of the nightshift's security squad. It was now situated directly behind the two office desks, where it remained all week, along with fax machines, computers, and copiers. Braun also wanted Rosier to secretly bring and install a 'state of the art' mini-cam, which Rosier did, neatly hiding most of the tiny security camera within the room's crown molding ceiling. It now covered the desks and all the file cabinets. "You can never be sure", Braun had sternly warned his security man.

As Sandy took down the doctor's lengthy dictation, her rapidly growing suspicions about him still troubled her. Braun had apparently held back everything of importance from her during the past six months, and this added to her qualms. *Could it somehow be tied into the snake/Ripper thing after all?* Following her recent talks with Christopher Seven, Sandy was almost sure of it.

Even without Chris asking her to, the last month or two, she'd privately been toying with a quick look-see through some of the doctor's records on her own, should the opportunity ever present itself. Klaus Braun's beautiful assistant wanted to see for herself what was *really* transpiring. For one thing, she certainly didn't want to be part of anything patently illegal. And if this was indeed the situation, she now had major choices to make. Including whether to stay or quit.

"Come on now, Miss Kent!" Dr. Braun barked, breaking off her thoughts. "Stop your daydreaming and pay attention! I need those Chicago files *now!* What's the matter with you today?"

"Oh, sorry" she mumbled. I'll get to them right away, Doctor."

Picking up the papers, and hurriedly placing them in order, Sandy handed her boss the thick folder just as the phone rang. She answered it promptly, not wishing to raise his ire any further. "Dr. Braun's suite. Miss Kent speaking."

"Sandra," said the masculine voice on the other end, "this is Dr. Rosella." Floda Braun's private physician sounded extremely worried and Sandy immediately wondered if Klaus' father was all right as the physician informed, "Floda came in here a short while ago for his afternoon checkup. I'm afraid there's been some complications. I need to have a word with Klaus *immediately.*"

"Certainly, Doctor. He's right here." Turning toward Klaus Braun she spoke slowly. "It's Dr. Rosella. He'd like to see you about Floda."

Practically ripping the phone from her hand, Braun quickly answered, "Yes, Rosella. What is it?"

"You asked me to check on your father's breathing, Dr. Braun."

"Yes?"

"Well, he's in my cottage right now and I'm afraid he's had a turn for the worse. Floda's breathing is extremely labored and his condition may be serious. You'd better come over right away."

"I'll be right there!" Klaus Braun's expression showed genuine apprehension. Leaping up from his desk he turned toward Sandy. "It's my father. He's taken very ill. I've got to go immediately. You stay here. Don't let anybody in, no matter *who* it is! I'll be back when I can." And, with that he ran out, slamming and locking the front door behind him.

Alone in Braun's vast bungalow, and worrying about frail old Floda Braun, ill down the street, Sandy sighed and slowly got up from her chair. While reaching over Klaus Braun's larger desk to pick up the Chicago papers, she noticed that the keys to his *restricted* file cabinet, his private papers, were surprisingly still in the keyhole of his confidential cabinet. In his excitement and haste to rush to his ailing father, Klaus must have forgotten to take his keys and locking up. This was something he'd never done before.

Sandy looked around the empty chalet and began to contemplate the unthinkable. Here was a golden opportunity! The chance to take a peek at Dr. Braun's hidden files and perhaps review the snake logs that Elsa Dykstra had taken over from her. Maybe it would throw some light on everything and reveal if Chris was right or not. *Yes,* thought Sandy, *a quick look may indeed uncover what Dr. Braun has delegated to Elsa, and why. It might also provide some answers as to the reason I've been steadily fazed out of the loop.*

For a brief moment Sandy felt a pang of guilt for even thinking of doing such an uncharacteristic thing. She felt much like a high school student deciding to cheat on an exam for the very first time. Yet Sandy knew this opportunity was just too good to pass up. Consequently, and for the first time in her life, Klaus Braun's loyal secretary decided to break her own steadfast rule and glance into someone else's personal papers. With her hands actually trembling, she unlocked Braun's private cabinet, using the main key that was dangling from it, and began her look-see. She did so with a strange feeling of foreboding, aware that her boss could come charging back into his cottage at any moment. If so, the uncomfortable and embarrassing result would truly be unthinkable! Nonetheless, Braun's heretofore devoted assistant slowly opened Braun's cabinet and took out the familiar red logbook.

Peering into the cabinet, she quickly sensed that something was amiss. In the same file space where the reptile tracking log was stored, there was a *second* one just like it. An exact duplicate! For some reason, there were now *two* sets of logbooks, one underneath the other. As she perused Elsa's *second* logbook, an identical looking snake tracking register, Sandy saw that it contained completely *different* entries and figures. Sandy Kent was totally at a loss. Dr. Braun had always insisted on only *one* fastidiously accurate log for his reptiles, and there had *never* been a second copy. This was the Center's singular bible and it only left the premises in Braun's briefcase, or under armed guard. What was this *second* logbook all about?

Sandy kept investigating. The duplicate logbook had a yellow note taped inside its cover. This yellow note, marked *Public,* was in Klaus Braun's familiar large handwriting. Leafing through the pages of both record books she recognized her own handwriting in book *one*, almost a year of her precise recordkeeping, comparing it with Elsa's new entries of the last six months. Glancing at book *two*, marked *Public*, Sandy could see that Elsa had obviously replicated it and, like Sandy's, that it exactly covered the last twelve months as well. Yet there was one glaring discrepancy; Elsa's recent entries in book two were far *different* from Sandy's book one.

The stunned Sandy now wondered which book contained the *real* snake movements and locations of the past twelve months. In her heart she already knew the answer. Book *two* with the public entries, the one Elsa Dykstra had done under Klaus's directions, was bogus! The snake movements shown in this book were undoubtedly fabricated, obviously meant to deceive the authorities. Or in the event the feds subpoenaed the log to view it. As for why Dr. Braun didn't want the *actual* movements of his reptiles seen? The answer was also clear. Braun was hiding something! There was no time now, but perhaps inside logbook two was the answer to any Ripper connection.

What's going on here? Sandy again asked herself. She then examined some of the file cabinet's other contents. The next folder she came across was even more puzzling. It contained various automobile invoices for recently purchased vans. Each one from *different* auto dealerships located up and down the Florida Coast. There were ten in all. Every purchase order was for a plain white cargo van. Yet strangely, instead of showing *Braun Industries* as the buyer, which was normal procedure, every new van order was in the name of Donald K. Gent, Dr. Braun's uncultured brute from nighttime security. *Why?*

For as far as Sandy could recall, all company vehicles had always been purchased at *Central Auto World* in Lake Worth. Why was Klaus buying trucks at *other* places? And, why were the vans in *Gent's* name?

Suddenly Sandy froze, hearing a noise coming from Braun's master bedroom! Her hand instinctively went to her mouth in shocked fear, knowing there was a separate back door in the bedroom. She called out, "Doctor? Dr. Braun?" Nothing but silence greeted her query. Sandy slowly turned around to look. Thankfully, no one was behind her yet, and the room was completely still. Save for the ticking of a small decorative wall clock.

Sandy frantically called out a second time. "Dr. Braun, is that *you?*" Again, there was nothing. She was about to get up and walk over to the bedroom, when the noise began again. This time she recognized it as only the loud, periodic compressor humming of a small refrigerator in the mini-bar of Klaus Braun's plush bedroom. It had just been her frayed nerves, or perhaps her guilty conscience, believing the sounds had come from another person. Greatly relieved, she sat back down in front of the filing cabinet and continued her foray, now sweating profusely. There was still no sign of Braun returning, so Sandy continued sifting through his papers.

She next came across a list of parking garages located throughout the United States. All of them were owned and operated by the *Keller Parking* chain, a nationwide parking consortium. Dr. Braun had circled several locales, including New York and Denver. There were others circled as well. Sandy had no clue as to what this meant. Shouldn't these rather mundane routines be in the hands of the doctor's large and very capable transportation department? She shrugged. The only clue to it all, if you could even call it that, was a large letter on top of the list. A large capital D. - *What does 'D' mean?*

The last file Sandy saw was in the distinctive handwriting of Elsa Dykstra. It was labeled, *Final Move - Prior to D.* Again, this was all gibberish to her. Numerous Swiss bank accounts were listed, along with a long directory containing the names of several key Braun employees. All of the names Sandy saw were from the nightshift - all except one - her *own!* Even more mystifying, after Sandy's name there was a large question mark, along with a handwritten notation, again in Dr. Braun's handwriting. It read, - *Personal decision - will advise.*

The whole thing was beyond her comprehension. Certainly nothing she'd ever been in on, or even heard being discussed. And heaven knows what this large letter D meant. *So much for still being an important and trusted worker for Dr. Klaus Braun*, Sandy mused.

Deciding not to press her luck, and expecting her boss to come barging in the front door at any time, Sandy closed all the file drawers, shut the cabinet, and left the keys dangling in the unlocked cabinet, exactly where they'd been. She then returned to her own desk and hastily began working on the Chicago papers.

Five minutes later, Klaus Braun returned to his chalet, looking greatly relieved. He glanced at Sandy and smiled as he spoke. "Father is fine now. He's sleeping under a nurse's care next door. He seems pretty much back to normal, thanks to Dr. Rosella."

"That's wonderful," Sandy replied, happy for the old man. She then held her breath, wondering how long it would take Braun to realize that he had absentmindedly left his keys hanging in the cabinet's lock. At first, it didn't appear he noticed them at all, as he merely sat back down behind his desk and wiped his brow.

"Dr. Braun," Sandy asked, trying to remain calm. "Do you want me to print those Chicago letters I've been working on?"

"No, they can wait. It's tough to concentrate now, after that scare with my father. Why don't we just knock off for today?"

"Very good, sir," Sandy replied, happy that her boss still hadn't observed the keys hanging from his file cabinet. She began to relax, thinking he might not even notice them till later. Her tranquility was short-lived. For just as she was getting up to leave, she saw Dr. Braun gaze over at his file cabinet for the first time and immediately spot the dangling keys. Grabbing them roughly, with a trace of self-directed anger, he locked the file doors. He then slid the keys into his pocket and his eyes slowly rose up to meet Sandy's. "One moment please, Miss Kent." A curious expression showed on Braun's hardened face. "Was anyone besides you in here while I was gone?"

"No, sir. I was alone the entire time, working on those letters you asked me to do. And you told me *not* to let anyone in."

His gaze held hers for a moment as he gauged the veracity of the statement. Then, as if divining her words to be true, Klaus Braun nodded. "Very well." He gave another angry glance at his cabinet.

"Is everything alright?" Sandy asked, timidly.

"Quite," Braun responded, confident that in all the years as his most loyal employee the always innocent and faithful Sandra Kent had never once betrayed him. "It's just that I must remember to discipline myself for an inexcusable lack in concentration. He smiled at her rather oddly. "Enjoy your evening, Sandra."

The snake man waited a few minutes for her to leave. Then, after reflecting a moment, he picked up his cellphone.

"Rosier?"

"Yes, Doctor."

"That video surveillance camera you people secretly set up in my suite. Is it operational yet?"

"Yes sir. It's been working perfectly since yesterday."

"Good. I want to review the tape of the last half-hour or so. Specifically my office and file areas.

Following the exhausting work session with Dr. Braun, complete with her nerve-wracking *spying* sortie into his private files, Sandy Kent was physically and emotionally drained when she met Seven for drinks later that evening. Nursing an apple martini, she moodily explained what her day of snooping had revealed. "There's no doubt that I'm being squeezed out, and no doubt about Klaus hiding things."

"Care to talk about it?" Seven gently asked.

She looked up at him. "For one thing, you were right about the snakes. Klaus is definitely covering up something. I discovered that there are now *two* logbooks. It's obviously being done to confound any potential inquires. I likewise learned that for some inexplicable reason there's a bunch of new vans secretly being purchased, as well as several listed parking garages. Beats me what it's all about. I was never informed about *any* of these this. And unless I read it wrong, there's apparently a big corporate move to a new location being planned. Something *else* I was never told about. Guess I'm out of the loop on everything now. Wouldn't be surprised if Klaus lets me go soon."

Seven squeezed her hand tenderly, hoping to console her. He then asked, "Did you run across anything utilizing the letter ***D?***"

"As a matter of fact I did." Sandy was surprised and a bit irritated that Seven was aware of it. Hearing that he, an absolute outsider, knew something about this mysterious letter D, while she herself was in the dark on it, seemed to increase her frustration. "I guess Klaus told you a lot more about his plans than he did me, Chris." Clearly upset, she filled him in on the rest of her findings.

Christopher Seven listened attentively, increasingly troubled by all he heard. Growing more concerned about everything, he nevertheless held back his mounting trepidation. The worried agent wanted to be absolutely certain that some of the disturbing possibilities he now suspected were even viable. Make sure he wasn't overreacting before upsetting Sandy or anyone else with them.

Of course, Seven would certainly mention all of this to G5 headquarters, putting a low-key, *wait-and-see,* spin on it like before. Time enough for the Super Stud to get even *more* tangible info and evidence from his Super Stud target, Sandy Kent.

As for what she'd *already* discovered, for all he knew these nondescript vans were just being used to deliver the bogus drugs to their territories. And regarding the quick getaway of Braun's nightshift workers, to a new, insulated location, Seven still suspected that some type of *Bernie Madoff* type scam was stirring. Only this time via *sham* pharmaceuticals. If that was the case, Braun's team would naturally want to get away swiftly, *before* the scandal unfolded. Yet, for the wily Braun to take this big a gamble, millions in profit had to be at stake.

The secret agent nervously wiped his forehead. If Dr. Braun was indeed planning some hugely profitable drug swindle on an unsuspecting public, Christopher Seven hoped that Sandy wouldn't be implicated or associated with any of it. For it was almost certain that the FBI, the Justice Department, and several other government agencies would soon be converging on Braun Pharmaceuticals. In fact, Seven himself would be recommending they do just that. But *not* until he found out for sure what was being planned, and where the feds should look for solid evidence. There was still plenty of time left to foil Klaus Braun's plans. Seven's closet foray had revealed Dr. Braun's target date as July 4th. Today was only May 12th. Operation D was still nearly two months away. Seven just hoped the FBI, and the other Federal agencies, would allow him the time needed to stop Braun.

Reflecting further on what Sandy had uncovered, the G5 operative silently began focusing on a potentially larger and much more sinister scenario. He shuddered uncomfortably and asked himself, *What if all this wasn't just a simple drug scam? What if there was something far more ominous in the wind?* He looked away from his beautiful target a moment, and contemplated the unthinkable.

For starters, what if Dr. Braun was part of some illegal weapons sale? With the appearance of the two Norwegian nuclear experts on the scene, supposing Braun and his cohorts were trading in armaments; or weapons-of-mass-destruction technology? Developing, and then selling them to America's enemies. Could those recently purchased company vans be part of some type of illicit shipping? Transporting weapon components over the border and then getting them to corrupt buyers overseas? It was a longshot for sure, but who *really* knew what went on at Braun's complex during the night?

Christopher Seven pondered these admittedly implausible and *unsubstantiated* possibilities, knowing it would be folly for one of the richest men in the country to sell his soul simply for more money. Yet somehow he knew that a man with Dr. Braun's bizarre eccentricities, and his propensity for dominance, definitely had something like this in him. The maddening part of it was that Seven, as the only government operative on the scene, just didn't know for sure.

The G5 operative nodded, resignedly. There was no doubt about it. He'd somehow have to clandestinely get onto Braun's island for the start of this nightshift weekend gathering. The doctor's private atoll would almost certainly be the outpost where Braun's covert operational planning would be discussed and formulated. One thing was certain. The mysterious nightshift team hadn't been flown down to Dr. Braun's private island merely for hotdogs on the beach.

Yes, Seven mused. *A quick spying foray to Klaus's island was the only option now.* As the anxious agent pondered this dangerous and perhaps reckless undertaking he again shuddered. *Oh well, no sense worrying about the risks. It has to be done. Hopefully this island espionage will prove more revealing than my closet escapade.*

Seven quickly but emphatically made up his mind about something else. Although Colonel McPhail, the FBI, and even the President, had left the ultimate decisions and timing of things up to Seven; if he found anything at all of a ominous nature being planned on Braun's island, it would definitely be time to call in the cavalry. To heck with his original assignment, and some Florida serial killer. He'd let the other agencies go after Dr. Braun, while he got himself, and hopefully Sandy too, safely away from all of it. There was still ample time and Seven again took solace that Operation D wouldn't begin until July 4th.

The Super Stud tenderly looked over at the beautiful girl sitting beside him, the one with whom he knew he was falling in love. What would this lovely young woman think if she knew why he'd been sent here from the start? And what would Sandy say if he revealed these new worries about Klaus Braun to her? Would she believe him, or would her admirable but misguided belief in her boss' altruistic work still be strong? Seven sighed. There was no sense telling her anything yet. All he needed to do now was to get to Braun's private island and find out what he could.

As per this shadowy island outpost, where Sandy informed the nightshift clan were now gathering, waiting for their esteemed leader to arrive from Paradise Island. Seven had already begun making tentative plans to sneak in. Earlier that afternoon he'd phoned Jack Hanover's Cuban friend, Eduardo Valdez. Valdez quickly agreed to take Seven over to Braun's Royal Keys Island via his charter fishing boat, landing the vessel on the far, uninhabited side of the island. Eduardo insisted that this was the only way to make sure Dr. Braun's well-armed sentries wouldn't spot them. The two men agreed to meet at Eduardo's home the following afternoon, to plan their covert trip.

Of course, this was something else Seven couldn't tell Sandy, for many reasons. Though he didn't like lying to her at this point, there seemed to be no choice. He'd just have to invent an excuse for being away during this upcoming weekend, although he knew she'd be keenly disappointed about it. Purposely avoiding her eyes, he guardedly began, "Listen, Sandy. I have to fly over to Turks and Caicos tomorrow. *Global* hired a private seaplane. I'll only be away for a few days, but it's got to be done. Some travel feature my editor wants me to handle for him. In the meantime, I want you to promise me that you'll stop spying on your boss, take no more chances with Braun's files, and simply do your job. Hopefully, I'll only be away 'til Monday."

"Be *away?*" she protested. "But Klaus likewise leaves for his private island weekend tomorrow. He's got a Friday evening flight so they'll be no one around to bother us the next three days. In case you've forgotten, those were supposed to be the three days you promised *me*. Days for you and I to enjoy here on Paradise Island."

"I know, Sandy, but I've got a better plan than that. Instead of you and me flying back to Florida with Dr. Braun on Tuesday, perhaps we could fly over to St. Barths for a week or so, on our own. I've been thinking about it all afternoon. It's only a short flight from here and I've got a buddy down there with a small boutique hotel in Gustavia. I'm sure he could fit us in. Talk about great food and beautiful beaches; that place is the tops!"

The change in her expression was remarkable. "Do you really mean it, Chris?" Her enthusiasm was obvious. "Actually, I do have some vacation time saved up, and I know Klaus wouldn't mind my taking the week off. Particularly this time of year. The Reptile Center is closed for renovations the next few weeks. We always shut down during the last three weeks of May. Nothing much really happens around the Center then, so Dr. Braun encourages us to consider taking vacation days during this slow period. Practically orders us to. And while it's short notice, I'm quite sure he wouldn't have any objections to my taking next week off."

She beamed excitedly and continued, "I'll have to run it by him of course, but I promise to do so first thing tomorrow morning. We're supposed to be visiting one of his associates bright and early tomorrow. Some herpetologist he's known for years. In fact, Klaus just phoned and told me about it. Said we'd be out at Dr. Gavin Cisco's villa, working most of the day. So it should be a perfect opportunity to bring up taking next week off."

"Just don't tell him you'll be vacationing with me," Seven retorted caustically. "If you do, he'll *never* give you the time off."

"I won't. And, you're probably right about that. I'll call you tomorrow morning. When are you leaving for Turks and Caicos?"

"Oh, sometime tomorrow afternoon," Seven answered, evasively. "And do me another favor, Sandy. Please don't mention to Klaus that I'll be away for a while. You know him. He'd probably blow a gasket thinking I won't make his precious deadline."

"Won't say a thing. Promise." She giggled. "See that? You've not only got me spying on my boss, you've got me fibbing to him as well. Some nun I would have made!" They both laughed as Seven called for the check.

~

The following morning was cloudy and cool and Seven ran his morning jog in relative comfort. After a relaxing shower and change of clothes he cell phoned Sandy in her room. She quickly informed him about her just-ended phone conversation with her boss. "Like I thought, Chris,

I'll be with Dr. Braun all day today. To take dictation from him and Dr. Cisco over at Cisco's place. Regarding next weeks' vacation request, I told Klaus I'd be taking it with an old sorority friend from California". Sandy giggled, conspiratorially. "Dr. Braun agreed that having next week off shouldn't be a problem. He promised to think about it, saying he'd let me know sometime later this afternoon. Certainly before we return to the hotel at 5:00 p.m. The doctor will then be taking the corporate seaplane over to his private island to join the nightshift weekend clan."

"Sounds okay," Seven replied.

"And listen to *this,* Chris. Dr. Braun stated that he assumed I'd be with *you* this weekend and he didn't seem to mind at all. Said he hoped we'd finally enjoy being alone together. I told him that would probably be the case. So see. Everything's working out."

Though Sandy's news sounded positive enough, the Super Stud suddenly felt a strange feeling of danger. Especially about her being alone all day with Braun. He chalked it up to frazzled nerves and said nothing about it. In any event, at least she'd be in the company of this noted herpetologist Gavin Cisco and Cisco's wife. So, why worry?

Hanging up the phone, Seven glanced over at the far wall and noticed a small hotel calendar hanging above the writing desk. For the first time all day he realized it was Friday; Friday the *thirteenth!*

Chapter 33

"Come into my Parlor"

Christopher Seven was a bit uneasy as his taxi pulled up to a small shack in a poverty-ridden section of Nassau's outer suburbs. A loud boom-box was playing music somewhere up the street, and the faint, but unmistakable, scent of marijuana wafted through the air. Warily approaching the front door of a yellow shack in severe disrepair, the Super Stud knocked twice. He was greeted by a tough looking, muscular man in his mid-forties. A shy, teenage girl with dark hair stood beside him. Seven smiled at the man and asked, "Eduardo?"

"Who wants him?" said the rough looking hombre.

"I'm Seven, friend of Hanover's. Jack told me to give you this code word when we met in person; *bluebird*."

The man's expression changed immediately and he grinned broadly. "Come in, my friend. Yes, I'm Eduardo Valdez. And please forgive me for being suspicious, señor. I'm always on guard." He grinned once more. "Even here your government has enemies. There are some bad people in the Bahamas who don't forget that I once helped the Americans." Valdez, pointed toward the attractive young girl. "This is my daughter Edie."

"Hi, Edie, I'm Chris." There was absolutely no response. The girl seemed in a permanent trance, with a dazed, melancholy look about her. Valdez quickly explained, "My daughter, she no longer says too much, señor. It's a sad story. Four years ago, two drunken thugs tried to abuse her when she was out walking. I found out later that these two animals were Klaus Braun's men. Thugs from his security squad, off-duty at the time."

Eduardo sighed, as he relayed more of the details. "Braun's men stumbled upon my Edie and began to grab her. She screamed and tried to fight back. One of them then used a blackjack on her. Caused much damage to her brain. She fell to the ground, bleeding and unconscious as the men quickly ran away. A woman passerby found my daughter, out cold, and losing much blood. She somehow dragged Edie to a neighborhood doctor." The big Cuban wiped a tear from his eye. "After checking on Edie I then rushed to the police. Klaus Braun was already at the station. He had bribed the police chief liberally and every magistrate in the district as well. We thus received no justice. Ever since that day, my daughter hardly speaks. Barely lives anymore."

Seven gritted his teeth, knowing he now had another reason to go after Klaus Braun. He listened attentively as Eduardo finished. "I can still see the grinning face of that pig, Braun. I thought about killing him myself that night, but you can't get near this man with all his bodyguards. I couldn't take the chance anyway. I knew my daughter, would need me more than ever now."

Valdez shrugged his shoulders. "No matter. Someday, when my Edie is better, I will kill this Klaus Braun. Or he will kill me. But not before I take him and some of his goons with me. Until that time, I will do everything I can to annoy or disrupt Braun whenever he comes here. That is why I readily agreed to help you when Jack called. But as God is my witness, my daughter and I will one day have our revenge on this man, Klaus Braun." Eduardo forced an awkward smile and motioned to a dusty couch. "Now come. Please sit down so we can go over my ideas for getting you safely to Braun's private island. It's a difficult task, but not impossible. "The two men then plotted for over an hour, as the Cuban outlined his strategy for sneaking Seven onto Royal Keys.

"After we get close to Royal Keys in my fishing boat, I'll drop anchor at least two miles out. This way we won't be detected by Braun's radar. We'll then lower my rubber life raft. It's powered by a small *Evinrude* outboard motor - quiet and sufficient. We'll ride the dinghy to a rocky cove on the far, uninhabited side of Dr. Braun's island. The deserted side. As far as I know, Braun's people don't usually patrol that side. It's nothing but swamps and overgrown thorn bushes. There's a small cliff you'll have to traverse as well."

"Wonderful", joked Seven, not a fan of heights.

"Once I land you there, you can use the map I'll draw up for you", Eduardo explained. "I used to visit this island a lot before it was sold to Braun. So I know it quite well. My map will help you find your way to Braun's side of the island. But bring a small compass with you."

The G5 agent nodded as Eduardo went over the timing. "It should take you two or three hours to trek to Braun's outpost from the deserted side. And about the same to hike back, where I and my boat will be waiting. I'll come back for you at whatever agreed time and date you say." Valdez grinned. "That is, *if* you survive."

Seven grinned back. "You just get me there, Ed. I'll survive. Then, if something *big* is stirring, Jack and will be sending in a whole army. Klaus Braun won't know what hit him."

And for the remainder of the afternoon, the two men went over their planning under the glazed but watchful eye of Valdez's daughter Edie. All in all, it was a good and useful afternoon for Seven, and his confidence in this sortie to Dr. Braun's island soared.

~

Regrettably for Sandy Kent, her day was not going to be quite as agreeable, though it would be one she'd never forget. The morning began innocently enough as Dr. Braun softly knocked on her door promptly at 10AM, shortly after her phone conversation with Seven.

"Had breakfast yet, my dear?" Braun asked thoughtfully.

"Yes, sir. I had room service earlier."

"Good. Then we can leave for Dr. Cisco's right away. Cisco and his wife have a small villa up on Nassau's north side. Mrs. Cisco said they'd be downtown shopping at the straw market for a while. But they've promised to join us for lunch a bit later. This way you and I can finish our dictation, and you can formulate our notes on it."

"Will we be taking a cab, sir?" Sandy asked, trying to appear interested.

Braun frowned. "Heavens no. You know I can't stand those island drivers. I've asked Gent and Slade to rent a car. They'll be coming with us, along with Rosier."

"I see," Sandy replied, not quite sure why three security men would be going. *Oh well*, she mused. *Klaus always has his reasons.*

~

The long ride up to Gavin Cisco's home was initially quite scenic. After a while, however, there were hardly any signs of life. Just an occasional island farmer and a few stray goats. As their crowded vehicle, a rented minivan, finally reached the top of a tree lined hill, they came upon an isolated stone house, one in shoddy condition. Sandy wondered how anybody could possibly live in it, least of all, a feeble older couple like the Ciscos. No one seemed to be home yet, just as Dr. Braun had explained earlier.

When the van finally came to a stop in a short, gravel driveway, Ted Slade, the more muscular of the two security men, came around to open the back door for Dr. Braun. The burly guard hardly even looked at Sandy, nor did he or his two cohorts, Gent and Rosier, help her out of the van. In fact, everyone now seemed to be staring at her a bit crossly, and something about the entire situation just didn't feel right.

"There doesn't seem to be anybody here yet," Sandy commented nervously. "Perhaps the Ciscos are running late."

Klaus Braun, with a glare that Sandy found both strange and frightening, sneered his reply. "Change of plans. We'll be alone today. By now the Ciscos are undoubtedly in some gin mill getting drunk. Everybody knows those two old fools are hopeless lushes. In any case, I had Gent phone them from the hotel to tell them we wanted complete privacy today. He ordered them *not* to return until late tonight. Since they're both on my payroll they obediently agreed to stay away. Especially after Gent promised to leave several bottles of whisky when we left." He looked at her coldly "We won't need the Ciscos for our business here anyway."

Dr. Braun glanced around a moment and then called out to Rosier. "This place should serve our purpose perfectly, Alvin. There's no one around for miles so we shan't be disturbed." Braun frowned at Sandy, menacingly. "Now then. Let's go inside, shall we, Miss Kent? As they say in children's books, come into my parlor." Klaus Braun's words were somehow terrifying. He smiled evilly. "It's time we had a nice long chat."

For the first time that day Sandy Kent felt alarm. Slowly turning around, she saw Braun's three goons standing behind her. Alvin Rosier, the maniacal security chief, motioned for her to keep moving. She had no choice but to follow Braun into the house, as beads of worried sweat began to form on her forehead.

The front door was unlocked and Rosier practically pushed it off its hinge as he stormed inside. After taking a quick look around, the brawny Haitian motioned them all inside. Dr. Braun strolled over to a dark green armchair and sat down. He then pointed to the brown leather couch to his right, waving her forward with a single finger.

Sandy paused a moment, not sure what to do. Without warning Slade grabbed her arm with a tight grip and practically dragged her over to the couch beside Klaus Braun's chair. He then shoved her down roughly onto the sofa. The violence of his manner fed the flames of terror now welling up inside her.

"Look here, Dr. Braun," Sandy interjected, nervous and shaking. Then, in a desperate show of defiance, she attempted to stiffen her shivering spine. "I demand to know what's going on."

Sandy Kent wasn't at all prepared for what came next. Klaus Braun stood up, staring at her with contempt for a moment, and then slapped her hard across the face. The impact of his severe backhanded smack made her cry out loudly.

"Silence, you double-crossing fool!" he screamed. "Just shut your mouth and listen. You will only speak when I demand an answer! Do you understand?" With a quick snap he pulled back his hand and cocked it, ready to hit her again if she didn't comply. The quivering girl nodded slowly, her eyes welling in tears. Her face whitened with an expression of shocked disbelief. Still feeling the heat on her cheek where she'd been slapped, Sandy looked up in abject fear as Braun spoke again. "Your little game is over Miss Kent. You've been brought here for interrogation. What you say now will determine whether you leave alive or dead. And in what state of pain. If you attempt to lie to me at any time I will know it. The consequences," he nodded toward his security guards, "and the suffering, will be unbearable for you. These three men here have all wanted to ravage your admittedly lovely body at one time or another. Today, they may very well get that chance." Klaus Braun's eyes bore into her. And then, with a sinister smirk, he added, "I trust I've made your position quite *clear?*"

Almost mechanically Sandy nodded again, not wanting to do anything that would anger these horrible fiends. "Good," said Dr. Braun. "Then let's begin." He glanced at Rosier. "Alvin, light up one of your 'persuaders'." Alvin Rosier grinned and took out a long, fat cigar. While he deliberately lit it very slowly, Sandy saw the end of the stogie grow red-hot, with a bright glow and a deep orange hue. She could smell the smoke. Rosier then walked over to her and held the lit cigar inches away from her cheek. As Rosier finally pulled the stogie back, Sandy had felt its heat dangerously close to her delicate skin.

"That's enough for now, Alvin", Braun ordered. "You've made your point nicely." The doctor turned his gaze back to her. "My dear, Sandra," he continued. "I can assure you that Mr. Rosier is an artist with that cigar. He paints with it as if its burning embers were a delicate brush. However, the portraits he creates are those of excruciating pain and disfigurement. I have watched him keep prisoners screaming for hours." Klaus Braun paused, purposefully, and then added, "By simply holding his red-hot persuader onto certain sensitive areas of your fine young body, he will create that same pain in you. He is quite capable of causing unending agony, pain you would have thought unimaginable. Of course his two colleagues will be holding you down tightly as he does so, after they've disrobed you completely, of course. So let's not kid ourselves. You will eventually tell me everything I want to know anyway. Either simply and quickly, or through the screams and tears you'll be shedding."

Still on his feet, he warned her again. "Now, my dear woman, I'm going to get a drink of bottled water from the kitchen. When I return, there will either be a full confession, and a full reply to anything I ask you, or we shall have the sickly sweet odor of burning flesh. Yours!"

Dr. Braun glared at the trembling girl with a sinister expression, one she'd never seen him display before. He then made his exit, purposely leaving Sandy Kent alone with his three ogling workers.

Chapter 34

Screams from Hell

*O*h my word! Sandy silently said to herself. *What type of awful nightmare have I gotten myself into? How could I have been so naïve? To not know that Klaus Braun was actually a vicious fiend and quite possibly insane as well. To not see that he was becoming madder by the minute these past few months! He and his henchmen are planning to torture me, horribly, yet I don't even know what it is that they want me to reveal. Is all of this a result of my seeing a few of Braun's private files without permission? Yet how could Dr. Braun have even known?*

She shook her head and continued conjecturing on the situation. *Chris was right, There's something evil happening here, something very ominous. The FBI ought to have been told months ago. I should have cooperated fully with them when I had the chance. Perhaps even called them the other day after I heard Braun's remark about the cobra. Instead, I kept on following Dr. Braun blindly. What will happen now?*

Klaus Braun reappeared in the living room, carrying a bottle of water. He sat down beside her on the worn leather sofa and spoke. "First off, there's no sense denying that you betrayed me, woman. A hidden video cam in my suite caught you spying. Luckily my man, Rosier, installed one. Since I doubt you'll be around much longer, I want to tell you who we *really* work for. Who we follow and worship."

Braun beamed proudly. "All of my nightshift workers are sworn disciples of the Yozem, the most ardent of all the devil worshiping clans. We freely worship Satan and know he will soon rule this Earth. As his devoted disciples, we'll stop at nothing in our quest to serve him. Including killing and torturing those who stand in our way!" He glared at her cruelly. "So don't expect any mercy today. No mere slap on the hands. We practice quite the opposite. Inflicting pain and torture on an *unbeliever* is something we actually relish. It's been practiced by our sect for centuries. Thus, I warn you. If you don't confess everything to me today, you will rue the day you were born!"

Sandy stared at Klaus Braun in utter disbelief and horror. *So that was the score,* she mused. *These men are all devil fanatics and I'm alone in their hands.* She again looked over at Braun. *How could I have been so wrong about this man? What a fool I've been.*

Dr. Braun inched closer toward her. He was all business now. No more small talk, no more explanations. "I know you went through my private files yesterday," he declared. Most likely on orders from that so-called magazine reporter. First of all, how much of what you discovered did you reveal to Seven in that hotel bar last night? Some of my undercover people observed you there. I want *every* last detail, including Seven's comments and reactions."

"Yes. I, - I told him about my looking into your file cabinet," Sandy answered obediently, now realizing how naïve it was for her not to have assumed that the makeshift office in the doctor's suite was under surveillance. As she spoke the condemning words, Sandy realized she might very well be convicting Christopher Seven to a similarly horrible fate. But, abject fear was controlling her now, and she quickly told her captors everything.

"We decided I should take a quick look at your files yesterday" Sandy confirmed. "Just to see if there was anything with your snakes connected to that Ripper killer." Dr. Braun's face reddened with anger as she continued. "I also couldn't figure out why you'd lost faith in me these past few months. I thought something in your private files might tell me why. I didn't think it would upset you so much or I wouldn't have done it. I swear! Half the things I saw, I didn't even understand."

Braun glared at her frostily. "Go on."

"As for Chris, he only planned to briefly help the authorities with their Ripper investigation if he could. Some media colleague inquired about it. That's all. He simply asked me to see if one of your cobras was involved. Nothing was done to get you or the Center into any trouble. He personally assured me of that. We, I mean he, just thought it might help find the serial killer through our snake log. Nothing else. You know I've always been loyal to you."

Instead of being satisfied with her explanation, Klaus Braun went berserk! Jumping up in anger, he ran over and grabbed Sandy by her hair, pulling it violently. Slapping her viciously, he screamed, "You unfaithful little fool!"

It was Gent who had to pull Braun off the girl, shouting, "Doctor, please, let us handle it. We'll get her to talk."

"I *am* talking!" screamed Sandy through her tears. "I'll tell you anything you want. Just ask me, please!"

Klaus Braun released his grip on her hair and tried to compose himself. "I'm sorry, gentlemen," he said, apologetically, completely ignoring the battered and terrified girl. "I lost my head a moment. Won't happen again. It's just that I gave this unworthy woman everything; power, prestige, money, and an important role in my organization. I had even thought of bringing her along to our new home after Operation D. Teach her the satanic mantra. Perhaps, over time, she could have ruled with me. But now, she dares do *this?* There's nothing I hate more than betrayal!"

The angry snake man motioned to Rosier and ordered, "Alvin. Give her a taste of what's in store for those who deceive me."

"Yes, doctor." Rosier sneered widely. Sandy watched in dazed horror as the three guards approached her. She tried to flee from the couch but Slade quickly grabbed her and held her securely. Gent then ripped off her blouse with one quick swipe, exposing the white lace bra she wore, and her soft, smooth midriff. More importantly to Rosier, Gent's actions had also exposed the girl's bare back. Gent and Slade held her tightly and turned her body so that her posterior now faced the approaching cigar.

Rosier studied her superb pink flesh for a second. He then pointed the lit stogie toward her uncovered back. Slowly and methodically he guided it forward, deliberately waiting a moment with an expert's timing. He knew the terror of not knowing when the searing pain would begin would add to the girl's torture. Then, just at the right instant, he skillfully pressed the cigar's red-hot end firmly against Sandy's tender skin!

The Haitian had instinctively known where it would hurt the most, the soft lower arch of her spine. He pressed the scorching stogie there for a while, bringing about instant, piercing screams; screams from hell at the hands of the drooling Satanists! Finally, as the initial scent of smoldering flesh arose, Rosier leisurely withdrew the still-glowing cigar. The agonizing demonstration had made its point.

Rosier knew this brief sampling would be quite enough for now. Though he'd be more than happy to *really* work on her later, as soon as his master gave him the *full* nod. To Sandy Kent, who hadn't seen it coming, the shock and pain of the scorching cigar was horrific. The torture, though relatively quick, still made her sob uncontrollably.

"Stop your blabbering!" Klaus Braun yelled. "That wasn't so bad. It's just a reminder of what we can do to you! Braun wiped his sweating brow. "For now, the punishment has stopped. But if you fail to answer *any* of my questions, it will begin again in earnest."

Sandy didn't really hear much of Braun's threats. Numbed by the veil of pain and shock, she'd become a terrified puppet, simply hoping there'd be no further torment. Dr. Braun could sense this as well. And for some inexplicable reason, perhaps the years of his secret admiration and desire for her, he too didn't want the real torture to ever have to begin. He wanted her to simply confess and be done with it. She'd have to die of course, but at another time and place.

Nevertheless, driven by his crazed zeal for Operation D and his higher devotion to Lucifer, the vindictive doctor was fully prepared to give Rosier the *complete* go-ahead if this beautiful traitor didn't talk.

Klaus Braun needn't have worried. His quivering secretary quickly told him everything. In between sobs, she informed him that Seven knew about the vans, the parking garages, the second logbook, the overseas move, and several other details the files had mentioned. As she fully confessed, Sandy knew she was signing Christopher Seven's death warrant. Yet, at this terrifying moment, it didn't matter. Nothing mattered except avoiding more pain.

The harsh questioning continued for some time, with the frightened Sandy giving out answers as quickly and accurately as possible under the fearsome circumstances. Near the end of the interrogation, Dr. Braun asked her specifically about Christopher Seven. "Is this man, Seven, some sort of policeman?" Braun demanded to know. "Have you ever once suspected as much?"

"What do you mean?" she asked, not quite understanding.

"You know. Has Seven ever told you that he was not really a reporter? Or, have you ever suspected it?" Klaus Braun was now trying to obtain her uncannily correct readings on most people. "With your admittedly profound gift for sizing up individuals, surely you've had your own doubts about this man? Perhaps doubted if Seven was what he claimed?" Braun looked her straight in the eyes.

Sandy was silent for a brief moment, thinking about how she should answer her demented boss. She'd certainly suspected all of those things about Christopher Seven. As recently as just a few days ago on the beach. In truth, she'd formed some private doubts about this handsome journalist early on, at one time even toying with warning Dr. Braun about it. But always, something inside her had cautioned her to refrain. Now, she was thankful she had. *Yes*, Sandy silently recalled, *Chris has certainly mentioned going after the Braun lately. And he has continually pushed me for answers exactly like a policeman or an FBI agent would. He may indeed be something other than a reporter.*

As she remembered her suspicions about the man she loved, Sandy was surprised that her hitherto loss of will and courage slowly began to return for a moment. Perhaps the old adage was right. The one that said: *Love sometimes has a strange way of bringing about bravery.* For Sandy Kent the adage had suddenly come true. Though still fraught with fear, she valiantly decided to keep her suspicions about Chris to herself. No matter what the penalty would be if the perceptive Dr. Braun saw through it. The question on her mind now was - *would these satanic fiends buy her explanation?*

She looked up at Klaus Braun and answered decisively. "No, of course not! Christopher Seven has only been interested in typical media facts. Routine information for his magazine story. If not, I certainly would have warned you long ago. For despite how you feel now, you know my past loyalty to you and our work has been unwavering. Besides, you yourself said his credentials were sound."

Despite his secretary's rather brusque answer, Dr. Braun believed her. She wouldn't dare lie to him now with the threat of scorching torture so close at hand. Amidst Sandy's sobs Braun calmly informed, "This pathetic little coward is undoubtedly telling us the truth, gentlemen. If Sandra says she never once suspected that Seven was a police officer or federal agent - and that he's in fact just a reporter - then it is almost *certainly* true. At least as far as her own intuition is concerned. Over the years, Miss Kent's keen reading of people has always been *remarkably* accurate. And she'd indeed know Seven best, making time with him instead of being loyal to *me*."

Rising up from the couch, Dr. Braun looked away forlornly a moment and added, "Nonetheless, despite her usually correct instincts about people, she too could have been fooled. This so-called journalist may still be some sort of undercover cop, or agent, although it's most unlikely. One way or the other though, Mr. Christopher Seven is now a dead man." He glanced down at the weeping girl in front of him. "We're therefore going to need your help to lure your handsome friend into a little chat with us, my dear woman." Frowning at her he asked, "When were you planning to see him next?"

Still sobbing, Sandy looked over at Rosier's gleaming cigar, knowing there was no choice but to tell them, "Chris will be away in Turks and Caicos for two days, doing a travel feature. He said he'd return Sunday night. We then planned to go on to St. Barths for a week or so. That's why I asked you for the time off."

"How charming," sneered Braun, "a romantic week in the Caribbean sun. Well, we'll just have to use this little St. Barths jaunt of yours to finish off Seven once and for all. And as a way to keep the authorities at bay for a few weeks. That's all the time I'll need."

Braun grinned at the shaking girl. "You're going to phone Mr. Seven a bit later, my dear, and fill him in on a few things." Dr. Braun glowered at her again. "With Rosier standing by you, you'll be telling Seven *exactly* what we want. Including the pleasant news that you'll be staying the weekend here in this villa with your friends the Ciscos. In reality, though, you'll actually be coming with us to my private island, where your final fate awaits you. Your reporter friend will likewise be brought there, upon his return to the hotel on Sunday night."

Klaus Braun cleared his throat and then gave more of the appalling details. "As to your own unfortunate future, short as it will be, you'll soon be destined to be the star of a very unique and painful satanic show. Something we like to call 'a punishment session'. I haven't yet decided if it will take place on my private island or back in Miami. Either way, you will die in agony."

Sandy stared blankly, her mind still paralyzed with fear and incredulity. Nothing made sense any longer. Dr. Klaus Braun, hero to millions, and at one time to her as well, was a fanatical devil worshipper. One who was planning to murder the man with whom she'd fallen in love. The handsome young man she had betrayed so quickly under the threat of torture. Sandy sighed, sadly. Now, it was never to be, those dreams of a life with Chris. Her iniquitous boss would see to that, and she herself would help him do it.

Yet, while thinking about Christopher Seven, Sandy suddenly felt a slight glimmer of optimism. An implausible beacon of light amidst the current darkness. This slim hope was based on the one thing she *hadn't* revealed to Klaus Braun, even under the threat of searing pain. Sandy had courageously and purposely withheld the admission of her growing instincts that Seven really *wasn't* a reporter. Keen intuition was now telling her that Chris was indeed some sort of agent gunning for Klaus Braun, and that he had been doing so right from the start! Closing her eyes, Sandy once more thought about the man she loved. As she did, she smiled inwardly. *How incredible*, she thought. *A smile in a fountain of tears!* Maybe, just maybe, Christopher Seven was indeed the one person who was on to Dr. Braun. And on to Braun's horrific plans as well.

Yet could it be true? Or was this just the dying dream of her tortured soul? *It just has to be*, she pleaded silently through her tears. *Yes, Chris, it's only you now. You're the only possible hope. But act quickly, my love. Please, before this madman destroys anyone else. At least then, I'll be able to die in peace.*

$\mathbf{A}$fter borrowing Eduardo's battered pickup truck, Seven took a drive to the nearby *Sunrise Mall,* Nassau's only genuine shopping center. He returned back to Valdez's home around five o'clock.

The Super Stud agent had purchased several items for his sortie to Braun's island, which included a small knapsack, some water, snacks, and food supplies, a small compass, and a sinister looking hunting knife.

Earlier in the day, while shopping for these items, Christopher Seven received a somewhat puzzling cellphone call from Sandy. Tense and brusque during the conversation, she stiffly informed him that she'd decided to take Mrs. Cisco's kind invitation to stay overnight, borrowing some clothes and cosmetics from Dorothy Cisco.

While Seven was a bit baffled at Sandy's edgy tone, at least he was happy she'd have something to do for the next few days, since neither he nor Dr. Braun would be around. Little did the G5 operative know that during this rather curious call from Sandy, Klaus Braun and his henchmen were standing right behind her, making sure she obediently followed their exact directives.

Seven had also conferred with his chief, Colonel McPhail, in New York headquarters, updating the Colonel about his plans to take Sandy to St. Barths for a week or so, to see if he could get any more info on Braun. During their talk, McPhail formally informed Seven that Washington was now growing quite concerned by the sudden appearance of the two Norwegian nuclear experts. Consequently, the FBI would soon be taking over the entire Braun case, doing so a month from now, sometime after June 10th. This decree had come directly from the President, himself. Until then, however, Seven would be allowed to proceed, unabated, with fully turning his female target.

Glad he'd still be left alone, at least for the short run, Seven said he fully understood the President's decision. And though he'd soon be bowing out of the Sandy/Braun assignment, the disappointed operative took solace in the fact that when the feds finally did step in mid-June, they'd have nearly a month to put a stop to Operation D, *whatever* it involved.

Now, back at Valdez's diminutive shack, after changing into an all-black outfit Seven had also bought for his mission, the G5 agent heard a soft knock on the bedroom door. It was Eduardo, who casually mentioned that his young daughter, Edie, would be coming along on their voyage to Royal Keys. Over Seven's adamant protests, Valdez informed, "My daughter *always* comes with me on the boat, señor. Even in her present mental condition she can handle the fishing craft as good as me. And get us back quickly if need be. Ever since her childhood I've taught her how to navigate safely. She is quite capable of sailing back to Nassau, on her own, from *any* of the Bahamian seas. And if I was injured, or suddenly took sick, she knows to take me and the boat to safety, and then go directly to her Aunt Marta's. We call this our 'peligro drill', and we've practiced it many times in case of any unexpected emergencies. When my daughter knows for certain that it is *peligro*, believe me, she will know *exactly* what to do. So, my Edie is coming. I will hear no more about it."

Knowing he couldn't prevent it, Seven reluctantly agreed. "All right, Ed. Yet I still think it's too risky. But, if you say so."

"Yes, I say so, señor. On a trip like this, things can happen."

~

An hour later Valdez's twin-motored fishing vessel pulled out of *Strawman Harbor* and was soon cruising in the open sea. Seven, sitting next to Eduardo in the co-pilot's seat, closed his eyes and tried, in vain, to relax. He just couldn't stop thinking about Braun's mysterious outpost, and decided to quiz Valdez on it. "What have you been told about Dr. Braun's private island, Ed?"

The big Cuban was reluctant to mention the ghastly rumors he had heard regarding Braun's Royal Keys over the years. Strange stories about tortured wails and screams coming from the isle during the middle of tropical nights. Or the eerie tales of Braun's big reptiles roaming the grounds. Instead, Eduardo stuck to what he knew to be the truth. "Of course one hears many things, señor, mostly from superstitious fishermen. What I do know for certain is that Klaus Braun bought his island some eight years ago. In addition to the cruise line companies and the big hotel chains, many wealthy individuals similarly purchase these small, Bahamian 'out islands'. For the rich they're a haven on which to build their private domains."

Eduardo explained more. "Braun purchased his island for just one thing; *total* privacy. His money has bought off most of the government officials and they therefore allow him to have his own soldiers and gunboats patrolling the area. Naturally, Braun claims he needs this heavy security to protect his secret formulas from rival drug companies. Most likely, that's just a cover story. Maybe, as you say, this island is where he makes larger plans."

After checking the radar and compass, Eduardo stood up from his captain's chair, stretched his legs, and resumed. "Klaus Braun himself comes to the island maybe eight or ten times a year. A few of these visits are probably legitimate. Like once a year he throws a big party for his workers. But the other times on his island? Who knows what takes place?" The Cuban shrugged his shoulders. "Crabbers and lobster boats talk of odd ceremonies and snakes roaming the grounds." Valdez noticed Seven's anxious expression. "Probably just made-up folktales. No worries, amigo."

Edie suddenly appeared from the small hold area down beneath the main cabin. She handed each man a can of cold soda, and then went back below. Seven watched her leave and then turned toward her father. "She's a fine girl, Eduardo."

"I know, señor. And sometimes she still seems to comprehend things pretty good. Someday, when I have enough money, I will send Edie to your American hospitals. Maybe they can help."

"I'm sure of it, Ed." The Super Stud made a mental note to urge Colonel McPhail to try and use his influence in order to help this loyal friend of America with his daughter's plight.

The next few hours of the voyage went routinely, with Eduardo and Edie sharing the steering. Then, Valdez excitedly exclaimed, "The island's dead ahead, amigo!"

After a steady course of nothing but blackness, Seven, too, could sense something different in the air. There were no lights or sounds, just a definite feel that land was near. As the fishing boat slowed to a stop, Eduardo and Edie quietly dropped the heavy sea anchor, using the boat's mechanized pulley. They next inflated and lowered the small rubber dinghy and then attached a small outboard motor to it. Seven and Valdez quickly climbed onto the raft as Valdez's larger boat bobbed lightly in the soft swell.

Eduardo waited till Seven was safely seated before starting the engine. "We can use the outboard to get in closer to the shore and then paddle the rest of the way toward the deserted side. We've anchored nearer the uninhabited side of the island rather than Braun's."

Seven nodded as Eduardo further explained, "There are two small oars under the seats. But even while rowing we must be quiet like cats. You never know, amigo. And caution is always a good companion."

Motoring through the calm seas in the dinghy, the ocean's gentle spray felt good on their faces. Ten minutes later they came to a shallow cove where the raft bumped gently over some small rocks and shells, bringing it to an abrupt stop. For better or worse, Christopher Seven had arrived on Dr. Klaus Braun's mysterious island!

The two men hopped out, pulled their rubber craft from the water and beached it near a large clump of trees and vegetation. They crouched down for a few moments and surveyed their surroundings.

"It is all clear," whispered Eduardo. "I can smell a man a half-mile away. No one's near. Still, we must whisper at all times."

"Let's go over the rendezvous plans and our timetables again," Seven suggested, in a similarly soft whisper.

"Okay, amigo." Valdez looked at his watch. "Right now, it is Friday night, five minutes before midnight. I will take the dingy back to my fishing boat, but I will be here at this exact location every six hours. Starting now

at midnight, of course. I've marked this spot in red on your pocket map."
He pointed toward the mark on Seven's map. "Every day and night that
you're on this island I'll come back here with the dinghy, always on the
sixes. Six a.m., 12 noon, six p.m., midnight, and so on. The last time I will
come, however, will be six o'clock Sunday evening." Grinning wryly, he
commented, "After that, it's *vamos* for my daughter and me. If you're not
back by then we will assume you're either dead or captured. Anyway, that
is all we can do."

Seven nodded again, but then firmly cautioned, "It sounds fine,
Eduardo. Just as long as you don't decide to go hunting for Klaus Braun
on your own. I've been meaning to talk to you about that. Our mission
is to simply get verification of the doctor's actual plans. That's far more
important than any personal revenge. I'm counting on you to simply wait
quietly and get me back to Nassau. I mean it. No heroics and no personal
agendas."

"But of course, señor." The Cuban's tone and mischievous grin was
one that Christopher Seven didn't care for, or entirely believe. Seven sighed
and shook his head. At this point he was squarely in the wily fisherman's
hands.

The Super Stud opened his small backpack, rechecked his snacks
and equipment, and then took a final glance at the map via one of his two
waterproof flashlights. It was time to go.

"Remember, amigo," instructed Valdez. "Go up that hill, stay on the
sand path, and head due north. After the stream, just follow the map,
north. My fisherman friends say you'll eventually see the lights of Braun's
camp. Maybe two to three hours later."

"I've got it, Ed. Fortunately I should arrive while there's still some
cover of darkness. And I'll only do my spying at night. I can rest and
eat during the day. Once I find Dr. Braun's locale, I'll tiptoe toward that
area whenever it's safe." Seven pointed to his knapsack. "I've got a small
listening device with me called a *Thrombor*. It's a bit like a stethoscope.
Paparazzi and tabloid reporters often use them in a pinch. If I get caught
with it, my alibi will simply be, 'the eagerness of an overzealous reporter'."
Seven frowned inwardly, knowing that excuse probably wouldn't wash
with Braun or his security thugs should they discover him. "Anyway, if I
can get one good piece of damaging evidence, or Braun's upcoming plans,
I'm out of there."

"Be careful when you get close to their camp," warned Valdez.
"Although *surprise* will certainly be on your side. They'd never suspect that
anyone would be foolish enough to actually sneak around in their midst.
Even so, keep your eyes open." He teased, "Sleep with only one eye shut."

Seven nodded his head. "You're right, Ed. Hopefully, security *inside*
the place will be minimal. Then, if I can just pinpoint one of Braun's staff
meetings, I'm sure to stumble onto something."

"Just make sure it's not one of his snakes," said Valdez.

Seven smiled and bid Ed farewell. "Well, Eduardo, I guess this is it. See you back here sometime between now and 6:00 p.m. on Sunday."

"Vaya con Dios, Christopher." Valdez bowed and crossed himself.

"Gracias, Ed." And with that, Seven was off.

~

Swiftly traversing the sandy path that Eduardo had mentioned, the G5 operative soon came to a small flat field. Taking out his compass and flashlight, he made sure to head due north and then quickly continued. It was easy going for a while, as the terrain was smooth and arid. Ten minutes later, Seven heard the soft sound of flowing water and knew he had arrived at his second landmark, the small stream. Resting a moment, he sat down on the ground, momentarily wondering if a cobra or mamba was somewhere nearby. *Did Dr. Braun actually bring snakes to this island, as those old fishermen friends of Eduardo's alleged?*

Thinking on it, Seven warily took out his light again and shined it around the immediate area. Nothing at all stirred and he was now satisfied that no reptiles were slithering around. Smiling to himself for half believing these old salt tales, the agent relaxed and enjoyed the tranquil beauty of the night. The cool air was pleasant and comforting. For a moment the Super Stud thought about Sandy, hoping the elderly herpetologist couple she was staying with weren't too boring. He glanced at the illuminated dials of his wristwatch. Twenty past midnight. Time to get moving again.

Now the going wasn't so easy. There were several clumps of trees and heavy undergrowth, with no real trail to follow. It was as if a maze of different paths had been purposely put there to confuse him. There were also a number of sticky thorn bushes that pricked at his legs as he traversed a small uphill rise. One or two of these encounters bringing about a trickle of blood. After a brief pause the G5 agent wiped his bleeding leg and took out the compass and flashlight again. Valdez had said to keep heading north, and only one of these vegetation-lined trails did so. Seven followed it and was soon back on an easier path toward the Braun encampment.

After another hour or so of monotonous walking he knew he must be getting close to Klaus Braun's outpost. Moving swiftly he came to another pile of thick undergrowth, this one much larger and denser. Making his way through the jungle-like vegetation, the G5 operative hoped there wouldn't be any more thorn bushes. Suddenly Seven stopped dead in his tracks! A faint rustling noise could be heard to his right. He listened again. Yes, there it was. A definite sound coming from his right side! Was it man or reptile? Christopher Seven hastily wondered which would be worse!

Frozen like a statue Seven waited in the darkness, not daring to take out his flashlight. All of his senses were now heightened. Beads of sweat trickled down his forehead as he listened for any signs of life. A few silent moments passed. Then, he heard it again, a clear-cut crunching noise from below! He was now sure that the rustling was from something on the ground. Cautiously, he turned on his flashlight and pointed it toward the sound. As he did, a stout, six-foot-long rattlesnake stared back at him!

Fighting panic, the sweating agent wondered what he should do. At this point, several more rustling sounds, these from his left, could be heard. Seven slowly turned his body and shined the light in that direction. Two more massive rattlesnakes were inching their way toward him. Had he stumbled into a den of these deadly serpents? If so, what did he know about them? They certainly weren't indigenous to the islands, so they must have been planted here by Klaus Braun and his crew. Were they placed there to take care of any trespassers? Praying these snakes weren't aggressive killers like some people claimed, Christopher Seven waited breathlessly.

Seven could actually feel his skin crawl as he shined the light on the reptiles. They were not rattling yet, so hopefully they weren't agitated. As far as he knew, rattlesnakes never deliberately attacked humans, unless stepped on, or in self-defense. Nonetheless, he was in their territory and recognized that he'd have to walk out of it very carefully. Keeping his flashlight on, he kept a close watch on both his sides, hoping there weren't any more snakes with which to contend. Just as this thought crossed his mind, he felt something gliding over his feet. Glancing down, he saw a large rattlesnake unhurriedly crawling over him! His heart pounding, he froze statuesque, trying to *will* the snake to go.

A tense-filled minute went by as the big serpent had now stopped, right atop Seven's shoes! Then, mercifully, it slowly slithered over him, crawling away leisurely toward its rattling brethren. As the massive rattler neared the other snakes to its left, all four of the reptiles seemed to stop moving at once, as if tensing up in unison. What was happening? Had they sensed the human intruder and were they now readying themselves to attack? Or was it merely some posturing over territory?

Seven didn't wait for the answer. Instead, he shined his light up ahead and noticed a small clearing. Almost at a snail's pace, he began edging steadily toward it, away from the posse of deadly serpents. At last reaching the clearing, he directed the flashlight beam along the ground to make sure it was empty. Only then did he stop to wipe the sweat from his forehead. *So,* Seven thought, *those fishermen buddies of Eduardo were right. Klaus Braun had indeed brought some of his reptilian friends to this island. Perhaps they were placed on the perimeter of Braun's complex to confront any unwelcome visitors. The question now was: were there any more of them?* The Super Stud knew it didn't matter. He'd just have to trudge on.

Still a bit apprehensive, he walked up the small hill in front of him. Reaching the top of it, his ears quickly picked up on another new sound, this one, definitely human. It was the distinct beat of a large kettledrum, its methodical, melancholy rhythm booming from afar. Seven narrowed his eyes and looked out ahead. When he did, he saw the unmistakable glow of lights in the distance. He had arrived! Here, at last, was the secret island outpost of Dr. Klaus Braun, his final destination. Just *how* final? That was the crucial question.

Christopher Seven whispered a silent prayer.

Chapter 36
Silence of a Lamb

Seven would now have to plan his next moves carefully. Obviously, he'd need to get nearer Braun's headquarters in order to make a visual reconnaissance of the compound. Do so *before* trying to sneak down into it. Getting closer shouldn't prove too difficult. Unless the edge of Braun's enclave was crawling with security guards. Or worse, more deadly snakes.

But then what? Perhaps there'd be a way to stealthily approach the main buildings, utilizing barrels, tents, bushes, or anything else that was around for cover. Just like he'd been taught during a summer session at Quantico's FBI Academy. Using the present cover of darkness, Seven's first objective would be the outside walls of Dr. Braun's meeting rooms. Once near them, he could effectively use his *Thrombor* stethoscope listening device. Odds-on, no one below would be looking for intruders. *Or would they?* Seven dismissed the thought and cautiously made his way toward the lights. And nearer the pulsating beat of the kettledrum as well.

Ten minutes later, he was crouched behind a thick shrub on a small rise overlooking the entire Braun compound. After using a quick burst of his red-lens flashlight, primarily to make certain that no serpents were in the vicinity. With Braun and his reptiles, you never know.

Seven dropped down to the ground. He was now close enough to the camp that being spotted by Braun's roving security squad was a definite danger. While he contemplated his next move, voices suddenly came out of nowhere! Seven looked up and noticed two large men approaching directly in front of him. Rising to one knee, and still concealed by a thick bush, the G5 operative slowly unsheathed his hunting knife. Armed but tense, he waited in nervous silence.

"How's your gal, Pete?" one of the walking men asked.

"You mean Sally? I dumped her a while ago. Got a new one now. Decent looks, but dumb as an ox!" Both men laughed and continued strolling up the hill, moving straight toward Seven. With a hasty plan of escape in mind, the Super Stud gripped his knife.

Now only a couple of yards from Christopher Seven's camouflaged hideout, the two patrolling sentries unexpectedly veered to the left, thankfully moving away from the Seven's hiding spot. With a sigh of relief, the G5 agent waited another minute, and then noiselessly slid his knife back into its scabbard, knowing he'd only use it as a means of self-defense.

"No sense going any farther," the shorter man said to his sidekick as they began leaving the area. "Don't know about you, Gus, but I ain't taking a chance on stepping on one of them rattlers. The doc's electronic monitoring system places those snakes fairly close by. Somewhere south of here."

"You got a point there, Pete."

"You bet I do. We can't risk spending the night in the infirmary and miss tonight's big stage show. It's scheduled for 2:00 a.m., on the podium. And I hear there's a good looking female involved. The doc's also planning to make some important announcements about the operation. Can't miss that either."

Gus grinned savagely. "I heard tonight's chick detainee is a real looker, Pete. Been a long time since I've seen a punishment session involving a pretty woman. So let's head back. Ain't nothing up here."

"I'm right behind you."

With that, the pair ambled back down the hill, leaving Seven to evaluate what they'd just said. *So*, the G5 operative reflected silently. *I've come at a good time. There's going to be a big announcement concerning Klaus Braun's Operation. There's also a female facing some sort of punishment. Knowing Braun's callous group, her chastisement will most likely be severe. Too bad for the woman, whoever she is, but there's no way I can help her now. Probably some nightshift worker who broke one of Braun's silly rules. Hope her chastisement isn't too severe.*

With the two sentries now gone from the area, Seven cautiously moved forward, working his way from one camouflaged hideaway to another. Eventually, after hiding awhile behind a large pile of rocks, he crawled close enough to see the staging platform, illuminated brightly by several towering gaslights. On this makeshift podium, an odd-looking, robed figure steadily banged his huge kettledrum. According to the guards Seven had overheard, this was obviously where Braun would be staging his punishment gathering, and likewise addressing the night staff. Puzzled by the bizarre setting, the Super Stud agent glanced at his watch. In less than an hour, he'd find out.

Seven took out his cell phone again and rechecked for a signal. As expected, there was none. Maybe when he got closer to Braun's compound. Shrugging, he grabbed a breakfast bar and some water from his knapsack, and quietly wolfed them down. He followed this up with his travel tooth care kit and laughed inwardly as he brushed his teeth. *Who was he trying to seduce out here?"* he grinned. The Rattlers? Still smiling at the thought, he sat and waited, serenaded by the lonely, beat of the drum.

For the next forty-five minutes or so, he observed a sizeable audience gathering in front of the stage. At exactly 2:00 a.m., the drumming grew to a crescendo. Seven took out his small binoculars, and with an unobstructed view of the podium, noticed two more robed men marching to the center of the stage, their steps in time with the beat of the drum. They looked like monks, with one notable difference. Outlandish demonic skeletal masks covered their faces, giving them the semblance of zombies from a Hollywood TV melodrama. Obviously this was some sort of cult observance for Braun and his nightshift clan. The FBI girl had obviously been right about that.

At this point, four additional masked men walked onto the stage, followed by Klaus Braun and his father, Floda. The elder Braun was being carried high in a chair, presented in pharaoh type fashion by two brawny security men. The eerie participants onstage, as well as the stupefied audience in front of them, looked odd and foreboding, and the ritualistic venue was hard for Seven to grasp. It brought to mind an old Salem witchhunt gathering. Again peering through his binoculars, Seven took a close-up look at Klaus Braun, who was now walking up to the podium's single microphone. Braun's voice boomed loudly through two large speakers sitting on each end of the stage. With muscles tensed and his senses heightened, Christopher Seven leaned back and listened carefully.

"Ladies and gentlemen of the Yozem!" roared Dr. Braun. We come here tonight as servants of the Dark Lord, Lucifer, the Son of the Morning Star! May *he* be well pleased with our labors!"

The crowd immediately chanted a singular response in practiced unison, as if at a mass. It was an odd, distant chant, and from it, Seven could clearly make out the words *blood* and *vengeance*. Klaus Braun bowed his head slightly before going on. "We are now on the precipice of a momentous occasion. A time when Satan's power, revealed through us, his devoted servants, will be unleashed on an unsuspecting world. May the Dark One rule on Earth forever!"

A chorus of high-pitched wails immediately interrupted him. Astonishingly, several men in the crowd began rolling on the ground, howling loudly at the half moon while violently scratching their naked chests. Dr. Braun held up his hands and decreed, "The fools of the West have scoffed at our mantra. Ignoring the epoch satanic message, even though it is clearly written in their own religious scrolls. That is why we will strike at the West first; assaulting America, the most decadent of their nations."

There was immediate riotous cheering from the crowd, along with lewd body gyrations, as men, and a few of the women in the crowd, tore off most of their clothes and embraced one another passionately, howling in high-pitched squeals. Seven was truly stunned by the display below him. Nonetheless, he dutifully watched, as a beaming Klaus Braun grinned his approval and spoke again. "As many of you know, we were planning to launch Operation D on July 4th, America's Independence Day. It was to be a fireworks display America would never forget!"

Pausing for the raucous laughter of his audience, Braun likewise laughed. He glanced toward his father, and acknowledged the old man's feeble smile with a nod. Dr. Braun's voice then turned serious. "However, situations beyond our control have forced us to implement the operation a bit *earlier* than we'd initially intended. Operation D will now commence in just three weeks. On *June* fourth, a full month *earlier* than the July 4th we planned."

Many in the crowd gasped in dismayed disbelief, apparently shocked by Braun's announcement. Seven likewise wondered why the doctor had changed his operation's scheduling. Klaus Braun again held up his hands for silence, and promptly explained, "Do not be alarmed, fellow Satanists! Except for this admittedly annoying change in timeframe, everything will proceed in accordance with our original strategy. You will all be safely out of the country with me, serving Lucifer, in our new Mid-East home, exactly as planned. Just a month earlier than we all thought."

Relieved murmurs arose from the audience, as Klaus Braun bellowed out more details. "Our contingency planning was indeed wise, allowing the operation to take place a whole month earlier or later. These emergency backup intricacies are now fully underway. Other than advancing our strike to this new June date, nothing has changed. Ten of the most vital and populated North American cities and economic centers will be destroyed forever! The nuclear bombs planted in these sites will make 9-11 look like a schoolhouse fire drill!" The crowd cheered wildly and many began howling again.

Christopher Seven paid little attention to their antics. Instead he remained frozen in utter astonishment and incredulity. *So,* he mused. *The unthinkable is happening. Klaus Braun is not planning to simply fleece ten American cities with some pharmaceutical scam. Nor is he preparing to develop or sell weapons to our enemies. He's planning to unleash them himself on June 4th, in some type of 9-11 sneak attack on America! Braun is a raving madman, a practicing Satanist with a warped spiritual agenda. Furthermore his cataclysmic operation is going to happen in just three more weeks.*

Feeling the sweat of worry and shame dripping down his sides, Christopher Seven suddenly realized what a fool he'd been. He, the suave secret agent they called a Super Stud. Well, this time he hadn't been so super. In fact, quite the contrary. He'd been careless and overconfident, brazenly wanting to act alone and keep the FBI and the other agencies away so as not to be disturbed. All because his vanity had convinced him that he could handle Klaus Braun himself by simply using Braun's pretty secretary and some clever gamesmanship. How wrong he had been. And now Dr. Braun, the diabolical snake man, was going to unleash horrifying terror on the United States. Destruction that according to this madman would be much more devastating than 9-11! Seven pounded his fists into his hand in disgust.

Seven then thought of Sandy, worrying that she might now be on Braun's hit list. As if in answer to his fears, several more men, dressed in parallel demonic attire walked onto the podium. They were leading a pretty brunette, scantily dressed in an erotic thong outfit, to the center of the stage. A tall masked man, expertly holding two large rattlesnakes, then made his way closer to the female prisoner. He promptly began taunting her with the snakes, skillfully holding them by their necks as he brought their deadly fangs frighteningly close to the horrified woman. The girl's shapely body had been roughly painted in hideously bright colors, and the Super Stud didn't need binoculars to see who she was. It was a terrified Sandy Kent, trying unsuccessfully to pull away from her devilish captors as the audience jeered and booed her unmercifully.

Seven struggled to resist the rage to run down and take his knife to Braun and everyone else on the podium! Instead, he closed his eyes to the horror, and coldly listened to Klaus Braun's speech.

"The woman before you is the traitor responsible for our inconvenient change in scheduling. She and that lying journalist." Braun shook his head, angrily. "I had initially planned to punish her *here* for you tonight. Perhaps roast her at the stake, or let my giant anaconda, the huge snake we keep on this island, slowly crush her."

Braun smirked callously. "But I have since developed another idea." He glared at his pretty captive and announced, "We could take this disloyal ingrate back to Miami with us. Back to the Reptile Center. It could be there, in Florida that her agonizing death would occur. Fittingly at our very last Miami punishment session. Then, at midnight on May 28th, the hallowed night of Satanic Reparation by the way, she and her meddling accomplice, Christopher Seven, will die by way of the great Komodo dragon! After their eyes are first cut out, and tossed to the sacred dragon, they themselves will be thrown into the dragon pit alive!"

As the spectators screamed with glee, an even more bizarre scene took place, momentarily halting Seven's thoughts of vengeance. A group of repulsively tattooed men and women danced onto the stage, naked except for the garish, painted designs that adorned their bodies. Two of the men carried a small lamb, which looked as frightened as Sandy. Drums and horns began playing alien, repetitive music, as the guttural moans of the mob grew louder.

While this haunting scene played on, one of the painted men took out a long carving knife and placed the blade against the lamb's exposed neck. His two tattooed cohorts held the unfortunate creature tightly. Seven looked away, always repulsed by any cruelty to animals. A raucous roar from the crowd caused him to look back toward the stage. The lamb's head had been completely severed from its body, and blood was everywhere on the podium. Promptly, all of the tattooed figures on stage began dipping their hands in the gory mess, rubbing blood all over their bodies.

Loudly wailing and dancing wildly, the mob below barked and bayed at the moon. For a moment, Christopher Seven thought he'd be sick to his stomach, as the whole nauseating setting was straight out of hell itself!

The distraught operative picked up his binoculars and reluctantly focused it on poor Sandy. Her eyes were blank and motionless like those of a scared rabbit, and her panic was evident. *What have I gotten her into?*

Seven screamed, inwardly. He cursed McPhail and himself as he gritted his teeth. At that juncture, Sandy was dragged off the stage, while the crowd hurled more insults at her.

Klaus Braun waited for his men to remove the trembling girl from the stage. He then raised his hands for a final decree. "Fellow believers of the Yozem. Tonight, the lamb, instead of the woman, has been sacrificed. But soon, either back in Miami, or right here tomorrow night, *she* will indeed be the chosen victim! We will see where and when she gets her just retribution. Either here or in Miami. Yet, wherever, Satan will be well pleased. "

With a final wave toward the crowd, Klaus and Floda Braun slowly exited under the eerie glow of the gaslights. The crowd then vanished into the night, hoping to find new perverted pleasures.

A stunned Christopher Seven sank to his knees, his mind racing furiously. There were so many things to consider. First and foremost, to quickly get back to Eduardo's fishing boat and immediately warn the FBI of Braun's plans from there. Do so by way of the boat's powerful radio phone. If that signal was also blocked, Seven would order Eduardo to leave him the rubber raft, and for Edie and Ed to sail back to Nassau in the larger boat *without* him. Valdez could then call Jack Hanover and Washington from the mainland.

Secondly, there was the fate of Sandy Kent to consider, the woman he'd dragged into all this. The innocent bystander now facing a heinous, unspeakable end. Seven would somehow have to get to where they were holding her. If only to mercifully kill Sandy himself, should Braun and his ghoulish maniacs change their minds, and decide to torture her here tomorrow night.

Yet the G5 operative knew that, despite Sandy, his first duty was to get back to Eduardo via the planned 6 a.m. timeslot. Then, once Valdez and Edie were safely cruising toward Nassau, Seven would take the rubber dinghy and return to Dr. Braun's outpost. This time to find Sandy, and either put a quick bullet or knife into her, or miraculously whisk her away with him. That was the least he could try to do for her, even if it meant an agonizing death for both of them, if he failed.

With bowed head, the Super Stud whispered a short, desperate prayer, one that included Sandy, the people in those ten American cities. And, of course, for his own upcoming fate. As always, he ended his praying with, *"Not my will, but yours, Lord."* The prayer helped calm him a bit and also buoyed his confidence. Yet many things were still on his mind and he knew the next few hours would be the most important of his life. The anxious agent sighed and silently tried to assure himself. *If I can just prevent Sandy from further torture and shame, and somehow, through Eduardo and Hanover, stop Klaus Braun and his Satanists from carrying out Operation D; then my own death will have then been well worth it.*

Wiping his brow, Christopher Seven rose to a crouch and began contemplating the lonely trek back to the other end of the island to meet Valdez at the cove. Suddenly, a single bullet whizzed by his left ear, followed by another shot that barely missed his arm. Before he could turn and run, the beam from a bright flashlight hit his eyes.

"Freeze!" yelled an angry voice from the darkness.

"**P**ut your hands in the air and slowly move forward!" demanded the harsh, masculine voice. Christopher Seven did as he was told, and soon came face-to-face with a brawny security guard. Seven recognized him in the moonlight as one of the two that had been guarding this area earlier. Pointing a long-barreled revolver at Seven's chest, the guard was obviously pleased with himself. "Thought I sensed something fishy up here before, when I was patrolling with Paul. Heard a sound from behind the bush and felt someone might be around. When I came back up to check, I spotted your searchlight. Also heard you digging in your bag for something. What was it, a gun?"

"No," answered Seven, "my binoculars. Why would I need a gun? I'm just a reporter doing a tabloid story on Klaus Braun and his pack of weirdoes. Quite a freak show they just put on." Thinking of rushing the man with his knife, Seven was first trying to anger him. Anything to throw him off his guard. "I don't suppose you're one of those satanic morons yourself? If you are, where's your toy rubber mask?"

"Shut up! You'll soon see what type of morons we are, you worthless unbeliever." The guard raised his gun. "A shot or two in your knees and elbows ought to teach you some manners, before I drag you down to the interrogation room." The man began breathing heavily with obvious eagerness, and Seven recognized the telltale signs of a genuine sadist. Aiming the pistol at Seven's left elbow, the panting guard asked, "Any final words before you start screaming? Wouldn't mind hearing you beg a bit."

Now sweating profusely, the G5 agent was just about to try offering this crazed gunman a last-second bribe, when suddenly Seven felt a whizzing sensation fly by his ear, similar to a bumblebee. The buzzing sound was immediately followed by a dull pop coming from behind. The face of Seven's sadistic captor immediately changed. It now sported a third eye, a small round hole right above the nose. Blood started to slowly trickle from it. With a blank expression, the security man gurgled and fell backward, disappearing over the edge of a small rocky overhang. Quickly turning around, the Seven saw the grinning face of his rescuer, Eduardo Valdez.

"I'm fairly certain that man was one of the pigs who did bad things to my daughter," the approaching Eduardo exclaimed, holding a pistol with a silencer on its end. "Not that it would have mattered. I would have shot him all the same. Lucky for you, I too want to visit Klaus Braun and his compatriots." Valdez nodded toward his revolver. "I still have some unfinished business with them."

Seven grinned back at the Cuban. "You're a Godsend, Ed. But I'm afraid there's bigger trouble for us now. For a lot of people, really."

"What do you mean amigo?"

"We've got to get back to your fishing boat as quickly as possible and inform the FBI that Dr. Braun is planning some type of nuclear holocaust for the United States. It's set to go off on the fourth of June, and the lives of millions of people are at stake."

Eduardo Valdez gave out a low whistle. "Dios mio! What can I do to help, senõr?"

"Let's get back to your fishing boat, Ed and figure out the best way to warn the feds. We can use your marine VHF radiophone and call the FBI and the Bahamian and American Consulates as soon as we get the raft back to your fishing boat. You can phone Hanover and the FBI as well."

Valdez looked at him apologetically, as if remembering something. "The radiophone on my boat, senõr. Unfortunately it's conked out. We'll just have to rush back and warn them *in person.*"

Seven shook his head angrily, unable to hide his displeasure. "Well, with your radio out, I guess that's our only option now. My cell phone's no good here. I tried it before. They've probably got the whole island jammed."

"Sí, amigo. I tried my iPhone back at the cove as well. No signal."

"Then, you'll just have to contact everyone the minute you're back in Nassau, Ed. That's your first priority now. So let's get moving."

Valdez nodded his agreement, as Seven told him the rest, including Seven's decision to stay on the island for a while. Knowing he'd have to try to save Sandy, or never be able to live with himself, the Super Stud casually explained, "You see, Ed, I won't be going back to the mainland with you, so you'll have to be the one who makes those phone calls. After I borrow your gun, I'll stand guard for a time. To make sure that you and Edie get away safely in the fishing boat. But then, I'm coming back here in the motorized raft. Hopefully we'll have made those calls, and that they'll arrange to pick me up here at noon."

Eduardo gave him a cynical stare. Purposely avoiding Ed's eyes, the G5 operative sheepishly explained, "First of all, one of us still has to keep an eye on things here. To make sure Dr. Braun doesn't get away. The authorities will definitely want to wring the truth out of him, so we can't let Braun out of sight."

Seven looked down at the ground and awkwardly continued, "Secondly, Braun is holding a captive. That girl I told you about, Sandra Kent. She could be an important material witness for us, so I've got to make sure nothing happens to her." As the Super Stud mouthed the lame words, he could tell Valdez wasn't buying much of it. The Cuban obviously felt that most of what Seven was saying was purely personal. It was clear he didn't approve by the frown on his face.

"I see, amigo," was Eduardo's only reply.

"Regardless of me, Ed, you've got an urgent assignment and several emergency phone calls to make. And you've also got your daughter to think about. You'll both have to get away from here before all heck breaks loose. That guard you just killed. They'll undoubtedly find his body before too long and start looking for us immediately."

Only the thought of his daughter's safety, along with Seven's potentially catastrophic news, stopped Valdez from protesting further. The big Cuban still wanted revenge on these people, yet his duty, both as a father, and as a patriot, trumped his vengeful fantasies. He thus reluctantly agreed. "OK, Chris, let's get back to my boat and make those calls. Follow me. I found a better route back. Easier and faster. We'll go *around* the thorny forestry rather than through it."

Eduardo's new route back was indeed quicker, as it circumvented almost all of the heavy vegetation. And thankfully, it was clear of rattlesnakes as well.

Two hours later, they came to the small stream, and then to the clearing. A relieved Seven knew it was only another twenty minutes or so to the dinghy's hiding place. It now seemed certain that they were going to make it without any problems. Suddenly the big Cuban held up his hand. "Stop," he whispered. "I hear something." He sniffed. "Smell something too." Eduardo paused a moment and then confirmed, "Yes. We're being followed. Two, maybe three men. Close by."

"What now, Ed?"

"Those trees over there. It's the only cover around."

They hunched low and scampered toward a thick grove of palm trees. Just as they dove behind them, a bevy of gunshots rang out, several bullets ricocheting off the tree trunks.

"Three men," Valdez whispered, as they crouched behind the trees. "One rifle, two pistols. By those rocks." He pointed to his left.

"That's just great," Seven grumbled. "And me without a gun."

"Don't worry senõr, assured Eduardo. Mine will be enough. I'm a top marksman, FBI-trained. But shooting in low light is not so easy. You must look for moving shadows. Like this." Eduardo took aim in the direction of the three stalking pursuers, fired two shots, and immediately rolled to his right behind another tree. Seven saw two of Braun's men grab at their chests and fall forward.

"Incredible shooting, Ed! Two down, one to go."

Valdez grinned, excitedly. "This is why I came, amigo! To kill as many of these rats as I can." There was now only one more of Braun's goons with which to contend.

They waited in tense silence before Seven broke it. "We can't stay here all night, Eduardo. You've got to get back to the boat. Give me your gun. If I can keep this last man pinned down, maybe you can make a run for the dinghy."

A few more shots came toward them. From his slightly higher position the third man seemed to have them pinned down. Then, from their right, a single round from his high-powered rifle hit a rock, ricocheted, and with a dull thud, found its mark. Eduardo Valdez went face down in the sand. "I'm hit," he groaned. "Badly, I'm afraid."

Christophe Seven swiftly made his way toward his wounded comrade. "Keep low, amigo!" Valdez warned through clenched teeth. "This last shooter is an excellent marksman."

Seven ripped opened Eduardo's shirt and surveyed the damage. It appeared the bullet had missed the heart, landing a few inches away from it. But there was still copious bleeding.

Valdez tried to sit up, but could only rise up on his elbows "Now it is *you* who must go on, amigo, without me," Ed said, through labored breaths. "Forget capturing Klaus Braun by yourself." Eduardo then winked. "And forget about that girl you love. You can find her later when the police come for the snake man. Just get to my Edie, and tell her to sail to Nassau so you can warn the Feds. Go now, while I try to hold off this last hombre."

Knowing there was really no other choice now, Seven immediately consented. Even with Eduardo's wound and Sandy in the hands of the Satanists, warning the Feds of Operation D's catastrophic plans trumped everything else.

Valdez moaned in pain a moment, but then an eerie stillness set in. Seven looked over at his injured friend. "I've got to get out of here now, Ed. Even if that last man's a good shot."

"He's gone, Chris."

"Gone?"

"Yes. I heard him run away just now. Have a look."

Christopher Seven picked up the binoculars and caught a glimpse of a lone figure dashing off in the distance. "I guess he'll be heading back to his outpost to bring reinforcements," Seven exclaimed. "But it'll take him a good two hours to get there if his home base is where that satanic podium was. And at least that much time to get back. After that, though, there's no telling how many will be here."

Eduardo smiled. "Don't worry, senõr. By the time Braun's men finally finish me off, you and Edie will be long gone."

Seven shook his head in argument. "I'm not leaving you, Ed, even if I have to carry you. It's only twenty minutes more to the raft."

"No can do, amigo. I'm not bandaged. Any bumpy movement and I might bleed to death. I wouldn't make ten feet without some medicine and bandages. The blood is spurting even now." Valdez looked up at the night sky and sighed. "Too bad we weren't back on my boat. There I have good medical supplies. Enough to patch me up to safely move. No time now. You must leave for Nassau to warn the FBI."

Seven thought on it a minute, and then hastily decided. "We still have plenty of time left before Braun's reinforcements can get back here, Eduardo. *Minimum*, four hours. That sentry needs at *least* two hours to travel to his outpost. And another two hours to get back here. That's at least four hours on foot. It should only take me thirty minutes or so to get to the fishing vessel and another half-hour to get back to you." Seven smiled encouragingly at the Cuban. "You say you have medicine and bandages on the boat?"

"Sí. There's a full medic's kit. But -"

"Just relax, Ed. Believe me, I know the mission comes first. But we'd be back on your boat, cruising toward Nassau, *hours* before they return. There's plenty of time, so why not give it a try?" Seven smiled again. "Besides, like you said. Edie will need her dad now."

"Gracias, senõr. But please promise me, amigo. The second you get onboard my boat, tell Edie this code word; *peligro muerto.*" Valdez made Seven repeat the code phrase twice, and then said a quick goodbye. "Vaya con Dios, Christopher!"

~

Thirty minutes later, the yellow dinghy pulled up to Eduardo's fishing boat. "Edie, it's me, Chris. Hurry!" Rushing out from the hold below, Edie grabbed and fastened the dinghy's tie rope. She was smiling widely. That is, until she realized Seven was alone. Knowing she'd be wondering where her father was, the Super Stud hopped onboard and took her gently in his arms, praying she'd understand.

"Edie. Your father has been wounded. But don't worry, I'm going back to help him. I'll need the medical supplies Do you understand?" Surprisingly, the girl nodded, but when she brought him a bottle of soda from below, Seven knew she was hopelessly confused. "What now?" he muttered.

Seven's mind raced rapidly. He was fully aware that his number-one priority was warning the FBI. Yet he also knew there was still plenty of time left to go back for Valdez. To not do so now, with hours to spare would be tantamount to killing a wounded comrade for no reason. Weighing Seven hurriedly decided he'd go ahead with his rescue attempt of Eduardo, providing he could *hedge* his bet.

He looked up at one of the shelves and spotted a pen, an assortment of envelopes, and some writing paper. Taking the items down from the shelf, the G5 agent frantically began composing a warning note for the authorities, just in case he found himself stuck on the island with no possibility of return. That was highly unlikely, as he'd solemnly promised himself that he'd be back on the fishing boat in twenty minutes or less.

Come back to the big boat no matter *what*. With or *without* Eduardo. Nevertheless, he still wanted to be cautious. He'd thus give Edie this warning note, along with definite orders for her to leave for Nassau if he wasn't back in thirty minutes. Seven was certain he could make Edie understand. Sitting down at the hold's small table, he hurriedly addressed the largest envelope:

> *Extremely Urgent! – <u>Attention</u> any Bahamas Government security offices, Nassau <u>Police</u>, United States Council, American or Canadian Consulate offices.—<u>Full and Huge Reward</u>! (International crime enforcement code 119 B.—US agent code 65334, out of New York.)*

Inside this larger envelope he placed his actual warning notes, all of them written in the standard simplex fed code. The coded note read:

> *<u>To FBI</u>: This is an urgent note from agent C7, US 65334, via your agent <u>Jack Hanover</u>, Miami: − Dr. Klaus Braun has kidnapped Sandy Kent and plans to execute her at the Miami Reptile Center; most likely on or <u>before</u> midnight of May 28th. If I'm captured, he will undoubtedly attempt to execute me as well.— <u>More</u> <u>importantly</u>, Braun and his team are planning something calamitous, involving nuclear weapons to be used on the USA; something called 'Operation D'. Braun plans to destroy ten cities, and said operation will commence on or before <u>June 4th.</u>*
>
> *After finalizing all aspects of the nuclear attack, Dr. Braun and his cohorts are planning to leave America for the Mid-East sometime between June 1st and 4th; destination unknown. Suggest <u>immediate</u> all-out assault on Braun's Miami Reptile Center and pharmaceutical offices! (Braun and his nightshift are scheduled to be back at their Miami Center sometime soon.) Klaus Braun's reptile hub will be well guarded and well armed. A surprise assault is thus the only method to save the girl, capture Braun alive to reveal full details, and prevent the destroying of evidence hidden there. All gates at Braun's Miami center are heavily fortified. Yet some spots are not as well patrolled. Particularly the south gate and the public entrances. - Thus extremely urgent! <u>You must stop Klaus Braun at all costs</u>, and if possible, <u>rescue the girl</u>. Again, you <u>must</u> stop Klaus Braun at all costs! - Seven*

The G5 agent signed his name and placed the most important notes he'd ever written inside the larger envelope. They were addressed to several assorted homeland security and police agencies. He sealed the bulky envelope tightly and underlined: - <u>*HUGE REWARD!*</u>

Seven then glanced at his watch. He'd only been gone from the island for half an hour. He grabbed two large bags of medical supplies and prepared to get back into the small raft. *But first. How do I tell Edie about her dad",* he silently asked himself. *And make simple, uncomplicated arrangements for her to deliver the warning notes; in the unlikely event that I don't return within half an hour.*

Recalling that Eduardo had mentioned his daughter could sometimes *'fully comprehend'* what was happening, Christopher Seven raced up to the top deck to face young Edie. With a gentle smile, he pointed to the large brass clock on the wall of the bridge and gave it a try. "Edie, it's now 4:50 a.m. Do you understand me? It's almost 5 o'clock?" She surprised him with an affirmative nod. "Very good," urged Seven. "If I don't return to this fishing boat within forty minutes, you must leave and go back to Nassau." Again, the girl nodded knowingly. *So far, so good,* Seven mused.

Seven then walked up to the wall clock and pointed to the numbers in childlike emphasis. "If your father and I are *not* back by 5:45 a.m., you must leave here *immediately* and take this letter directly to the Nassau police – *police!*" When she nodded affirmatively Seven sensed he was definitely getting through.

He next handed Edie the large sealed envelope, in which he'd put all of the individual SOS letters, and pointed to the large letters on the outside that said *Police*. Raising his voice for emphasis, he exclaimed, "Police! Give *this* to the police." This time, Edie merely shrugged her shoulders apathetically.

The Super Stud began to worry. Perhaps he wasn't getting through after all. Although this note was merely a precautionary hedge, the G5 operative fought back his mounting panic, and toyed with simply leaving for Nassau now and forgetting about Sandy and Eduardo. Does Edie comprehend *any* of this? *What should I do?*

Seven stared at the young girl again. Her forlorn, innocent expression quickly made him forget his thoughts of deserting her father. He looked down at his watch again. Time was wasting. He simply *had* to make her comprehend the warning notes!

Knowing there was only one thing left now, Seven slowly, repeated her father's code words to her. "Edie. You must understand me! You must! It's condition peligro muerto. *Peligro muerto!*"

The girl threw her left hand to her mouth and gave a low moan. The noise startled Seven, for it was the first time he'd ever heard her utter a sound. The anxious agent immediately wondered what the *real* meaning of this secret family code between father and daughter meant. He likewise wondered if Eduardo had deliberately misled him about it in some way. Seven saw tears well up in the girl's eyes and tried to calm and hold her, but she angrily pulled away. Realizing there was nothing more he could do, he hopped back into the dingy, with the medical supplies in hand, knowing there was still a good chance of saving Valdez. The G5 agent untied its rope, and was soon motoring back to the island as fast as the raft could go.

The sea had kicked up, and the ride back was chilly and rough. Now, even the ocean seemed against him. As Seven wiped the sea spray from his forehead, he turned around to have a quick look back at the comforting fortress of the larger fishing vessel. When he did, his heart literally sank. The fishing boat's engines were running, and, inexplicably, the big craft was starting to speed away! The girl had obviously misunderstood everything Seven had said. Either that, or somehow Ed's dire code words had made her leave the area.

Christopher Seven, on the verge of complete panic, knew there was no other option now. He'd have to get to Valdez and rescue him. Then, if the bandaged Ed could be moved, to see if the two of them could motor the tiny dinghy all the way back to Nassau!

As soon as Seven reached the shoreline in the dinghy, he placed the first-aid kits under one of the seats, and then began pulling the raft up a small hill toward his wounded comrade. His plan was to bandage Eduardo as best he could, after first treating him with some strong medication and pain killers. Then, using the raft as a moving stretcher, transport Valdez down the hill and out into the ocean. Hopefully Seven could then pilot the small, motorized craft back to the mainland, guided by Eduardo and Seven's pocketsize compass.

As he grabbed the tie rope and began to pull, Seven's mind was spinning with a myriad of possibilities, including the condition of his wounded friend. Would the medical supplies he'd brought back be enough to save Ed's life? With any luck they would, for Seven desperately needed the Cuban's keen navigational skills if he was going to successfully pilot the small raft back to Nassau to call the FBI.

Dragging the dingy uphill toward Valdez, the sweating G5 agent labored feverishly. It was still dark out but the approaching dawn was unfortunately beginning to bring in some light. Just as he reached the palm grove area where he'd last left the injured Cuban, Seven saw something moving in a large palm tree directly up ahead. Was it man or reptile? The Super Stud couldn't tell for sure. The suspended object was partially hidden by the tree's windblown branches. The swaying object appeared to be large and bulky, and Seven wondered if it might be some type of giant constrictor, like Braun had mentioned in his podium speech. Leave it to Klaus Braun to have brought one here.

Fingering the large knife at his side, Seven approached the dangling object guardedly, cautiously getting close enough to see it more clearly. When he did, Christopher Seven was instantly overcome with shock and grief. Hanging from one of the tree's broad limbs, was the lifeless and horribly mutilated body of Eduardo Valdez!

The Cuban's corpse was suspended by his feet, tied tightly to one of the highest tree branches. Eduardo had obviously been beaten and tortured, since there were several long knives protruding from his chest. Fresh blood and bruises could be seen near the gun wound.

As a disbelieving Seven began rushing over to the hung body, an angry voice cried out, "Hold it, bub! Don't move an inch or you're a dead man. And throw down your weapons." Simultaneous clicks of several rifles and handguns immediately told the shaken G5 operative the rest of the bad news. He was completely surrounded by several of Braun's security thugs!

The posse stared at him with professional aloofness, as the confident voice of their lead man exclaimed, "Hello, pally, I'm Sam. I see you finally came back for your wounded friend. Thought you might. But you're a tad late." The man barked out a cruel laugh. "Dickson told us there were *two* men tangling with him here. Figured the second man had gone for medical supplies at whatever spot you guys hid your raft. We couldn't find it."

The guard looked over at the dinghy and shook his head. "You two must have been crazy, coming all the way from Nassau in that thing."

Seven said nothing, but was inwardly pleased they hadn't spotted Edie and the larger fishing boat. He slowly surveyed the six burly sentries and wondered how they could have arrived here so quickly. Klaus Braun's main camp was over two hours away, and Seven had only been gone thirty-five minutes. This lead guard, Sam, a lanky man with a horribly scarred face, moved forward and began explaining.

"I see by your expression that you're surprised to find us here so soon. Guess you didn't count on the fact that we all have ATVs". You know, those speedy off-road vehicles." Sam pointed to a bunch of them parked in a small clearing "They can go anywhere on this island, in less than a fraction of the time. Plus, we know all the shortcuts. Most helpful, we have small outposts everywhere now. Even on this deserted side of the island, which is *our* standard home base." The man grinned widely.

"Anyway", he continued, "We were riding the ATVs on routine patrol when we found our man Dickson running back to base. Dickson is the one sentry you guys *didn't* kill. He quickly filled us in on the score. Told us you fellas shot two of his team. We were headed toward the island's back cove anyway, so we made it here pronto on our motorized vehicles."

The scarred security man beamed in triumphantly. "The six of us easily overpowered your wounded buddy up this hill a ways. Worked him over pretty good during our short but sweet interrogation. The fool screamed a lot with the pain, but stubbornly refused to tell us anything. Wouldn't sing, no matter how hard we were on him. A real wise guy too. Claimed he was a Cuban travel agent on holiday here. I really lit into him after that wisecrack, but he still wouldn't spill. It was clear your pal wasn't going to talk, so we finished him off with the knives. We then tied him in this tree for our little surprise to you."

Seven looked up at Eduardo's suspended body. His faithful friend and companion, so virile and alive just a short while ago. Now dead. He thought of poor Edie, and then glared back at Braun's pack of sadistic thugs. For the first time in Seven's life, coldblooded murder was on his mind.

The G5 agent listened half-heartily as Braun's group leader warned him, "So since your Cuban pal wouldn't tell us what's up, we'll just have to get it out of you, bub. First of all, where did you guys come from and how did you get on this island so easily? Talk, or your death will be as painful as your friend's."

The Super Stud knew he'd better protect Edie at all costs. Do so, in case Braun's people had a speedboat able to catch up to her. He also decided to use his knowledge of some of Dr. Braun's key people, in order to gain some time. Or perhaps even save his life. Seven faced his captors and began addressing them firmly.

"I'll tell you *what's up* all right. Since you and those rifles of yours leave me no other choice. About how I'm desperately needed at Klaus's base camp ASAP. And how you and your trigger-happy gorillas might have critically delayed some of the Dr. Braun's urgent needs."

Seven paused a moment, for dramatic emphasis, and then added, "My name is Christoph. Dr. Steven Christoph. Last night, I was called by Dr. Braun and Alvin Rosier and told to rush to this island in *absolute* secrecy. Klaus was worried about a possible spy hiding amongst the night shift clan. You know how concerned he is about privacy."

Seven knew his story was having an effect by the look in Sam's worried eyes. He thus continued, "We were ordered to motor here at night from the mainland, via a small craft. The smaller the better, in case the Bahamian coast guard had radar or ships near the island. Then, upon arrival here, slip in through this back cove, and make our way to Klaus at home base. The old man, Floda, knew all about it too, as did Elsa. I was assured there'd be no problems getting on Royal Keys, provided we came in through the uninhabited part of the island. Even so, we were ordered to kill *anyone* who got in our way. Friend *or* foe."

Seven shrugged his shoulders and declared, "Obviously, some signals were crossed on that part of it. That's probably why you guys weren't informed. Like I said, our coming here was to be done in *total* secrecy. In case there was a spy within the nightshift gathering. Regardless, I was instructed to bring Klaus my thoughts and the new calculations for the nuclear planning he wanted those Norwegian scientists, Schilling and Gustaff, to revisit."

The G5 agent motioned toward Eduardo's body. "That Cuban you butchered was strictly transportation. Although he, like me, was a true devotee of Lucifer. Our mission was crucially important to Operation D. We thus swore to Klaus that we'd give our lives rather than reveal anything. The Cuban did so gallantly, as you saw. Me? I figure I better stay alive if I'm to get the nuclear data to Klaus."

The Super Stud wiped his forehead, in fake trepidation, and opined, "Revealing these facts to you now will probably mean my agonizing death. Along with *yours,* once Klaus hears about it. But since the doctor desperately needs me and my new calculations, I'll presume that's more important than my vow. So take me to the camp base pronto! Maybe I can then explain what's happened, and prevent us from all being thrown to the sacred dragon!"

The confident tone of Seven's words, plus the very specific VIP names and details he'd thrown about, startled his captors. The entire security squad became uneasy and confused. Their head man, Sam, was the first to reply, doing so almost apologetically.

"Look, mister, it's like you said. We don't know nothing about all this. I'll get you to Dr. Braun alright, and we'll let him sort it out. But technically, you're still a prisoner. At least for the moment. Unfortunately, I can't call in to verify anything. There's no cell signal of any kind here on Royal Keys. The doc has a powerful jam on the island that blocks any and all transmissions. All they know back at the *main* base is that I'm bringing in a couple of intruders. I told Dixon, that guard we ran into, to inform headquarters about it once he returned there. Yet, if you really *were* part of Dr. Braun's work, why didn't you just say something to the other guards?"

"Those three predators didn't give us that chance," Seven angrily explained. "They starting shooting at us from the beginning, so we had to shoot back. Like I said, it was critical I get my information to the doctor. Anyway, let's get to headquarters!"

Scar man tried to force an overly friendly smile. "Sure, fella. We'll take you there. And if what you say is true, I know Dr. Braun will understand." The head man's demeanor had become one of a worried colleague. He looked over at the prisoner, apologetically. "I'm still gonna have to put cuffs on you, however. For the ride back to camp. That's standard procedure. I'm sure you recognize that." Seven nodded as Sam added, "You can ride in the lead ATV with Brenner. Naturally, we'll also have to bring the Cuban's body in as well. For possible identification." Sam then yelled out to his crew. "Ok, boys. We're going to the main building. Let's move out!"

Calmly trying to contemplate his next moves, the handcuffed Seven settled in for the bumpy ride back to headquarters. For the moment, at least, he'd taken the initiative from his captors. He knew it would be a far different story once he was back in the hands of Dr. Braun. *Oh well*, Seven mused. *It'll be interesting to see Braun's face when his favorite magazine reporter comes strolling into camp.*

~

The ATVs rapidly made their way to Dr. Braun's main base, traversing the same jungle-like trail Christopher Seven had taken earlier. The sun had finally come up and Seven could now clearly see the terrain he'd previously trekked during the night. Shuddering as they drove past the rattlesnake area, the G5 agent vividly recalled the unnerving feeling of the big snake crawling over him in the darkness. He shivered, and then leaned back for the rest of the ride.

Soon they passed the area of Braun's Devil-worship podium, and Seven thought of Sandy again. *What have they done with her?* He silently asked. *Could he really find and rescue her?* The odds were slim, but the Super Stud was trained to always focus on the positive.

The off-road vehicles easily navigated the small hill directly above. The spot of Seven's narrow escape from the sadistic security guard; the crazed sentry that Valdez had shot in the head, saving Seven's life. The bittersweet memory made him think once more of his gallant rescuer. Eduardo's dead body now lay slumped in the back of one of the other vehicles. The brave Cuban soldier had died a hero's death, revealing nothing. But soon, when Braun's people identified Eduardo Valdez as a part-time FBI operative - one who'd publicly sworn he'd get Klaus Braun - Seven would have run out of plausible cover stories as to why he was on this island.

The ATVs motored down the hillside and soon arrived at a small guardhouse manned by two heavily armed sentries. This was obviously the gated entrance to Klaus Braun's island headquarters. One of the gatekeepers excitedly greeted the incoming group leader. "Hello, Sam, glad you guys are finally back. Dr. Braun was only told that you were bringing in two intruders. He figured it was merely a couple of island fishermen. Was that all it was?"

"You'll soon see," was all Sam said, still worried about his own hide. The guard grinned and promptly let the ATV caravan through.

Seven tried to observe as much as he could on the way over to the main building. Braun's island complex was enormous, a working hub and housing area smack in the middle of nowhere. He shook his head as they pulled up to the main building and laboratories.

"We've arrived, bub," Sam informed. "We'll soon find out if you're supposed to be here or not. Brenner and I will escort you inside. And remember, we've got guns. And you're officially still a prisoner."

Tightly handcuffed, Christopher Seven said nothing. Sandwiched between Sam and Brenner, he slowly followed them through the building's entrance, and up to a private office door with Klaus Braun's name on it. *This is it,* thought Seven. *What will happen when Braun, who's apparently expecting some meddling native fisherman, sees that it's me?* He waited uneasily as Sam knocked on the door.

Dr. Braun, hearing the knock, deliberately chose to ignore it for a moment. He and his four visitors, now fully informed that only a single prisoner was being brought in, wanted the trespasser to sweat outside the door a bit longer. This game of tormenting a waiting captive always amused them. The snake man smiled to his guests and explained further. "That will be my security guards with their trespassing prisoner. It's undoubtedly some curious fisherman who, despite our posted warning signs, nonetheless chose to have an unauthorized look around. I'm afraid it will be his last look at anything. Let's have some fun with the captive, shall we? Before I give him to Rosier for Alvin's cigar burning artistry. Enter!" he exclaimed loudly.

The doctor's deep, authoritative voice was exactly as Seven remembered it. Sam nervously nodded to his sidekick, opened the door, and slowly entered the room with the captive. Klaus Braun, who'd been conducting an informal staff meeting, at first didn't even bother looking over at the three entering men. Neither did any of his four VIP attendees, which included Braun's father, Floda, the two Norwegian nuclear scientists, and Alvin Rosier, head of security.

Nursing a glass of sherry, Dr. Braun finally glanced over, fully expecting to see some cringing native islander being roughly escorted in by the sentries. As Klaus Braun turned and looked, his mouth slowly fell open. The wineglass he was holding tumbled to the floor, its crystal shattering into pieces with a noise that pierced the thick silence. The other men, who'd been sitting calmly, immediately turned to look as well. When they saw it was Christopher Seven, they too all gasped!

The G5 operative, sensing their utter astonishment, was unexpectedly encouraged by the look of fear and shock in the group's disbelieving eyes. Seven quickly took the initiative.

"Hello, gentlemen. Good to see you all again. I've come to get Miss Kent." The Super Stud then directed his gaze pointedly at Klaus Braun. "And to put a stop to this lunatic's Operation D."

Chapter 39

The Eyes of Death

The frail oldster, Floda Braun, was the first to actually react to Seven's astonishing appearance. Old man Floda slumped down in his chair and gasped loudly, coughing while laboring to draw in a breath. Seven hoped it was a serious malady. "Quick, you fools," Klaus barked at the two Norwegian scientists. "Do something for my father! You there, Rosier. Get him some water!"

Floda gradually began breathing normally again and in a heavy accent informed, "I'm all right. Just the shock at seeing this man here."

Klaus Braun, after making sure his father was all right, turned and glared at Seven. It was a strange look, an odd mixture of both hatred and respect. His lips turned up evilly as his eyes zeroed in on the captive. "Hello, Mr. Seven. Nice to see you again. We have so much to ask you and you have so little time."

~

Twenty minutes later, the handcuffed Super Stud was sitting at a large conference room table located inside the island's cavernous warehouse. He'd been coldly informed that he was going to be asked some key questions by members of Dr. Braun's executive staff. This, in order to better facilitate what should now be done. Klaus Braun firmly explained that the captured journalist's answers would determine how and when Seven, and presumably also Sandy Kent, would be dealt with; either harshly or reasonably. It would depend on the accuracy and input of what Christopher Seven decided to reveal at this point.

The G5 agent was well aware that Klaus Braun's promise of a fair bargain, and potential leniency for detailed information, was undoubtedly just a ruse. Something to get him to confess everything he knew or had done. Seven was quite certain that his days were already numbered, despite Braun's surprising civility and decent treatment of him so far. The Super Stud had no illusions on that score. He'd be lucky if he wasn't thrown to the rattlesnakes soon.

Seven tried to calmly weigh his options. Even with his own inevitable death at the hands of these maniacs in the offing, he realized that the only possible hope of preventing Braun's diabolical operation was to keep stalling. Perhaps there was some way to dissuade Dr. Braun from further accelerating Operation D. If Seven could delay things, even briefly, maybe a miracle could yet take place. Conceivably, Edie Valdez might get Seven's warning note to the right people.

Christopher Seven knew that the first priority was to try and assure Braun and his cohorts that there was absolutely no threat to their current plans. No reason to expedite their already adjusted June 4th timetable.

Unfortunately, with the dubious mental state of Eduardo's young daughter, this was most likely true. Thinking about it in dejected hindsight, Seven realized that Edie Valdez was clearly the unlikeliest of people he'd have chosen to convey his SOS messages. Even so, there was always the thin hope that the notes he left with her back on the fishing boat would somehow get through. And the G5 operative had been trained to act on even the slimmest of hopes.

There was also Sandy's fate to consider. The worried agent hadn't seen her yet and he wondered if she was even alive, despite Braun's assurances. If she was still living, Klaus Braun's goons would surely work her over if Seven didn't seem to be cooperating. The anxious agent glanced at the time and the small date window on his wristwatch and saw it was 8:17 a.m., Saturday, May 14th. Was Sandy's pending execution extravaganza still scheduled for two weeks hence; midnight of May 28th? Or, had they killed her already? Seven contemplated in silence as he waited for Dr. Braun to begin.

Gathered around the long conference table, Seven saw some familiar faces, and a few he didn't recognize. Sitting close by were Dr. Walter Schilling and his fellow nuclear scientist, Neil Gustaff. Braun's father, Floda was also there, seemingly making a full recovery from his earlier breathing problems. Among the other attendees was Alvin Rosier, Braun's muscular Haitian security chief. A Middle-Eastern gentleman Seven didn't know was seated to Rosier's left, clothed in his native robed regalia. Additionally, a well-dressed, but strange looking man sat at the far end of the table. This man's peculiar facial features were extremely haunting, and he had an ominous, ghoulish aura about him. There he sat, staring out, a large notepad and pen near his hand.

What's this all about? Seven wondered. *Could Braun suspect that I might have sent a warning?* As the secret agent tried to focus on things, Dr. Braun called his emergency gathering to order.

"Gentlemen, for those of you who haven't yet met him, this is Mr. Christopher Seven. I'm sure you've all heard about him by now. He is allegedly a reporter for *Global Magazine*, one who unfortunately stumbled upon some of the details of our operation. How much he's actually detected, we do not know. Yet, as always, we will soon find out. For those of you wondering how Mr. Seven got onto this island unscathed, our security team was indeed about to eliminate him just a short while ago. But this Mr. Seven plays the game well. And through a series of clever bluffs, he is somehow inexplicably still with us."

Christopher Seven immediately felt the frosty, angry stares of all the attendees. Klaus Braun waited, looked over at him, and then continued, "Mr. Seven, most of the men seated here make up my executive planning committee. They're the most essential warriors of those who make up my little domain. As you rightly stated, our present undertaking is indeed called Operation D. How you even know this codename mystifies me. We will certainly want to know that. In fact, we will want to know many things."

"So will I," Seven replied, cynically.

Dr. Braun ignored him and went on with his talk. "Along with my entire group of nightshift workers, we are practicing worshipers of Satan. Our mantra is from the sacred sect and traditions of the Yozem, the most zealous of all the satanic clans. I won't bore you with our beliefs, other than saying we firmly believe that Lucifer is the true sovereign of this universe. And that he will soon rule it for all time."

"What's that got to do with me?" asked Seven with a smirk. "I don't even own a pitchfork."

Klaus Braun gave the prisoner a menacing glare, and his voice began to rise. "I see you haven't lost your annoying trait of being sophomoric and insolent, even though your life hangs in the balance!" Braun quickly calmed himself. "To answer your question though, you have been brought here so that we can evaluate what you actually do know or might have possibly told others. And how this may affect the timing of our actions." Dr. Braun pointed to the well dressed mystery man who Seven had noticed earlier. "Allow me to present my head cleric, Lucas Yezid. Using his unique satanic gift, Lucas can readily discern a prisoner's fraudulence, discover any threats to us, and divine a prisoner's fate. How he does this, even I do not fully understand. Yet his demonic gift of prophecy produces uncanny, supernatural accuracy. He is practically infallible."

For a brief moment, Christopher Seven wondered if this so-called mystic actually *was* able to detect the truth. Seven had read about such people. Clairvoyants who, at all times, could do just that. Seven had always been skeptical about most of them. As for some diviner being given this power by the devil, the G5 operative knew that was quite impossible. The Bible clearly stated that only God actually knows what will befall mankind, saying this resolutely. Seven remembered the theme of those biblical passages. *The gift of discernment is a gift from God alone, according to the Word. One that the Prince of Lies doesn't have the power to give.*

Seven momentarily closed his eyes and silently petitioned God for help in overcoming the evil around the table. He relaxed a minute, as Klaus Braun preached on.

"Any good operation or plan has to have well thought-out contingencies in the event of unexpected problems. Such is the case with ours. We will now question you to see if we must further change or advance our operation's schedule. Perhaps strike even quicker. Maybe even in a few days. Although that would admittedly make things much harder. And maybe a tad less effective as well."

Braun angrily shook his head at the thought, and then went on, "As you undoubtedly must have overheard, we've already decided to move up our operation a whole month earlier, due to your, and Miss Kent's, meddling. We can do so again if necessary. Yet, if we can wait until our present June 4th target date, so much the better. We therefore need to know everything you've discovered regarding my operation. And what, if anything, you've revealed to any others." Braun frowned with genuine concern.

Seven remained silent for a moment, frantically trying to decide what, if anything, to say. While he certainly wasn't willingly going to tell this madman anything about G5, or about the warning notes he'd left with Eduardo's daughter, could there be a way to stall? Coax Braun into delaying Operation D in order to give every chance for Seven's SOS to get through? The Super Stud hurriedly pondered the possibilities and then gave his reply. "Whatever I say to you now will be the truth, Dr. Braun. Man to man. I hope you'll respect that."

"I understand, Mr. Seven. One warrior to another."

After a short pause, Christopher Seven began the most important recitation of his life. He spoke calmly and confidentiality, something he knew would impress his satanic audience. Seven remembered and used his early training on being interrogated or tortured by enemy agents. *Always give them plenty of snippets of truth,* G5's intelligence instructors had taught him. *Never make up total whoppers or lie excessively,*

It took Seven over an hour to assure Braun's crew, but he convincingly stated that since he hadn't left the island after last night's bonfire ceremony, there was obviously no way he could have told anybody on the outside what he'd overheard. As to informing anyone *prior* to that, Seven stuck to the same story. He was just a magazine correspondent and had known nothing about any bomb plot. In fact, he and Sandy thought they'd actually be *helping* Dr. Braun by finding the missing cobra. As for Operation D, Seven swore that the first time he ever heard the operation's name, or any details about it, was when watching the gas lit ritual the night before. He wrapped up his recitation by credibly informing them that he likewise knew nothing at all about Eduardo Valdez being a part-time FBI operative. Or Ed's wanting to kill Dr. Braun. He'd merely engaged the Cuban for transportation, after Valdez was recommended by his FBI media friend. And as for sneaking onto Braun's island? It was simply done to make his exposé more exciting. After an hour of this persuasive logic, Seven was certain that most of the table attendees had believed him. The pseudo reporter thus ended his remarks.

Klaus Braun initially said nothing, not wanting to give the prisoner any hints of his thoughts. However, everything Seven had stated made solid sense. Surely if this journalist had been with the police, or was working with some Federal agency that suspected anything as bold as Operation D, that agency would have been here already to arrest everyone. Or they would have done so in Miami.

"Thank you for your recitation, Mr. Seven," Dr. Braun finally exclaimed. "And now, it's time for Cleric Yezid, our infallible diviner of truth. He alone will decide if what you have just told us is a lie or the truth. He will likewise reveal how the Dark Prince below will want your death and your punishment handled, if either is required."

Klaus Braun nodded to the mysterious priest. Lucas paused a moment and then slowly stood up, like a corpse rising from its casket during a wake! Lucas Yezid appeared to be in some sort of powerful trance, as sweat poured from his face and guttural moans spewed from his mouth. His eyes, now bored in on Seven's, were glazed in a stony, pallid hue, truly the eyes of death! After several minutes of this spell, the satanic mystic seemed to snap out of it. Turning toward Seven, Yezid began his decree.

"By the power of Lucifer within me, I have divined that the prisoner spoke truthfully when he claimed he knew nothing of our operation prior to last night. Satan's revelation has likewise assured me that this man has done *nothing* to prevent or hinder us. There's not one thing to fear from this captive. Either now or in the future." Yezid nodded, affirmatively. "Your operation is quite safe, gentlemen. There's no need to begin it any sooner or later. June 4th should still be our target date." The high priest then concluded, "Regarding the prisoner's fate, Satan's instructions were also clear."

Seven watched with a distant feeling of both trepidation and curiosity, as the ghostly prophet gave the guilty sentence. "The Dark One has decreed that this reporter shall be fed to the sacred dragon, alive, at midnight, on Friday, May 28th. He will join Sandra Kent in agonizing death at our final Miami punishment session!"

Chapter 40

Operation D

Christopher Seven, trying to outwardly appear calm, showed absolutely no emotion, hoping to deny these killers a groveling dog-and-pony show. Turning toward Braun, he exclaimed with an assertive smirk, "So much for the mercy of the court, and getting off easy via your phony-baloney high cleric. I agreed to tell you the truth and did. But as usual, you and your people turn out to be filthy liars."

Dr. Braun's reply was cold and unemotional. "You had a fair chance, and that's all I promised. Frankly, after weighing the counts against you, I find the punishment just. You will die on the twenty-eighth of May at midnight, along with Miss Kent. Die in the manner foretold. That's a consecrated revelation from Lucifer himself."

Seven calmly looked at his fingernails, as if not having a care in the world. He'd been taught never to give up, no matter how dire the outlook, and hoped his training would keep him strong. His mind still clung to the slim hope generated by the SOS note given to young Edie Valdez. And, as always, on escape. His duty as a secret agent was to garner as much information as possible and to then to somehow flee with it. If there was to be any chance at all, he'd have to know more about Klaus Braun's plan. With that in mind, he decided to goad Braun into revealing more. Perhaps the egotistical snake man would be swayed by his fawning audience sitting around the conference table.

With all the scorn he could muster, Christopher Seven began his taunts with a derisive chuckle. "You know, Klaus, everything I've heard so far is just a bunch of wishful nonsense. The only *dark one* I can see is the fool who dreamed up this silly little operation of yours." Seven laughed, loudly. "Do you actually think a few sticks of dynamite, or whatever homemade explosives you've cooked up, are going to hurt the most powerful country in the world? It's all a pipedream, Klaus." Seven shook his head, derisively. "As for you or your old man enjoying any satanic revenge, I wouldn't be surprised if your father, the so-called Floda Braun, or should I say, Martin Bormann, croaks before long anyway. He may not even live till June fourth."

The tactic worked perfectly. Klaus Braun's response was immediate, and laced with fury. He rose up from his chair in a rage, stormed over to where the handcuffed Seven sat, and slapped him hard several times across the face. "You are the foolish one, Seven!" Braun screamed between blows. "And since you will soon be dead, devoured without eyes, while your flesh is chewed into mush by my dragon; it will amuse me to tell you about our *'silly'* little operation', as you've called it. Something for you to take to the grave." The doctor cleared his throat, as the Super Stud, ignoring his stinging cheeks, tried to focus solely on what Braun spat out.

"Operation D will *indeed* hurt your filthy country! Millions will die, and economic chaos will ensue on a scale that will make 9-11 and the COVID pandemic seem like child's play!"

Dr. Braun waited for his words to be absorbed. Observing, with satisfaction, the captive's suddenly concerned expression, he then went on with his explanations. "All of my life, for as far back as I can remember, the West, particularly the United States, has been the decadent catalyst for ruining mankind. Your religions, your democracy, and of course your constantly butting in on other nations. From father's time to mine."

Seven sneered. "We're *asked* to butt in, Braun."

"Yes. Asked by other even *weaker* democracies. All the same, your wretched country has always been soft and corrupt."

"You seem to like it, Klaus. Your mansions, your expensive wines, and your stacks of money. It's your way of life too."

Klaus Braun's nervous habit of laughing sarcastically surfaced again as he spoke. "I only wanted to prosper in the United States, and use those temporal things you mentioned, as a way of showing my Satanist brothers how easy it is to succeed in your pathetic country. I've lived to bilk the American public out of billions of dollars, and then utilize their *own* money against them. Utilizing an enemy's own resources, while opposing him, is looked upon highly in the satanic world. That's why it was so important for me to exploit your magazine article. To sway the United States Senate into giving me a sizable grant. It was the only reason I even tolerated you. That would have been the final icing on the cake, getting that senate pharmaceutical grant. The sweetest irony of all. Your foolish government actually helping finance Operation D.' Braun frowned. "Unfortunately, your and Miss Kent's brainless meddling forced me to rush everything, so now it isn't to be."

"Too bad," answered Seven with a smirk.

"Yes, it is too bad, Mr. Seven. Oh well, one can't have everything." Dr. Braun gave a cynical shrug. "Generally, I get what I want. Or I use my brain and my power to make things go the way I desire. Take this New Ripper ruse, for instance." Braun sneered at the name. "Father and I devised all of it. Planned it to the last detail some time ago as a prelude to D." Braun nodded his head. "You'd be interested to know, Seven, that two of my *own* men, professional killers from the Middle-East, are actually the so-called Ripper."

So! Seven had wondered how the Ripper thing tied in with Dr. Braun and his Operation. Thus far, the Super Stud had thought it was merely the use of a rare Braun snake. But now, who knew what the doctor had really planned? And *why?*

Klaus Braun, seeing the puzzled expression on his captive's face, quickly informed, "You see, Mr. Seven, when a major operation is planned against any large country, a few obscure rumors concerning the potential attack are bound to leak out. It even happened with 9-11, though those leaks went unheeded."

Christopher Seven silently agreed, but he remained quiet while Dr. Braun explained more.

"Because there are so many terrorist rumors constantly floating around, most of them are taken lightly. Every month or two your government gets a lead on something, which inevitably turns out to be a false alarm. Even so, when governments think of possible major operations carried out from within, they initially focus on people or organizations rich enough to carry them out. Like bin Laden, for instance. Or even me."

Seven had to admit this was true. It was always well-funded enemies that proved the most dangerous.

"I knew there might eventually be suspicions about me and my secretive billion-dollar company," Braun acknowledged. "Particularly if word ever leaked out that someone might be financing an internal terrorist plot. Hence I took the initiative *before* it happened and purposely let them think I was involved in something *else*. Like giving a venomous snake to a serial killer. Or harboring an old war criminal. My tactics worked flawlessly. Even you would have to acknowledge that." Seven nodded inwardly as Dr. Braun added, "It's just like I taught you about apprehending a cobra. Always focus the attention on your left hand while you actually plan to attack with the right! Keeping your opponent off balance; that's the key. Whether it's human or reptile."

Christopher Seven shook his head in self-disgust. *Yes,* he thought. It had worked perfectly. We all suspected Klaus Braun might be up to something. Perhaps deliberately hiding the fact that one of his snakes had been lost or stolen. Or possibly pulling off some type of pharmaceutical scam. But that was small potatoes compared to Braun's actual plans. The snake man's subterfuge had come off flawlessly. The old carnie slight-of-hand gambit. Even G5 was taken in, along with the FBI. The agent turned away to hide his shame and anger, as Braun's boasting continued. "By the way, my two top assassins, the *real* New Rippers, Rahmad and Amir, have been keeping tabs on you from the start."

Seven laughed mockingly. "I hope you've got better men than that, Klaus. I snuck onto this island rather easily."

Braun shrugged his shoulders. "Perhaps. But most of the time my very proficient security squad does not fail me. Anyway, as I was saying, I used the New Ripper gambit to divert attention. By occasionally using a snake, something I knew might attract the authorities to me or my Center, I deliberately pushed the envelope. Just to see if the police or FBI would even think of me."

"They did, Braun."

"Yes," the doctor acknowledged. "But they never connected on the *real* thing. Or even on the fact that I was a practicing Satanist. The closest to discovering the truth was that FBI female agent, Loretta Swanson. My inside sources quickly warned me about her. That's why she had to go. As for her FBI colleagues, by the time they ever do associate me with the actual plot, or with your and Miss Kent's upcoming disappearance - Operation D will have already done its job. And we'll be safely out of the country."

"Operation D?" asked a chuckling Seven, hoping his scorn would keep baiting the doctor into revealing more of his plans. "How do you know the inane thing will even come off? The little guy, standing on the corner with a nuclear bomb in his lunchbox, never seems to work. How can you be so sure *your* operation will?"

Dr. Braun's exhilaration began to build. He rubbed his hands excitedly as he spoke. "Have you ever heard of the Russian M89 compact nuclear bomb, Mr. Seven?"

"As a matter of fact I have," admitted Seven. "I wrote an article about those missing soviet weapons for the *Washington Star.*"

Braun's mention of the bombs brought Seven back to another Super Stud assignment. One in which he was dispatched overseas to ferret out some information about these explosives from a pretty Russian socialite, who was having an affair with her Soviet boss. The mission had been only partly successful, and most of the M89s were never found. To this day, Colonel McPhail worried about some rogue country or independent power getting its hands on one, via the expanding Russian weapons black market.

"The M89s are small but formidable nuclear bombs," Seven affirmed, hoping to keep the dialog going. *Dirty bombs* in a carrying case, they called them back then. A compact bomb that can take out a whole city. The Soviets produced quite a few of them before Glasnost. From what I recall, no one was particularly concerned about their being lost, as most experts felt that the M89s were hopelessly unworkable. In fact, my story centered on the well-established reality that getting them to detonate properly was almost impossible. That was always the problem with those particular bombs. They were worthless without a feasible method to set them off."

The Super Stud was suddenly wary of the direction this was heading, as Klaus Braun pompously asked, "What if I was to tell you that I'd arranged for ten of these undersized nuclear bombs to be smuggled into Canada from Russia? And then into the United States from there. And what if I told you that these ten bombs, armed and ready to blow, will soon be sitting in some of your most vital cities?"

Christopher Seven considered the effect of Braun's scenario, and then with sudden sweat dripping from his brow responded, "I'd say I hope you haven't found a way to detonate them."

"Oh, I haven't," Klaus Braun admitted. He paused dramatically. "But Doctors Gustaff and Schilling have."

Seven watched speechlessly as the two nuclear experts from Norway stood up and bowed slightly to him. They then sat back down.

"It took them almost two years," continued Braun. "And a lot of my money. But with some external help, they eventually devised a new linear timing device that can detonate the M89 weapons flawlessly. I'm not much of an expert on nuclear gadgets but they tell me it has something to do with fusion and a slow dripping acid timer. In any case, it works, and all ten bombs will be set to go off and destroy their target areas simultaneously. When they do, your Homeland Security Department and your first responders will be overwhelmed. It will make Hurricane Katrina and the COVID pandemic seem like a day in the park. The economic and psychological impact will last forever!"

So that's it, thought Seven, now half in panic. *This madman really does have a way to destroy much of the United States and kill millions of people in the process. Not with pharmaceuticals, but with powerful nuclear devices! And here I was trying to stop him with nothing more than my looks and a liaison with his pretty secretary. What fools we've all been, worrying about a single serial killer instead of planning to stop a major assault on the country.* Braun's voice interrupted Seven's distressing thoughts.

"And do you want to know the best part, Seven? It doesn't matter *what*, or even *who*, you've told about this. The bombs will soon be sitting snuggly in various parking locales. They'll be hidden inside ten non-descript vans, and some SUVs as well. Expertly programmed to explode on our new date, June the fourth." Dr. Braun again rubbed his hands gleefully. "That's just three weeks from now. And even if they found out some of the details, your government certainly couldn't check *every* city, *every* similar vehicle, and *every* parking option in the country. Not with only three weeks left to do so. Braun frowned slightly, "Of course, due to you and Miss Kent possibly stumbling on a critical fact or two, I'll have to change some of my original targets and parking venues. Regardless, the vans will be leaving for their *final* destinations very shortly. They'll soon be sitting safely in their indoor or outdoor parking cocoons around the country, ready to do their explosive tasks on D-Day." And only I will know the targeted cities."

Dr. Braun then gave a look of counterfeit sorrow. "Unfortunately our well-paid van drivers, who think they're delivering stolen aircraft parts, by the way, will have to be eliminated. That will be done quickly. Hopefully an hour or so, after they arrive and have parked their vehicles. We'll instruct each of the drivers to simply collect the remainder of their hefty fees in various back alley addresses we'll give them. Sadly, but as a necessary precaution, that's where all of the drivers will be eliminated. Shot by local hit men, contracted by an 'anonymous source'. Hopefully their deaths will be painless."

"But of course," frowned Seven.

"So no matter *what* you've done, it's too late to stop my operation now!" Braun roared. "And as I've told you, only I know where all the fireworks will be. Accordingly, in the unlikely event of capture, I carry this." He waited a moment and then patted his right pocket. Seven wondered what it meant, and watched as Dr. Braun took out a small packet containing a lone, green capsule, He then explained, "Cyanide, Mr. Seven. My father carries one as well. Quick and painless. Should any of your police friends surprise us before June fourth, we'll simply bite down on these, and that will be that. Yet all provisions have been made, so Operation D will commence even if we're dead."

"Why don't you try the pill now to see if it works?" asked Seven.

"And miss your and Sandra's May 28th punishment extravaganza in Miami?" Braun countered. "Certainly not." The snake man laughed triumphantly. "So there you have it, Seven, Operation D. What do you think of my *silly* little operation now?"

Christopher Seven sat silently. There was really nothing to say. Nothing to do either. Except hope and pray that somehow Edie Valdez would get through. Yet even if the authorities eventually did get the note, what good would it really do?

"Incidentally," added Braun, "there's one more thing."

"I can't wait to hear it," Seven retorted, sarcastically.

"I myself can't take *all* of the credit for this glorious operation," Dr. Braun admitted. "It was actually my revered father who designed much of it. The brilliant man over there who you mistakenly thought was Martin Bormann."

"Oh come off it, Klaus," Seven bristled. "What's the point of denying that he's Bormann at this point? I've heard all about the Nazis trying to add years of life to people, using their sordid experimental drugs. So why deny it? Rumor has it that your father is indeed Martin Bormann. And that you've somehow slowed down his aging process." Seven glared at the oldster. "They'll soon be chasing your old man from every part of the globe, despite the fact that you've probably added eighty years to his disgusting life."

"Actually only seventy-eight, Mr. Seven," corrected Klaus Braun. "Father should be about one hundred and thirty-five years old now. But you're right in some respects. Thanks to my formulas, we've indeed had some success in the area of slowing down aging." Then, with a twinkle in his eye, Braun winked at the men around the table and asked, "But what's all this about *Martin Bormann?*"

"I know the whole story," Seven retorted, "about those last days of the Third Reich. The shadowy tale of Adolf Hitler's funeral procession.

When Hitler's dead body was wrapped in heavy black sheets, and then quickly burned, along with his wife's corpse. All done in a showy gasoline funeral pyre. And then, years later, the witness who claimed he saw an unknown mystery man in a demonic mask walking behind Hitler's procession." Seven glanced at Klaus Braun's elderly father. "Two guesses who that was. Mr. Bormann over there. You people know I'm going to die soon. So why don't you at least admit to that?"

"Perhaps I should explain it myself, Mr. Seven," said someone else sitting at the table. The voice was very soft and frail, with an unusual European accent. Seven looked up and saw that it was the old man himself, Floda Braun, who was speaking. His son, Klaus, immediately stood and interrupted him. "You don't have to tell this fool anything, father."

"Oh, but I want to, my son. I too, have longed for an American or British audience to whom I could tell my story. Let it be this man, ironically a journalist, who hears it now." Klaus sat back down and reluctantly let his father, Floda, begin.

"Martin Bormann died via suicide on the very day you've described, Mr. Seven." Floda Braun looked upward as if recalling the whole thing again. "He died, along with Hitler's faithful wife, Eva. Martin Bormann, like Eva, willingly committed suicide to serve an important purpose. He died so that a clever deception could take place. One that was deemed *Sehr Geheim*, and ultimately *Chef Sache;* the uppermost classification of Nazi secrets in the Third Reich.

Floda took a small sip from the glass of water that someone had placed near his chair. "You see, Mr. Seven, it was actually Martin Bormann who lay dead under the black sheet, *not* Hitler. And it was actually Bormann's body that was burned along with Eva's. Hitler was still very much alive. In fact, it was Hitler himself who was the mysterious masked man, walking off to the side in his *own* funeral procession. By the way, that mask is called a *Yucid*. It's a satanic death mask honoring Lucifer. The same type of skeletal mask we use today in many of our Yozem vengeance slayings."

The old man smiled thinly and then concluded his account. "The Bormann deception worked without a hitch. Even the most powerful Nazis attending that day never realized the switch of Martin Bormann for Adolf Hitler. The allies never knew either. They simply thought Hitler dead, and Bormann alive, and therefore the world kept on looking for Martin Bormann without success. In the meantime, Hitler, alive and well, secretly escaped to South America with his young son. It was he, *not* Bormann, who was kept alive all these years. Through a venom-laced vitamin drug Klaus developed."

"How could you possibly know all that, Floda?" Seven asked.

"Because, Mr. Seven, I am *not* Martin Bormann. I am Adolf Hitler. And this is my son, Klaus!"

236

Chapter 41
Diary of a Madman

Seven fell back in his chair as if punched in the stomach, the wind literally knocked out of him by the old man's incredible revelation. Then, after thinking on it, he just couldn't make himself believe Floda's claim. It had to be some sort of clever deception. A gambit to somehow influence the hateful nightshift lunatics Klaus employed. Yet why would they lie about this Hitler thing now, knowing their condemned prisoner was going to die soon? Furthermore, if one believed in the possibility of a hundred-and-thirty-year-old Martin Bormann, being kept alive by a miracle drug, then why not an equally old Adolf Hitler?

Seven looked over at the feeble old man. His facial expressions were harsh like Hitler's, and though there was no mustache, his angular face, stooped shoulders, and piercing eyes could indeed be the matured features of the hated Nazi dictator. *Yes,* thought Seven, *it just might be. Yet how could this bizarre story be true? Was it simply an expedient narrative that Dr. Braun and the oldster had fabricated for some warped political or satanic reasons? A devoted 'espirit de corps'?*

Nonetheless, when the G5 operative thought back on the whole scenario, he had to grudgingly admit that many things fit. There was the vengeful and grandiose plan of Operation D for instance. And the cruel extremism of Braun's inner circle. Even the way these nightshift zealots worshipped Klaus himself, and revered his father, Floda. Whoever he was.

Sitting perfectly still, the stunned Super Stud decided to say nothing for a few moments. Everything was going far too fast now. Braun's cataclysmic plans, Sandy's and his own brutal death sentence, and of course this unbelievable Hitler business. Klaus Braun interrupted the tense silence.

"I know you find father's story hard to believe, Mr. Seven, but it's absolutely true. He is indeed Adolf Hitler, and I'm his son, Klaus. Born out of wedlock in 1943 at Berchtesgaden, Bavaria."

"Sure, and I'm Winston Churchill," sneered Seven.

Braun ignored the derisive remark and calmly continued, "After my mother's death, as the Russians were rapidly closing in on the fuehrer bunker in Berlin, father and I were secretly shepherded out of Germany by a special undercover SS unit. Of course there first had to be a grand deception and my father used the one he just revealed to you. He and his two-year-old son, yours truly, were flown out clandestinely, eventually settling in the rural outback of South America, along with several other prominent Nazis. We had tons of money in gold bullion from the Reich treasury, but obviously, we couldn't use father's celebrated last name. So we instead chose to use my mother's maiden name, *Braun.* She was, of course, Eva Braun. I retained my actual first name of Klaus, but father cleverly inverted his first name, Adolf, into Floda. Floda is the reverse of Adolf. It's an amusing gambit, and we've used variations of this inversion ploy many times since." Dr. Braun smiled at the old man, well pleased with their inside family joke.

"I spent many happy years in South America," Klaus continued. "Father and I treasured our daily sessions with the satanic ministers flown in. Father's always been interested in the occult, especially astrology, and he became a devout Satanist the last year of the war." Braun smiled. "South America was also where I became adept at handling snakes. Even the most venomous ones. At thirteen, I was introduced to medicine, another subject I became proficient in. I studied under the best medical brains of the Reich. True geniuses who relocated to our community through Buenos Aires. Many of the Nazi doctors were there. Vickstrom, Heiks, and the brilliant Dr. Mengele."

"What a lovely bunch of medical misfits," stated Seven.

Again, Braun pretended not to hear the insult, simply going on with his story. "These men showed me the secrets and discoveries learned, in part, from various medical experiments at the camps. The more mundane drugs they developed, like the headache and arthritis pills, I later mass-produced in Florida. Made me a blooming fortune. But the *real* Nazi secrets, such as the anti-aging inroads and the cloning advances, I kept to myself. When they're fully developed, I'll use them to force Lucifer's will."

"I'm sure the world can't wait," Seven interjected.

This time Braun gave the reporter an angry glare, but then went on. "Several years later, father and I quietly immigrated to America via our satanic contacts in immigration. And also by way of many sizable bribes. We then opened the Miami Reptile Center, and the rest, as they say, is history. Soon after, with the invaluable help of Cleric Yezid here, we put together a solid core of nightshift Satanists. We've worked steadily ever since for satanic revenge, and Operation D will be our most intricate endeavor yet. Sadly, since we have yet to find an unending fountain of youth, it may well be father's last."

"I'm so terribly sorry," smirked Seven.

Braun, still trying hard to ignore Seven's insolence, continued, "It was during my late teen years in South America that I learned about Vitimultin. The amazing vitamin mixture developed for father during the war by Dr. Theo Morell. Based on Nazi poison theories, I came up with the idea of mixing this vitamin formula with Bushmaster venom. Low and behold, it worked! We had found our fountain of youth."

Klaus Braun took another sip of water and further explained, "Regrettably, though, Dr. Morell died a few years after the war's end. And there was never any diary or notebooks kept on the exact ingredients of his Vitimultin. Try as we could, even later with intricate computer analysis, we just couldn't duplicate Morell's precise formula. We still can't, and that's the problem. All that was left of the vitamins were the hefty batches Dr. Morell had already mixed for my father. The huge vats of Vitimultin that were flown out with us when we escaped to South America. Although we still had it in sealed bulk, and the stuff has an almost endless shelf life, it was really only a sufficient amount to give to *one* individual over the years. And now, it's nearly run out. Yet what better person to have preserved than my father?"

"What about Genghis Khan?" asked Seven, sardonically.

Dr. Braun finally showed anger. "Listen, Seven, I've tried to be patient with you, so stop your childish insults!" Still irate, he nonetheless countered, "At least father will be around long enough to enjoy the Operation D fireworks. And *your* torturous death"

Seven grinned his next reply, "Yeah, maybe he'll live another month or so. Then he'll kick the bucket as he should have long ago. And even you, and your sordid scientists, can't prevent *that.*"

"Regrettably, we can't, Mr. Seven. Unless our chemists can come up with a last-minute breakthrough. But no one lives forever. And my father will live to carry out what Satan willed for him years ago!"

"And what's that?" Seven asked. "To temporarily cripple a country that kicked his butt back then? I'd say that's carrying a persecution complex a bit too long."

Interrupting the dialog, the elderly Floda Braun interjected, "Oh, it's nothing like that at all, Mr. Seven. There are no longer nations or governments that concern me. My planning is solely for Lucifer now. Not some man-made boundaries. Countries are merely land masses to be used and discarded. I could have risen to the top of *any* country! Even yours. Germany was simply a convenient spot on the map."

Seven nodded. "You're right about that, old man. Hatred and bigotry can be found *anyplace.* If you're really who you say you are, and I doubt that very much, then it was you and your political ring of murderers, and *not* the German people that was really to blame. Something like Nazism could have happened anywhere, even in America. Look at the Ku Klux Klan, and the Neo-Nazi movements. Ignorance and prejudice can fuel the worst instincts of *any* people."

"Father no longer discusses politics," Klaus interrupted.

"Too bad," chided Seven. "And too bad your daddy's Flintstone Vitamins are running out, and he'll soon be a *dead* dictator."

"Whatever time my father has left, he will live longer than you!" Klaus Braun screamed. "And he'll die a lot less painfully!"

"We'll see," was Seven's rather intriguing reply.

The snake man shrugged his shoulders, and then spoke in a controlled, almost conciliatory tone. "Today is Saturday, May 14th. We'll let you and Miss Kent relax here on my island for the next twelve days or so. Albeit with the help of an injected drug that will make you both sleep a lot, as well as make you extremely cooperative. I may need a few photos of you both, to go along with the lovely letters I'm forcing Miss Kent to write to her friends in her own handwriting. Some sophomoric dribble about Sandra running off to St. Barths with a handsome 'mystery man'. These letters, bearing an actual St. Barths' postmark, should keep the Miami police fools guessing for a few more weeks. And that's all I'll need."

Christopher Seven took in everything carefully as Braun informed, "On Thursday, May 26th, you and Miss Kent, in a sleepy, drugged stupor, will be quietly smuggled back to the Miami Reptile Center via one of my corporate planes. You'll be landing at the Pompano Beach commuter airport where I pay hefty bribes for just such purposes. And though I doubt we'll need them, I'll have the necessary forged passports and papers just in case." Dr. Braun looked around the table at his colleagues, purposely ignoring Seven. "Then, gentlemen, at midnight, May 28th, Miss Kent and Mr. Seven, along with a ravenous, Komodo dragon, will be the main attraction at our very last Miami punishment ceremony!"

Klaus Braun walked over to his handcuffed prisoner, and savagely pulled Seven's hair back. "You stupid unbelieving meddler!" Braun screamed. Quickly calming himself, the snake man let go of Seven's hair. With an evil smirk of dismissal he said, "Until the 28th, then, Mr. Seven. When we shall first cut out your eyes and then throw you to the sacred beast." He smiled, maliciously. "Pleasant dreams."

The next twelve days on Braun's Royal Keys Island were a series of sedated blurs for both Christopher Seven and Sandy Kent. Neither saw the other, as they were housed and tightly guarded in separate quarters. Continually drugged to be more compliant, via a new venom-based drug, Seven vaguely recalled posing and smiling dutifully for a few pictures taken of him in a bathing outfit. The crafty Dr. Braun planned to keep the photos handy, in case they were needed to keep the Sandra's 'romantic vacation' story alive. They might be helpful to go along with the letters he'd forced her to write to some friends. Letters which mentioned that she and her 'mystery man' were vacationing together for two dreamy weeks in the Caribbean.

In the meantime, Klaus Braun and his nightshift crew, now back in Florida, were working diligently on Operation D, along with honing their elaborate 'getaway' plans. Just like every other year at Braun's Miami complex, the reptile park and pharmaceutical laboratories were now 'closed for annual renovations', during the slow, pre-summer period. Unlike past years, however, this time Braun's Miami facilities would *not* be reopening.

On Thursday morning, May 26th, at precisely 10:00 a.m., one of Dr. Braun's company seaplanes took off from Royal Keys for the short flight to Florida. Onboard, slumped dreamily in opposite corners of the aircraft, were the heavily sedated Sandy Kent and Christopher Seven. Braun's excellent forgery team had come up with perfect counterfeit passports for his two young captives, complete with photos and new names. Shortly after landing, the heavily bribed Pompano airport administrators laughed loudly as the 'intoxicated' young couple staggered off the plane. Sandy and Seven were quickly whisked away, and were soon ensconced at separate dorms near the Reptile facility.

~

The following day, a cloudy May 27th Friday afternoon in New York, G5's director, Colonel Peter McPhail, was worried sick after not hearing anything from his Super Stud agent in nearly two weeks. "Any contact from Seven?" he repeatedly asked his staff.

The answer was always the same. "Nothing so far, sir."

By two o'clock, Colonel McPhail had finally had enough. He called in Henry Carson, knowing his second in command had been on the phone all morning with the FBI. "What's the score, Hank?"

"Not much to tell you, Colonel. We discreetly checked on that FBI fisherman, Eduardo Valdez. He's the Cuban who Seven was working with. No one in Nassau has heard from Valdez, or has even *seen* him lately. Or his daughter, for that matter. It doesn't look promising."

"What do you suggest?"

"Well sir, after my conference call with the FBI this morning, and as per your instructions, we've agreed to let them take over completely, starting late next week. They're aware that Seven's last estimate was that this Operation D thing, whatever it entails, wouldn't commence until July 4th; a little over a month from now. So that still gives the FBI plenty of time to act once they take it from us next week."

McPhail nodded as Carson further informed, "Then, sometime around the middle of June, they intend to really put on a full court press. They'll confront Klaus Braun, grill him hard, and, via search warrants, thoroughly scrutinize his books." Carson shrugged. "Of course the FBI says they'll still give Seven the next ten days or so to resurface, and hopefully come up with something on his own. That is if Chris is still alive. If not, they're very sorry about it. A nice guy and a brave agent, but after all, they can't force a separate investigation about some missing journalist. Or anything regarding Dr. Braun for that matter, until they've got their ducks totally in order."

"I understand the FBI's position completely," said McPhail.

"No one's come right out and said it, Colonel, but I'm sure they all suspect that Christopher Seven is in all likelihood dead. Especially since Valdez has also gone missing. Everyone figures their island foray didn't go well. They got caught, and that was that."

McPhail nodded his head as Hank Carson added, "No one is sure about Sandra Kent though. Or whether Braun would do anything foolish regarding her. But Florida has no record at all of a Miss Sandra Kent returning to Miami with the rest of Braun's staff.

Carson cleared his throat. "Just yesterday, however, Miami PD came up with a few travel tidbits from some of Miss Kent's female friends. Letters from the Caribbean written in Sandra's handwriting. The letters and postcards say that she's having a great time visiting the various island hot spots. So it seems Miss Kent is island-hopping around the St. Barts area, romancing with someone."

"What about Braun's take regarding all this, Hank?"

"Dr. Braun claims he knows little about it. Aside from a brief note Sandra left for him at the hotel, just before they were scheduled to return to Miami. Braun is absolutely livid with his secretary. Says it's not at all like her to just take off and leave him a cursory memo. Braun's blaming Christopher Seven for the whole thing, who he claims hasn't been around either. The doctor says he'll be issuing a formal complaint to Seven's editors. "Neither Carson nor McPhail bought much of Braun's story, but knew they were helpless to intervene.

McPhail heaved a sigh. "Not much we can do at this point, Hank." The

Colonel sighed again. "I guess Seven and Valdez were eliminated during their spying attempt on Royal Keys, Hank. Either by some trigger-happy guard or on direct orders from Klaus Braun himself. Perhaps this Kent woman was somehow mixed up in it as well. But we certainly can't force an investigation. Security of G5, along with that of the Super Stud section. Chris knew the risks. He also knew we could never really protect him or go searching for answers if anything happened. Especially on someone's private island. No civil liberties there. We'll just have to assume the worst. Maybe the FBI can sort it out once they take over. Let me know if anything further turns up."

~

Locked in a heavily guarded employee dorm on the deserted outskirts of Braun's Miami Center, Christopher Seven knew nothing about New York's present dilemma. He had his own problems with which to contend. So far, Seven's day had been absolutely dreadful, waiting around helplessly for his pending execution scheduled for midnight tonight. It had been made even worse by the constant taunting of the sadistic guards. One sentry in particular, Rosier's young security lieutenant, Rick Clemons, was especially disagreeable. The Super Stud longed to get his hands on this cocky punk. But, being handcuffed, and frequently chained, Seven knew that was quite impossible at present.

This guarded dorm, which had been serving as Seven's prison was Spartan but functional. In addition to a small kitchen area and living room, there were two bedrooms, each with an adjoining bathroom. Seven's four guards all slept in the larger bedroom, with one of them always awake, and posted outside the prisoner's room. Surprisingly, Seven had been allowed his own bedroom and bath, though each night he was chained to his single bed by way of a long shackle. One which was removed every morning. Fresh clothing and toiletries were supplied daily, but all of Seven's toiletries were now in plastic containers. There were no glass bottles, and the shaver they had given him was electric. The wily Klaus Braun wasn't allowing his captive any item remotely usable as a weapon. Or anything which could be used to commit suicide before tonight's torture ceremony.

On this dreary, rain-filled Friday afternoon, Seven finished up an hour's worth of strenuous calisthenics, and then, still loyal to his Super Stud routines, showered, shaved, and brushed his teeth. Just as he finished, sudden footsteps approached his bedroom. "Time to get moving, pretty boy," prodded the smirking Rick Clemons. "We're taking you to see your Kent girlfriend over at the woman's quarters. Last chance to say your tender goodbyes." Clemons laughed loudly.

The security van took the long way over, passing through most of Dr. Braun's massive complex. Still handcuffed, Seven looked out the window and tried to take in everything. As he watched Braun's nightshift staff loading boxes and crates, it was quite obvious that final moving preparations were in motion. Clemons asked the van driver to stop by the Komodo dragon's habitat. "Let's show pretty boy what's in store for he and his woman tonight."

Except for a handful of nighttime workers by the dragon area, Braun's entire complex was now completely deserted. There was therefore no point in trying to scream for help. The guards led Seven closer to the Komodo's enclosure, where they soon were staring up at a towering podium, purposely being built directly over the dragon's sizable fenced-in habitat. There was no sign of Braun's monstrous beast, but two carpenters were warily putting the finishing touches on the newly constructed platform. This satanic punishment stage hovered directly above the big reptile's pen, but remarkably there was no railing or barrier around it. Accordingly, the cautious carpenters took great care not to accidentally fall off and land in the lair of one of the world's most dangerous creatures.

Rick Clemons chuckled as he explained, "This is where it all happens tonight, pretty boy. Where you and your girl will be thrown to the Komodo for his dinner."

"Maybe the dragon won't be hungry," Seven retorted.

The sadistic guard grinned. "Oh, he's always hungry. But just in case," Clemons pointed to a large pail on the far corner of the stage. "You see that bucket up there? All the way over in the corner. That's a mixture of melted chicken skin and offal. We have to keep it away from the gaslights because it's extremely flammable. Anyway, they spread that gunk all over the condemned prisoners. Just the smell of it drives the huge reptile wild. Normally the Komodo Dragon is a cautious attacker, merely biting a prey with its venomous teeth and then waiting for the quarry to fall. But if anything lands in his pit with *that* goo all over it - well, let's just say, the dragon goes crazy and devours its victim immediately. Dead *or* alive." Clemons laughed loudly again. "And you and the Kent woman will be coated with that stuff."

Christopher Seven didn't hear much of Clemons' laughter. Instead, he concentrated on the guard's statement about the combustible chicken fat. Glancing around, the G5 agent noticed there were several towering gaslight stands surrounding both the stage and the dragon's lair. Tonight they'd presumably all be lit, flaming torches to give the event the demonic appearance that Braun and his devilish creeps seemed to love. Seven had seen similar gas-lit poles back on the island, during the satanic ceremony there. *Well, well,* he contemplated, silently. *Gaslights and an extremely flammable bucket of chicken oil. There might be a chance after all!*

~

Ten minutes later, the blue minivan came to a stop in front of an ivory building marked *Women's Quarters*. Seven and his four guards were soon standing inside a modern residence containing a small but well-appointed living room, a spotless kitchen, and two back bedrooms. Elsa

Dykstra, dressed in black leather, greeted them, gun in hand. She stood alone in the middle of the small foyer leering at Seven with both desire and scorn. "So," she exclaimed. "Our handsome young reporter has been caught with his hand in the cookie jar. It will be good to hear his screams tonight."

Elsa motioned toward a tall Asian guard who was holding a snub-nosed revolver on Seven and barked out an order. "Sit him down and bind his legs with those irons. You can then unlock his cuffs." Mercifully Seven's uncomfortable handcuffs were soon removed and he was then led to the couch. "Bring out the Kent girl!" Dykstra commanded. "Sandra's not cuffed, but that doesn't matter. She's nothing but a docile weakling. Elsa sneered at Seven. "Heaven knows why you find her appealing."

The guards quickly returned with Sandy Kent, holding her tightly by the arm. Thrilled to see her again Seven smiled warmly. As always, her incredible natural beauty, even in this environment, struck him. Other than a few small bruises about the face, she looked undamaged. Both Sandy and Seven were genuinely grateful that the other was still alive.

"Thank God," Sandy exclaimed. "I've prayed and prayed every night. When they told me this morning that you were alive, I didn't believe it at first. I thought it was just another one of Elsa's sadistic tricks. I can't tell you how wonderful it is to see you."

"It's wonderful to see you too, Sandy." He frowned at her bruises. "What's this Dykstra witch been doing to you?"

Sandy put her hand to her face. "Oh those," she said. "It wasn't Elsa this time. It was Rosier and Clemons. They roughed me up when I didn't write those letters fast enough to suit them."

Seven glared directly at Clemons. "Those two punks are pretty tough, as long as they're fighting women, or a cuffed prisoner. The G5 agent motioned toward the couch. "Sit down, Sandy. We've got some catching up to do."

"Klaus said to allow you exactly fifteen minutes," Elsa barked, gruffly. "Not a second more!" She then turned and walked into the far bedroom, accompanied by Clemons and a well-built black security man. The Asian overseer, Chang, strolled to the kitchen, sat down at a wooden table, and kept an eye on the captives with bored efficiency.

Sandy was anxious to hear the details of Seven's miraculous reappearance. "Are you really alright? How did you get back alive? They told me you tried to come for me on the island."

Seven didn't want to tell her too much in case Klaus Braun was setting up some type of last-minute interrogation. He accordingly downplayed it. "Oh, I'm a pretty persistent reporter. I needed an inside story on Braun's island for a supermarket tabloid I sometimes ghost write for. Didn't want to tell you about it for fear of worrying you. That's why I made up that Turks and Caicos story."

She looked at him caringly. "You make it sound so easy, but I bet it was terrifying. Anyway, you were right not to trust Dr. Braun. He's quite mad. I guess I've been the foolish one all along."

"Don't be silly, Sandy. Braun had everyone fooled."

"Tell me something, Chris. Is this evening, with that Komodo dragon beast, really going to be as bad as they say?"

Seven didn't have an adequate response. His main objective now was to keep her hopes up and her fears down without telling her the unthinkable truth about their almost certain future agony. "Listen, I'm not going to lie to you. We're in a heck of a mess and there's no sense denying it. But we're both still alive and that in itself is a miracle. So who knows what can happen?"

"My hero," Sandy said with a gentle touch to his cheek. "Always trying to make me feel better. But don't worry. I want you to know that I'm at peace now. At peace with myself, and at peace with God. I wasn't before all this, but I am now." She again smiled at him warmly. "Whatever happens, even if it's very painful, we'll only feel it momentarily. Then we'll be reunited in heaven."

"That's my girl." Seven took her hand gently. "That's the best way to look at it. Everyone faces death and people die each and every day. It's your faith in God that will bring you through it."

The two of them sat in silence for a few minutes. It was Sandy who tearfully broke the silence. "Elsa told me they'll be wiping out ten major cities and all of the inhabitants. It's unimaginable." More tears rolled down her cheek. "What a madman Dr. Braun turned out to be. I should have seen it coming."

The Super Stud said nothing. Her statement of 'I should have seen it coming' was indeed something that had grated on Seven ever since he heard Braun's incredible plans. Contrary to 9-11, where there were very few definitive clues beforehand, this time, he, a federal agent, knew exactly what was coming. Yet he was now powerless to prevent it. And unlike Sandy, Seven had been trained to spot enemies of his country. Sadly, Klaus Braun had fooled him too. It weighed heavily on him, and would be hard to die with tonight.

Sensing his frustration, Sandy looked at him caringly as she spoke. "You needn't blame yourself either, Chris."

Without hesitation, Seven grabbed her and kissed her passionately. This time the kiss was one of unmistakable love, at least on his part. "Well, I should have known one thing, Sandy. You're the most wonderful woman I've ever met." He kissed her again. "I should have told you earlier when I had the chance."

She smiled and put her hand on his. "I've thought a lot about our nights together in Nassau. I knew then that you still weren't ready for any permanent ties. Obviously, I wanted more, but you were still unsure; especially with me." He tried to interrupt but she would have none of it. "It's okay, Chris. I understand your point of view now." Sandy sighed. "I'm not sure of anything anymore. Except that I want to grow closer to God with the time I have left, as short as that will be. Yet if we ever do get out of this alive I want you to know that you'll have no obligations to me, nor I to you."

With a keen and loving eye, Christopher Seven looked at the beautiful woman sitting beside him and wondered mutely about the horrors facing them tonight. There was no sense kidding himself. Eduardo's daughter obviously hadn't comprehended anything about the warning note that Seven had given her back on the fishing boat. If young Edie had, the Feds would have been here already. The dejected agent sighed, trying desperately to hide his feelings. He knew the toughest part of the ordeal would be watching her go through the agony first. Clemons, the sadistic guard, had informed him that Dr. Braun had cruelly planned it that way.

Seven silently promised himself that if all else failed, he would attempt to somehow kill Sandy quickly, before her torture actually took place. There just might be the chance to grab a guard's gun, or to get his bound hands on one of the surgical instruments. If so, he'd slay Sandy without delay. And then in a wild surprise attack, turn the gun or knife on Dr. Braun and then himself. With these morbid thoughts twisting in his mind, he turned to her. "Sandy?"

"Yes, Chris."

"You trust me, don't you?"

"With all my heart."

"Promise me then, that whatever I attempt to do tonight, you'll understand."

"I promise."

And with that they lay silently in each other's arms until Elsa Dykstra returned to separate them.

Sandy, now with more tears in her eyes, was ushered back to her small room. Seven was led to the other bedroom by the sentries. Once inside, he was again handcuffed and his legs were chained to one of the bedposts. He was next ordered to sit down on the bed. Elsa Dykstra soon came in carrying a small pistol. "Wait outside," she ordered the guards. Clemons and Chang exited quietly, closing the bedroom door behind them. Elsa then walked over and locked it. Alone with the prisoner now, she smiled sweetly at him. "Well," Elsa purred, "We're finally together. I've been waiting a long time for this."

The Super Stud was half expecting a severe slap on the face

or perhaps a hard blow of the gun across his forehead. Instead, the unpredictable woman walked over and kissed him hard on the lips. The kiss tasted of gin and cigarette smoke, and Seven found it repulsive. Her excited breath still panting, she spoke again, "You are the handsomest creature I've ever seen - man *or* woman. I've wanted to do that for some time now. It's too bad we never really got to know each other. Tell me, do you like my passion?"

Seven wanted to tell her that he was revolted by the kiss but wondered if there might be a chance to use this horrid woman in some way. "What can I say, Elsa? You've got the gun."

"I know. But if you and I managed to enjoy ourselves now, perhaps I could help you."

"Just give me a car and let me out of here," Seven replied. Then I'll come back to you someday and give you *real* quality time."

"Oh, I couldn't do that, silly boy. Then I'd wind up in the jaws of the dragon instead of you. But I do have a pill I might give you. One that will deaden most of tonight's pain. Klaus developed it and it's quite effective." She came closer to him and stroked his hair longingly. "You just take it a few hours before they bring you to the punishment session, and you'll hardly feel a thing." Elsa grinned seductively. "So, is it a deal? You and I, for the chance to get this wonderful magic pill?" She rubbed her body against him, her intent unmistakable. "And I'll be a lot more interesting than your romps with that Kent weakling."

Christopher Seven summoned all of the hatred he could muster as he responded. "That's some choice, lady. The excruciating pain of my death tonight or the worse torture of having to be with you now. Frankly Elsa, I prefer the dragon."

His cutting words seemed to unleash a genuine monster inside Elsa Dykstra! Her neck reddened as did her face. Springing toward him in a mad rush, she began pounding him with her fists! The painful blows came rapidly, in a torrent of hard punches and slaps to his face. She kicked at his legs and other parts of his chained body. Her strength and fury were surprising, and Seven winced with the pain. The loud commotion quickly brought two of the guards to the locked door. They knocked frantically! "Miss Dykstra!" yelled a worried Chang. "Are you all right?"

"I'm fine!" Elsa hollered, calming herself as she walked over and unlocked the door "Get this unbelieving fool out of here!" she shouted, glaring at Seven with absolute loathing. "And one more thing. Make sure you save me a good seat tonight. I want to hear every one of his screams when the dragon rips him apart!"

S even and his guards left Elsa Dykstra's apartment a few minutes before 6:00 p.m. The Super Stud was thrown in the back seat of yet another van, this one a brown Toyota, driven by a heavyset blonde woman. Clemons, with his gun pointing directly at Christopher Seven, surprisingly announced, "You've got a quick appointment with Dr. Braun now, pretty boy."

Ten minutes later, the G5 operative was brusquely ushered into Dr. Braun's office. "Please handcuff Mr. Seven to his chair and wait outside," Braun ordered Clemons. "The cuffs should keep him still, and I'm armed as well." Braun showed a small gold plated double-barrel derringer. "Come back in fifteen minutes."

"Yes, sir."

Klaus Braun nodded toward Seven and greeted him. "Busy afternoon for me, Mr. Seven. In addition to all the moving details, I went over some final operational details with my father."

"And how is the little Fuehrer this evening?" asked Seven, derisively. "Has he conquered any countries today? They say France is still available."

Braun showed no trace of agitation. "My, my." He exclaimed. "You certainly are very witty for a man about to die. But Father is fine, thank you. Particularly so after he finally got the chance to tell someone from the West who he *really* is."

"Come on now, Dr. Braun. You don't really expect me or anyone else to believe that Hitler nonsense. Probably just something the two of you cooked up to impress your wacky followers."

"Believe what you want, Seven. But Father told you the truth the other day."

Seven frowned. "Enough of that Hitler baloney, Braun. When is this dragon sideshow of yours going to begin? If I'm going to die, why wait until later tonight? Why not get it over with now so you can concentrate on this maniacal new dawn of yours?"

There was a tense silence for a moment. Though it was probably just an unintentional throwaway line by the prisoner, the word *dawn* was both the initial name of the operation, as well as the codeword for activating the bombs. Klaus Braun gradually relaxed, dismissing his fleeting anxiety as simply coincidental wording. Looking up he replied, "You see, Mr. Seven, Father has always wanted to settle the score with your nation. Even during the war, he continually dreamed about what his Luftwaffe planners called the *New York Rocket*. A V2 missile that could reach the United States from Europe. They actually worked on such a weapon back then, along with experimental Messerschmitt long-range bombers that could potentially get to America. Sadly, nothing reached fruition." Braun smiled proudly. "But now, after all these years, Father's dream will indeed come true. And this time, it will not be for some singular nation, but for a higher cause. Lucifer's!"

The Super Stud scoffed at him. "You're completely barmy, Braun. As mad as that World War II moron you claim is your father. The only *dawn* you two should face is one with a firing squad."

"You called it a 'new dawn', Seven, and that's exactly what it will be. And why Father and I chose that particular name." Braun grinned. "We found it quite amusing when your government likewise used that *same* nickname for one of its inane Mid-East plans."

Dr. Braun stood up from his desk and further explained, "Incidentally, the 'D' of Operation D is for dämmerung; Operation Dämmerung, or Dawn to you. It will indeed bring forth a brand new era. For when the world sees what we've done, and the international media asks *why*; our satanic brethren will finally have a forum to preach our whole dogma." Braun wiped his brow. "You see, I've studied your Bible, Mr. Seven. Look at Ephesians 6:12; how Lucifer will fight you! Or in your Old Testament, Isaiah 14: 12-14. How Satan was once esteemed on Earth, and will again triumph."

"Those are false interpretations of the passages, Braun."

"False in your eyes, but not in mine, Mr. Seven. The world will soon learn the *truth* from Operation D!"

"You haven't done anything yet, doctor. And you may or may not do anything next week either. Even if you do, you'll merely be viewed as another homicidal maniac; a Manson, bin Laden, or Timothy McVeigh. Simply a brief footnote in history along with those other losers who tried to take revenge on a world they couldn't fit into."

Pounding his fist on the desk, Klaus Braun shouted, "Many people have underestimated me in the past! I am not afraid of you *or* your country. That's why I changed *nothing* regarding my current timetable, even after the meddling of you and Miss Kent. And why I have insisted, despite the nuclear scientists' admonitions to strike sooner, that we *don't* move up D-Day." Klaus Braun screamed his next words. "We will alter *nothing!* The bombs will indeed ignite on June 4th, *exactly* as I have decreed!"

So, thought Seven. *There is a way to move up, delay, or perhaps even prevent the detonation of those bombs.* He decided to keep angering the egocentric snake man in the hopes of getting more out of him.

"Things can always go wrong, Doctor. Even with the best of plans. Perhaps you've targeted the wrong cities. Or the bombs fail.

Braun promptly stopped his boasting, and, with a knowing grin, indicated for the first time that he was aware what the captive was trying to do. He nodded admiringly and replied, "You are indeed a character, Christopher Seven. Always trying to get information, and always thinking of impossible escapes. It's either the reporter or the policeman in you. Whichever, I admire your spirit and optimism. Although in this case, they're both misguided. It's a good thing for us you're going to die tonight. For like I've said, you play the game well. We're indeed better off without you."

An odd expression suddenly came over Braun's angular face, a gaze the G5 agent had never seen before. *Was it a look of madness?* Seven wondered as Braun expounded. "Yet, I will tell you this, Seven. Something you can take to the grave. There is one other entity that indeed knows *every* detail and design of my operation. My inner power and soul mate. My best friend so to speak. Just find him, her, or it, and that will tell you everything."

The Super Stud was taken aback. Who, or what, was Dr. Braun's trustworthy secret ally? Was it an actual person? His father for instance? Or a group of men like those two Norwegian scientists? Or could Braun be speaking metaphorically? Just an expression referring to his inner being, or his own satanic power? Seven calmly looked up and posed the question directly. "Why don't you tell a condemned prisoner the facts then?"

"Oh, but I already have," Mr. Seven. "I just told you the whole thing. And I think I've said quite enough."

Disappointed that the doctor wasn't going to reveal anything further, the Super Stud decided to try and switch gears. "What will you be doing in your new home abroad?"

"Oh, we still plan to be very active", answered Klaus Braun, evasively. My Mid-East friends are giving me a new base of operations in a remote part of Iran. They've told me I can have my snakes with me there, and that will come in handy for my next little venture. My herpetology team and I are planning to introduce deadly sea snakes into the decadent travel spots of the West. Places like the French Riviera, the Mediterranean's luxury beaches, and even your Hawaii."

Dr. Braun beamed proudly as he talked about it. "In order to see if this plan will work; introducing dangerous reptiles into places where they aren't indigenous. We've done it successfully before. My team covertly introduced the *Burmese Python* right here in Florida. Despite what you might have read about uncaring pet owners, it was actually *my* people who planted most of those huge constrictors all over your touristy Sunshine State. Thanks to us, this massive killer will soon be creating havoc on the eco system. And hopefully on residential areas throughout the entire south!" Braun's chest puffed out, pompously. "But my proudest success occurred in Guam several years ago. My associates and I secretly introduced some extremely venomous tree snakes there. It succeeded beyond our wildest dreams, and Guam is now crawling with deadly serpents."

"I hope the Chamber of Commerce rewarded you."

"No, they didn't, Mr. Seven. But my reptiles managed to kill or injure many of your fellow non-believers via Satan's power."

"That's pure nonsense, Klaus. It's you who should read the Bible more carefully. Like 1st Peter, 5:8, which states the devil is evil. And that Satan's followers never succeed."

Tiring of arguing philosophy, Dr. Braun took his usual glance at his watch and said, "Well, we obviously disagree. I'd love to go on with this, but I have many other things to do at the moment. And you too have much in store. Any last questions?"

When Seven said nothing, Klaus Braun walked over to where Seven was cuffed and addressed him again. "I have given you these moments of explanation out of respect. You were indeed one of the cleverest thorns that ever graced my garden, and, for that, I once more salute you. I never did find out if you were some sort of policeman or not. No matter. Your knowledge will die with you tonight. As for any alarms you might have been able to raise, I am now quite certain there were none. Or that they went awry. For undoubtedly had you been successful in reporting anything about my upcoming operation, your colleagues from the authorities would have raided us by now. My cleric was right. We have nothing to fear from you."

Christopher Seven sighed, knowing Braun was unfortunately correct. Two full weeks had passed since the G5 operative had given the SOS letter to Edie Valdez. Had his notes reached anyone by now, help certainly would have come already. The Super Stud shook his head dejectedly, just as Rick Clemons reentered Braun's office. Seven gave one last glance at Klaus Braun and advised, "There's a biblical edict, one that comes from the book of Job and also from James 4:7. God lets Satan go only so far with His servants, and then acts to rectify the situation. Remember that, Braun."

"In that case, Mr. Seven, you better hope He rectifies your present situation before midnight tonight!"

~

Two hours later, as Christopher Seven and Sandy Kent waited nervously in their separate apartment prisons, Rahmad and Amir arrived punctually at Dr. Braun's office. "Sit down," Braun ordered. The doctor stared at them a moment and then spoke. "Tonight, shortly after midnight, you'll be carrying out the *last* of your serial killings. The only murder *not* taking place on the first of the month. As homage to reparation night, you'll strike this evening." Waiting for further instructions, the two killers suddenly felt aroused as they toyed with images of tonight's victim.

Dr. Braun stood up and silently looked out the window. *This next part might be a bit tricky*, he mused. Braun looked directly at his henchmen. "Gentleman, I must now ask you to reaffirm your *Purus* pledge. That should I ever be killed in action, either here, or later in Iran, I am fully expecting you to avenge me as per your sworn vow."

The two henchmen bowed respectfully. Both knew that the *Purus* was a blood oath to Lucifer. A private agreement between Satanist colleagues to avenge the death of a chosen leader. But those acting as avengers *also* had to die, slaying themselves right after they slaughtered a chieftain's killer. Rahmad and Amir had previously been chosen as Klaus Braun's method of revenge, and it was one of the highest honors ever bestowed on them. "We shall willingly carry out the Purus if it ever comes to that," Amir vowed solemnly. "And immediately sacrifice our own lives afterward, as a tribute to both you and the Dark Lord!"

Braun nodded with quiet satisfaction before responding. "Thank you. Of course, I expect no such action to be required for many years. Hopefully, never, should I die a natural death."

With the Purus now fully reaffirmed, Dr. Braun began preparations for the ritual of satanic blessing before tonight's concluding Ripper murder. As on other such occasions, he took out a beaker of chilled human blood from a small refrigerator, and heated the vial over the blue flame of a small gas burner. Motioning his assassins over, Braun watched silently as they, in turn, took the beaker and slowly drank sizable mouthfuls of the warmed blood. Both killers immediately felt the customary surge of energy and power.

"May Lucifer be with you," intoned Klaus Braun.

Chapter 44
The Punishment Stage

Back at the small, shabby apartment in which he was being held, Christopher Seven was still trying to figure out what, if anything, he could do in order to change the horrific fate soon awaiting he and Sandy. His wristwatch read 10:40 p.m. and he knew they'd be coming for him at exactly 11:00. Nevertheless, Seven tried to remain calm, knowing that having his wits about him from this point on would be critically important.

The quick catnap he'd forced himself to take had helped a bit, giving him a needed boost of energy. But the *real* coup had come some fifteen minutes earlier, when he was about to step into the shower. Noticing a slight crack in the vanity mirror above the bathroom's grimy sink, Seven had somehow managed to pry a piece of jagged glass from it. This he'd done, undetected, by gently banging the mirror with his shoe while running the shower water loudly. Thankfully none of the guards had heard or seen anything, and his only worry now was that they might check the bathroom area when they came for him.

Carefully fingering the piece of broken glass, he hurriedly began to dress. After first wrapping the sharp glass piece in a heavy covering of Kleenex tissues, taken from the cardboard box on the counter, the G5 agent gently hid the six-inch sliver of mirror on the inside of his undershorts. His primitive stabbing weapon would be fairly safe now, though he'd still have to be careful not to let it drop or cut his skin. Any blood oozing from his clothing would certainly call attention to it.

Twenty minutes later, security guard Rick Clemons walked into Seven's bedroom where the prisoner was quietly sitting on his bed. "Eleven o'clock, pretty boy, time to get going. We can't keep the dragon waiting for his dinner."

As Clemons began meticulously checking the bedroom, Christopher Seven nervously held his breath. Would Braun's sadistic watchdog carefully survey the bathroom next? A few anxious moments passed. Mercifully, Clemons seemed satisfied, and only took a quick, cursory glance into the bath area. He then expertly tied Seven's hands together with a leather binding and pointed his gun toward the door.

~

After driving a short while, the security van neared the Reptile Center. Seven felt the tissue covered glass piece pushing against his thigh. The solid feel of it was somehow reassuring. Knowing he might be able to use the jagged glass as both a primitive weapon, and as a way to cut his leather bindings, the Super Stud smiled inwardly. He then glanced around at his four overseers and their spectacled van driver. They too were nervous, knowing it was their responsibility to get the prisoner to the satanic staging area without a hitch. At precisely 11:20 p.m., the van arrived at a small, isolated building, a concealed structure that housed the private files and coded records of Braun's nightshift. There was a sign out front, which read: _Private_ Restricted Zone—_Mortal Danger_—_No Admittance._

"This is where we caught that industrial spy, Ken Fusco, snooping at some old documents belonging to the Dr. Braun's father," Rick Clemons informed. "I suppose that's where Fusco stumbled onto that Martin Bormann stuff. As well as the age inhibitor files we heard Fusco was gabbing about in the ambulance." Clemons grinned. "We took good care of Fusco with the Taipan."

Seven was then ushered out of the van and led down a flight of steps to a small, hidden prison cell located in the building's dank basement. He wondered if the rest of Klaus Braun's nighttime workers even knew this makeshift jail cell was here. As Seven thought on it, Clemons began telling him what would happen next. "I'm going to explain this to you one time, and one time only. So listen up.

Seven nodded, still trying to show that he was a meek, compliant lamb going to the slaughter.

"It's my responsibility to get you over to the ceremony platform at exactly five minutes to midnight", Clemmons explained. "Sandra Kent will likewise be brought there by her guards." Clemons looked directly into Seven's eyes. "Now, here's the deal that Dr. Braun told me to offer you. If you cooperate fully and go to your execution quietly, like a man, Miss Kent will not be mistreated prior to her death. But if you make _any_ trouble at all, Sandra Kent will be given to her guards for some pre-punishment fun. So if you care about the Kent dame, my advice is to do as you're told. From what I hear she's already terrified."

Seven again nodded his head meekly. Clemons nodded back and said, "A wise choice. At least for the girl's sake. You'll both be kept in separate holding cells until approximately 11:50. That's forty minutes from now. Dr. Braun is gracious enough to give each condemned captive some personal time to reflect, and to recognize that Lucifer is truly the Earth's king. The supreme one they _should_ have served."

"So you lunatics claim," replied Seven.

Rick Clemons simply shrugged his shoulders. "Suit yourself. But you're the one who's going to die soon. Anyway, the time alone is yours. We'll come back here for you at exactly 11:50." He locked the cell door and added, "Sorry, we don't have a prison chaplain." Laughing loudly, the guards then left the building.

Seven waited until it was perfectly quiet. After thoroughly inspecting for any hidden cameras, and fortunately finding none, he reached into his undershorts for the glass piece and then awkwardly began working on his leather bindings. The G5 operative gamely persevered, nearly cutting the vein on his wrist a few times in the process. Undeterred, he continued sawing. At last, his progress was exactly where he wanted it. Then, with one stiff pull, the binding gave way, and his hands were free!

Sweating profusely, Christopher Seven relaxed a few moments, justly proud of himself. He rewrapped the jagged glass piece in the tissues and tucked it back into his undershorts. Thinking about the glass piece, and his soon to be unbound hands, Seven smiled slyly. His stabbing glass and free hands would certainly be an effective surprise on Braun or some unsuspecting Satanist. Though sadly, Seven knew he might first have to use it to slice the neck of the girl he loved. This he would attempt at just the right moment. *Before* his startled captors had composed themselves. Perhaps he could likewise do the same thing to Klaus Braun and then to himself before they stopped him.

Seven sighed. If he were successful, would the killing of Sandy, as well as his own suicide, be viewed as murder and sin in the eyes of God? He wasn't sure. Suicide and murder were always deemed wrong in the Bible. But perhaps it might be viewed much like in Genesis. When Abraham was willing to sacrifice his own son, Isaac, on the altar.

Grimly reflecting on it, Seven loosely retied the torn leather strap around his wrists to give the appearance that he was still tightly bound. At this point the leather strapping could easily be pulled apart when required. Yet outwardly he still appeared to be bound tightly. Even so, he'd have to keep his hands close together at all times, in order to hide his handiwork from Braun's entourage on the stage.

Staring up at the ceiling, the agent gloomily thought of Sandy, knowing she was waiting alone in a similar holding cell. The poor thing. She must be in a state of shocked terror by now. The Super Stud agent now wondered if she blamed him for everything. While mulling over these disconcerting thoughts, he heard footsteps coming down the hall. Soon, the large cell door was opened. Grinning with his sidekicks, Clemons announced, "It's time, pretty boy."

~

Over at the far section of Braun's enclave, appropriately called the *Large Reptile Display Area*, the overflowing crowd of devil devotees was now wild with expectation! Robed men with long pole lighters began igniting gaslights and torches everywhere, including the four corners of the newly constructed punishment stage. The whole area was soon illuminated in a hazy, amber glow.

A number of items were already in place on the raised staging site, including a large kettledrum. And some menacing looking surgical instruments had neatly been placed on the sanctified *retribution table*. Most ominous of these was a ceremonial cutting sword, its ax-like blade glistening in the amber hue. Beakers of human blood, cased in ice, were also on the table, as the satanic stage was now ready.

The nightshift audience, eagerly anticipating the torture and death of Christopher Seven and Sandy Kent, was literally high with excitement. Many were clad in lurid ceremonial outfits, such as the feathered capes of the devil bird. This was the *Tammuz*, a cloak made from the wings of vultures. Several men sported wild tattoos on their half-naked bodies, most of these depicting strange images of the Black Sabbath. Others wore hideous skeleton death masks, and some in the crowd were attired in the *Oemis*, a rare satanic vest made partly of human skin.

The few females in the mob looked the strangest of all. They sported tiny thongs, and their bodies were painted with bright red and yellow stripes, the favored colors of the Dark World. Together with their male compatriots, these fanatical devil worshipers literally howled for blood. The whole scene was something out of Dante's depiction of hell!

At precisely 11:55 p.m. all eyes in the crowd became glued to the punishment platform where a lone kettledrum began beating out its rhythmic introduction. The drumming was followed by a cloud of slickly produced, 'special effects' smoke, virtually encasing the entire stage. Three men appeared out of the haze, as if magically coming from nowhere. When the audience saw them, their screaming became even more thunderous. It was Klaus Braun and his father, Floda, accompanied by Lucas Yezid, the High Priest of the Fifth Order. Several eerily hooded, monk-like disciples followed them out on the stage, and their sudden appearance indicated that the ceremonial first phase was starting. The screaming and singing abruptly came to a halt.

Lucas Yezid held up his hands and walked over to the single microphone. "Brothers and Sisters of the Son of the Morning Star. The moment of retribution has arrived!"

Wolf-like howls from the audience were followed by several shouts of "Kill them now! Kill them now!"

Again, Yezid held up his hands and grinned. "Patience, my friends. Their time will come in just a few more minutes. But first, it is my great honor to bring to you the two men who have been chosen by Lucifer himself to guide us in our upcoming Operation D. Fellow believers; I give you, Dr. Klaus Braun, and his esteemed father, Floda!"

Klaus Braun waved to the cheering throng as he guided his father over to the single chair on the stage. Facing the crowd with a proud expression, Dr. Braun walked over to the microphone and announced, "Before we begin with the punishment session, there are two gentlemen I want to bring out to you. Two of my most loyal servants." Braun smiled proudly. "Amir and Rahmad have worked tirelessly to ensure the success of our operation. We wish them well in their Ripper task tonight."

The two henchmen awkwardly made their way onto the stage. Though uncomfortable in the spotlight, they reveled in the applause. They then fled into the night for their final serial murder.

Braun then motioned to his high priest, Lucas Yezid to take over. It was almost time for the punishment ceremony to commence. At that exact moment, the van bringing Seven and his three security watchdogs to the staging area arrived right on time. Exiting the van, Seven and his guards paused a moment by the steps leading up to the podium; waiting for Yezid to finished his satanic blessings.

Christopher Seven glanced around the stairway area leading up to the stage. Although he saw no sign of Sandy, he did catch a glimpse of two men, one tall, and the other rather short, running off the platform and into a waiting car. As Seven watched their vehicle speedily pull out of the compound, little did he know that these two Satanists were Amir and Rahmad. The *real* New Ripper killers.

The barking voice of Rick Clemons quickly brought Seven back to his present nightmare. "Let's go, fella. Up the rest of the steps, nice and easy. We'll wait by the landing till I'm given the signal. Then we'll walk you out to the center podium. And no tricks. Remember the girl."

As Seven and his guards began the short climb, the G5 agent concentrated on keeping his hands tightly together. His release of the leather binding would come later when he pulled his arms apart. Clemons, noticeably more tense, glared at him. "You'll be going out on stage in exactly one minute. As soon as you're out on the podium, we'll be leaving you. But there'll still be at least four guns on you at all times, aimed to maim but not kill. And don't forget. What I said about your girlfriend still goes. She's in that white trailer over there with her guards. Should you try anything funny before she's brought out, they'll be a short pause in the ceremony, which will be enough time for those men to ravage her. So no juvenile theatrics."

Again Christopher Seven nodded meekly as Clemons finished his directives. "There'll be four robed men in hoods when you first get out there. They're the high priest's disciples. But don't let their monk outfits fool you. These men are also armed and likewise trained to maim. And Lucas Yezid, our high priest, is very capable with the rough stuff. He trains and lifts weights daily."

Rick Clemons looked over at Seven for a reaction. When there was none, the sadistic security man merely barked out his final instructions. "The four disciples will eventually make their way over to you when they're given the orders to do so. Their job is to hold you and the girl down on the surgical table when it's time for the ceremonial surgery. This will occur to the woman first. They'll remove her legs, as an extra punishment for her treachery, and then cut out both her eyes. After that, they'll throw her down to the dragon." Clemons grinned, sheepishly. "Sorry about that, but there's just no easy way to put it." A drum signal from above interrupted them, indicating that it was time. Leading their victim to slaughter, the guards slowly walked Seven out.

The first thing Christopher Seven noticed, once on the stage, was the nearly deafening crowd noise. Most of it was aggressive cries and jeers directed at him. The spectators taunted him, shouting obscenities, and watching in sadistic glee for any signs of his losing it. Just as she had promised, Elsa Dykstra stood right in front, a cruel grin pasted across her ugly face. Only Seven's training allowed him the ability to appear calm and detached so as not to give these sadists the freak show they wanted. Inwardly, however, the agent felt real fear, along with repulsion, and resignation. Seven closed his eyes and whispered a silent prayer.

With the kettledrum pounding in the background, the G5 operative tried desperately to clear his head of all the yelling and terror in order to think. He began to will his brain into survival mode and gradually that mindset took over. Alert and surprisingly calm, the sweating agent began looking around for any hints of escape.

Glancing to his right, Seven saw that the very end of the stage was situated directly over the Komodo dragon's habitat. He was surprised to see that there was no wall, fence or barrier anywhere. A careless stagehand or guard could easily fall right into the dragon's lair if that worker wasn't careful. Could this fact be useful? Seven wasn't sure. Obviously the stage had been purposely designed this way so Braun's crew could throw the condemned captives down to the reptile without having to lift them up over any obstacles. They would naturally assume there'd be no struggle from two wounded and blinded prisoners. All of this could very well be true, but without any barrier on that side of the podium, the Super Stud might at least be able to push Braun, or a couple of his men, off the ledge in a surprise, suicide struggle. Just before they shot or subdued him. Additionally, no one would be expecting the prisoner's hands to be free, or for him to have his primitive glass piece weapon.

As for the rest of the area, there were several gaslights on poles, just as Seven had hoped. Thankfully, the large container of flammable chicken offal was not too far to his left. He also noticed a large axe and several knives on the surgical table. Conceivably, they might be used as surprise weapons once he got his hands free.

Seven's thoughts were disrupted by new, frenzied sounds and yearning moans from the crowd. Looking to his left, he saw Sandy being dragged out onto the stage. She was dressed in a revealing black leather thong and Seven could sense her shame along with her obvious fright. Her hair had been tied up in a strange bird's nest arrangement, and parts of her nearly naked body had been painted in the sect's preferred red and yellow. She was literally panting with fear, her eyes wide, as if a deer caught in headlights.

The Super Stud gritted his teeth with guilt and revulsion. *How I wish we'd never met*, he screamed to himself, cursing McPhail, G5, and himself for everything. Seven's shattered conscience, brought on by the pathetic sight of the terrified girl, was now telling him that all of this was *his* doing. Trying to control himself, he hoped these waves of culpability wouldn't hinder his spirit, or destroy his hopes of fighting to the end. The operative sighed. Somehow, he'd just have to forget his feelings of guilt and concentrate on disrupting this sickening spectacle. And on mercifully killing Sandy before they could torture her.

Suddenly, he heard the booming, acerbic voice of the bizarre priest, Lucas Yezid, who was now pointing toward the two prisoners. "There they are!" yelled Yezid to the roaring mob. "Two conquered enemies of the Prince of Darkness! Their moment of agony and death has come. It's time for them to witness the power and wrath of our Dark One!" With the crowd again going crazy, the cleric grinned savagely and shouted, "Let the punishment begin!"

Chapter 45
A Glimpse into Hell!

With the appearance of the trembling girl, the satanic spectacle had reached its zenith! Cleric Lucas Yezid, reveling in his role as judge, jury, and executioner, walked up to the microphone, sneered at Sandy Kent and Seven, and announced, "By the power of darkness within me, I declare these two prisoners guilty! They will now be executed in the manner decreed." He pointed down toward the dragon's pit. "But first, let us witness the sacred beast."

As of yet there had been no sight or sound of the giant Komodo Dragon in the pen below. The creature was still hiding in its straw shed, a bit alarmed by all the noise and vibration from above. A worker in a white cloak suddenly hopped on stage carrying two dead cats. Next, in some sort of customary ritual, one that everyone seemed familiar with, the bowing worker dutifully delivered the dead felines and the bucket of liquefied chicken fat to Klaus and Floda Braun. Both Brauns then began liberally coating the dead cats with the pungent offal. As they coated the carcasses, large amounts of the flammable chicken grease spattered on them. Glancing toward the gaslights, Christopher Seven made a mental note of it.

This cat sacrament completed, the white coated worker again bowed respectfully, and cautiously made his way out onto the edge of stage right, standing precariously over the platform's unsecured perimeter. Hovering directly above the dragon's lair, he threw the grease covered cat bodies down into the reptile's habitat.

At first nothing happened. Then, gradually, a rumble emanated from below, along with a distinctive hissing noise. Seven looked down at the dragon enclosure and immediately spotted the grotesque Komodo lizard poking its huge head out of the straw hut. The big reptile glanced around cautiously for a moment. Then, without any hesitation, the creature's muscular body swiftly slithered out of its shed, moving sideways, in a shimmying motion toward the dead cats. The Komodo came to an abrupt stop a few feet from the carcasses. *My word,* thought Seven, glancing down at it. *The thing is massive, and looks like some prehistoric monster!*

The G5 operative watched, transfixed, as the huge lizard began moving again, this time even faster. Opening its mouth for a second, the dragon exposed long, pointed teeth, with thick, poisonous saliva dripping from them. Then, in a lightning fast swoop, it pounced on the feline carcasses and devoured them in two quick bites! As blood oozed down its repulsive jaw, the reptile shook its immense head. Now getting aroused with hunger, the agitated Komodo had suddenly gone into a 'feeding mode', a state in which nothing could quell its voracious appetite. Striking out at the air, it began pacing around its domain in small nervous turns, circling the den in a furious search for more food to devour. Having seen enough, Seven turned his head away in revulsion.

"The sacred beast seems hungry enough," grinned Yezid. "And it shall now be fed the two human sacrifices!" The satanic priest looked to his right, over at a shadowy figure dressed in black who had just come onto the stage. This was the man they called the 'Carver', a tall, muscular executioner clad in heavy leather. He was carrying two menacing looking hatchets, obviously to be used for his perverted butchery on the captives.

With intentional dramatic flare, Lucas Yezid then called out to his hooded disciples. "Bring the woman forward to the surgical table and hold her down tightly. After the carver cuts off her legs and plucks out her blasphemous eyes, toss her to the dragon!"

As Yezid's two disciples grabbed Sandy, and began roughly dragging her forward, she suddenly came out of her dazed, submissive state and tried to pull away. The sound of her pleading sobs told Seven it was now or never! Not knowing or caring what he would do next, the G5 agent raised his arms and pulled his hand binding apart with one strong tug. The previously cut bindings broke easily and his hands were now completely free. He swiftly grabbed the piece of jagged glass from his midsection and readied himself!

At first, no one on stage comprehended what had just happened, their attention still focused on the struggling woman. Seven was about to rush over and try to wrestle the large hatchet from the Carver, when to everyone's surprise, loud, steady gunshots rang out from directly behind the audience. The sound of numerous automatic weapons being fired, along with several booming explosions, caused immediate chaos and panic! Stunning the assembled crowd, and also those on the stage. Seven had absolutely no clue as to what was taking place. Together with everyone else on the podium, the Super Stud turned and watched the mounting pandemonium. It was as if a movie director, orchestrating the whole scene, had suddenly yelled, "Action!"

All at once, a torrent of bullets whizzed by, going right over the heads of the frightened audience below. Unlike Dr. Braun's security professionals up on the stage, the startled, half-drugged spectators in front of the stage did not stay put very long. In a panic-stricken attempt to seek safety, most of them began running uncontrollably toward the direction of the Center's front entrance. A few of Braun's followers in the audience did try to stand their ground, doing so with varying degrees of success. They were quickly pushed forward by the moving sea of humanity, and several of them were knocked down and trampled in the process. *So much for Braun's 'loyal satanic fanaticism'*, mused Seven. *These people are deserting like rats!*

As the G5 agent watched from the podium, a huge explosion caused him to look to his left, the general direction of the blast. Through thick puffs of smoke, he saw several of Braun's armed gatekeepers running from their outside posts toward the stage. They were being chased by numerous riflemen in dark blue jackets.

More gunfire rang out, and in the confusion, almost everyone on stage began yelling diverse orders and panicked advice. Additional armed invaders in blue began storming in from the other end, the Center's west gate entrance. Braun's few remaining security men, up on the podium and down below, fired swiftly and somewhat effectively, forcing the new attackers to take cover. Frozen in uncertainty, Seven still kept a close eye on Sandy and the two robed disciples who were holding her.

Out of nowhere a motorized roar came from the sky, along with the illumination of several bright spotlights blanketing the entire area. Three helicopters appeared overhead, one hovering directly above the stage. As the choppers descended, the Super Stud heard the most gratifying words of his life coming from the helicopter's speakers. "FBI!" boomed the voice from the sky. "Drop your weapons and raise your hands. Do as you're told and you will not be harmed."

As more FBI reinforcements swarmed in, the numbers became overwhelmingly against Klaus Braun's squad. Even the most zealous of the doctor's loyalists quickly began to realize it. During a brief lull in the fighting, one of the federal agents, standing behind a thick tree trunk, called out to the stage area, using an amplified megaphone. "All of you Braun people. Throw down your weapons and put your hands up immediately. The folks who've already dispersed are surrendering. Turning themselves in at the front parking lot. You must do the same. You're completely surrounded and we have a lot more reinforcements and armaments on the way. This is your *final* warning!"

Almost as soon as the announcement was made, nearly all of Braun's remaining followers, both down below and up on the stage, surrendered. This included Lucas Yezid's two robed disciples, who ran down the podium steps with their hands up. Only Yezid, the two Brauns, and the sinister looking Carver, who was now holding Sandy, were staying put. Seven heard Braun's father, Floda, cursing in German as the old man watched the mass desertion.

Glancing around the stage, the G5 operative weighed the odds. Now only four men remained. Two of them, Klaus and Floda Braun were cringing under the ceremonial table, hiding behind one of the table's thick legs near the bucket of chicken offal. They were obviously no physical threat. The third, the now trembling 'carver', appeared to be wavering. Though still holding Sandy by her arms, he nervously looked around. Only the fourth man, High Priest Lucas Yezid, seemed firmly resolved to stay. Seven fingered his jagged glass piece weapon and waited for his chance.

A round of warning bullets whizzed over the heads of the two remaining Satanists on the stage, aimed high so as not to hit the girl.

Yezid didn't flinch, but the beefy carver had seen enough. He let Sandy go and ran off to capitulate. Now free, Sandy quickly ran toward Seven and grabbed his hand. "Get behind me! Seven yelled.

With a wary eye, Christopher Seven looked directly across at Lucas Yezid. Would this bizarre zealot stay and fight. Or would he, like his cowardly brethren, finally flee? Seven wasn't sure.

Abruptly, the amplified voice of the FBI man rang out again. "You there, the hooded man on the stage. Up with your hands. Now!"

At first it looked like the crazed cleric was obeying the order. But as he slowly began to raise his arms in counterfeit compliance, Lucas Yezid casually reached into his pants pocket and threw a small round object onto the ground. Almost immediately, a thick cloud of smoke began to engulf the entire area. Yezid had obviously ignited some type of smoky effect capsule, similar to the one he'd used for his dramatic entrance during the start of the punishment ceremony. This current cloud of smoke was even denser, and the entire stage was instantly engulfed in a copious, covering haze. As the smoke grew thicker, Yezid laughed sinisterly, and then disappeared into the foggy mist.

Seven knew the crazed priest was still around. He could almost *feel* the man's presence. *Yet where was he? Darn the smoke!* Suddenly Sandy screamed loudly! Out of the fog came the zombie-like face of the demonic cleric, his astonishing gray eyes blazing with hatred. Yezid was holding a small cutting instrument up high, the surgical knife intended to hack out his captives' eyes! Seven pushed Sandy away and roughly grabbed the cleric's arm. As their furious battle began, the two men tumbled to the ground.

The demented Yezid was quickly on top, his fists pounding away at Seven's midsection! The G5 agent instantly recognized the strength of his assailant, and knew he was in for a life-or-death struggle. Seven was well aware that a crazed opponent is often the hardest one to defend against, as temporary frenzy can often give a combatant what seems like superhuman power. This quickly appeared to be the case with Lucas Yezid. His savagery was overwhelming, effectively preventing Seven from utilizing his glass piece weapon. All the agent could do now was counter the cleric's powerful blows, and try to keep Yezid's surgical knife away from his face.

The veracious fighting continued to rage in the thick smog, each man at times rolling dangerously close to the wide-open right-side edge of the podium. The exposed side, with no wall or security railing, hovering directly over the dragon's lair! As the two combatants clashed, their bodies frequently came near this dangerous edge, which was right over the famished reptile below. Seven could clearly hear the Komodo's loud panting and prancing as he fought the cleric.

Somehow, Lucas Yezid was getting the better of him, dominating via his being on top. The devilish madman was trying to choke Seven with his strong left hand, while trying to free his right hand to stab his opponent with the surgical knife. Several times Seven attempted to roll his adversary over, but the enraged Yezid was either too strong or too crazed with power to budge. Then, to Seven's dismay, he saw Yezid finally free his right hand and hold the surgical knife directly over him! The silver blade glistened in the gaslight, ready to carve out Seven's eyes! The Super Stud struggled mightily to fend it off, desperately trying to keep the razor sharp instrument away from his exposed face.

"I shall yet feed your eyes to the dragon!" screamed the Satanist, trying to pound the dagger directly into Seven's left eye. The cleric grinned as his knife came down, straight toward its eyeball target. Fortunately for Seven, he managed to turn his head at the last second. Despite doing so, the sharp weapon still caught him on the cheek and blood gushed out all over Seven's face, momentarily blinding him. "The eyes!" Yezid screamed again. "Give me your eyes!"

The thick smoke surrounding the stage was finally beginning to dissipate. Christopher Seven looked up at his powerful adversary, staring directly at the man's pale, skeletal face. Now it was Yezid's eyes that seemed to stand out. The G5 operative could actually see the reflection of the gaslights in the man's pupils. It was truly the face of the devil that Seven was now staring at, more dead than alive. A ghastly glimpse into hell. Yezid again raised his knife, ready to inflict the killing blow!

From his prone position, Seven knew he was losing the battle. There was only one chance now. A basic move the agent had practiced many times during martial arts training. He brought up his right knee as hard and as fast as he could, performing the classic *Handou* knee jolt. It caught Yezid in his vulnerable crotch, a perfect shot right between the legs! The cleric screamed out in pained surprise, dropping his knife in a reflex reaction.

This brief pause was all that Seven needed! He forced his jagged piece of glass deep into Yezid's left wrist, grabbed the cleric's arms and quickly pushed him straight up and off his body. The momentarily stunned priest was instantly propelled into the air. Upon landing, Yezid's body bounced violently and began rolling uncontrollably over the side of the platform. The screaming Satanist frantically tried to grab onto the edge of the platform as he tumbled, but to no avail. Yezid yelled loudly and rolled uncontrollably into the dragon's lair below!

Seven was up in a flash, looking over the side, and taking great care not to stumble and fall into the dragon's den himself. Glancing down, he saw the bloody horror unfold below him. It was a dreadful scene, and Seven again felt he was getting an image of hell. The *real* hell, not the fairytale world that this man and his followers extolled.

What he witnessed next was truly appalling. Yezid didn't have a chance. He was still alive, but lying face up on the ground with the snarling reptile directly over him. The Komodo Dragon was clawing and biting at will, brutally devouring its helpless prey. The giant lizard kept grunting as it viciously consumed the wailing victim in large pieces. Ripping and tearing the man's flesh with savage efficiency, the dragon twirled its giant head. Twisting pieces of body parts in its jaws, much like a rag doll in the mouth of a puppy.

Seven instinctively thought of somehow trying to help this unfortunate man, now in the clutches of the great reptile. For a moment, he actually felt sympathy for the screaming cleric, although he knew that this demented prophet had earlier pronounced the same horrific fate for him and Sandy.

Still hearing the awful high-pitched wails, the Super Stud lowered his head in disgust. In another thirty seconds or so, the horrible screaming had ceased. The exhausted G5 agent turned his head and slowly walked away.

Chapter 46

"Satan Shall Be Avenged!"

Tired and disgusted with all of the brutality and killing that had taken over his world and his mind, Christopher Seven staggered away from the edge of the platform. Half in a trance, he stood in the center of the punishment stage trying to erase forever what he'd just witnessed below in the dragon's lair. Wiping the blood from his face, the exhausted agent hardly noticed the superficial cut near his eye. He glanced up toward the sky. The smoke was finally clearing and it seemed to be turning into a beautiful night.

Still dazed, he looked over to see the smiling faces of FBI Agent Jack Hanover and Sandy Kent. Hanover had a warm smile on his face, but Seven was too spent and too numb to smile back. Behind Sandy and Jack, four FBI agents had their guns trained on Dr. Braun and his father. Both Brauns had their arms held high. Caught by surprise, just after Seven's fight with the cleric, the Brauns had been unable or unwilling to take their cyanide capsules.

"Hello, Chris," Jack greeted. "We tried to get here as quickly as possible. Only received the facts a few hours ago, through Bahama's American Embassy. A local policeman received one of your notes via Eduardo's daughter. We know about Braun's plan to blow up half the country, thanks to your warning notes left with the Valdez girl. Since your message also mentioned this satanic hoedown here tonight, we rushed over as fast as we could."

Hanover shook his head. "It was a close call, Chris. The Bahamian authorities almost didn't get your message at all. Edie Valdez held the note for nearly two weeks after running to her aunt's house. Apparently, Edie was in a bad way, knowing her dad was dead. She stayed alone in a spare bedroom most of the time and sulked continuously. But then, just this afternoon, Edie saw a police car go speeding by, in front of the aunt's place. For some reason, and who knows what with that girl's confused mind, young Edie made some sort of connection with your letter and the police. Whether it was the word *police* casually mentioned by the aunt, or the actual sight of the patrol car, something clicked. Whatever it was, Edie ran to her room, grabbed your letter, and handed it to the aunt who immediately called both the American Embassy and Nassau's Government House. I got word about 8:00 p.m. this evening. We then scrambled like crazy to get the proper warrants and to arrive here before midnight. That was the time your note said Sandy would be executed."

Jack motioned toward his small army of agents. "Our little attack group included snipers from my office, a SWAT division from county, and, thanks to the Florida Governor, the best marksmen of the State police.

There were even a few Navy Seals with us. Your letter sounded pretty ominous, so Washington brought in the big guns." Hanover grinned. "The President got things moving a lot faster than he did those healthcare bills of his."

Seven chuckled as Jack further informed, "Of course, still being the consummate politician, the President naturally had a few reservations. Didn't want a Waco type debacle to ensue, I guess." Jack shrugged his shoulders. "It went pretty well, all things considered. Only a few casualties, all on their side. Most of Braun's people are now in custody and they're singing like canaries."

"It was a fantastic job, Jack", said Seven. "I'm extremely grateful."

Hanover again shook his head. "No, it's *we* who should be grateful to *you* Chris. The whole country should be if this Operation D thing can somehow be prevented."

Glancing around, the Super Stud spotted Klaus Braun and his father. Seemingly still in stunned disbelief, their hands were held high as several FBI men surrounded them. Seven suddenly remembered what they both were carrying and yelled to the agents, "Quick! Grab the cyanide pills from their pants pockets!"

Before either Klaus or his father could react, a powerfully built black agent named Morgan grabbed the deadly pills from the Brauns' pockets. "My, my," the FBI man commented, wryly. "These old guys were planning a little going away party. But now, they're going away tablets are gone." Two more agents rushed toward Klaus Braun, smiling at Seven and Sandy as they passed. "The two captives are clean now," Morgan reported to the new men, after carefully frisking both Brauns again. "No guns or knives, and no more pills."

Seven looked over at Sandy Kent. "You okay, Sandy?"

"I'm fine."

"She's fine, alright," said Hanover with a friendly wink at her. "For a person who's been threatened, beaten, scared stiff, and nearly devoured by a giant reptile."

Christopher Seven walked over, put his arm around her, and then glanced toward the posse of agents surrounding the Brauns. Agent Morgan strolled over. "Here's what I found, sir." He showed Seven the two confiscated tablets.

The Super Stud nodded his head. "You better hold on to those pills. Like I said, it's cyanide. They were planning to take it before you had any chance to grill them."

Standing over by Klaus and Floda Braun, Hanover wrinkled his nose. "Boy, these two Brauns smell like a butcher shop."

Seven laughed and explained, "Klausie and daddy have been playing with a bucket of chicken grease, Jack. Some gunk they and their satanic cohorts were going to spread all over Sandy and me. They spilled most of it on themselves during their silly cat ritual."

"Whew," said Hanover. "They reek of it."

"Don't sell that chicken aroma short, Jack," replied Seven. "The dragon simply loves it."

Hanover gave him a puzzled look. "If you say so, Chris."

Seven heard an agent address Klaus Braun. "Alright, Doctor, you have the right to remain silent. Anything you say may..."

Dr. Braun and his father only halfheartedly listened to their Miranda Rights being administered. Another FBI man, a short chap with red hair, waved off the handcuffs that a younger agent was taking out for the Brauns. "They're a bit too elderly for those, Al. We'll be keeping a close watch on them from now on. No cuffs needed. At least eight agents will be surrounding these two at all times."

Klaus Braun kept staring at Seven. Then, as if suddenly deciding on something, the snake man slowly began to speak. "Remember what I told you, Seven. You'll *never* escape Satan's wrath, not even now. The Dark One's avengers will surely find you. And when they do, Lucifer shall yet have his revenge!"

Though smirking, Seven was inwardly troubled by the confident manner in which Klaus Braun had just threatened him. Despite that, the Super Stud grinned at Hanover. "Satanic gibberish, Jack. These freaks actually believe in it. Don't give it a second thought."

The entire assemblage of agents and captives then began walking toward the compound's main exit, passing a few of Braun's slain workers lying on the ground. Seven noticed that one of the dead men was the punk with the facial scar, the sadistic security guard from the island who had organized the butchering of Eduardo Valdez. Seeing this man's dead body instantly made him think of Eduardo and a small token of payback for the heroic Cuban.

Seven, and a now drained Sandy Kent, walked in the front group of agents, along with Jack Hanover. Braun and his father, guarded by a small army of FBI men, took up the rear. Slowed by the elderly Floda Braun, this second group soon lagged well behind. Floda was having trouble walking, breathing irregularly as he labored to keep pace.

Far behind the first group now, and knowing he was out of Seven's earshot, Klaus Braun turned to one of his captors with a gentle, disarming smile. "Excuse me, gentlemen. Father needs to rest a moment. He's very old and all this is a bit much for him."

The lead agent looked over at Floda and felt a twinge of genuine sympathy. He nodded, knowing the two Brauns were no longer a threat, especially the frail old man. "That's fine, Doctor," agreed the FBI leader. "But please, sir, not too long."

"Thank you," Dr. Braun replied. "You're very kind."

The elderly Floda seemed relieved to rest a while. He too, smiled warmly at his captor, and with the agent's help, awkwardly sat down on the ground directly under one of the gaslight poles. The elder Braun's breathing was loud and uneven now, and the lead FBI agent, a man named Simmons, was starting to get concerned. *Was this oldster, Floda, having a medical problem?*

"Is your father alright, Doctor?" Simmons worriedly inquired.

Dr. Braun nodded. "He should be fine in a minute or two. Walking always does this to him."

"Perhaps we can make the journey a little easier for him," said Agent Simmons. He called out to one of his colleagues. "Baines! Get a medic and a stretcher for the old fella."

"Yes, sir." Baines took out his wireless communicator. While he called for the medical equipment, Klaus and Floda Braun, sitting quietly on the ground, casually looked at each other. Unbeknownst to the federal agents, the Brauns were silently communicating with their eyes, both thinking about the detailed plans they'd made while hiding under the table during the raid. Plans involving the heavy coats of chicken fat that now covered their clothing and bodies.

A few minutes later, as two paramedics carrying a stretcher neared the area, Klaus Braun abruptly leaped to his feet and grabbed a nearby gas-lit lamp pole out from its metal base! He waved the flaming torch menacingly at the startled FBI agents, who immediately reached for their weapons. The FBI team couldn't believe this ridiculous escape attempt, if it was one. There were at least twelve guns pointed at Klaus Braun, and every inch of the Reptile Center was now completely guarded by the Feds. Any chance of Dr. Braun escaping was utterly impossible, especially with his aged father along.

Knowing all this, Agent Simmons held up his hands to calm his crew, fully aware that Jack Hanover had given strict orders to keep these two captives alive at all costs. Still, the FBI men were prepared to fire if necessary, but only to wound instead of kill.

In his role as lead agent, Simmons was getting ready to calmly order Dr. Braun to drop the fiery pole. But then, without warning, the crazed snake man, with a look of triumph in his fierce eyes, screamed, "Satan shall be avenged!" With the flaming torch still in his hand, Klaus Braun promptly touched the gas flame to his father, who was sitting underneath Klaus, and then to himself. Their bodies, soaked with the liquefied chicken fat, instantly went up in a gigantic blaze!

The startled agents, who certainly hadn't expected such an occurrence, had no blankets or equipment to combat the increasing inferno. They were completely stunned and, for the moment, totally helpless. Waiting a few minutes to approach the towering blaze, so as not to catch fire themselves, the FBI squad at last reacted. While the flames and screams came forth, they vainly tried to move toward the captives, the smell of smoldering flesh almost too much to tolerate!

When they finally managed to safely approach the smoldering bodies, it had mercifully ended. The impromptu Viking funeral suicide of Dr. Klaus Braun and his father, Floda, had swiftly taken its toll. Both men were dead, lying in a smoky heap of charred remains. More unfortunate was the chilling fact that Klaus Braun could no longer be interrogated about his upcoming Operation D targets. There was virtually nothing left of him.

Hearing the screams and the distant commotion, Christopher Seven and Jack Hanover, well in front of the Braun party, rushed back to see what was taking place. "Stay here with this officer!" Seven yelled to Sandy, handing her over to a stocky southern agent.

Suspecting that it was some type of Braun rescue attempt, or planned escape, Hanover drew his pistol. However, as he and Seven approached the dying flames, and saw several stunned agents standing around a thick cloud of smoke, they quickly realized what had occurred. Arriving at the scene, rife with the pungent odor of burnt flesh, Hanover and Seven looked at one another in shocked disbelief. Jack finally broke the stunned silence. "Unbelievable! Why did they do it?"

"No different than a Taliban suicide bomber or those Japanese kamikaze pilots killing themselves for a cause," Seven answered. "Remember Jack, these men were fanatics, believing in a false but explicit doctrine. To them, this was a logical step."

The G5 operative slowly made his way closer to the smoky mess. He looked down at the charred remains; two men who'd been so alive and menacing only a few hours earlier. Now, both were gone, most likely condemned to the *real* hell below. It was ironic that these two had died by fire, the never-ending torment decreed in the Bible. "Fire," Seven muttered. And to himself added, "It's fitting that the old man, if he was in fact who he claimed to be, died by fire. Hitler had sent many innocents to burn in the fires of his holocaust and blitzkriegs."

The Super Stud silently pondered the question again. *Was this mysterious old man, Floda, actually who he professed to be? Or was it all some elaborate Klaus Braun ruse?* Perhaps they'd never know for sure now. No matter what, however, the son, the notorious Dr. Klaus Braun, had proven to be just as villainous as the alleged father. Together, they had planned Operation D, their cataclysmic *new dawn*, which now seemed impossible to avert.

Seven shrugged his shoulders and turned to face Hanover, grudgingly acknowledging his dead adversary. "Klaus Braun was truly one of a kind, Jack. I guess he just couldn't risk our finding out anything more about his upcoming operation."

"I suppose," Hanover agreed. "But now what? We've only got a day or two to try and prevent a full-blown catastrophe. Time is our real problem. We can't evacuate every major city in the US, although that's what they'll probably attempt to do. It won't be practical though. And think of the panic it will cause, and the resulting economic woes."

Seven worriedly nodded his head as Jack pleaded, "Somehow, we've *got* to find out more of the details concerning Braun's operation, Chris. Let's get back to my office and see what we can come up with. Maybe we've overlooked something."

"Fine. Just as long as you have a bit of food, a hot shower, and some clean clothes for Sandy and me."

Hanover smiled at them. "Don't worry, folks. We'll have all those things back at the office, even at this hour. I'll phone ahead and have everything ready." He winked at Seven. "I assume you'd also like to check in with your, ah, editor, although it's late. I'm certain Global magazine is wondering where you've been lately." Seven nodded, knowing Jack really meant for him to call G5 headquarters. The Super Stud had almost forgotten that Colonel McPhail and G5 didn't even know he was still alive.

Hanover then looked over at Seven, somberly. "But make it a quick call, Chris. If ever time was short, it's now!"

Chapter 47
A Hill of Beans

An hour after leaving the chaos of the Reptile Center raid, Sandy and Seven each took a soothing, soapy shower in the FBI locker rooms. They now sat refreshed in an empty office at the Bureau's North Miami Beach headquarters, clad in some clean clothes loaned them by a few generous agents.

Christopher Seven had briefly spoken with a greatly relieved Colonel McPhail via Hanover's cell phone, doing so shortly before leaving Braun's reptile hub. Thanks to this emotional conversation with his chief, the G5 operative was pleasantly surprised to find a Super Stud *care package* awaiting him upon his arrival at the FBI's offices. Since all of Seven's personal items had been confiscated by Braun's henchmen, McPhail's gift package consisted of a new wallet, filled with six hundred dollars in cash, replacement Visa and American Express cards, plus a new working cell phone. And, of course, the Colonel's bundle also included the required Super Stud oral hygiene kit, complete with toothbrush, mouthwash, and Colgate paste. Inside was an uncharacteristically jocular note that said: *You're back on the job! - Use these hygienic products with care. - McPhail.*

Seven grinned as he read the note, knowing it was just like the old man to think of business first and his agent's welfare second. Nonetheless, he dutifully used his new tooth care supplies after snacking with Hanover and Sandy, and the normalcy of this standard hygiene routine made him feel somewhat human again.

Though it was now going on 4:00 a.m., Hanover gently reminded Sandy and Seven that there was no time for the frazzled couple to rest. The FBI desperately needed their help in trying to dissect everything they knew about Braun. Despite the urgency and time constraints, however, Jack had thoughtfully given them a few moments alone, right after everyone had shared a meal of sandwiches and coffee.

For Seven, this brief, but welcome, respite with Sandy was heaven sent. It was good to finally be alone with her again. Thanks to Dr. Braun's security goons, they'd hardly spoken to one another without being closely watched the past two weeks. Let alone been able to privately talk about their growing relationship.

Realizing that his time with her now would necessarily be limited, Christopher Seven looked over at his beautiful companion and spoke softly. "The terror and danger are finally over, Sandy. We're safe and sound. No more demons and no more danger. As far as you and I are concerned, we've got a lifetime to enjoy each other." The Super Stud suddenly wondered if his words would be taken as a marriage proposal, and somehow didn't care if they were. He was now certain that he was in love with her.

Sandy said nothing for a few moments. She merely smiled at him, staring at this handsome enigma, who, even now, still steadfastly claimed to be *just a reporter*. Somehow she knew there was a lot more to him than that. Yet Sandy also knew, instinctively, that he wouldn't want her to ask about it. This incredible looking man had entered her life, swept her off her feet, and then brought her along on a staggering journey into hell. Not certain what to say, she simply gazed at him.

Christopher Seven couldn't help noting Sandy's faraway expression. He'd half expected as much, knowing her nerves were probably still numb by all that had occurred. His heart pounded excitedly at the very sight of her, and he silently wondered, *Was this love, lust, or perhaps merely relief that they were both still alive?*

Sandy finally began to speak, disrupting Seven's feelings. "A *lifetime* to enjoy each other, you say? Well, we'll have to see about all that, Chris. At this point, everything's a confusing blur to me. And most likely to you too. All I really know is that you've saved my life, or attempted to, several times in the past few weeks. I'll never forget that." Tenderly taking his hand, she said, "But I also believe that God is trying to tell me something. Something I'll have to sort out myself. Right now, though, we need to forget about our own concerns and plans, and start concentrating on preventing the terrible fate that Klaus Braun has devised for our country. So let's put all of our efforts into that first. To help Jack and his agency anyway we can. Hopefully there'll be plenty of time for us to work out the rest when that's over."

Seven leaned over and kissed her tenderly on the lips. He was surprised by her response. Though warm, it had no hint of desire or emotion in it. *Probably all the trauma of the past week,* he surmised. He'd have to be very careful to be gentle with her for a long while.

"You're right, Sandy," Seven replied awkwardly, still somewhat taken aback by the strictly platonic reply to his kiss. "Anyway, thanks for understanding the FBI's dilemma. What's that line Humphrey Bogart says to Ilsa in Casablanca? *'At present, our own problems don't amount to a hill of beans compared to what the world is facing'.* Well, it happens to be true at the moment. We'll just have to put our heads together and give the government any help we possibly can."

Sandy nodded just as Jack Hanover reentered the room. Two other FBI agents accompanied him; Tyler Wheaton, a friendly black agent, and Brenda Cunningham, an attractive blonde. As everyone shook hands, Christopher Seven couldn't help noticing Brenda Cunningham eyeing him longingly. This typical female response to his looks, just like the tooth care routine, brought him back to reality. Like always, the Super Stud smiled politely toward Brenda and tried to ignore her staring at him as Jack began his recitation.

"Obviously we don't have much time, people, so let's get started. Washington informed me that they'll supply anything we need, as did the Florida Attorney General. Search warrants, wiretaps, manpower, equipment - *anything* at all. I'll temporally be heading the task force until my chief arrives from DC to take over. So let's begin."

For the next hour everyone in the room wracked their brains trying to figure out what, if any, clues could have been left by Klaus Braun. Seven said very little during most of the session, simply trying to analyze everything being discussed. But then, when he heard Hanover ask Sandy if Klaus Braun, or his father, Floda, had a private safety deposit box, or personal vault, a hitherto forgotten detail suddenly began gnawing at Christopher Seven's memory. It was something Dr. Braun had carelessly revealed, obviously assuming that Seven couldn't make use of it since he'd shortly be dead.

The G5 operative frantically tried to remember the exact details of the conversation. *Yes, there it was!* It had been during his final talk with the doctor yesterday. Braun's candid admission about entrusting Operation D's secrets *'to the one who knows everything.'* The Super Stud definitely recalled it now. Dr. Braun had told him: "*Find this soul mate, my one equal, and you've solved the riddle of Operation D. The answer to everything.*" At the time, Seven had wondered if it was a figure of speech or an actual person. The G5 agent again asked himself. *Just who is this Braun friend?*

As he half heard the others in the room, Seven's mind raced for the answer. Klaus Braun had had no real friends. He had acquaintances and coworkers, of course, but oddly enough, no pals. Braun wasn't the sort of person who liked any human being. His only friends, the ones he thought he could trust, were his snakes. But *which* snake? Which serpent in his collection would he consider his equal? Which creature was on the same level as its master?

"That's it!" Seven suddenly yelled out, startling everyone.

"*What's* it, Chris?" asked Hanover.

Christopher Seven didn't respond immediately. He was still busy trying to work out his hypothesis. Dr. Braun had repeatedly avowed that he would "much rather trust a snake with his life, and with his really *important* secrets then with any mere mortal." As for *which* snake to guard his top secrets? There was only one. Braun's true equal. The singular living thing he considered on par with him. And this so-called *friend* of Braun's now stood guard over the doctor's unique, homemade safety deposit box. Seven had seen it all back at Braun's *Mi Casa* mansion.

"Chris, Chris, *what* is it?" pleaded Jack Hanover.

Looking up at Hanover, Seven calmly replied, "Listen, Jack. I know it's almost six in the morning, but can you get a search warrant for Braun's home, *Mi Casa*, as soon as possible?"

"Certainly. I can have one in twenty minutes."

"Good," replied Seven, grinning triumphantly. "We'll also need a snake-handling expert. One who isn't afraid of confronting a King Cobra. Have him meet us at Braun's mansion ASAP!"

~

A stunned Miles Hoffman, head butler at Braun's *Mi Casa* estate, sleepily greeted the small troop of early morning visitors now waving badges and search warrants at him. Jack Hanover's investigative group, standing at the massive front door with Sandy and Seven, had been hastily put together in a little over an hour. It included three men from the Miami-Dade bomb squad, two FBI code-breaking specialists, and a pair of highly qualified Palm Beach locksmiths. Others in the group included two prominent snake handlers from the County Zoo; Dr. Benjamin Littman, and his fellow herpetologist, Andy Choy.

"Mr. Hoffman," Hanover ordered the butler. "Please point us toward Dr. Braun's private office."

"I'm afraid it's locked, sir," Hoffman replied. "But I can have Mr. Wilcox down here in a few minutes. He's sleeping upstairs. Mr. Wilcox has the only key to the office when the master's away. He cares for Dr. Braun's snake that's housed there."

Ten minutes later, Hanover's group, now accompanied by Klaus Braun's head herpetologist, Kevin Wilcox, entered Braun's plush office. The room was just as Seven remembered it. The large, elaborate desk, the fancy chairs, and of course, the ornate snake habitat where the King Cobra was kept. After clearing the room of everyone but the snake handlers, the three herpetologists extracted the big snake from its cage and then brought it out to a waiting van in a large travel crate.

Following that, it was the bomb squad's turn to check out the now empty Cobra coop. After carefully brushing away some straw to expose the false bottom, where Seven said Dr. Braun's safe was hidden, they held a small explosive-detection device over the cage. They then checked the needle gauge.

"It's hot, alright," one of the team warned. "Probably a small bomb set to destroy everything inside. And to likewise kill any intruder, should it be tampered with improperly."

"Can you guys defuse it?" Hanover asked.

"No problem," one of the men replied. "My guess is that Klaus Braun didn't think any explosives experts would be having a crack at it. Shouldn't take us too long to deactivate it."

It took exactly twelve minutes. Following that, the locksmiths cracked opened the safe, and then the FBI code breakers went to work examining Braun's notebooks and private papers.

After waiting a while, an impatient Jack Hanover called over to his code experts, "What about this Operation D thing of Braun's? See anything that might be connected to that?"

"Not yet, sir," answered Peter, a tall FBI code breaker.

Peter's colleague, Gary Stein, likewise thumbing through some of the material, suddenly yelled out, "Here's something, Pete! A notebook with names of various planets. After each planet there are a few lines of irregular letters and numbers."

"What's on the cover of the notebook?" Peter asked.

Stein glanced at the front of the ledger. "Four large letters, NWAD." He frowned. "Makes no sense, except maybe the **D** part."

Hanover couldn't hide his frustration. His voice rose angrily, "Come on guys, you've got to do better." He wrung his hands and commented, "Too bad Klaus Braun isn't here so I could squeeze it out of him! Or that father of his, Floda. Or whatever his *real* name was."

Mention of the name *Floda* immediately jarred Seven's brain into action. "That's it!" Seven yelled out, excitedly. "That notebook with the planets. That's definitely the one, Jack!"

"*What's* the one, Chris?"

Seven grinned smugly and explained, "That notebook your agent Gary has. Don't you see? Braun and his old man's big joke on the world was that his father was called Floda, the reverse of Adolf. Well, that notebook is called NWAD; at first glance, pure gibberish. But the reverse of those letters is DAWN. Klaus and his father called Operation D their *New Dawn*. So that brown notebook *must* be it!"

Hanover glanced over at Peter Mews, a specialist on all forms of past and present codes. "What do you think, Pete?"

Mews slowly nodded his head. "It could just be. During World War II, the Nazis had several primitive interoffice house codes based on the planets. Keeping it easy for the old man to read. We'll take all of it back to the office. I know time is pressing, but give us a few hours with the rest of the code crew and we'll try to decipher it. I'll let you know, Jack, if it's anything significant."

Hanover promptly approved, so Peter Mews and his partner quickly gathered up Dr. Braun's papers, pads, and notebooks and left with them. After they departed, Jack looked over at Seven and Sandy.

"Listen, you two. We're going to go through this house with a fine-tooth comb. It could take us three, four hours. Maybe more. And it will take the code boys every bit of that back at headquarters. Why don't I ask that butler to show you to a couple of spare bedrooms and let you both finally get some well-deserved sleep? They've certainly got enough rooms in this place. So, whatdaya say?"

Sandy and Seven both nodded appreciatively.

"Then it's a deal," Jack exclaimed. "But I have to insist on *separate* rooms. Wouldn't do for the FBI to condone anything improper." Seven and Sandy laughed, and were soon sleeping soundly in two large guest suites above the main floor.

~

Three hours later, Jack Hanover excitedly approached the bedroom where Christopher Seven was sleeping soundly in the room's full-size bed. Quickly opening the door, he rushed over and began shaking Seven awake. "Chris, Chris. Wake up. We did it!"

"What's up?" the Super Stud asked groggily.

Jack grinned. "We've done it pal! Completely foiled Klaus Braun's Operation D." Seven shot up like a bolt as Jack further explained.

"A short while ago, I received a cell phone call from those two code breakers informing me that it was indeed that primitive wartime Nazi code after all. With the help of the other codebreakers, our encryption people cracked it! The planets were the key to the letters. After they established that, the rest was easy, and they quickly broke it. There were several other coded messages, including one that said: *For Father - In the event something happens to me,* followed by all of Operation D's actual details." Hanover grinned. "That NWAD notebook was the one all right. Just like you said. Guess it was meant for the old man to work with in case something happened to Klausie." Jack slapped his thigh. "Boy, oh boy, we uncovered Braun's entire plan!"

"Thank God," said Seven, with real feeling. "Does Sandy know?"

"Not yet. She's down the hall, still sleeping. I'll have one of the maids wake her and then you can tell her the good news yourself."

Seven nodded.

"There's no doubt about it now!" Hanover exclaimed. "The list in the cobra cage was the genuine article. Thank goodness you recalled Braun's hidden safe. Seems the doctor was a real stickler for documenting everything, yet Klaus wanted to give his old man simple, and specific orders. That vault notebook revealed the precise ten cities *and* the exact location of each van. They've already found the first truck at the list's precise address. The local FBI team there will soon be disarming it, with phone help from those two Norwegian scientists. Those two are singing like birds, obviously trying to save their skins."

Seven again nodded as Jack added, "Apparently Klaus never really changed the locations from his original sites, even though he told the workers he was going to. There were ten explosives all right. Nine in the US, and one in Canada. Weaponry experts will soon defuse all of them." Hanover grinned, still elated. "I guess that whacko Braun never dreamed anyone would look in his King Cobra vault. Well we did, thanks to you. And we hit the jackpot!"

An overjoyed Christopher Seven sat up and thought about the King

Cobra a moment, the world's deadliest snake. Looking over at Hanover, the Super Stud told him about the old legend. "You know, Jack, Klaus Braun always feared that his King Cobra might take him down. He had a premonition about it. Some ancient Malaysian folktale about this species of snake having human, vindictive qualities. I guess he thought the cobra might kill him with a deadly bite, never dreaming the snake would take him down by revealing Braun's entire Operation D plan." Seven paused, reflectively. "The King Cobra got its revenge, but in a way Braun never imagined."

"Well, whatdaya know?" Jack replied. "I guess old Klausie was right about that one. Thanks to the cage notebook we'll soon have all ten weapons under control. And with three full days to spare." Hanover chuckled. "Heck, Chris, we should get a bonus for coming in *ahead* of schedule." Seven laughed loudly as Jack looked over at him happily and exclaimed, "So, what say you kiddo? We done did it!"

"I say it's great, Jack. And as soon as I take a shower, and call my chief, I'm going to wake up Sandy and tell her that the entire Braun nightmare has finally ended. After that, I'm going to devour the biggest steak and eggs plate in Florida, and then go back to sleep forever!"

T wo hours after Sandy Kent and Christopher Seven heard the wonderful news about the FBI's code-breaking success, they were being driven away from *Mi Casa* in an FBI pool car. The driver, a chatty young agent named Josh, was first taking Seven to the Carlton Hotel in Palm Beach, where G5's travel department had secured him a room for the night. And from there, driving Sandy to her place in Ft. Lauderdale.

Just before he dropped Seven off at the hotel, Josh received an excited cell phone call from headquarters. After clicking off, the thrilled FBI driver informed both his passengers that all ten Braun bombs had been found and diffused. Overjoyed, Seven and Sandy agreed to meet up later at her condo around eight o'clock.

Sandy had turned down Seven's offer of a celebration dinner at *La Maison*, telling him that she had something very important to discuss, and that they'd need the time for that. Left to his own devices for dinner, the Super Stud decided on something quick and casual. Driving yet another rented Mustang convertible, this one procured at the hotel's Hertz desk, his destination was a fast-food stand he'd heard good things about; one ironically called *Jack's*. He followed the tasty hamburger meal with his practiced tooth care routine in the restaurant's empty men's room, and then excitedly drove up A1A toward Sandy's condo.

Wondering what was on her mind, he hoped she, like him, was ready to talk about a lifelong commitment. Having thought about it the entire day, Christopher Seven had come to the conclusion that he'd never find a better match. Sandy was intelligent, beautiful, and fun to be with. He was now certain of his love for her, and felt that she loved him as well. That afternoon he'd reflected on all of the wonderful things marriage could bring them; togetherness, the shared highs and lows of life, and, hopefully, a family.

Of course, he'd have to inform his boss, Colonel McPhail about it. And as soon as he was a married man, permanently retire from the Super Stud section. Morally, after getting married, Seven realized there could be no further wooing of women like headquarters required of all its Studs. With any luck, the colonel would offer him another position in the G5 agency. If not, there were always those modeling jobs he'd repeatedly been offered, or that screen test out in Hollywood his brother, Tim, wanted him to take.

Yet whatever career moves came his way, Seven was certain that he and Sandy would be just fine. The only thing on his mind now was how to propose to her. And to remember to be patient and gentle despite his zeal. After all, she'd been through a lifetime of terror with this recent Braun nightmare. All the same, he hoped his planned marriage proposal tonight would help lift her spirits. Turning into her condo's large parking lot, Seven grinned widely at the butterflies building up inside him. With all the snakes, dragons, and death he'd just faced, the G5 operative was surprised to find that proposing to a beautiful woman made him feel almost as nervous. He locked his car and swiftly made his way toward the building's lobby.

Sandy's sexy voice over the outside security intercom caused his heart to instantly begin racing, and he was promptly let inside by the electronic unlocking buzz from above. As the elevator made its climb, Seven wondered what he should say to her upon his arrival. Hopefully he wouldn't be too corny with the usual overused clichés about marriage. Actually finding himself a bit edgy now, he pushed her doorbell and waited.

As Sandy opened the door, Seven contemplated putting his arms around her and surprising her with a sensual kiss. However, while glancing to his left, he saw two nuns sitting on the couch of Sandy's small but elegant living room. He immediately wondered if his timing had been right, hoping she'd indeed said eight o'clock.

"Hi," Seven greeted. "Didn't know you had company. I was certain we said eight o'clock, but I've been wrong before."

She smiled, gently. "No, you're not wrong, Chris. Please come inside. I'd like you to meet two very special people." Her lead was easy to follow and Seven did as he was told. He saw the radiant faces of the two nuns beaming at him, as Sandy made introductions. "This is Sister Rosemarie and Sister Teresa, Chris. They've been here for several hours, almost from the time that FBI lad dropped me off this afternoon. We've been talking about the future; my future. I thought you'd want to hear everything directly from me, and from them too, if need be. Sorry to surprise you like this, but I thought it the best way."

Sister Rosemarie spoke next, doing so in a kindly, polite manner. "Perhaps you two should first speak alone, my dear. This handsome gentleman deserves as much. Sister Teresa and I will be right down the hall in the sunroom should you need us."

The two nuns stood up and walked into the hallway, closing the front door softly behind them. Seven, still a bit bewildered, barely heard Sandy's voice. "Please sit here, Chris," she said, pointing to the couch. The confused Super Stud again followed her cue and waited for some type of explanation.

"I wasn't sure when and how I would tell you," Sandy began. "As you probably know, I've prayed a lot during these past few weeks. Prayed for you, and prayed for me. One thing I *especially* prayed for was that millions of people wouldn't die because of something I did to help Dr. Braun."

Christopher Seven frowned at her guilt. "I've told you before, Sandy.

You had nothing to do with that madman's plans."

With her hand held up she tried to continue. "Please, let me go on, Chris." Seven nodded and continued listening.

"When you and Jack told me this morning that all the bombs had been located, and that no one would now die by way of Braun's operation, I knew my prayers were answered. But they had been answered with a condition. You see, Chris, I promised God that if everything worked out, I would dedicate the rest of my life to Him. I thought about it endlessly while I was a prisoner, both on the island and in Miami. I also realized that my life had been going nowhere, even before this recent nightmare."

The girl's face took on a glow as she looked at him tenderly. "I promised God that I would do something about getting my priorities straight, if only you, I, and those cities could be spared. I thought about it again when we faced our execution by way of the dragon. Knowing I was giving my life to God, no matter what was going to happen, gave me some unexpected peace of mind. Something I can't easily explain."

Sandy looked away from him a moment and then went on, "When you reappeared at Elsa's place, and when we were later both rescued, I knew *His* hand was in it. And now that we, and all of those innocent people, are safe, I also know what my sacred duty is to be. I'm dedicating the rest of my life to God. I'm going to try and become a nun, if I can. Sister Rosemarie and Sister Teresa believe it possible if I'm willing to apply myself. And I am. Of course, there'll be long, hard roads ahead. Becoming a candidate, the aspirant period, a postulant, and then the vows. But other women my age have done it, and I'm determined to try."

Seven remained silent as Sandy continued, "There's now a worldwide shortage of nuns. Especially here and in Europe. That's why you don't see many of them around these days. So perhaps I can be of help in some very small way." Looking at him for his reaction, she smiled gently. "And remember. I once told you I'd thought about becoming a nun when I was younger. Maybe it's always been my calling."

"I guess I should have paid more attention," Seven said softly.

"Perhaps, I should have too, Chris. Paid more attention to the voice of God. I believe you were somehow sent to help show me the way." She looked at him pensively. "And perhaps the horrible experiences of the past week were also a sign. I think this longing to be a nun was always inside me. It only had to be revealed. The trials we went through did that. Now, I'm certain I'm making the right choice."

"Are you, Sandy?" Seven asked, a bit selfishly. "I'd never want to change your mind about something like this, but we've both been through the ringer. Sometimes people react with a knee-jerk reaction, and later live to regret it."

"I know, Chris. That's what Sister Rosemarie said too. But I've never been so sure of anything in my life. I want to do this, with all my heart." She took his hand in hers a moment and then quickly let it go. "The only worry I had was telling you. I wasn't sure if your plans had me in them, or not, and I didn't want to hurt you in any way."

Christopher Seven looked over at her, knowing what he now needed to do. And it would be more difficult than anything he'd faced with Klaus Braun or Braun's satanic crew. Somehow he'd have to exit this girl's life for good. Do so without saddling her with any feelings of guilt or regret about her decision. The agent shook his head. The whole thing had suddenly become completely surreal. Here was the woman he thought he'd be proposing to just a few minutes earlier, and now he had to find a way to let her go. Do so with no strings attached. Yet Seven knew it had to be done. He wouldn't dream of competing with God, and understood he'd never win if he tried. He too believed in God, and knew one's life choices must always include putting Him first.

With great tenderness, the Super Stud gazed at her and replied softly, "To tell you the truth, Sandy, I'm not sure I could ever really be tied down to anyone. Not for a while, anyway. I was actually planning to tell you that tonight, but didn't know how you'd react either. It's just like I mentioned back on Paradise Island. I'm not ready to settle down with any one person yet. Not that a women like you wouldn't have been tempting, mind you. You're beautiful, caring and exciting. But me, I've got a lot of irons in the fire. I'd like to see the world, maybe write that bestseller. And, yes. There'll probably be more women in my future."

Filled with relief, Sandy chuckled for a second. "I know that *last* part is true!" She then turned serious again. "Maybe someday, when you're ready, you'll find that perfect girl, Chris. And when you do, she'll get the best man in the world. And one of the handsomest too!"

Seven, a bit embarrassed, tried to make light of the situation. "I bet you nuns say that to all the guys who show interest."

They both laughed, though Seven's laugh was forced. Sandy gently took his hand again. "Deciding on a life without you is one of the toughest things I've ever done, Chris.

"Come on now," he replied, fighting to keep the conversation light. "How many people can say they faced down a Komodo dragon? Now *that's* tough!"

Again the couple laughed, and the initial tension that had threatened them for a while was eased. It was almost as if they were back on that Nassau beach, enjoying themselves in the sand. Seven, sensing he might not be able to fake it much longer, decided it was time to make his exit. "Listen, Sandy, I wish you the very best in your new life and with your future plans. I'm sure your devotion is sincere and I know it's the right move. I'm confident you'll make it just fine. One thing I would like to say though. No matter what happens, no matter where we go or what we do, you'll always be a part of my life."

"And you mine, Chris." Her reply came with a genuine show of affection, as a small tear welled up in her eye.

Just then, the two nuns knocked lightly on the partially-opened front door. "Okay to come in now?" Sister Teresa asked.

"It's fine, Sister," Seven assured her. "I was just on my way out. Sandy's told me about her decision. I think it's great, if that's what she wants to do. I only want the best for her."

"We've talked to her at length," Sister Rosemarie declared. "And we're convinced it is. Of course, we've both told her about the hardships and the challenging road ahead. But she's so inspired and sincere. I'm certain that, with God's help, Sandy will succeed." The smiling nun then asked, "What about you, young man? What does your future hold?"

Seven grinned. "Well, I hope you aren't going to try and talk me into becoming a priest. First of all, I'm not Catholic. And second, I've never played bingo!"

Everyone in the room laughed. "We're all God's children," Sister Teresa exclaimed with a warm smile.

"We feel privileged to have met you, Mr. Seven," said Sister Rosemarie. "Sandy told us a bit about how you saved her life. You're quite a young man!"

"It was nice to meet the two of you, as well," Seven replied, standing up to leave. "May God richly bless you."

"You too, my son," the nuns said in unison.

With Sandy at his side, Seven began walking to the front door. Suddenly, a wave of nostalgic melancholy hit him, one he'd never experienced before. Perhaps it was the suddenness of saying a final goodbye to the woman he'd been prepared to marry. Or perhaps it was all of the incredible memories coming back. Now he'd have to leave them, and this beautiful girl, forever, knowing it'd be better that way.

"Well, I guess this is goodbye, Chris," Sandy whispered, trying to avoid his eyes. "I won't ask about your future or what you really do for a living. I just know it's for good and important things, and I'll pray for you often."

She was still trying to shun eye contact with him, knowing it might bring tears. He, however, looked directly into her eyes, wanting to remember forever more the lovely face of this incredible woman. The one with whom he'd shared so many stirring moments. Sandy had grown from being merely a beautiful target to the woman he loved, and she'd done so in such a short time. Yet now, it was suddenly all over, and he gently told her so.

"I guess it *really* is goodbye, Sandy."

"God bless you, Chris. I'll never forget you."

He desperately wanted to take her in his arms and kiss her one last time, but instead reached out and shook her hand. "God bless you too, Sandy."

And with that, they walked out of each other's lives forever.

T he following day, the golden Florida sun came up bright and early over
West Palm Beach. Waking to the opulence of the Carlton Hotel on this
dazzling Sunday, Christopher Seven felt surprisingly refreshed, despite
tossing and turning much of the night when thinking of Sandy. Fortunately
he had been lucky enough to get the hotel's last available room, albeit for
one night only. After tonight, the hotel was fully booked with an upcoming
convention.

The shortage of rooms at the Carlton didn't really matter to Seven.
During last night's phone conversation with headquarters, he'd agreed
to catch a 7:00 a.m. flight to New York, first thing Monday morning. With
tomorrow's early departure in mind, the G5 operative decided to stay at
the *Airport's Hilton* for his final night in Florida.

After showering, Seven hurriedly finished his room-service
breakfast, brushed his teeth, and was off to church. The sermon, given at
a small Baptist church down the road, was comforting and timely. Seven
listened sternly as the reverend read from 1st Peter, Chapter 5, verses 8
and 9, the exact passages he'd quoted to Klaus Braun. Seven's role was
not to judge, leaving that up to God. Yet he was almost certain that the
malevolent Dr. Braun was now spending a terrible eternity with the devil
he'd so faithfully served.

After checking out of the Carlton, the Super Stud heard the familiar
high-pitched tone of his cell phone ring out just as he was getting into
his rental car. It was his chief, Colonel McPhail, calling from New York,
sternly reminding him to be courteous but discreet during Seven's
scheduled meeting with the FBI brass later that afternoon. Tiring of these
inter-agency squabbles, Seven nonetheless assured his boss that he'd be
prudent. The call ended on a happier note, with the colonel assuring him
that young Edie Valdez would be getting financial help and treatment, and
would soon be flown to a top clinic in Minnesota. This was in answer to
Seven's request, which was formalized yesterday on direct orders from the
President.

~

An hour later, Christopher Seven was sitting in a large office at the
North Miami Beach FBI headquarters, with Jack Hanover and Hanover's
illustrious chief, Benjamin Winslow. Mr. Winslow began the session by
announcing his strategy for the inevitable media blitz.

"As for the press, all they'll initially be told is that Dr. Braun
temporarily went off his rocker, and committed suicide at his Reptile
Center. Afterwards, my spin doctors will leak some general snippets
stating that Braun may have also been involved in financing a covert

satanic group. We'll try to downplay the nuclear threat, saying only that there were some terrorism worries, which we managed to foil. Of course there's no such thing as *total* secrecy in these types of stories, so, undoubtedly, a few of the facts will become known over time."

Mr. Winslow took a sip of water and continued. "There'll be absolutely no mention of Braun's father or his wacky Hitler claims. Though in fairness to Floda's assertions, there are some puzzling details you might find interesting, Chris." Winslow opened a thin folder. "Among the other items our investigators found in Klaus Braun's private lockbox were several handwritten letters in Hitler's actual writing. Some of those letters were written well *after* Adolf Hitler was said to have died. Quite baffling, that part. There were also a number of rare personal photos of the Nazi dictator and his mistress, Eva Braun. In one of the pictures they were holding a baby boy. Don't know where Dr. Braun picked all this stuff up. Must have cost him a fortune at some collector's shop."

"Unless," exclaimed an excited Jack Hanover, "Klaus Braun's father *really* was -"

"Now, now, Jack!" Winslow admonished. "There can be absolutely *no* discussion on that - Washington's orders."

"What have you heard about Braun's Mid-East assassins, Mr. Winslow?" Seven asked.

"Oh, those two, Amir and Rahmad." Winslow's face showed genuine anger. "We've been looking for them for quite some time. Our best guess is that they're probably in Cuba by now. Or in the process of sneaking back to the Mid-East through some satanic pipeline. Either way, there's been absolutely no sign of them. Most of the stool pigeons we captured in the raid say those two terrorists are definitely gone. Claimed Braun had contingency plans to whisk them away in case of trouble. And obviously there's no reason for them to stick around any longer. Not with their leader dead." Winslow sighed. "Oh well, at least this Ripper charade is undoubtedly over now. No need for it anymore. Although we'll hold off warning people till we're sure."

"They sure sounded like nasty customers," Seven exclaimed.

"I'll say," agreed Jack Hanover. "We'd love to get our hands on them. Since Rahmad and Amir were really the New Ripper, they were the fiends who butchered our agent, Loretta Swanson."

Seven's tired eyes blinked a moment, and his two FBI colleagues could plainly see that he was exhausted.

"There's a lot more we need to get from you, Chris," said Winslow. "But I can see you're still bushed. Can't blame you, after all you've been through. So Jack's come up with a good idea."

Hanover nodded and explained, "I thought you and I could have a working supper in Boca tonight at *La Maison*. On *us* this time. Afterward, we can go back to my beach house and finish those reports that Washington wants done. You can then bunk at the beach home with me tonight, and I'll arrange for your airport ride and rental car return."

Sensing a bit of uncertainty on Seven's part, Jack quickly added, "Don't worry. There's plenty of room at the beach home now. The spare bedroom is finally empty again. Only little old *me* living there, as of this morning." Jack grinned. "Since this Ripper thing is over, my watchdog security roommates have finally left. Mr. Winslow had insisted those two hulks stay with me after the Loretta tragedy. Anyway, they finally checked out earlier today, so I'm free. *Halleluiah!*"

"Don't sell those guards short, Jack," scolded Winslow. "Remember, Loretta Swanson was murdered in that house. The security men were there to protect you from anything similar." He then glanced over at Seven. "So, how about it, Chris?"

Though Christopher Seven nodded his OK, his thoughts quickly turned to the FBI's lonely beach house in which he'd just agreed to bunk. Reflecting silently, a chill ran through his body. *Darn that Braun,* he mused. *Even now he gives me nightmares!*

As Seven and Jack began walking out of the office, Mr. Winslow suddenly called out to them. "Hold up a minute, fellas. I almost forgot. And Washington would never forgive me if I had." The FBI chief proceeded to bring out a long cardboard box from the closet, which he neatly pried open with a letter opener.

Christopher Seven couldn't believe his eyes! Inside the box was an ornate scabbard housing the beautiful Jean Lafitte pirate sword, the very gift with which Klaus Braun had tried to bribe him. The shiny sword glistened in the air with polished splendor, and Seven was surprised to see it again. He wondered what was up.

Ben Winslow gave a crafty grin and explained, "We at the Bureau would like you to have this, Chris. All of Dr. Braun's other items will eventually be auctioned off, but we managed to, shall we say, *liberate* this one for you. It's apparently your property anyway. After all, we found a perfectly legal receipt in that safety deposit box of Braun's. One that says you're rightfully the lawful owner."

"But, -" protested an astonished Seven.

"No *buts* about it," ordered Winslow. "And I've been told that giving you this sword, along with the legal receipt showing you purchased it from Braun, has been cleared at the highest levels." He grinned again. "Although everyone from the President on down will deny any knowledge of our giving it to you."

Seven was stunned and genuinely moved. He was also amused that the nation's highest law enforcement agency had pilfered a personal gift for him. Doing so from a criminal's private collection no less! Of course he'd have to clear it with Colonel McPhail. Just how would G5's old man react? Did he already know about it from the President? If so, would the colonel allow him to keep it? Seven wasn't sure. He reluctantly took the sword and thanked his friends with a playful wink. "Thanks. I just hope I don't bring the police down on you."

Both grinning, Seven and Hanover then strolled out to the FBI's main reception area where four secretaries were busy at work. Jack called out to one of them. "Do me a favor, Lois and make a 6:30 dinner reservation for me at *La Maison* tonight. My two watchdog security shadows have finally gone home and I'd like to celebrate my newfound independence. Yes sir! I'm living all alone again at my bachelor pad, *without* those muscular nannies."

"Sure thing," agreed Hanover's attractive assistant while winking at the other girls. "But do tell me, playboy. Since you're all alone tonight, are you taking Julia Roberts or Gwyneth Paltrow to dinner?"

While everyone laughed at this jocular and seemingly innocuous dialog, neither Seven nor Hanover noticed one of the recently hired file clerks standing well behind them. She was a thin lady with dark rimmed glasses, trying to act and look uninterested, while stationed inconspicuously over in a corner.

Despite her polite disinterest, this spectacled woman was actually paying very close attention to Jack Hanover's every word. Especially Jack's saying that the FBI security guards had left him, and that Hanover would be alone in the beach house tonight.

The reason for the woman's interest was simple. Although this stern looking file clerk had passed the FBI's difficult screening process with flying colors, she was a practicing devotee of Satan. She was also a well-paid spy. One who'd been planted in the Miami FBI offices a few months earlier by her now deceased satanic leader, Klaus Braun!

With his meeting at FBI headquarters concluded, Christopher Seven drove north to the *Delray Karate Center* for his 4:00 p.m. appointment, his last martial arts session in Florida. The hour lesson was as rough as anticipated, with the instructor freely tossing him around. While they worked on several defensive holds and counter moves, the G5 operative thought back to his fight with Braun's crazed cleric. *Thank goodness for these instructional classes,* he reflected.

Exhausted by the rugged exercise, Seven showered again and changed into some casual clothing. He threw his damp workout garments into the plastic laundry bag provided in the Center's locker room. Hopping back in his rental car, he headed south toward the FBI beach home, located on the outskirts of Deerfield.

As Seven weaved through the inevitable rush-hour traffic on US-1, he wondered what the infamous beach house would actually look like. The Super Stud had pictured it many times in his mind, but had only seen a few obscure file photos. On a more mundane level, he hoped there'd be a decent washing machine and dryer there.

Twenty minutes later, Seven pulled into the short gravel driveway of the FBI hideaway, got out of his car, and stared at the remote white structure a moment. The diminutive dwelling looked just as lonesome and serene as he'd imagined. Its secluded setting, with no neighbors or streetlights, almost seemed planned. As if it was meant to keep to itself the dark secrets of murder and terror that had taken place here.

Seven sighed and took out his suitcase and laundry bag from the trunk of the car, along with the precious silver pirate sword. Like a kid with a favorite play toy, he didn't want to let the Lafitte cutlass out of his sight now, hoping he'd somehow be allowed to add it to his private collection. He was even mildly upset that the airlines had naturally insisted he check the sword through to Newark, via their *"special baggage department"*, storing it in the hold area as "antique weaponry". Grinning at his childish possessiveness, the Super ambled up to Jack's front door.

Although he had the extra house keys Jack had given him back at the FBI offices, Seven rang the doorbell anyway, receiving no reply. After giving it one more try, he unlocked the door and walked into the cool, dark residence. "Jack?" he called out, knowing by the absence of Hanover's car that there was probably no one home. His calling was met with silence. Shrugging his shoulders, he turned on the kitchen light, and immediately noticed a yellow note stuck on the refrigerator door, held there by a small, decorative magnet. It was from Jack.

Dear Chris: I've just been summoned to Washington for a meeting with the Vice President and some other bigshots. I may also have a short conference with the President. (A bit nervous about that one!) - I only had time to hurry back here and throw a few things in my suitcase before rushing to the airport. Sorry I missed you. Nothing short of this Washington summons would have kept me from our dinner, but when those two esteemed politicians call upon you, there's no turning them down. By the way, I'm not trying to stiff you out of a paid meal if that's what you think! Anyway, my apologies. - I've taken the liberty of sending you the FBI report sheets we need completed. You can send them back to me via the standard bureau courier pouch. - A driver will pick you up at 5:30 tomorrow morning for the airport. I've also made arrangements to have your rental car returned to Hertz. Hope I catch up with you next time you're in DC or Florida. It's been a blast working with you! - Jack

PS: Please feel free to use the master bedroom tonight instead of the shoddy guest room. I've just put on some clean sheets, and it's the only room in this archaic dump where the air conditioning works well.

Seven smiled at Jack's thoughtfulness, while admitting to himself that he was glad the dreaded paperwork could wait. He was likewise pleased that it would be an early night. Carrying his suitcase and treasured pirate sword into the master bedroom, he placed them near the side of the queen-size bed. After unpacking a few clean items for the following day, he returned to the kitchen area, and thankfully found a small washer/dryer combo in one of the larger kitchen closets. He promptly threw in his wet workout clothes.

While the laundry continued washing, Seven went back into the master bedroom and lay down on the bed. Only then did he remember that this was the hallowed ground. The spot where FBI Agent Loretta Swanson had been brutally butchered. Quickly sitting up, Seven bowed his head and said a short, silent prayer. He then got up from the bed and strolled into the living room.

The Super Stud stared out the picture window, toward the lonely beach. *Yes,* he thought, *this must have been where the killers had made their forced entry.* He could almost see them doing so in his mind, and visualizing Loretta's terror during their attack. Shuddering, he walked back to the kitchen.

When the laundry finally finished, he stacked the clean clothes neatly on the kitchen counter. "I'll pack them later," he said aloud, while wondering what to do next.

Deciding on a quick, but hearty, meal somewhere close by, he hopped back in the Mustang and drove down US-1 to Pompano Beach. His destination was *Billy Rodino's,* the famous barbeque restaurant, for a platter of the best St. Louis ribs in the country. As always, Seven dutifully ducked into the bathroom after finishing his meal, and quickly brushed his teeth. He grinned after doing so, knowing that no matter how long he planned to stay on with G5, this toothcare ritual would probably still remain a lifelong habit for him. The Super Stud wondered if it had become excessive compulsive behavior. Chuckling at the thought, he slid into the Mustang for the short drive back.

~

At the same moment that Seven was languidly enjoying his pleasant car ride home, two stalkers, holding a small bag of tools, and a black carrying case with air holes, were stealthy arriving on the rocky shoreline of the FBI's beach house. They'd come in accordance with their *Purus* pledge, the vow they'd made to their now deceased chieftain. *"To brutally slaughter anyone who'd orchestrated the death of their leader."* In this case, Jack Hanover was definitely one of them.

Hanover was the FBI infidel who'd led the raid on Dr. Braun, so, in their minds, at least, he, along with the detested magazine reporter, Christopher Seven, was one of the two rats who'd planned the murder of their ruler.

This was not the first time Amir and Rahmad had been here, and as they settled in behind the large sand dune, it all began coming back to them. The delicious memories of the night they'd slain the FBI girl. The two assassins realized that events surrounding their last act of revenge were much different than when they had come for the woman. For one thing, it would be their final satanic act. A sacred, irrevocable promise. Both men had reaffirmed this earlier in a moving, ritualistic suicide prayer, solemnly swearing to slit each other's throats after killing Hanover. Tonight's Purus would be their ultimate sacrifice. In essence, their *final* curtain.

At least their closing target was a fitting one. For in their minds it had been Jack Hanover and Christopher Seven who'd brought about Dr. Braun's tragic end. Doing so during the FBI raid. True, Hanover was probably second in responsibility. Second only to that hated magazine reporter, Christopher Seven. Yet Hanover had equally put his filthy hands in it as well, so he would therefore be viciously slain!

Earlier that afternoon, via an excited cell phone call from a mole working within the FBI itself, Rahmad and Amir had hastily been informed that Jack Hanover would be 'all alone' at his beach house tonight. The informant was certain that there would be only *one* occupant in the FBI home. Hanover's bodyguards were gone, as of this morning. So conditions were therefore favorable for his slaughter.

Settling in on the beach for what they assumed would be a long wait, the two killers crouched behind the now familiar dune. The darkened home and the driveway still remained vacant. Stretching their arms, they both glanced at their watches in eager expectation.

Surprisingly, the two killers didn't have to linger very long. For in only twenty minutes their timing was rewarded. A lone car pulled up, and their victim was soon standing inside his dwelling. Amir spoke first. "Rahmad. This Hanover comes back early tonight. Use the long glasses and watch the lights. As always, we'll strike after the target has gone to sleep."

Amir's partner reached for his binoculars just as the front door closed. As Rahmad focused in on the foyer, a bright hall light came on, illuminating the entire area. But then, when Rahmad saw the lone figure enter the hallway, complete dejection filled his soul. Though the man walking into the house was partially hidden from view, Rahmad could plainly see that this person was definitely *not* Jack Hanover. This man was thinner and not nearly as tall. Rahmad had studied photos of Hanover all afternoon and knew the target's face and features.

Rahmad sighed at their cruel fate, wondering if they should simply leave now and try to flee the country. He almost didn't have the heart to inform his partner, but knew he must. Readying himself to tell his sidekick the disastrous news, Braun's henchman took one last look through his binoculars. When he did, his disappointment and gloom abruptly ended, instantly changing into sheer elation! The thrilled assassin quickly realized that he knew the man who'd just entered. Dr. Braun had sent them to spy on this target several times. Grinning from ear to ear, the ecstatic Rahmad couldn't believe their amazing good fortune. He was certain it was a blessing from below.

Breathlessly, he glanced through the field glasses once more to make certain. Yes, it was true! And had he not been efficiently trained to speak noiselessly on covert assignments such as this, Rahmad would probably have screamed out in joy! Instead, he whispered his jubilation. "Amir. Satan is truly with us tonight. Our fondest wish has been granted. It is that filthy reporter Seven. *He* is the one that stays in the house alone tonight."

Amir was likewise incredulous! Quickly composing himself, the tall assassin closed his eyes in silent homage to Lucifer. He then spoke slowly, in a cold, hateful tenor. It was a tone his partner had never heard before.

"We shall kill this man Seven *very* slowly tonight. Slay him in such a fashion that even the Dark World below will find shocking!" The killers licked their lips and waited.

~

Christopher Seven had entered the beach house through the front door, switching on the light in the hall and those in the living room. He then walked into the master bedroom, removed his shirt, and reached for his new cell phone. Calling New York, he found that both McPhail and his secretary had left for the evening.

After clicking off, the tired agent went back into the main living room and rested a few moments on the couch. Looking out over the beach he noticed the bright full moon above. It appeared to be playing tag with the clouds, darting in and out of sight every five minutes, and making the evening seem particularly eerie.

Seven's thoughts turned to poor Loretta Swanson again, the attractive FBI agent who'd been murdered in this very house. It must have been horrible for her. Seven had read the full reports on the slaying. How the killers had entered through the same front window he was now glancing at. And how they'd surprised Loretta while she slept. The case notes were horrific. Of course Seven and the authorities now knew that it was Braun's two men who were actually the New Ripper. Not some serial killer madman.

Shuddering slightly, the G5 operative realized that it must have been even more dreadful for Loretta than the file had described. The terror of the snake on top of her bed, followed by the two henchmen overwhelming her with their heinous butcher knives. Seven had seen some of those satanic instruments of death at Braun's punishment show, ready to be used on he and Sandy. He therefore knew, first hand, what these devil worshiping fiends were capable of doing. With another shudder he closed his weary eyes for a second and rested his head on the back of the sofa.

Looking to his left, he noticed a framed picture of Loretta Swanson on the far end table. The Super Stud easily recognized her from the mission file. Perhaps Jack had placed the girl's photo there after her murder. Or maybe it'd been put there by Loretta herself. Seven vaguely remembered Jack telling him that he'd left a few of Loretta's remembrances in the house, using them as a daily reminder to do his best to catch the killer. *At least Loretta Swanson would have been proud that Klaus Braun's plans had all been foiled*, Seven reflected.

Seeing this picture of a pretty young woman turned Seven's next thoughts to Sandy Kent, the beautiful woman he could no longer have. Was she likewise thinking of him at this moment? He sighed, knowing it was best to try and forget about her.

He turned on the television in the living room, directly opposite the couch, and watched a rerun of an old NHL playoff game for a while. Seven loved hockey, and the action of this Stanley Cup final was fast and furious. It now seemed ironic to him that his favorite hockey team had always been the *New Jersey Devils*. Seven laughed loudly. "After Klaus Braun and his devilish followers, do I dare root for *that* particular team any more?"

Looking at his watch, he saw that it was almost eleven o'clock. He watched the game for another forty minutes or so. But then, finding it impossible to keep his eyes open, he decided to call it a night, knowing he'd have to be up very early tomorrow morning. Turning off the TV, he slowly walked into the master bedroom.

After a relaxing shower, Seven chose his travel clothes for the morning, placing them on the room's small dresser. He then packed and locked his suitcase so that he'd be able to get going as soon as the alarm rang. Glancing around the room to make sure he hadn't forgotten anything, the agent spotted the ornate scabbard holding the Lafitte pirate sword. It was now standing right near his bed. Smiling contently, he touched it a moment, still incredulous that this beautiful weapon might actually be his to own. His brother, Tim, would be ecstatic. Beaming at the thought, Seven hopped into bed.

Unlike the others who'd slept in this room, the G5 agent didn't bother to close the heavy curtains, knowing he'd be rising before the sun did. After saying his evening prayer, the Super Stud looked out the small bedroom window and noticed for the first time that the bright glow of the full moon was finally coming out from behind its cloud cover. He hadn't noticed its brightness before, and this substantial amber glow was now shining brightly. It was akin to having a powerful nightlight on in his bedroom.

On any other evening, Seven would have immediately gotten up and closed the curtains, as this much light in a bedroom would normally disturb him. Tonight, however, he was much too tired to care. Rolling over on his side, away from the glaring moonbeam, the weary Super Stud shut his eyes, and was instantly asleep.

Chapter 51
An Appointment with Death

As planned, Braun's avengers watched the darkened house from their shoreline hiding place for the required two hours. Satisfied that their victim was sound asleep, the stalking assassins silently crept up to the front picture window. Then, deftly using a noiseless glasscutter, and a suction cup plunger on it, they pulled out a small entranceway. Crawling through it, they were soon standing inside the dark living room, staring at the closed master bedroom door.

Their covert entrance had gone as smoothly as it had on the night they'd butchered Loretta Swanson here, perhaps even better. The duo bowed to each other and put on their repulsive death masks.

Amir reached down for the small carrying case that held the deadly cobra. While picking it up, he heard a soft, rustling noise as the disturbed snake began to crawl around inside. With a sinister smirk, Amir followed his partner toward the bedroom door.

The two stalkers had decided that the plan of attack for Seven would be similar to that on Loretta, although it would definitely not be as easy. This was a strong man they were after, not a terrified female. The shock from the cobra bite might soften him up a bit, but they'd have to pounce on their victim much more rapidly this time. Perhaps slice up his arm so there'd be no fighting back. Nonetheless, Rahmad and Amir wanted this brash reporter to remain alive for as long as possible. To be fully conscious while they took out their ruthless revenge on him. The insolent Mr. Christopher Seven was going to die very *slowly* tonight.

In the eerie silence of the living room nothing but the ticking of a small wall clock and the dull hum of the central air conditioning could be heard. When they arrived at the closed bedroom door, Amir motioned to his sidekick, the break-in expert they called the *ferret*. Rahmad, the ferret, clasped the door handle with an expert's touch and slowly opened it, as always doing so with skilled precision. But then, just as Rahmad was halfway through the process, something inexplicable happened! For the first time in his long career, his opening of a door was just a little less than perfect. Rahmad silently cursed the soft clicking noise as his partner cringed angrily. Both men nervously waited for any reaction. Thankfully there was none. The sleeping man was completely still.

Glancing around the bedroom, the satanic duo observed another unexpected complication; the inordinate amount of moonlight in the room. They much preferred to work in the dark with only their tiny penlights when and if needed. This full moon illumination was like having a bright nightlight on in the bedroom. Yet, moonlight or not, turning back *wasn't* an option.

Slowly inching closer to the foot of Seven's bed, both intruders were now standing statue-like in the stillness of the master bedroom. True to his practiced routine, Amir noiselessly opened the black carrying case and carefully released the cobra onto the bed. This part was always dangerous, as the snake could sometimes become angry when let loose. Accordingly, Amir took great care *not* to get bitten. For to die by this particular serpent, the snake used solely for unbelieving enemies, was an unforgivable disgrace; a deplorable offense in satanic eyes. Fortunately for Amir, no such trouble ensued and the deadly reptile was now resting quietly on Seven's bed. The stalkers then silently dropped to their knees, just below the bed's footboard. Once there, they waited patiently for their victim to scream out in horror, just like their other sleeping target had done when she was confronted by the lethal Egyptian cobra in this very same room.

Unlike the unfortunate Loretta Swanson, however, Christopher Seven was now wide awake, having been roused by the silhouettes in the moonlight and the clicking noise from the bedroom door. Rahmad's first mistake in years, as well as the two shadows on the wall, had indeed given them away. Quickly coming out of his restless sleep, Seven realized that two prowlers now occupied the room. Even so, he certainly wasn't aware that a deadly cobra had just been dumped on his bed and that it was only a few feet away from him!

Rapidly becoming more alert, Seven was still unsure why the two men crouching below the footboard were hiding there. Weren't they afraid that he might jump up and get ready for them?

Remembering the case notes on the Swanson murder, and the very specific details given from one of the stoolpigeons captured after the raid, the G5 agent thought on it a moment. He soon realized that there was only one answer. Braun's goons must have placed a deadly snake on his bed! Focusing his eyes straight ahead, he spotted the cobra's prone body glistening in the moonlight. Though the snake had not yet reared up, the Super Stud now knew what was coming.

Drenched in sweat, Seven immediately contemplated rolling off the mattress as fast as possible. As he slowly raised his head, however, it became painfully clear that it was too late for that. This slight movement of sitting up had caused the hooded reptile to angrily rear into its famous striking position, poised and ready to attack! Now only a few feet from Seven's face, the cobra's shiny body looked powerful and dangerous.

The assassins remained crouched on the floor, confidently expecting the bitten man to panic and let out a scream. That would be their cue for the follow-up attack, their signal to spring from the floor. All of their other snake victims had shrieked out in horror, and they would give this one a few more moments to do likewise.

Yet unlike those panicked, flailing victims, and unlike Loretta Swanson with her lifelong fear of reptiles, Christopher Seven simply froze like a statue. He did so not out of terror, but out of respect for the cobra's reflexes. Seven knew that any more quick movements on his part would surely bring about a strike from the serpent.

But, now what? Staying frozen forever was not an option. Sooner or later the snake would attack, or the two men would leap from the floor. And, if he tried to roll off the bed, the deadly reptile would surely nail him. The sweating Super Stud hurriedly weighed his options. As he did, his mind raced back to what he'd seen Klaus Braun do several times, both at *Mi Casa* and at the Reptile Center. Back then, Dr. Braun had willingly showed Seven the secret of snake capturing. "Anyone can do it," Braun had said. "Even a child. It just takes is a lot of nerve."

Okay then, thought Seven, *why not me? Besides, there's really no other choice now*. Slowly, ever so very slowly, he sat up a bit higher. The snake eyed him warily, though it didn't move a muscle, seemingly transfixed with watching its victim's eyes. *Come on now*, Seven willed himself. *You can do this. Your reflexes are as quick as that old man Braun's were. Perhaps even quicker with all of your martial arts and tennis practice.* The Super Stud clearly recalled Braun's snake handling technique. "Remember," Dr. Braun had instructed, "the secret is all in the left hand. Keep the snake occupied with *that* hand while you grab it from behind with your right. Anybody can do it." *All right*, agreed Seven, silently. *Then I can do it too.*

Delicately placing his left hand in front of the cobra's face, Seven moved it very gently in a swaying circular motion. *That's it*, he encouraged himself. *Nice and easy. That's perfect, you're doing fine. The snake looks mesmerized. Careful now.*

The reptile stared at the moving hand as if hypnotized, exactly as Klaus Braun had said it would react. While the cobra intently watched Seven's circling left hand, it didn't notice the agent's *right* hand reaching up behind its neck. The snake merely kept staring at the gyrating left arm. Seven waited a few more seconds and then inched his right hand up ever so gingerly, directly behind the serpent's thin neck. *Steady Chris, almost there. — Now!*

With immense concentration and determination, Seven's right arm sprang out rapidly and firmly grabbed the snake from behind. Clutching the cobra's neck tightly, the G5 operative literally held on for dear life. The startled reptile wriggled wildly, but at this point its deadly fangs were safely being held away from its victim's face.

Now for the final act of courage, Seven reflected, knowing it had to be done quickly. He grabbed the snake's neck with *both* hands and firmly wrung the cobra's neck, doing so in one strong and quick snapping motion. He immediately heard a sharp crack and felt sure that he'd broken the creature's neck. Then, without further delay, he tossed the snake as hard and fast as possible against the far bedroom wall. The flying reptile struck the wall with a sickening thud! Landing in a corner the serpent began to writhe slowly, most likely in a lingering death throe. Was the thing still alive? Seven didn't think so. Either way, there was no time to spare! He quickly turned on his bedside lamp, jumped off the bed, and readied himself for the inevitable attack!

While Seven instinctively went into the classic martial arts defensive stance, the two hideously masked intruders finally sprang up from the foot of the bed. One held a polished weapon that looked like a sharp hatchet, while the other appeared to be unarmed.

Both assassins believed they'd be facing a terrified and wounded victim of the lethal cobra attack. To their utter dismay, Christopher Seven was neither, and the agent took brief satisfaction in seeing his attackers' grins turn to somber surprise through their masks. Instead of confronting a traumatized man on the verge of death, Amir and Rahmad were now facing an angry, alert, and completely healthy opponent. And from Seven's structured, defensive pose, someone obviously schooled in martial arts to boot. Additionally, Seven knew that these men would be coming for him right after the snake. He was therefore neither shocked nor surprised by their sudden appearance. That was something else his assailants hadn't expected.

Even so, the ghoulish masked faces staring at Seven were initially startling, for it was akin to being attacked by the boogieman in the middle of the night. Regardless of their bizarre looks, Christopher Seven was ready and waiting for them. He knew they were only human, not two mysterious devils from some dark world below.

A poised opponent with all of his wits about him was something Braun's men hadn't counted on, and it threw the two terrorists off guard. Sensing their brief uncertainty, Seven launched a quick, powerful *savate* kick to the chest of the shorter one, bouncing him off the back wall. As this shorter man slowly came back, now in a defensive crouch of his own, the G5 operative narrowly missed being hit by the swinging hatchet of the taller one. There was no doubt about it. The two thugs had regained their wits and were fully intent on killing him!

Seven was immediately up on the balls of his feet, poised to fight and counter any attack. He decided to show them he was calm and confident, although he knew the odds were clearly against him. "Sorry, I don't have any candy, fellows," the agent smirked, sarcastically. "But I thought Halloween was in October."

The scorning words had their effect. Both attackers snarled and growled in anger. The shorter man, now recovered from the kick, spit at him and cursed savagely. The two invaders then began communicating with each other in some type of Arabic dialect, obviously trading signals or instructions. Whatever they were saying Seven didn't like the sound of it. He watched them warily.

The taller man came forward first, swinging his hatchet lazily in a circular motion. His partner, who was standing off to the side, suddenly pulled out a short icepick-type weapon from his back pocket. While the taller thug approached with his ax, the other man, holding the ice pick, moved toward the opposite side of the bedroom.

Christopher Seven realized it was going to be extremely tough to fend off two professional killers, both wielding deadly weapons and coming at him from different directions. Especially since he'd be doing it unarmed, with only the use of his bare hands. Seven took a deep breath, clenched his fists, and decided he'd just have to give it a try. *Better to go down fighting and hopefully take one of them with me.*

Then, blessedly and unexpectedly, it hit him. *There just might be a chance after all!* Within easy reach, to his right, the Super Stud noticed the slender case of the Lafitte pirate sword by his bed. Neither of his assailants knew of its existence. As he reached behind and swiftly grabbed the cutlass out of its scabbard, he heard a piercing, animal-like roar come from the short goon he had kicked. This smaller man, armed with his ice pick, began charging wildly from the far side of the room. There wasn't a moment to lose!

As the screaming Rahmad raced toward him, Seven grasped the pirate sword by its handle, pulled it out of the holder, and in one neat, cat-like motion, turned it forward to face his charging assailant. Seven pointed it forward just in time to meet the unsuspecting on rusher. Seven's timing was perfect. The force of the man's wild charge, directly into the gleaming sword, forced the blade right through his heart, and the impaled Rahmad was instantly killed! Seven pulled the sword out of the dead man and then looked over at the taller attacker.

Amir, still holding his hatchet lazily, stared in shocked disbelief. After a few dazed moments of silence, the stunned terrorist screamed out in anguish. Amir's eyes blazed wildly. He was now truly a man possessed, revenge his only guide! Amir had just seen his lifelong partner die instantly. Yet, instead of charging Seven, he spoke, doing so very softly. "Lucifer, Dr. Braun, and now, my dead brother, all demand a slow and painful death from you. And I shall be the sacred instrument who claims it for them!"

Christopher Seven said nothing, concentrating solely on his foe, and a ghostly silence now filled the room. The stillness was deafening after all of the previous screaming and turmoil. Then, without warning, Amir charged wildly, swinging his weapon like a Samurai warrior with the fury of a wounded animal! Seven knew that this was the hardest type of attack to repel. An assault with no pattern, coming from a crazed opponent with nothing to lose.

Amir's suicidal attack had been impossible to predict or elude, and it worked perfectly. One of the terrorist's swinging blows immediately caught home and badly gashed Seven's left arm. The force of the blow was terrific. It knocked Seven off his feet, causing him to drop the pirate sword. The staggered Super Stud now lay on the floor weaponless and bleeding.

Though he was hurt, Seven was also angry, upset with himself for allowing this wild man get the better of him. The crazed suicidal charge now gave Amir, who was soon standing directly over him, the uncontested opportunity to kill him.

Lying on the floor and bleeding, the G5 agent looked up at his victorious opponent's face. He could clearly see the man's grin of conquest through the skeletal mask's thin mouth hole. As the gloating assassin slowly raised his hatchet, Seven glanced dejectedly over his shoulder to where the Lafitte pirate sword was lying uselessly, a few feet to his right. It would take a miracle for him to regain it, and the agent was now out of miracles.

Christopher Seven stared transfixed at the triumphant Amir towering over him. The killer's huge hatchet glowed harshly in the hue of the bedside lamp. It was now ready to slice him to pieces!

"I'll not kill you with the first blow," Amir informed his fallen opponent, doing so with obvious, vindictive pleasure. "Nor with the second. Instead, I will simply cut off both your arms, and then perhaps your right leg with another jolt. I am an artist with this hatchet, so I plan to keep you alive for several hours." The ghoulish masked figure giggled excitedly. "I may also chop off some of your more sensitive masculine parts. My promise to you, made in hallowed memory of Rahmad, is that your last moments will seem like years. When you finally expire, I'll take pleasure in drinking your blood."

Christopher Seven said nothing. Though he remained on the floor, a helpless, bleeding prisoner waiting for more crippling blows, the G5 operative still thought about the pirate sword laying to his right. Seven knew his only chance now was to cause his opponent to lose concentration, if only for a brief moment. Yet, the odds of that happening, especially to a professional killer, were slim indeed. Nevertheless, it was his only hope. The wounded agent desperately needed some type of diversion so that he could regain the cutlass. Could he say or do something that might throw this man off guard?

Seven desperately tried to concentrate on that, and not on the negatives. Yet, as he observed Braun's assassin holding the hatchet firm, with an expert's confidence, the reality of the situation was obvious. This man was a cold-blooded professional, one thoroughly trained by al-Qaeda. Looking up at the two legs standing over him, Seven glumly mused, *I can't see anything I can do or say to distract him.*

The Super Stud was now trapped in what is known as '*reckoning time*' in the game of chess, the precise moment a player realizes the contest is over. Seven, a skilled chess competitor, knew he'd arrived at his final move. This was it. Check mate. His reckoning had come.

As he waited for the first searing blows to hit, for some curious reason, the face of Loretta Swanson appeared. This vision was as real and clear, as if the pretty FBI agent was standing right there in the room with him. Was she telling him they would soon be joined as tortured and mutilated victims? When the grinning Amir slowly raised the hatchet over Seven's right leg, the Super Stud's spirits sank completely. He mouthed a quick prayer and gave into the inevitable.

Then, inexplicably, instead of carrying through with his first crushing wallop, Amir suddenly stopped cold, his hatchet frozen in midair. Was it just another sadistic touch? Seven wasn't sure. In this moment of strange confusion, Braun's top assassin slowly looked down in horror at his left leg and noticed a trickle of blood. The Egyptian Cobra, which had been dormant for such a long while, was now right by the henchman's foot. It had somehow gotten up the strength to crawl over and strike, biting Amir twice on his ankle.

The shock of the snakebite had momentarily taken away Amir's ability to concentrate, and that was all Seven needed. In one adroit move, he deftly rolled to his right, picked up the sword and was back on his feet, holding his pirate cutlass firmly. As Amir stared at him with a dazed, spellbound expression, Seven thrust the sword savagely, driving it deep into Amir's chest several times, the last one going straight through him! The lanky killer dropped his hatchet and slowly fell to his knees, the point of the sword's blade now protruding in his back. Amir gave a low gurgling sound and fell forward.

With a weary eye on the cobra, which was lying motionless, but still breathing next to Amir's lifeless body, Seven slowly backed away. Picking up the dead man's hatchet, he chopped off the cobra's head in one swift motion. He felt a bit underhanded in doing so, since the reptile had just saved his life. Yet, knowing that a recently killed snake could still bite, the agent took great care not to touch the serpent's decapitated head. He had once read that, even if severed, a dead snake's head could still deliver a lethal reflex bite.

Seven looked down at the Cobra, admitting he felt more pity for the serpent than he did the two dead men lying next to it. Using the flat end of Amir's hatchet, he scooped up both halves of the snake and threw them in the tall wastebasket by the bed. After pausing a moment, he walked into the bathroom and vomited copiously.

~

Ten minutes later, Seven bandaged his wounded left arm as best he could and then took a long cool shower. Afterward he automatically brushed his teeth, and gargled with Listerine. These familiar practices helped make him feel alive again. He then surveyed the horrible scene in the bedroom. It looked like something out of *Friday the Thirteenth*. As he mopped up the mess with some old beach towels he found in the linen closet, the G5 agent was certain that during the violent fighting his own blood had mixed with the blood of Braun's two devils, and also with the snake's. Seven found this fact somewhat curious, being blood brothers to three of the deadliest creatures he'd ever encountered.

Thinking on it, the agent unemotionally pulled the Lafitte cutlass from Amir's chest. The dead man's face was cold and white. Taking his cherished sword into the bathroom, Seven again hopped in the shower, washed some more blood off himself, and then painstakingly rinsed and cleaned off the pirate cutlass. Drying off the sword gently with a soft towel, he held it up to the light. The silver rapier gleamed brightly, and the smiling agent was inordinately proud of it now. The shiny weapon that had twice saved his life.

Still a bit dazed, Seven changed into a new pair of white Levis and a clean white tennis shirt taken from his suitcase. He walked out into the living room, dotingly carrying the cutlass with him, as if never wanting to offend it. His first duty now was to call the Miami FBI offices. Picking up the house telephone by the couch, he noticed a cool breeze of air coming from his left. For a split second, he thought a ghostly apparition had entered the area, and it momentarily startled him. Then he saw the large hole in the front window. Of course! Braun's assassins had neatly cut it out for their clandestine entry.

Proceeding with his phone call, Seven was soon speaking with Special Agent Jed Parnell. The Super Stud calmly told the astonished Parnell all that had taken place, leaving out nothing.

"Do you need emergency medical attention, Mr. Seven?"

"Not right away. I've bandaged it up, a bit. Seems okay."

"Stand by, sir. Be there within the hour with a paramedic."

Fifteen minutes later, the phone rang. It was FBI Director Ben Winslow. His tone was serious and businesslike. "We'll take over from here, Chris. Get you to a hotel too, if you'd like."

"Thanks anyway, Mr. Winslow, but it's almost 2:30 in the morning. No need for that. I have to be at the airport in a few hours anyway. Could you do me a favor, though, and notify my chief? Tell him my replacement cell phone was broken in the struggle."

"Will do. I'm sure he'll want to know all the details." Winslow paused a moment. "Glad you're okay, son, but I'm afraid we're all going to be in for a media blitz soon. The death of the New Ripper is going to be big news. That's why you'll probably have to scram, as I know your boss insists on anonymity. While you're getting your stuff ready to go, I'll call Colonel McPhail myself. Stand by. One of us will call you back."

Twenty minutes passed before the living room telephone rang out again. Seven figured it wouldn't be McPhail though, as the security conscious colonel would be aware that this open FBI line might presumably be bugged. Sure enough, it was Ben Winslow calling back.

"Colonel McPhail says he doesn't want you or your department to have *any* further involvement in this whatsoever, Chris. He's certain the President would agree. So we're going to get you out of there before the press and the local police are called in."

Seven was relieved. "Thanks, Mr. Winslow."

The FBI chief explained further, "We've worked out some of the details for a general cover story. Your boss has agreed to them. To make a long story short, here's the deal. We're going to announce a bit later this morning that the New Ripper killer was finally apprehended. Not one lone killer, as was first suspected, but a *pair* of lunatics, in this country illegally.

Last night, they tried unsuccessfully to kill another FBI agent at the beach house. This time, though, our men were ready and waiting, and they nailed both suspects and their pet snake."

Seven could almost envision the watered-down accounts in the newspapers. Chuckling to himself he heard the FBI chief say, "Sorry, you won't get the credit for it, but you know."

"That's quite alright, Mr. Winslow."

"We'll play down the terrorist angle," Winslow continued. "That is, if we can. But nothing about any Christopher Seven will be mentioned. I was told by the colonel that it has to be that way." Ben Winslow grunted affirmatively and added, "By the way, I've already picked out the agents who we'll say were at the beach house tonight. Two good men who know how to be vague with reporters. They're being briefed now in preparation for meeting the press. Don't like playing with the truth, but it can't be helped this time. National security, and that top secret department of yours."

"I understand."

Director Winslow explained the rest of it. "Our profile boys downtown will tell the media that these two psychotics were most likely doing their sinister deeds for their pet snake. Much like that *Son of Sam* serial killer in New York was acting for his dog. At any rate, we'll proclaim that South Florida is safe at last!"

Seven nodded with satisfaction and continued listening.

"And like I told you and Jack earlier. There'll initially be no mention of Klaus Braun's role, the bombs, or that old man Floda."

"Yes, sir."

"Although I've got to tell you. The two archive experts we hired said the handwriting in those Operation D exchanges from Floda to Klaus was nearly *identical* to Adolf Hitler's. Bit of a mystery there, I'll admit that." The FBI chief waited for Seven's response, and when none came, he simply finished up. "If the press pries too much into the satanic end of things, we'll slowly drip in some crazed cult angle. Your boss can fill you in on the rest back in New York. Well, so long, Chris. And once again, well done."

Chapter 53

Final Chapter

Christopher Seven strolled into the kitchen and grabbed himself a cold soda from the refrigerator, still thinking about the enormity of the entire Operation D case. The general public would never know how close to genuine disaster they'd come. Just like so many other ominous plots uncovered by G5's Super Stud section. The agent sighed and walked out of the kitchen.

Plopping down on the comfortable living room couch, he knew it was time for some thoughtful reflection. For one thing, he was now certain he wouldn't be quitting the Super Stud unit. How could he, with foes like the Brauns, and Amir and Rahmad, around? He now felt foolish for even thinking of resigning; Sandy or *no* Sandy.

With regard to these types of enemies, the despots and madmen whose sole purpose in life is to destroy the United States, they had to be confronted. Even if other people and other countries didn't understand America's need to fight back. Seven thought about those other countries a moment. He also thought about his many friends living in Europe, Africa, Israel, and in the Middle-East. Good people, all who wanted nothing more than to live in peace, and the chance to raise their families in freedom. He recalled what he had recently said, ironically to oldster, Floda Braun. '*People* aren't the problem. It's the oppressors and their so-called governments'.

And what about his *own* government? Well, the United States certainly wasn't perfect. Seven himself had occasionally criticized America's handling of race relations, the environment, its early treatment of Native Americans, and, at times, even her foreign policy. But overall, he was quite proud of his country. *Especially* when she stood up to terrorists and tyrants. Seven could never comprehend why some nations didn't understand that America *had* to protect her security. She was still vulnerable to threats, such as suicide bombers at our military bases, or psychos trying to fly hijacked planes into our skyscrapers again. To counter that, vigilance and strength was *always* the best defense. If that sounded like an 'America first' view, so be it!

As for these types of spineless enemies, men like Braun, the cowardly Mohammed Atta of 9-11, the late bin Laden, or the sadistic Amir, the Super Stud was now certain of one thing. Every terrorist is basically just a jealous coward, and certainly *not* a courageous patriot. Seven had always laughed at those ignorant American television commentators and celebrities who called these terrorist thugs 'brave'. Or excused them as 'freedom fighters'. They weren't brave in *any* way, shape or form, and they certainly *weren't* freedom fighters. Particularly since the regimes they represent never give freedom to its *own* people.

Tyrants such as these are not so invincible in a fair fight. And not so clever when the odds are evened. The two dead bodies in the bedroom proved that. And while any Timothy McVeigh or Atta type moron can do damage. Say, blow up a nightclub with a suicide bomb or indiscriminately kill civilians with automatic weapons. That's really not courage or war. That's murder, pure and simple. There was no doubt about it. Terrorism is simply murder, performed by cowards who sugarcoat it as politics.

Well, there were still plenty of these brutal sects and enemies around. Despots like Klaus Braun, who'll stop at nothing in their attempts to destroy America. In view of that, Christopher Seven now knew he would stay on with G5 and oppose these foes. Use all of his God-given gifts to do so. And if that included his looks and his expertise with women, so be it. It might have sounded corny a few months earlier, but after this case, the words rang true.

Still thinking about his private soapbox sermon, the Super Stud slowly got up from the couch. Feeling the sting of his reddened eyes protesting their lack of sleep, he rubbed them gently while looking admiringly at the Lafitte pirate cutlass by his side. Picking it up, the G5 operative held the silver sword high, smiled, and sat back down on the sofa. His thoughts then turned to the two dead men lying in the next room. Had they simply been born 'bad' or did they emerge that way? If so, he pondered their eternal future. Like them, Seven believed in a devil and an actual hell. Yet, he also believed in God, his Son, and in a *real* heaven. There was a definite choice between the two places, and a huge difference as well.

The G5 agent then considered his own beliefs. As he did so, he was still unable to dismiss the carnage that he himself had just wreaked, now the third time he'd killed in the line of duty. There was no getting around the fact that it had been *he* who'd just taken the lives of two human beings. In his heart, however, Seven was already at peace with his actions. He knew that the killings had been done purely in self-defense. He'd been savagely attacked, and there had been no other choice. To him, the commandment given to Moses by God was not strictly '*thou shall not kill*'. In Seven's mind it was rather; thou shall not *murder*. And just like a soldier in combat, Seven felt there was a vast difference between murder and protecting one's self. He hoped the God he worshipped in church every Sunday would understand.

Yet, as he thought on this, he also recalled the clear directive of Jesus; *pray for those who persecute you*. Accordingly, he said a quick prayer for the souls of the two men who'd just tried to murder him.

Opening his eyes and rubbing them once again, the sleepy operative was still puzzled by one final detail. Something he couldn't quite grasp. While fighting for his life in the bedroom, he had felt a powerful presence alongside of him. Just where had this invisible force come from? Was it simply a 'feeling', or an actual apparition?

Suddenly, Seven felt a gentle wind in the living room. Unlike the breeze he'd felt there earlier, this one was warm and pleasant. Looking to his left, he again saw the photo of Loretta Swanson, the attractive FBI agent who had likewise been ambushed here by the same two killers. Smiling up from the framed picture on top of the end table, Loretta appeared to be looking straight at him.

As Seven looked back at the photograph, he saw that the single thin drawer of the end table directly below her picture was slightly ajar. Funny, he hadn't noticed this partially opened drawer before. And he now felt compelled, almost ordered, to see what was inside. Sliding over to have a look, he found an unfinished letter in the girl's attractive handwriting. Attached to the note was a smaller color photo of Loretta. The letter, written to her dad, was obviously never completed. With mixed feelings about doing so, Christopher Seven nonetheless decided to read the partially written note.

> *March 31st, Nighttime—*
>
> *Dear Daddy,*
>
> *It's me, your angel. Tonight I had the strangest feeling that I'd never see you again. I know it's only one of my childish 'inner feelings' but it reminded me to tell you that I love you very much, and do hope you're taking care of yourself. Particularly your high blood pressure.*

The note curiously and suddenly ended with the next group of sentences. It was clear that Loretta meant to complete the letter at a later date, one that unfortunately never came. As the letter continued, it abruptly stopped with a second paragraph that read:

> *I know you always worry about me, Daddy, but please don't. And if you ever get nervous or sad about me, just remember my silly childhood dream of being a fairyland princess. Then you'll be sure to know that if any evil villain sends a terrible snake to slay me, my brave and handsome white knight, the one with the great silver sword, will avenge me for sure!*

Seven was truly startled by this letter's last paragraph. Unexpectedly, he felt the gentle breeze touch him again and the late girl's presence seemed very strong. Looking at his reflection in the mirror across the room, the G5 agent realized that he was now dressed in white, just like the knight. And in one hand, he was holding his Lafitte cutlass, which was indeed a *great silver sword*!

He again looked at the small portrait of Loretta Swanson attached to the letter. She seemed to be smiling at him knowingly. Somehow Seven was positive that Loretta knew he had killed the snake, the men who'd slain her, and that he had punished the evil leader who'd planned it all. The Super Stud had indeed avenged her, the beautiful fairyland princess.

Christopher Seven smiled back at the girl in the photo.